Temp Girl
The Complete Daily Serial

STEPHANIE BOND

INTRODUCTION

Hey, there.   It's me, the girl you probably hate—you know, the tall skinny blonde at the gym, the one who disses you at the water fountain? I'm here to tell you everything you suspect about me is true:

Yes, I have an easy job making ridiculous money.

Yes, I turned the extra bedroom in my fab Atlanta condo into a closet for my designer wardrobe.

Yes, I have a personal assistant.

And yes, as a matter of fact, my gorgeous boyfriend *is* a doctor.

My life is beyond amazing and more than I could've dreamed when I was growing up. My mother might say I've "gotten above my raisin'." I guess that's why I've become such a diva... and why a part of me has always been waiting for the other shoe to drop.

As much as you dislike women like me (rightfully so because, admittedly, even *I* kind of hate me), you'll be happy to know when the shoe finally dropped—Christian Louboutin, of course—it landed with a giant, life-changing crash.

I'm Della, by the way. Della Culpepper. And trust me—you won't want to miss my freefall into reality.

JULY

July 1, Saturday

"WHAT ARE YOU GOING to buy with your bonus?" my boyfriend Dr. Kyle Covey asked me.

I avoided making eye contact with the chatty concierge in the lobby of my condo building on my way to the elevator, then spoke into the microphone of my headset, trying to sound modest. "I might not get a bonus. They're not guaranteed at Traxton, you know."

A couple of smiley residents walked toward me. I gave them the "I'm-not-stopping-to-speak-to-you" wave and kept going. The only people in the building I hang with are Sabrina, an event planner, and Susan, a sales rep for a liquor distributor, and they're both working out of town through the Fourth of July holiday.

"Of course you'll get a bonus," Kyle said. "You crushed your sales quota for the quarter—again."

"I did," I admitted, jabbing the call button with my elbow in deference to my fresh manicure. "I even asked Anthony to hold back some of this week's orders to submit next week for the new quarter."

I stiffened when a woman walked up carrying a little wrinkly dog—a pug, I think. I'm not a dog person.

"How's your personal assistant working out?" Kyle asked.

"Great." I stepped onto the elevator and moved as far away from the pooch and its owner as I could. "He keeps me organized, and frees me up to make more sales calls."

The woman with the dog glared. "Do I have to listen to your conversation?"

I covered my mike. "Do I have to share my elevator with your ugly dog?"

The woman gasped. "I've heard about you."

"Believe it all," I shot back.

She turned her back to me.

"Everything okay?" Kyle asked.

"Just dealing with a rude resident," I murmured, loud enough for the woman to hear. "Before I was interrupted, I was about to say I'm glad you suggested I hire an assistant."

"Hiring someone to do the menial work is money well spent."

"True." I've learned a lot from Kyle and his family about how the Other Half lives.

The elevator dinged and to my dismay, the woman with the dog got off on my floor. They both gave me parting snarls as they peeled off.

Shrugging off the irritation, I turned to walk down a hallway that led to my unit. "I was thinking if I get a bonus," I mused aloud to Kyle, "I might have Anthony shop for a new leather sectional for the condo. Something Italian."

Kyle made a rueful noise. "Sometimes I think I chose the wrong side of the medical industry."

I knew when he was fishing for a compliment. "Right. As if your celebrity clients could do without you. Wasn't it just last week Toni Springer gave you a shout-out from the red carpet?" I stopped in front of my door.

"You're right—I'm happy in dermatology. Besides, I don't have the temperament for pharmaceutical sales. I'm too honest."

Panic blipped in my chest. "You think I'm dishonest?"

"I'm teasing," he said good-naturedly.

I exhaled. I was being too sensitive. Kyle had no idea how dishonest I've been.

"I'm happy one of us can cash in on the hottest selling weight loss drug in history," he said.

"It pays to be in the right place at the right time," I offered breezily.

"I just wish I'd bought stock in Traxton Pharma when Beltina first hit the market."

Like I did, I wanted to say, but didn't. No use to rub it in.

"Listen, I gotta run," Kyle said. "Want to grab dinner later?"

I eased two fingers between my belly and the waistband of my skirt as a gauge. "Something light?"

"Okay, I'll text you. Congrats, doll. I'm proud of you."

"Thank you."

I waited until the call dropped before emitting a little squeal of happiness. I had the perfect boyfriend. And the perfect job.

I punched in the key code to the door of my condo and pushed it open.

And the perfect home.

I live in a corner unit in a lux condo building in Triangle Point, Atlanta's premiere work/live/play development. I still got a thrill every time I walked through the door of my posh digs. High ceilings, hardwood floors, high end finishes, and—

An odor reached me and I wrinkled my nose. Dirty dishes?

As I went from room to room and took in the disarray—food containers strewn about my living room, wet towels on my bathroom floor, and my unmade bed—my anger mounted.

Everything was just as I'd left it.

My housecleaner Elena had been coming to clean every Saturday for months and had never missed a day... so why today? I checked my phone to see if she'd left a message, but found nothing. Beyond frustrated, I pulled up her name in my contacts, then hit the call button. It rang several times, then Elena's voice came on the line.

"This ees Elena," she said in heavily accented English, "leeve uh mess-eej."

"Elena, this is Della Culpepper. I'm standing in the middle of my uncleaned condo, which should be no news to you. I would've appreciated a call if you had an emergency. What am I supposed to do?"

I tapped my foot, then sighed. "Look...if this has anything to do with the broken vase last week, I'm sure we can work it out. Please call asap to reschedule."

I ended the call with a stab of my finger, and broke my nail. "Dammit!" I shouted to my dirty rooms. "Can't anyone be counted on these days to do their job?" I couldn't let Kyle see this unholy mess.

I brought my arm back to throw my phone against the wall, then caught sight of my reflection in a mirror over a side table and froze. I didn't recognize myself.

Most people would consider me beautiful, I suppose. I inherited a nice face and my height from my mother—the only good things she'd ever given me. Clever grooming and discipline accounted for the rest of my appearance. But in that moment I looked ugly and out of control. I slowly lowered my arm and found my hand was shaking.

It's my stress load, I reasoned. I have a lot of obligations and I've been pushing myself hard to break sales records in a city where the traffic alone can drive a person insane.

I walked to the refrigerator and removed a cold bottle of mineral water from the stockpile inside. I held it to my temple to calm the pulse pounding there and practiced deep breathing. Everything would be okay. I'd meet Kyle near his place for dinner. Elena probably had car trouble, would come by later. By the time I got home, everything would probably be in order.

I have an enviable life—everything I've always dreamed of. And there's more to come. I'm dating a doctor, for heaven's sake. My job is going gangbusters. I most likely have another fat bonus coming my way and, at this rate, the sky is the limit.

My life is good… perfect, in fact.

So why am I scared something bad is about to happen?

July 2, Sunday

THE THING I LOVE most about Triangle Point is everything I need outside of my job is within walking distance, which is almost unheard of in Atlanta. And it's the reason this little contained community is one pricey place to live. Some creative developer decided to take an abandoned manufacturing compound and turn it into a lifestyle playground for adults. From the windows of my condo, I can see high-end department stores, storefronts for any kind of service one can imagine, and mid-rise office buildings for companies looking for a hipster vibe, all stacked and packed into a cute five-square-block village. Everything is new and nice, the way I like it. The spotless sidewalks and manicured landscaping are a far cry from the conditions of my childhood.

Indeed, I often marvel how I got here from there.

Typically the route to my gym is straight-forward, but it's weigh-in day, so I'm taking a more circuitous route to offload some last-minute poundage. I churn my tongue to work up a mouthful of saliva, then discreetly spit into an empty Starbucks cup. Every ounce counts.

"That must be the worst coffee ever," a man said.

I lifted my head to see a stocky dark-haired guy wearing a white apron standing on the sidewalk ahead of me, holding a tray of—dear God—pastries. I'm half-embarrassed he saw me spitting into the cup, but wholly irritated he would comment.

"It's not coffee," I offered in deference to Starbucks, which I revere. "But thanks for minding my business."

I used the voice that typically stopped would-be conversationalists cold, but apparently this guy was an exception.

"Want a free donut?" He extended the carb-laden tray toward me, wafting a fried-sugar scent in my direction.

My mouth watered. I shook my head and picked up the pace so I could get away and spit.

"If you ask me," he called behind me, "you could use a few of these on your back view."

That stopped me. I wasn't going to let some fat guy skinny-shame me. I turned back. "You think so?"

He was still studying my ass. "Definitely."

I walked back. "They're free?"

He smiled. "Yeah. To celebrate a new restaurant." He gestured to the sign behind him—Graham's Eatery.

I scanned the colorful goods—mini donuts, muffins, eclairs, cupcakes, all drizzled and sprinkled to the extreme. "Mmmm," I murmured in appreciation. "Gosh, if you think I'm underfed, I might as well take more than one."

He grinned, pleased with himself. "Yeah, sure, take as many as you want."

"Okay, thanks." With my free hand, I took the tray out of his hands, then resumed walking.

"You're welcome," he called behind me. "What's your name?"

As I passed a garbage can a few feet away, I dumped the entire tray without breaking stride.

"Oh, now that's just not nice," he yelled. "I thought southern girls were supposed to be sweet!"

Without turning, I lifted my sweet middle finger, then spit into my cup.

I pulled my phone from my gym bag and called my assistant. Anthony Wazniak answered like he always did—promptly, and sounding out of breath.

"Hi, Della. How are you today?"

"I've been better. My housekeeper didn't show yesterday and she's not answering her phone."

"Elena? That doesn't sound like her."

"I didn't realize you knew her so well," I offered drily.

"I, uh, don't," he corrected. "She just seemed conscientious."

"Well, she's not. And frankly, I haven't been all that pleased with her work lately. Will you call the agency and ask them to send a replacement a-sap?"

"Will do. Anything else?"

"Actually, I'm considering buying new seating for the living room. Will you put together some ideas?"

"Sure," he said excitedly. Anthony had an unused degree from a private art school, and impeccable taste. And the man *loved* to shop. "Do you have anything special in mind?"

"Something white."

"Good choice," he oozed.

"I'm walking into the gym. Text me when to expect another maid."

"Okay, Della. Have a great day!"

I ended the call. Anthony had been a find. His mother was a friend of Kyle's family, so he came from good stock and he had good manners. His creative background and over-the-top enthusiasm for retail and pop culture didn't make him the best fit for corporate culture, but in the month he'd worked for me, he'd been a stellar personal assistant.

At the gym I carded in and managed to avoid the too-friendly gal at the counter by pretending to be on the phone, ditto for the knot of bouncy Zumba girls in the locker room. I preferred the high intensity interval workout classes and less socializing.

I dropped a tissue into the cup of saliva and discreetly disposed of it. A chunky girl gestured to my workout bag, tastefully branded with "Ask your doctor about Beltina for weight management."

"I see that drug advertised on TV all the time," she said. "Do you take it?"

I nodded. I didn't tell her I sold it because she would probably hit me up for samples.

"Is it expensive?" she asked.

"It's not cheap," I admitted. "But I think it's worth it."

The girl nodded. "You should do one of the commercials—you look great."

"Thanks." My mind bounced back to Donut Guy and I smirked. What a jackass.

I split the time until my trainer Jan arrived between the stair climber and the sauna to sweat off a few more ounces. I'd been watching my diet and taking Beltina twice a day, but I was still nervous when I stepped onto the scale under Jan's stoic gaze. Old habits die hard.

She slid the weighted needle across the numbers on the top of the scale, down, then back up, then nudged it down again. "One hundred twenty-one," she announced, then recorded it on the form on her clipboard. "You're down a pound and a half from last month."

I exhaled. "Good."

"At your height, you'd have to gain fifteen pounds before Traxton put you on notice."

She presented the form for me to sign. As part of my employment contract, I had agreed to "maintain a weight and appearance in keeping with the healthy focus of the Beltina brand." For their part, though, Traxton paid for my gym membership, and for Jan to train me twice a week.

"Are you feeling okay?" she asked.

"Sure." I didn't mention being light-headed and jittery.

"Any problems sleeping, or changes in your energy level?"

I frowned. "No. Why do you ask?"

She shrugged. "No reason." She put away the clipboard and picked up her bag. "Make sure you're eating enough, and stay hydrated in this heat."

I told her I would and waved goodbye. In the locker room I

pulled my phone out of my bag, along with a bottle of Beltina—I hadn't dared to swallow any water this morning. I took my overdue dose and checked text messages for some word from Anthony.

Agency sending replacement cleaner tomorrow.

I felt my blood pressure spike. Tomorrow? How hard could it be to find someone who could use a mop and a broom? I slammed my locker door, then realized in the ensuing silence how loud it must have been. I looked up to see everyone staring at me warily. And that, too, went all over me.

"What?" I asked, then turned and walked out.

If everyone would just do their job, I wouldn't have to get so worked up!

July 3, Monday

"WILL YOU COME TOMORROW, SIS? Please? My boss at the garage is giving me the day off."

I winced into the phone. My younger brother Donnie was the only person who could get me to make the three-hour drive to Dewdrop, Georgia for a Fourth of July family cookout. "Okay, I'll come."

"Hoo-ray!"

"But I don't know how long I can stay."

"You'll stay until the fireworks, won't you? That's the best part."

I swallowed hard. "Of course I'll stay until the fireworks."

"Hoo-ray! Will you bring beef jerky?"

"If I can find some," I promised.

My brother is autistic. He's on the mid- to high-functioning end of the spectrum and he's an excellent mechanic, but he has routines and particular likes and dislikes. Beef jerky is a like.

"Gil will be here," he intoned.

Gil Malone, my mother's shack-up, redneck boyfriend, is a dislike—for me as well.

"Thanks for the warning," I said, and he belly-laughed.

Donnie's laugh is maybe the happiest sound in the world. If I could bottle it to sell, I wouldn't need a wonder drug like Beltina.

"I'll be there around noon, Professor." His nickname since childhood. "Bye."

"Okay. Bye, Sis!"

I ended the call and sighed. It wasn't how I'd hoped to spend the holiday. While it would be nice to see my brother, I dreaded learning what new bad decisions my mother had made.

The ring of the doorbell broke into my thoughts and I bolted up. Finally—a maid. I wasn't sure how much longer I could stand the mess.

I swung open the door to a wisp of a young Asian woman wearing a baggy khaki dress, apron, and sensible shoes, carrying a bucket of equipment that dwarfed her. She hung back.

"Thank God you're here," I said, gesturing for her to come inside. "What's your name?"

She pointed to her name tag.

"Joon-woo," I read. "Well, Joon-woo, my other housekeeper left me high and dry. Everything needs to be done—dusting, mopping, both bathrooms need to be cleaned top to bottom, the carpet vacuumed, the bed linens washed and changed...and the kitchen—I mean, just look at it."

She surveyed the smelly clutter, wide-eyed.

"Do you understand?" I asked, enunciating each syllable.

She nodded, then set down her bucket, snapped on a pair of yellow rubber gloves, and set to work. I was dubious, but I left her to do her thing while I called Kyle to break the news I wouldn't be joining him and his friends on his boat at Lake Lanier the following day.

"Oh, no," he said. "Why not?"

"My brother called and he's having a family reunion in southern Georgia."

"Your brother the professor?"

"That's r-right." It wasn't a lie, not really. "It's a last-minute thing, and my mother really wants me to be there." Okay, that *was* a lie.

"Maybe I should go with you."

"No," I blurted. "I mean... no one there will know you."

He laughed. "That's kind of the point, isn't it? I'd like to meet your family one of these days, Della."

"And you will. But tomorrow's not the best time."

"I'm starting to think you're ashamed of me."

I gave a high-pitched laugh. "Not at all."

"I don't have a PhD like your brother, and I'm not an inventor, like your father—"

"Step-father," I corrected, and still almost choked on the word. The only things that idiot Gil Malone had ever invented were new ways to dodge work.

"—but I can hold my own in a conversation. And I give free skincare advice."

That would go over like gangbusters. "You'll meet them another time," I said. In an alternate universe. "Besides, you wouldn't want to disappoint your guests."

"Will you at least be back before the fireworks?"

What was it with men and fireworks?

"I'll try, but don't count on it."

He sighed. "Okay. At least let me know when you're back home."

"I will."

From the bedroom I'd turned into a closet came a loud thump followed by a cacophony of falling boxes.

"What was that?" Kyle asked.

"My housekeeper," I said through gritted teeth. "If she didn't kill herself, I might have to strangle her."

"Go," he said. "Bye."

I jogged to the room and shrieked. Joon-woo was clawing her way out from under a couple dozen designer shoe boxes she had apparently upended with the vacuum. She looked stricken, and rightfully so considering how many thousands of dollars of shoes lay around like bodies after a highway pileup. Angry tears gathered behind my eyes—I'd worked too hard to have nice things for them to be ruined by careless hired help.

"Get out of this room," I ordered. "Go clean the kitchen."

When she hesitated, I lost it.

"Joon-woo, go clean the kitchen!" I screamed, pointing.

She skedaddled, dragging the vacuum. I cursed and began to pick up the boxes. There went the woman's tip.

Good help was so hard to find.

I swiped at the tears, telling myself not to be so emotional, but in the face of tomorrow's dreaded trip to see my family, it felt as if the universe was trying to sabotage me, push me back down... put me in my place.

I squinted at a pink leather Aquazzura sandal and whimpered—it was scratched!

I was definitely being punished.

My phone rang and when I saw the name, my mood instantly vaulted. It was my boss calling... to congratulate me on a standout quarter?

I dropped the sandal and connected the call. "Hi, Portia."

"Hi, Della. Did I catch you at a bad time? Your voice sounds funny."

"No." I used a cloth Christian Louboutin shoe dust bag to wipe my eyes, then blow my nose. "Allergies. What's up?"

"Well, first, congratulations on a great quarter—your numbers have exploded. In fact, you're a big reason why Beltina is now the fourth most prescribed drug in the southeast."

I smiled. "I am? It is? That's terrific news. I hope that means everyone will get a nice bonus." I crossed my fingers and waited.

Portia made a thoughtful noise. "Actually, I'd like to talk to you about that in person, Della. Can we have lunch Wednesday?"

"The day after tomorrow?" I asked, surprised.

"Yes. I thought I'd fly in and sit down with you face to face to discuss a change in your responsibilities."

My pulse spiked with excitement, but I schooled my voice. "Of course. I'll have to move a few appointments, but that won't be a problem." For Anthony.

"Good. I'll have my assistant send you the details. Enjoy the holiday, and I'll see you Wednesday."

"I'm looking forward to it," I said, and managed not to squeal until I ended the call. When I did, Joon-woo peeked her head around the corner, her slender face creased in concern.

"I'm okay," I assured her, enunciating slowly and loudly. "I *think* I am getting a pro-*mo*-tion."

She nodded, gave me a thumbs up, then disappeared again.

Just for that, Joon-woo might get a tip after all, I decided. A small one.

July 4, Tuesday

"DO YOU THINK PORTIA wants to make me a sales manager?" I asked Kyle. I was driving south, heading for the rabbit hole of Dewdrop. From the background noise, I could tell Kyle was on his houseboat, soaking up the sun and clinking glasses with other golden people who couldn't imagine spending a summer day any other way.

"Seems likely since she's flying in from L.A.," Kyle said. "I did an informal survey on the boat and half the women here are taking Beltina, and those are only the ones who fessed up."

I frowned. "How many woman are on the boat?"

"Too many to count," he teased. "But none of them have your fire—or your legs."

I cooed.

"The point is this drug is selling as fast as they can make it. Traxton is probably going to have to hire new sales reps, and they're going to need someone with experience to manage the new people. You're a shoe-in, doll."

I groaned. "Don't mention shoes. I spent the better part of yesterday putting my shoe collection back after my bumbling housekeeper demolished it."

"Did you fire her?"

"I couldn't. She doesn't speak English. And other than the shoe disaster, she actually did a good job."

"As far as I'm concerned, you're lucky when the help doesn't steal anything. You did lock up your jewelry, didn't you?"

Dammit—I couldn't get used to this Other Half gig. "I don't really have that many nice pieces."

"Well, we'll have to remedy that," he said, his voice all low and sexy.

My heart jumped. If I married Kyle, we'd be a power couple, and I'd have the kind of life no one could take away. Kyle's parents had money, and their parents had money. The Covey family had pedigree.

The only Pedigree my family had was the dog food for the albino pit bulls Gil had penned up in the back yard of my mother's ramshackle house.

The thought of our families mixing was the stuff nightmares

were made of. And if Kyle knew the truth about me and my dubious relations, he'd wipe me from his life.

He sighed. "Are you sure your family can't do without you today?"

I glanced at the mile marker coming up. If I turned around now, I could be at the dock in a little more than an hour. It took all my willpower and the image of Donnie's face not to. "Duty calls," I managed to get out.

"I don't believe you've ever said the name of the town you're from."

"Dew... berry... ville."

"Dewberryville?"

"You're breaking up," I said, rubbing my finger over the mike on my headset. "Must be driving through a dead zone. Have fun with your friends!"

I kept Donnie's sweet face in my mind the entire depressing drive. The last fifty miles to Dewdrop were rugged and void of radio or cell phone reception. I was pretty sure Google Maps had no idea this place existed. I had to admit, though, the landscape was picturesque, if a little desolate. It was mostly farmland dotted with houses and barns. Corn and peanuts were the predominant crops, with strawberries here and there. My family weren't farmers—that would be too productive. My uncle Seth used to raise watermelons, but mostly to plug and fill with grain alcohol to sell to his buddies. And I have memories of my grandmother raising tomatoes that were ugly and bumpy on the outside, but tasted so good.

It occurred to me I hadn't tasted a good tomato since I'd moved to Atlanta over ten years ago to attend community college.

I zoomed down the SUV windows to inhale some fresh country air. But when the stench of country manure hit me, I remembered some of the less pleasant aspects of rural living, and zoomed the windows back up. My windshield was a polka-dotted mess of bug guts. I winced when the right side of the Audi lurched into a particularly deep pothole. When I returned home, my car would need a trip to the auto spa for sure.

Dirty or not, I knew my foreign vehicle would cause a stir when I pulled up to my mother's house and parked next to all the pickup trucks and domestic compacts, and I was right. A crowd of about forty people had gathered in the yard around long picnic tables laden with food. They all turned curious faces my way, and some pointed. I spotted Donnie, whose handsome face split into a big grin as he jogged to my car.

The boy could melt me into goo.

"Hi, Sis!"

"Hi, Professor." I was one of the few people he would embrace. At twenty-five, Donnie was a big man, tanned from fishing and strong from working on cars. I wrapped my arms around his wide chest and held him close for as long as I dared. "You're filling out."

"You're so skinny," he said bluntly. "And blond. I almost didn't recognize you."

It hit me that I hadn't seen him in over a year. "I've lost some weight," I conceded, then touched my light hair. "And I thought I needed a change."

"It looks pretty," he said with a grin.

"Thanks, Donnie."

"Cool SUV."

"It's my company car."

His eyes widened. "Your boss gave it to you?"

I nodded. "Because I have to drive to make sales calls."

"You must be really good at your job."

I smiled. "I am. I brought you some beef jerky—it's in the back with some other food for the cookout. Will you help me unload?"

"I'll get it. You should go say hello to Mom. She's surprised."

I glanced over and saw my mother standing at the corner of the yard, hugging herself and looking anxious.

"She didn't know I was coming?"

"I didn't tell her," Donnie said. "I was afraid you wouldn't come."

Which, I realized, reflected growth on Donnie's part. Keeping a secret required a certain amount of deception, which was difficult for him... but easy-peasy for me.

I walked to where my mother stood and conjured up a smile. "Hi, Mom."

Lisa Culpepper was once a pretty woman, but years of hard work and disappointment have taken their toll. Her face has taken on a harsh quality. "Hello, MaeDella. What have you done to yourself?"

I winced inwardly at the sound of my given name. "Lost a few pounds and changed my hair color—it's no big deal."

But she was still looking at me as if I were a stranger. "This must've been Donnie's idea."

I nodded. "He called me, I said I'd come."

"Well, hell-o, MaeDella."

I glanced over at the leering man who sauntered up to stand next to my mother. "Hi, Gil." He smelled like he'd fallen off a beer truck after drinking the cargo.

"You look different," he said, then licked his lips.

"You look the same," I returned.

"With your fancy car and your fancy clothes you must be doing well." He tipped his beer bottle to indicate my sundress and sandals.

"It's called a job, Gil. You should look into it sometime."

He frowned. "I guess you came down from the big city to save the day?"

I was confused. "What do you mean?"

My mother's body language grew agitated. "Gil, MaeDella came for a visit is all."

But something was up. I looked past them to a homemade banner that read "SaVE LiSA anD gILs HOMe." And beneath the banner was a large mason jar stuffed with coins and dollar bills.

I wanted to point out Gil was a squatter, but I needed to cut to the chase. "What's this about?"

"Donnie shouldn't have called you," my mother said.

"Bank called in a loan against the house," Gil blurted. "They're going to take it and the land."

The house and land where Donnie and I had grown up, the house Donnie still lived in with my mother and her ape of a boyfriend. The little green clapboard structure didn't hold a lot of good memories for me, but it had kept the rain off my head. I pressed my lips together. "What loan?"

My mother slid her gaze to Gil, who was posturing like a rooster. "See, there was this business deal I thought was a sure thing—"

"How much?" I asked my mom.

"MaeDella, I don't—"

"How much?"

"Twenty thousand will get us out from under," Gil said.

I blinked. "Twenty thousand?"

"Twenty-five would give us some wiggle room."

July 5, Wednesday

I DOUBLE-CHECKED the restaurant address Portia's assistant had sent, then groaned.

"This joint?"

Graham's Eatery was the place where Donut Guy had attempted to assault me with carbs. Maybe I'd get lucky and he wouldn't be working today.

I walked into the cool interior and glanced around. The décor was industrial chic—lots of stainless steel and reclaimed wood, with some farmhouse elements thrown in. I was immediately suspicious of the menu because the air smelled like yeast. Other diners didn't seem to have the same misgivings, though, since the tables were nearly full.

The hostess greeted me. "Do you have a reservation?"

"It's under Portia Smithson," I said. "I'm early."

"I can go ahead and seat you… right this way."

On the way to the table, I scanned for the dark-haired guy, but didn't see him. Not that he would recognize me anyway—I was wearing my favorite powder blue suit, a white silk tank, and classic Manolo Blahnik black pumps. I wanted Portia to picture me as a sales manager. Now that my savings account had been drained— How had the odious Gil known the exact amount I had in reserve?—I really needed the bonus and the promotion to materialize. I had financial obligations of my own.

Under the table, my leg jumped in trepidation. Portia was intimidating. She didn't remember our first encounter, but it had changed my life.

Four years ago I interviewed for a sales position with Traxton as Mae Culpepper. But I knew within a few seconds of walking in I wouldn't get the job. Portia had swept her cool glance over my plump figure, discount clothes, and blah brown hair, and instantly dismissed me as a candidate even though she asked a few rote questions as a formality. I had left the interview humiliated, but determined to change my image. After finding a mention of Beltina on the Internet—at the time it was available only in Europe—I used the Dark Web to find a black market supplier, and the pounds melted off. As luck would have it, Traxton became the North America provider of the drug. I reinvented myself as Della Culpepper, slender blond bombshell, and reapplied at Traxton. I'd maxed out my credit card on a designer outfit, professional makeup, and hair coloring by the most celebrated stylist in town, and Portia had offered me the job on the spot.

It had been a valuable lesson about projecting the person I wanted to be. And some part of me still worried something about me as Della would trigger her memory of me as Mae, and I would be revealed.

My mouth was dry. I glanced around for a waitress, hoping for a glass of water to calm my nerves. I spotted a waiter standing next to a nearby table and waved to get his attention.

"Excuse me."

He looked up and I balked—it was Donut Man.

"Yes?" he said, coming toward me.

I reached for my phone so I wouldn't have to make eye contact. "A glass of water, please?"

"Yes, ma'am." He moved to a water station and filled a glass with ice water from a pitcher.

I watched him under my lashes and pretended to check messages when he set the glass on the table.

"Can I get you anything else while you wait for your party?"

"No, thank you."

"Perhaps you'd like to flip me off again?"

I looked up into his mocking gaze. He totally recognized me.

"For the record," I said, narrowing my eyes, "you deserved it."

He opened his mouth to respond, but I saw Portia walk in and cut him off by standing.

"That's my boss," I hissed. "Scram."

Thankfully he moved away as I greeted Portia, who looked like a sleek cat in her tailored dress.

"Hi, Della," Portia said in her throaty voice, then she gave me a hug. "You look well."

She'd never given me a hug before. That was a good sign. "Thank you, Portia. You look fantastic, as usual."

"I forget how hot it gets in the South," she said, fanning herself. "How do you stand it?"

"I—"

"Unfortunately, I don't have much time, so I need to make this quick."

She reached for her briefcase, and my pulse ticked higher. She'd brought a written offer for the sales manager position. To hide my involuntary smile, I lifted my glass for a drink.

"We're letting you go, Della."

It took a few seconds for her words to sink in. When they did, I inhaled sharply and brought water into my lungs. I sputtered and coughed, fighting for air. My mind reeled.

"It's not you," she said, pulling papers from her briefcase. "The FDA has suspended sales of Beltina pending further clinical trials."

"Wh—why?" I managed to get out.

Portia gave a dismissive wave. "Something about a spike in reported side effects." Then she pointed her finger. "Actually, in a way, it *is* you. Sales in the Southeast have outpaced sales in the rest of the country, and this is where the complaints are being recorded."

I gaped. "It's my fault the drug has been suspended because I sold too much of it?"

"Ironic, huh? But don't worry. If all goes well, we expect to be back in the good graces of the FDA in six months. Then we'll hire you back."

"Hire me back?"

She handed me a pen and pointed to the bottom of a form. "If you sign here."

I frowned. "What's this?"

"Standard confidentiality agreement. You can't discuss anything you know about Traxton or Beltina, or the terms of your dismissal. The FDA will control statements made to the press so you can't tell a soul about the drug suspension. If you do, you could be prosecuted for insider trading since this could affect the company's stock price. Also, it goes without saying you can't sell any Traxton stock you might own. In return you'll get two weeks' base pay, and your quarterly bonus of—she consulted another paper—thirty-two thousand dollars."

I was still processing everything she said. "That's my best bonus yet."

She smiled. "You earned it. But you need to sign the papers, Della, for your own protection. And to ensure that when things blow over, I can hire you again—possibly as a sales manager."

My elusive promotion. "Sales manager?"

She nodded. "You're definitely management material."

That was bolstering. Still… "What if I don't sign?"

Her mouth formed a flat line and she sighed. "Then we'll have to get the attorneys involved. The severance package would be off the table… and you wouldn't be eligible to come back in six months." She looked pained. "We don't want that, do we?"

I swallowed. "No."

She tapped the bottom of the form, and I slowly signed my name. From her briefcase she pulled out a notary stamp and processed the document. Then she pulled out a handheld scanner and ran it over the form a page at a time. "I just emailed you a copy."

My phone vibrated in confirmation.

"You'll need to print that soon. Your Traxton email address will be suspended at midnight."

"O-kay."

"Someone from Human Resources will be in touch about other company property."

She zipped her briefcase and stood, then tucked a fifty dollar bill under a plate as a tip in exchange, I realized, for conducting unpleasant business in a public place that best ensured a jilted employee wouldn't freak out.

"Goodbye, Della. I'll be in touch sometime in December."

I wanted to stand but I wasn't sure my legs would support me. "What am I supposed to do for six months?"

She gave me a magnanimous smile. "Anything you want." Then she sobered. "As long as it's not sales."

"Come again?"

Portia tapped her briefcase. "Read the non-compete clause. Take care."

I watched her walk out of the restaurant and climb into a waiting cab. The whole thing had taken less than ten minutes.

"I take it that didn't go well."

I looked up to see Donut Man standing there. To my horror, I burst into tears.

He looked equally horrified, but before he could say anything else, I got up and strode out.

By the time I walked back to the condo, my tears had dried and stunned mortification had set in. I walked through the lobby like a zombie. This couldn't be happening. An hour ago I was contemplating what my new Traxton business cards would look like, and now, I'm unemployed. The elevator ride seemed to take forever and when I got off on my floor, I went the wrong way. When I finally found my door, I fumbled with the keycode for long minutes. When it opened, I was weak with relief. I just wanted to curl up in a ball and have a good cry.

"Surprise!"

I screamed, then recognized Kyle, Anthony, Susan, and Sabrina standing there with noisemakers, holding a cake.

Kyle stepped forward and kissed me. "We were so sure your boss had good news, we wanted to celebrate."

Anthony grinned. "So how did it go?"

"Did you get the promotion?" Sabrina asked.

Susan snapped a photo.

They were all so excited for me, I couldn't bear to burst their bubble. And my pride was still smarting. Besides, I wasn't allowed to tell anyone I'd been fired. And Portia had hinted she would be hiring me back as a sales manager....

I pulled a smile out of my canned behind. "I got it all right."

July 6, Thursday

I STARED AT THE orange pill in my hand. I'd been taking Beltina twice a day for almost four years, with no side effects. I scanned the side of the ten-tablet sample box for warnings I might have overlooked, but saw none. Once I became a sales rep for Beltina, I had access to an unlimited supply of samples, so I could skip the black market and a State-side prescription. And thank goodness I had just enough samples left to get me through the end of the year.

But should I stop taking it? Portia hadn't mentioned what complaints patients had made, but surely she would have if they'd been serious in nature.

Remembering the big piece of celebratory cake I'd had yesterday, I tossed the pill to the back of my throat and swallowed it with a drink of water.

Then I placed a call to Traxton Human Resources to get a date for when my bonus would land in my account. My monthly overhead, including four thousand for the condo mortgage and association fees, was about ten thousand. If I slashed all luxuries and food, I could get that figure down to about five thousand. My two weeks' base pay was a pittance, but my bonus would cover me for six months... barely.

The young woman on the phone made a rueful noise. "It's going to take a while to process your termination paperwork."

After being on hold for forty minutes, my patience was already worn thin, but I pushed down my rising ire. "How long?"

"The home office in Switzerland shuts down the entire month of July, so it'll be after that—maybe August?"

I bit down on my tongue until I tasted blood. "Can you be more specific?"

"No, sorry. And to be honest, we're probably looking at September."

My eyes practically crossed. "That's unacceptable! I have bills to pay—I need my money."

"And I need a new air conditioner in my car," the woman said flatly. "That bonus check of yours is more than I'll make this year."

I scoffed. "It's not my fault you have a crappy job."

She hung up on me.

"Oooh!" I started to throw my phone, then remembered I couldn't afford a new one. So I picked up the first thing I could get my hands on—a stainless steel water bottle—and threw it. It bounced off a tile wall into the mirror over my bathroom vanity, leaving a cobweb of broken glass in the frame.

Great—was that seven years of bad luck, or did inflation apply?

I leaned over to grip my knees. I had to think. I'd planned to replenish my savings by selling my Traxton stock, and now that wasn't an option. I had half a mind to call my mother and tell her I needed the money back, that she and Gil would have to save themselves from their own stupidity.

But that would leave Donnie out in the cold (or in this case, the heat), and he didn't cope well with change.

My phone rang and speak of the angel, it was Donnie calling. I didn't want to talk to anyone, but I couldn't risk that he was having an emergency.

I exhaled, then connected the call. "Hi, Professor."

"Hi, Sis. Gil's gone."

My first thought was Gil was dead, but people like Gil Malone don't die—they live on and on and on. Unless someone helps them along.

"Gone where?"

"Don't know. Mom's crying. She said he took the money."

My stomach cramped. *No, please God.* "Put Mom on the phone."

They argued for a few seconds, then my mom's tearful voice came on the line. "Hi, MaeDella."

"What happened?"

"Yesterday I deposited the check you gave me into our account… and this morning Gil was gone."

"And all the money?"

"He left me enough for groceries."

"That was big of him!" I exploded.

"MaeDella, Gil's not a bad man—he just can't catch a break."

Something in me snapped. "Mother, Gil Malone is an idiot, and so is any woman who would stay with him."

She gasped. "When did you turn into an awful person, MaeDella? You're nothing but a big fake."

While I processed my mother's assessment of me, Donnie's worried voice came back on the line. "She didn't mean it, Sis."

"Yes, she did. But that's okay."

"I have six hundred dollars saved up, but the man at the bank said they need at least ten thousand by tomorrow or they're going to throw us out."

"Don't worry, Professor," I said with as much good cheer as I could manage. "I'll take care of it. You take care of Mom, okay?"

"Okay," he said, sounding relieved.

I ended the call and scoured my accounts, near panic. If I

drained my checking and got cash withdrawals across my credit cards, I could cover it. With hatred toward Gil Effing Malone burning in my stomach and a migraine coming in for a landing, I made a call to the local Dewdrop bank. If there was an advantage to being from a small town, it was that everyone knew everyone and they wouldn't question Lisa Culpepper's daughter calling to arrange payment on her loan.

"Oh, hi, MaeDella, sure I can take care of that for you, and what a nice thing to do for your mama, she's so proud of you, says you've got a fancy condo in Atlanta, and a big job making a lot of money, woo-we, that must be nice."

I closed my eyes. Yes, that must be.

July 7, Friday

"THIS LOOKS LIKE A COOL PLACE," Kyle said as we were seated at Graham's Eatery. "Why didn't you want to eat here?"

"Uh... Portia and I had lunch here and it wasn't a good experience," I said. I glanced around for the stocky waiter, but didn't see him. But I was wearing a hat and sunglasses, so maybe he wouldn't recognize me.

"We can still leave," Kyle offered.

"No. It was nice of your client to give you a gift card." Besides, I would normally put my meal on my expense account, and that was no longer an option. For a free lunch, I'd take my chances.

"Libby says it's the freshest place in town."

"Libby?" I asked.

"Libby Lakes, you know—the reality show star."

"Ah. What dermatology work is she having done?"

He wagged his finger. "You know I can't say. But she's on the verge of turning thirty, so her face needs some extra care."

I blinked. "I'm on the verge of turning thirty. Does my face need extra care?"

He grinned. "The hat and sunglasses make it hard for me to tell. What's up with that?"

"Light sensitivity," I murmured, picking up a menu. Plus my dark roots were starting to show—I needed to get to the salon soon.

"Interesting selection," Kyle remarked, studying his menu.

"Lots of carbs."

"Yeah, stay away from those. When you hit thirty sugar goes straight to your ass."

I looked up sharply, then smiled. "And you like my ass the way it is?"

"I do," he said with a wink.

And Kyle could have just about any ass he wanted. He had patrician good looks and perfect skin, naturally. He stayed trim by running and juicing. And he'd just been named one of Atlanta's most eligible bachelors by *Biz Trends* magazine. I was a very lucky woman, and I was determined not to mess this up by turning into a dough-butt.

A waitress came by to take our orders. I chose a salad and Kyle ordered flank steak. Over our meal, he talked about his business, and I tried to be attentive. But I confess I was distracted by my predicament, and as embarrassing as it would be, I wondered if I should come clean to Kyle.

Or I could keep up appearances and when December and my promotion arrived, I could pick up where I left off with no one the wiser.

"Della?"

I startled. "What?"

He made a regretful noise. "Here I am rattling on about my practice when you must be overwhelmed with your new job situation."

"I am," I admitted. "In fact—"

"By the way, I called my broker this morning and bought ten thousand shares of Traxton."

My stomach pitched. "Ten thousand? Isn't it trading at—"

"Around fifty dollars a share, yeah. But after finding out how many women in my circle of friends alone are taking Beltina, I think it's a great investment." He grinned. "So we can both get rich off this wonder drug."

Well, that settled it—I couldn't say anything now. If I did and Kyle sold his shares, the SEC would lock us both up. And orange isn't a good color for me.

"How was your lunch?" the waitress asked, clearing our plates.

"That was the best flank steak I've ever eaten," Kyle said. "So tender."

The girl smiled. "I'll tell the chef." She looked at me. "And the salad, ma'am?"

"The tomatoes were bland. Otherwise, it was fine."

Her smile dimmed. "Sorry about that." She hurried away, arms full.

Kyle coughed. "You always seem to be a little hard on waitresses, Della. The quality of the food isn't her fault. Besides, aren't tomatoes supposed to be bland?"

"As a matter of fact, no, they're not." I leaned forward. "Can we go out on the boat this weekend?"

He grimaced. "Actually, I had an ulterior motive for lunch. I wanted to tell you in person I'm going to Sacramento for two weeks to learn a new procedure for injectables."

"When do you leave?"

"Tomorrow. They had a last-minute vacancy. I wish you could go, too, but with your new promotion, I'm sure this is a bad time for you to be away."

"Right," I said, trying to tamp down my relief. With Kyle out of town, it would take off some of the pressure of lying. "You should go alone and focus on work."

"I'm excited to try this new product. It's supposed to look great and last twice as long as anything else on the market." He angled his head. "And when I get back, maybe I can use it to fill in those laugh lines of yours."

"Excuse me," a man's voice said.

I was happy for the interruption, until I glanced up to see Donut Man standing at our table. I ducked my head and feigned interest in the strap on my sandal.

"Deidre told me how much you enjoyed your steak, sir, so I wanted to introduce myself. I'm Chef Charlie Graham."

Crap, this was *his* place?

Kyle stuck out his hand. "Dr. Kyle Covey—have we met before? I feel like I know your name."

"I don't believe so," the chef said. "But it's nice to meet you today."

"My steak was terrific. You have a great place here."

"Thank you. But the lady wasn't as pleased with my tomatoes, I hear."

I felt his gaze on me. Slowly I raised my head, still hoping he didn't recognize me under the hat and behind the glasses.

But he so did.

"It's hard to find good tomatoes," I murmured in concession.

"But I'll try harder," he said. "What's your name?"

"Della," I said reluctantly. "Culpepper."

He extended his hand and I had no choice but to put mine in his.

He covered my hand with both of his huge paws. "I hope you'll give me another chance, Della."

I tugged to withdraw my hand, then nodded. "Of course."

Kyle's phone rang. "Sorry—I need to get this. I'll take it over there, Della."

Great. Alone with Chef Charlie.

"I'm glad to see you," he said in a lowered voice. "I feel bad about what I said when you were here with your boss."

"Don't mention it," I said.

"It was none of my business."

I gritted my teeth. "I said, *don't mention it.*"

He held up his hands. "Got it." But he didn't leave, stood there studying me with a sardonic smile on his face.

"What?" I bit out.

"I'm just wondering."

I sighed. "Wondering what?"

"How you even *got* those laugh lines."

He walked away and I hoped the man could feel the eye daggers I threw at his fat back.

July 8, Saturday

WHEN THE DOORBELL rang, I was soaking in a jet bubble bath in the dark, drinking wine. My predicament was starting to sink in and to say I was feeling sorry for myself would be a bit of an understatement. I kept remembering my foreboding feeling one week earlier that things for MaeDella Culpepper were simply too good, so the universe was due a correction.

I was right. I usually loved being right, but... wait, I lost my train of thought.

A chime sounded.

Oh, right—the doorbell. It was probably Anthony or Susan or Sabrina, none of whom I wanted to talk to. If I didn't answer, they'd go away.

I had been clinging to the hope that Portia would call and say letting me go had been a big mistake and/or misunderstanding and I could hit the "resume" button on my career, but that was starting to seem unlikely. So I was considering faking my own death, or simply disappearing for a few months to see how things would shake out. If I said I'd been kidnapped, surely the bank wouldn't foreclose on the condo, if only at the risk of bad public relations.

How ironic that I'd saved my mother's house from foreclosure, and now I was wondering how I was going to keep my own roof over my head.

Suddenly I was blinded by the bathroom light. I squinted, a little too drunk to be afraid someone was in my condo. Plus from the startled gasp, the intruder seemed more scared than I was. When I saw the sensible shoes and the bucket of cleaning equipment, I smiled.

"Joon-woo, it's you." Then I laughed. "Hey, that rhymed."

But her eyes were bugged out of her small face in horror as she surveyed my red foamy bath. I looked down and realized why. "Don't worry," I slurred. "I didn't slit my wrists." I raised my arms, hefting an open bottle in each hand. "It's spilled wine."

She calmed visibly, her hand to her chest.

"I forgot you were coming today. I guess the agency gave you the code for my door?"

She nodded.

"Have you talked to Elena, my former housekeeper? I can't remember her last name."

She shook her head.

"Because if you hear a story about me throwing a vase, there was a very good reason for it."

She waited.

"Well, I don't remember the reason, exactly, but I'm sure at the time, it made sense."

She averted her gaze to the broken mirror over the vanity, and I covered my guilt by taking another drink—from each bottle. Then I gestured to the clutter on the counter and the dirty clothes in the floor. "You can clean around me, keep me company."

She began to gather up clothes and put them in the hamper.

"Joon-woo, do you think I have laugh lines?"

She walked back to my garden tub and I thrust my face forward for her inspection. She squinted, then shook her head.

"Good. Men suck, don't they?"

She nodded fervently.

The general assiness of men appeared to be a universal truth that crossed language barriers. I sighed and took two more drinks. The cleaning service was one expense I was probably going to have to drop, but I'd think about that later.

The small woman shook a plastic garbage bag to open it, then began to clear the counter of cups and tissues and corks.

"Joon-woo you aren't going to steal from me, are you?"

She looked at me, then shook her head.

"Please don't." I took another swig and swished fresh wine to dispel the taste of sour wine, then swallowed. "Because it might be something I'll need to sell."

July 9, Sunday

"HOW IS THE NEW housekeeper working out?" Anthony asked.

I hummed into the phone, wavering. "Joon-woo is doing a decent job, I suppose."

But I regretted letting her see me drunk—oh, and naked. What if she told the cleaning company? Or reported me for sexual harassment?

"You're already on a first name basis with her?"

"The communication is one way—she understands English, but doesn't speak it."

"But you like her better than the previous housecleaner?"

I made a non-committal sound. "Did the company say why Elena didn't come back to clean for me?"

Even with the headache of a hangover, I remembered the vase-throwing incident more clearly now, and I could see how she might have misconstrued the situation. But no one had been hurt—she'd had plenty of time to duck.

"The lady at the company didn't say," Anthony replied, "and besides, you said you weren't happy with Elena's work anyway."

I frowned. "I wasn't, but it's the principle. She should've at least let me know she wouldn't be back."

"I don't disagree," he offered sympathetically, "but it's probably best to just forget about it."

"I suppose." Still… I was perturbed with Elena for just dropping off the face of the earth like that.

"I'm emailing over your appointment schedule for the week," Anthony said. "You'll be in Peachtree City Monday, in Athens Tuesday—"

"Actually," I cut in, "I'm going to take off a couple of weeks, so I need for you to cancel all my appointments."

"Ah—I guess you want to get ready for your new position as sales manager?"

"Um, right. But until Traxton assigns someone to take over my accounts, don't say anything to the customers about the move. If anyone asks, just say something came up."

"Will do."

"And don't use my business email address."

"Of course, I'll use your personal email address until you get a new address from Traxton to go with your new title."

"Right," I murmured. "And since I won't be working the next couple of weeks, you can take some time off too." I paid Anthony by the hour, so I needed to find a way to ease into letting him go.

"Gosh, Della, I really need the hours to make my rent this month. You've been saying you were going to hire a kitchen and closet organizer—what if I do that for you?"

I winced, wishing I didn't like Anthony so much. "Okay."

"Super! And I'm still looking for your living room seating, but I hope to have some nice options to show you soon."

Right—the furniture I'd been planning to buy with my quarterly bonus. No way was that going to happen, but if I told Anthony I'd changed my mind, he might get suspicious. And if he found out I'd been fired, his connection to Kyle's family meant they'd find out, too.

"That sounds good," I said, trying to inject some enthusiasm into my voice. "Why don't you come by Thursday?"

"See you then," he sang.

I ended the call and sighed, then turned back to the job search engine on my laptop screen. I was hoping to find something low-key for quick cash while I waited for things to right themselves at Traxton. I read aloud from the helpful how-to's.

"Filter by including or excluding your wish list requirements for your dream job, then hit 'search' and start applying. You could be making money within hours."

My mood buoyed—this might be easier than I thought.

"Okay." I talked to the screen as I typed. "Include 'high compensation,' 'work from home,' and 'exciting.' Exclude 'sales'." I hit the search button and waited for a list of dream jobs to appear.

No results. Please adjust your expectations and try again.

I pursed my mouth. Hm… this might be harder than I thought.

July 10, Monday

SINCE IT LOOKED AS IF the only jobs I could get quickly to fill the six-month void involved skeezy telemarketing, I decided to take another route to restore some of my funds:

Hunt down my mother's boyfriend Gil Malone and wring my twenty-five thousand out of his lame, beer-soaked, country ass.

But I needed reinforcements.

I walked into the midtown Atlanta police precinct wearing hat and glasses on the off chance someone might recognize me. I expected to see tattooed felons handcuffed to table legs. Instead it was just a boring waiting room full of bored-looking people, and two windows with uniformed attendants. A red digital sign advised me to take a number. I did—number 237. But to my dismay, number 210 was currently being waited on. No way was I waiting that long. I backtracked into the hallway and looked for the nearest men's restroom. And waited.

A few minutes later a tall, rocky-shouldered guy exited and walked toward the stairwell. Underneath his sport coat I saw the flash of a badge at his belt.

"Excuse me."

He turned back. "Can I help you?"

"Are you a police officer?"

"Detective," he said. "Detective Jack Terry."

"I'm Della Culpepper. Do you have a minute for a question,

Detective?"

He nodded toward the stairwell. "If you can walk and talk. I'm on my way out."

He was already walking, so I hurried to catch up to him. If I'd known I'd be jogging, I'd have worn something other than platform sandals.

"What's on your mind, Ms. Culpepper?" He held open the stairwell door for me.

"I gave my mother a sizable sum of money to pay off a loan against her house."

"Nice of you," he offered, descending the stairs slowly in deference to me, I realized. He was wearing black western boots and I got the feeling it was a preference rather than a style statement.

"Er, thanks. The problem is, her assho—I mean, her useless boyfriend withdrew the money out of her account and took off with it."

He frowned. "Damn."

"I know, right? I'm wondering if anything can be done to the piece of sh—I mean, to him."

"How much money are we talking about?"

"Twenty-five thousand."

He whistled low. "Was there a written agreement as to how the money would be used—an email, for instance?"

"No."

"Where did this happen?"

"Dewdrop, Georgia. It's a little town—"

"South of here, I've been past it. That's actually good—small-town banks are usually more protective of their customers. Did you write a check?"

"Yes."

"And you made it out specifically to your mother?"

"I did."

"Was the boyfriend's name also on the account?"

"No. He likes to be, shall we say, off the grid."

"Does he have a criminal record?"

"I don't know, but I wouldn't be surprised."

"And what are the chances the people at the bank should've known not to give him the money?"

"Everyone in town knows Gil is a low-life."

We had reached the bottom floor. The detective stopped in front of a door that exited to a garage. "Then your mother probably has a case to press charges against him."

"My mother, not me?"

"Right. The money was a gift to her, and it was her account, so in the eyes of the law, she's the injured party."

I must have looked pained because he winced.

"Sorry." He reached into an inside jacket pocket and withdrew a business card. "Look, if you get me the guy's full name, DOB, and social, I can at least find out if he has a record."

I took the card. "Thanks for your trouble, Detective."

"No trouble." He pointed toward another door. "That'll take you to the lobby. Good luck."

He exited to the garage, but instead of going to the lobby, I sat down on a cold concrete step and weighed the anguish of another difficult conversation with my mother versus the humiliation of taking a slimy telemarketing job.

It was a coin toss.

July 11, Tuesday

"HI, MOM. How are you?"

"Hi, MaeDella." My mother sounded tentative. "I've been meaning to call and thank you for taking care of things with the bank. We should be fine until Gil comes back with the money he borrowed."

"You mean, the money he *stole*," I corrected. "Have you heard from good old Gil?"

"No," she murmured. "He's probably busy."

"Uh-huh. Mom, I talked to the police about you pressing charges against him."

"Oh, I can't do that."

"Yes, you can," I said, fighting to stay calm. "He took money out of your account without your permission. *My* money. But you have to let the bank know as soon as possible—there's a short window for making claims. Once you sign an affidavit, the police can put out a warrant for his arrest."

"Arrest? They'd put him in jail?"

"Prison, actually. What he did is a felony."

She gasped. "Prison? Slow down, MaeDella."

"Please call me Della," I said through gritted teeth.

"I won't do that," she said. "And I won't press charges against Gil. You don't know him like I do. He's a decent man."

"Mom, he's mooched off you for years, and you almost lost your and Donnie's home because of him."

"No one was more upset when that business deal fell through than Gil."

"Do you even know where he is?"

"No."

She sounded so agonized, I believed her. "Then at least give me his date of birth and social security number so I can have a cop friend try to locate him."

"Absolutely not—I won't be party to getting him into trouble with the law."

I pinched the bridge of my nose. "Mom, what has this man— and I use that term loosely—ever done for you?"

"Gil loves me. He rubs my feet when I come home from a long day of waiting tables."

"That's the least he can do, don't you think?"

"And he holds me at night, and tells me everything's going to be all right. Do you have someone who does that, MaeDella?"

Unbidden, hot tears burned my eyes. How dare she judge my relationship when she knew nothing about it. "I have a boyfriend," I said defiantly. "He's a doctor."

"Good for you. Is there a reason you haven't introduced him to your family?"

So many, my mouth watered to say, but I swallowed the words. "This isn't about me."

She gave a harsh laugh. "Of course it's about you, MaeDella. It's always about you. I wish you hadn't come. We would've been fine without your interference."

My throat constricted and I considered telling my mother because I'd given her the money she and Donnie needed, I was now in trouble myself, so I really, *really* needed for her to press charges against Gil.

But I didn't because deep down, I had a feeling even if my

mother knew my predicament, she'd still pick her lame bedwarmer over me. So instead I managed a little laugh. "Then I won't make the mistake of interfering again."

"Goodbye, MaeDella."

I heard the distinct click of a landline phone being hung up.

What was the saying—no good deed goes unpunished? I massaged at the sudden pain in my chest. Maybe so, but a telemarketing job was under the category of cruel and unusual.

July 12, Wednesday

"GIRL, I'VE HEARD dark roots are in on the West Coast," Johna said, painting dye solution on my hair with a brush "but this is the South and you're at least a week past your grace period."

"I know," I said, contrite. "It's been hectic lately."

"That doctor man of yours running you ragged?" Faye asked from the other station where she was sweeping up.

"Kyle is out of town. It's… other stuff."

"Did you lose your job?" Johna asked.

My head snapped up. "What? No. Why would you ask that?"

She pointed to the magazine open on my lap. "Five Ways to Make Quick Money."

"Oh—I'm reading it for a friend who lost her job."

"What does it say?" Faye asked.

I went down the list. "Become a driver for Lyft or Uber, sell your belongings, rent out a room in your house, be a pet sitter, sell stock photography."

Johna made a face. "That's a terrible list."

"Agree," Faye said, shaking her head. "I have a friend who drives for one of those car services and the process to be approved is *not* quick."

"Sell your belongings?" Johna asked. "Okay. But I say look around your house and see what you can take back to the store where you bought it to get a refund."

Faye nodded. "I did that with a space heater I bought for the winter. I didn't use it once. Took it back without the box and they still gave me my money back."

I pursed my mouth.

"Or sell your hair," Johna suggested. "That'll get you a fast Franklin."

"For extensions?" I asked.

"Sure. And some people buy human hair to make crafts with, like wreaths and shit."

"Ugh."

"Don't judge," Johna said, shaking her finger. "And rent out a room? Sure, if you want to be murdered in your sleep."

"Amen to that," Faye said. "Instead, just rent out your bathroom."

I squinted. "What?"

"Yeah. I have a friend who registered her bathroom on a website and if someone is walking past her apartment and nature calls, they can ring her up and pay to use her bathroom. She charges more for number two."

"Ew."

"But she makes an extra hundred bucks or so every month."

"I say be a lab rat," Johna said. "My brother did that and made good money." Then she scratched her temple. "Although he does stutter now."

"Is your friend cute?" Faye asked me.

I straightened. "Yeah."

"She could be a Cam Girl."

My eyes bugged. "You mean online porn?"

"It doesn't have to be full-on," Faye said. "There are all kinds of funky fetishes out there." She giggled. "I did it in college and pulled down *bank*, might still be doing it if I wasn't a mom."

"I sold my dirty underwear," Johna said matter-of-factly. "It was easy dough and there are a lot of freaks out there." She pointed a comb. "But if you can get into the prison system, that's where the real money is."

I was speechless. "Okay, the two of you should have written this article."

Johna laughed, then set a timer. "I'll be back in a few to rinse you out. Need another magazine?"

"I'm good," I assured her.

I pulled out my phone and typed in a few notes to myself the women's suggestions had triggered. Selling my dirty underwear was way down on the list, but it was higher than renting out my bathroom.

Another woman walked in and settled into the chair at Faye's station for a blowout. From the chatty conversation, I gathered the woman lived here in Triangle Point, but I didn't pay attention until I heard a familiar name.

"...Charlie Graham," the customer said.

"What's the name of his restaurant?"

"Graham's Eatery. My friends and I all have a crush on him. He's cute and funny and charming."

All eyes turned in my direction, and I realized I'd made a scoffing noise.

"Do you know him, Della?" Johna asked.

"No," I chirped. "Don't mind me."

Faye turned back to her customer. "What does he look like?"

A bowling ball.

"He's stocky," the girl gushed. "You know, the kind of man who could keep you warm at night."

Oh, brother.

"And he's single?"

"Yeah. He was just named one of Atlanta's most eligible bachelors in *Biz Trends* magazine."

I made a strangled noise.

"You okay over there, Della?"

"Yep," I squeaked, then looked back to the quick money article. "Just reading."

And mentally rolling on the floor laughing my skinny ass off. As if that toad of a man was in the same league as my Kyle.

July 13, Thursday

CHEF CHARLIE GRAHAM is set to take Atlanta by storm with the opening of his restaurant Graham's Eatery in Triangle Point. Graham hails from Nashville where he gained notoriety for being one of the youngest recipients of the James Beard Foundation Award for Rising Chefs. But what most people don't know about this handsome bachelor is his love for food comes second to his love for boxing.

I wrinkled my nose. "Boxing?"

Anthony stuck his head around the corner of a rolling clothing rack. "Did you say something?"

"No." I slapped the *Biz Trends* magazine closed, then gestured to the pile of unread fashion and design periodicals on the table. "I get too many magazines. Will you go through all these and cancel my subscriptions?" That alone would probably save me a couple hundred dollars a month.

"Sure," Anthony said. "Are there more clothes in here?"

I looked up to see him trying the knob on a narrow storage closet.

"No, just odds and ends. I keep it locked because family photos and other things I don't want to lose are in there."

Anthony was a handsome guy in his late-twenties with great skin and a bright-colored wardrobe. We were in my second bedroom I'd turned into a closet.

"Okay, I separated all the clothes that still have tags on them." He gestured to the bulging rack.

"Which ones are they?"

"All of them."

I masked my reaction—how did that happen?

"It's really generous of you to give these gorgeous clothes to Goodwill. Do you want me to drop them off on my way home?"

"Um, no, thanks. I'll take care of it."

He pointed to neat stacks of receipts. "And I matched them to as many receipts as I could find in your desk, like you asked."

"Great. This way I'll know what they're worth for my taxes."

"What next?"

"My insurance agent suggested adding a rider to my dweller's policy to cover my shoes and bags."

"Not a bad idea," Anthony said, glancing around the room at the stacks of boxes and designer dust bags.

"Can you look up the market value for each of them?"

"I'll get on it right now."

"Speaking of clothes, is that a new shirt?"

He frowned and shook his head. "It's from the fat side of my closet."

"What do you mean?"

"I have, like, four different wardrobes, for whatever weight I am. You're so nice and skinny, you probably think that's insane."

I didn't comment.

He patted his rounded stomach, and sighed. "No matter what I do, I can't seem to get this under control." Then he brightened. "But my doctor said if I lose ten pounds on my own, he'll write me a prescription for Beltina."

I managed a smile—I hoped it would still be available when Anthony was eligible for it. "I wish I could offer you samples."

"Oh, don't worry, I wouldn't want you to jeopardize your job."

I nodded, feeling guilty. I no longer had a job to jeopardize, but I needed the stash of samples in my closet for myself.

July 14, Friday

"BUT WHY THIS PLACE?" I asked, dragging my heels as we approached Graham's Eatery.

"Because," Sabrina, my event planner friend said, "it's the hottest place in town right now, and my clients expect me to be familiar with all the trendy spots."

My other friend Susan, the sales rep for a liquor distributor, leaned in. "And my boss wants this account, so what better place to come for happy hour?"

"See?" Sabrina said. "We can kill three birds with one stone."

"And it's on us," Susan added, pulling me inside. "To celebrate your promotion."

"We already did that," I protested.

"At your apartment, with a lousy supermarket cake," Sabrina said.

"Yeah, this is big, Della. You deserve something nice—and alcoholic."

I didn't, but it was easier to go along.

The restaurant had a different vibe for happy hour than for lunch. The lights were low and each table flickered with candlelight. The music was louder and more vibrant—wait, was that Bluegrass? Then I remembered Chef Charlie was from Nashville. Yee-haw.

"Wow, it's packed," Sabrina shouted, threading her way through the crowd. She was a vibrant redhead with energy to burn. "Wait, I know that waitress—she used to work at Mint Julep. Let me see if she can get us a table."

"The crowd is a good mix," Susan said to me, scanning. She was a brunette with an edge that helped her compete in an industry that was predominately male. "One-third wine drinkers, one-third beer, one-third mixed drinks."

"But you can't be everything to everybody," I said. "It'll peter out when the novelty wears off."

"I don't think so, not this time."

Sabrina came back. "Struck out."

Susan turned and waved to one of the bartenders. "That guy used to work at Tree Top, one of my accounts. Maybe he can get us a table." She moved toward the bar that was three people deep.

"This will be a great venue for work parties," Sabrina said, glancing all around.

"Don't you think the acoustics are bad?" I asked. "It seems really loud."

"No, this place is a goldmine."

Susan came back. "No go. Guess we should put our name in for the two-hour wait."

"Ladies?"

We turned to see the hostess smiling at us. "Table for three, please follow me."

We looked at each other, eyebrows high. "One of your contacts came through," I murmured as we were led through the mass of people waiting.

But when we walked past full tables, and headed toward the kitchen, Sabrina muttered, "What's going on?"

"Maybe they're going to make us wash dishes," Susan whispered.

I was worried Chef Donut Man had spotted me and was kicking us out the back door, but I held my tongue.

The hostess pushed open a swinging stainless door and held it. "Ladies, the chef's table."

Sabrina and Susan exclaimed in delight over the long butcher block table sitting in a corner of the bustling kitchen. It had been appointed on one end with three elaborate place settings. A waiter stood at attention next to the table.

"Ted will take care of you," the hostess said. "Enjoy."

Sabrina poked Susan. "You must've slept with that bartender to make this happen."

"Don't look at me, I thought this was your doing."

The waiter pulled out the seat at the head of the table. "Ms. Culpepper, if you please."

Both girls turned to stare at me. I gave a little shrug and went to the seat proffered. This was a nice gesture by Charlie Graham—maybe I'd misjudged the man.

From the table, the operations of the kitchen were visible, from the food prep areas to the stoves to the plating stations. Counter to the relative chaos in the dining room, the nerve center of the restaurant was running smoothly. Quiet acoustic music played overhead, and aproned workers moved in and out of their stations like choreographed dancers. But I didn't see Donut Man.

When my friends were seated, Ted explained we would be served a special menu, at the chef's pleasure. He asked if we had food allergies or special dietary needs. Sabrina and Susan were practically vibrating with excitement. I doubt they would've mentioned a lethal allergy if they'd had one.

"Very well." He waved over a server holding a tray. "For appetizers, may we present shrimp tarts, and for Ms. Culpepper, grilled tomato melts."

Ah, now I understood. This was reward—or payback—for the "bland tomato" comment.

When the waiter left to bring us wine, the girls pounced on me.

"You didn't tell us you know the chef!"

"Talk about burying the lead, Della!"

I lifted my hand. "I've only chatted with him a couple of times when I had lunch here."

"You must've made an impression," Sabrina said.

"Did he ask you out?" Susan demanded.

"No," I hissed. "I was here once with my boss, and once with Kyle."

They bit into their appetizers. "Oh, my God," Sabrina said.

"Amazing," Susan said.

I bit into a tomato melt—pepperjack jack cheese melted over a cherry tomato half, topped with diced green peppers and almond slivers—and chewed slowly. Not bad.

Ted returned with our wine. "Chef recommends a rosé for you, ladies," he said, presenting the bottle to them. Susan, our resident expert, peered at the label and looked impressed. He poured the pale pink wine into a glass for each of them. "And for Ms. Culpepper, from Chef's private stock, tomato wine."

I warily eyed the light golden liquid he poured from a decanter into my glass. Next to me, Susan was about to come undone. "What does it taste like?"

I sipped from my glass, then nodded. "Tomato. Interesting." I let Susan have a sip while Ted cleared our plates and served the next course.

"A garden salad with sunflower seed dressing for you ladies," he said. "And for Ms. Culpepper, tomato salad with edamame succotash."

I sampled the dish nursing a tight smile. The man knew how to make a point. I wondered what he had planned for my entrée. Tomato lasagna? Tomato quiche?

"Tomato cobbler topped with cheddar biscuits," Ted announced when he set it before me.

I pushed my tongue into my cheek. My tomato-themed menu seemed to have escaped Ted and my distracted friends, who had finished the bottle of rosé and were well into a bottle of pinot noir. But my anger was on a slow burn. Chef Charlie hadn't offered us his private table to be nice—he'd done it to teach me a lesson... and to load me up with carbs. The man obviously couldn't take criticism. I would've walked out, but Sabrina and Susan were having the time of their lives. Between courses, I spotted him twice moving around the kitchen, his back to me. But I was sure the man would eventually come around to gloat.

He did, after our plates were cleared and before we were offered dessert.

"Good evening, ladies." The big dark-haired man cut an impressive figure in his white double-breasted jacket and chef's hat. He looked robust and utterly pleased with himself when he nodded in my direction.

I inclined my head. "Hello again. Chef Charlie Graham, meet Sabrina Cutler and Susan Odom."

The girls gushed about the special treatment, and—no surprise—the man ate it up.

"You must have known we were celebrating Della's promotion," Sabrina said.

I froze. Oh, God.

"Of course he knew," Susan said to Sabrina. "Remember, Della's boss met her here to tell her the good news."

I met his gaze and silently pleaded with him not to rat me out.

"Ted," he said, "please fetch a bottle of champagne. And cheesecake."

"That's not necessary," I murmured.

"Of course it is," he said with a little smile.

Great—rub it in. I bit down on the inside of my cheek. I'd been right about Charlie Graham from the get-go. He was a jackass.

Ted was gone and back in a flash. Charlie uncorked the champagne with expertise. I sat stiffly while he filled our flutes himself. "Do you mind if I join you?"

"Not at all," Sabrina said.

"Please do," Susan added.

"Allow me to make the toast," he said, lifting his glass. "To Della. May she get everything in life she deserves."

"Hear, hear," Sabrina said.

"Congratulations, Della," Susan said.

We all clinked our glasses. I reluctantly clinked my glass with Charlie's. His dark eyes danced with mirth. I felt utterly humiliated, but took a sip of the champagne for appearances' sake. When the cheesecake came to the table, though, I held up my hand. "None for me, thank you."

"I made it myself," he said.

My mouth watered—I could smell the cream cheese and the vanilla. But cheesecake was my trigger food. I couldn't afford to take a single bite. I shook my head and pushed to my feet. "In fact, I have to call it a night."

The girls looked distraught. "No!"

"You can't. It's still early."

I pointed to my phone. "Work emergency."

"You've had your promotion for less than a week," Sabrina said, "and your boss is already pinging you after hours?"

I nodded. I glanced at Charlie—he, of course, knew I was lying.

"Thank you for dinner," I said. "It was... tomato-y."

He inclined his head, then said goodbye to the girls and returned to the kitchen. Sabrina and Susan waved off my attempts to leave Ted a tip—thank goodness. I didn't have a lot of cash on me.

Once outside, I gulped for air. My life was slipping through my fingers and I desperately needed to resume some control. On the walk back to my building, I stopped in the supermarket to get a couple of necessities. But somehow found myself in front of the bakery case surveying the selection of colorful carbohydrates on display.

"May I help you?" asked a woman behind the counter.

I hesitated, then pointed. "Cheesecake, please."

She bent over, wielding a spatula. "How many slices?"

"The entire thing."

July 15, Saturday

"YOU LOOK STRESSED," Kyle said, tilting his head. "Is everything okay?"

Damn the resolution of the new iPhone. FaceTiming made me miss regular old audio calling when you didn't have to worry about putting on mascara—or even a smile.

"It's pouring rain," I said, holding the phone up to the window for proof. (As if I ever lie.) "I'm just not looking forward to being cooped up all day."

"Too bad. The weather out here is terrific. I might drive to the coast, get in some sailing."

"Great." I marveled how casually the sentence had fallen out of his mouth. I wanted my children to grow up believing sailing was a normal weekend activity. Versus catching flies in a mayonnaise jar.

"Did you have a party last night?"

I frowned. "No. Why do you ask?"

"Your place is a mess," he said with a laugh.

I swung my back away from the kitchen and living area. Damn—I need to figure out how to blur the background in this app. "Anthony is helping me to get organized," I improvised. "We're still sorting through everything."

"Ah. Well, I'd better let you get back to it. I'll call you tomorrow." He puckered up and made a kissing noise.

I blinked—Kyle wasn't normally so… kissy-face. I awkwardly blew him a kiss, then ended the call.

That was weird.

Weird in the way that makes a woman think something about the relationship has changed… like he's cheating.

But I immediately dismissed the idea. Kyle said it himself: He isn't dishonest enough to do what I do, i.e., *lie.*

The doorbell rang and I winced. I forgot to cancel the cleaning service.

Although, considering the state of the condo, I needed it today. And after things were in order again, I'd discontinue the service and start being more careful with my money.

I opened the door and Joon-woo gave me a flat smile. I guess I hadn't scared her off last week.

"Come in, you can start in the kitchen."

She followed me inside and put her hand to her nose against the odor.

"I know, right? Why does coffee smell so good when you're making it, yet the grounds smell so bad when it's over?" I'd dragged a coffeemaker out of the cabinet to help curb my twenty-dollars-a-day Starbucks vice.

Joon-woo set down the equipment bucket and pulled out a garbage bag. When she saw the empty cheesecake container—with one fork—she slid her gaze to me.

I bristled. "Don't look at me like that."

I'd sat up late eating until it was gone. Afterward, I'd lain on the couch, miserable, wishing I could throw up. All that sugar on top of all the acid from the tomatoes did not make for a restful night.

Joon-woo averted her gaze and scooped the container into the trash, eliminating the evidence.

"I'll be in the bedroom," I said, pointing down the hall.

But the scene in the room I'd turned into my closet sent another wave of stress rolling over me. Anthony had done a great job of organizing the shoes and bags in their proper containers, and providing a spreadsheet of their resale value. He'd included a dozen coats from my clothing racks he thought also warranted insuring.

The sum total was gut-clutching—even more so because it

represented a fraction of what I'd paid for everything—but encouraging, too, because if I could sell some of this stuff on eBay, I might make enough to scrape by until my bonus arrived.

The operative word being "if." I sat down at my laptop and opened the *eBay for Dummies* book on my Kindle. I have decent technical skills, so I know most of my frustration rests in the fact that I've never done this before—and I really hated having to do it now. I thought by this time in my life, I'd be beyond scraping by.

But after a couple of hours, I'd clunked my way through setting up an account (TomatoGirl29—*ha*) and a profile.

Now all I had to do was decide what I could part with, create the listings, and take pictures to upload. From the book, I knew pictures would make or break a sale.

I set about the difficult task of sorting through my prize designer items. I decided to assign a code to how much I loved the item and compare it to how much I could get if I sold it, then rank everything and sell as far down the list as I had to. I wound up with an A, B, C, D, E ranking. I would start with the E's, and hopefully my cash flow would improve before I got to my most-loved A-items.

I set up a makeshift backdrop for the photos with a white sheet and floor lamp, and began snapping away, taking pictures of the angles the book suggested buyers would be most interested in seeing—the profiles, the bottoms (to show wear), a closeup of the designer tags, and any imperfections. The coats I hung on a hanger on the back of a door. But when I uploaded and viewed the photos on my laptop, I was underwhelmed.

Joon-woo knocked on the doorframe and pointed to the vacuum. The carpet in the room was littered with bits of paper, plastic tags, threads, and fuzz from my and Anthony's organizing, so I waved her in.

"Just be careful," I said. "Remember what happened before."

She remembered because she carefully avoided the stacks of shoe boxes as she pushed the vacuum that probably weighed as much as she did. Actually, she moved rather gracefully, even in those dreadful shoes.

I angled my head—she looked as if she wore about the same size shoe. I scrutinized the rest of her. With a little makeup, she could be quite pretty—and her slender figure was better than a coat hanger.

"Joon-woo?"

But she was intent on her cleaning.

Rather than yelling, I reached over and pulled the plug for the vacuum out of the outlet.

Her head came up in confusion.

"Joon-woo, put this on." I handed her a long red cape I'd loved in the store, but had worn only once.

She looked perplexed, but handled the garment carefully and settled it around her shoulders, covering her baggy dress.

Wow—she looked *nice*.

I dug through the shoes and handed her a pair of black patent Valentino pumps.

"And these."

She loosened the laces on her sensible shoes and toed them off, then slid her feet into the pumps, like Cinderella.

I handed her an oversized Chanel bag. "Put this on your shoulder."

The pieces overwhelmed her, but it was very now. I took a quick photo just to be sure what I saw translated digitally.

It did. *This* was a selling photo.

I turned the picture for her to see. Her face lit with surprise—and pleasure.

"Joon-woo, how would you like to make some extra money this week?"

July 16, Sunday

MY PHONE RANG and I smiled to see Donnie's name. I answered, praying nothing else was wrong.

"Hi, Professor. What's up?"

"I'm here, Sis."

"Here, where?"

"In your lobby."

I almost dropped the phone. "In my lobby... in Atlanta?"

"Yeah. I came to visit you. The guy at the desk says I have to call you to come get me."

"Are you alone?"

"Yeah."

Oh, thank God. "Okay. I'll be right down."

As I rode the elevator down, my mind reeled with questions. Donnie, nor anyone in my family, had ever visited me since I'd left home for college.

When I walked off the elevator, I spotted my brother talking to the chatty concierge guy I usually avoided.

"Hello, Ms. Culpepper. You have a visitor."

"I see." I smiled at Donnie, who had dressed up for the occasion in dark jeans and a pale blue button-up shirt I'd given him for Christmas. He was so handsome, my heart squeezed. I wondered when some Dewdrop girl was going to snag him. When it happened, I hoped she was a good person.

"Hi, Sis." He seemed awestruck. "This is where you live?"

"Yes, upstairs. Want to see?"

"Sure. This is so neat," Donnie said, looking all around the expansive lobby as we walked to the elevator.

A pretty young woman in a short dress walked by and smiled at him.

"Hello," Donnie said, and turned around to watch her walk away before catching up with me. "She's pretty."

"Yes, she is," I agreed. "How did you get here, Professor?"

He grinned. "GPS. My boss told me to drive a car we were working on to see how it ran on the interstate. I asked if I could drive it up here and he said sure, as long as I have it back by closing time."

I swallowed a reprimand. Donnie wasn't a child and he was an excellent driver. "Where did you park?"

"That guy in the lobby, Henry, told me where to go. He said it was free because I'm visiting you."

I felt contrite—I didn't even know the name of the concierge. "Good."

We walked onto the elevator and to my dismay, the woman carrying the pug got on with us. She moved to the other side of the car.

"Hi," Donnie said.

Her eyes were wary. "Hello."

"I like your dog. Can I pet him?"

She hesitated, then nodded.

Donnie reached out and scratched the dog under its chin, displacing lots of wrinkly skin. "What's his name?"

"Howard."

Donnie murmured to the pet as if it were a child, and the pug licked his hand.

"He's sweet," Donnie said.

"Yes, he's my little angel," the woman purred.

My eyes ached from wanting to roll, but I resisted.

"This is a cool elevator," Donnie said. "Henry says it doesn't have a machine room."

"And that's very different?" I asked.

"Yeah, it takes up less space, and it uses weights and counterweights to operate instead of hydraulics and cables. That's why the ride is so smooth and quiet."

"It is a quiet elevator," my neighbor agreed. "The elevator in the building I used to live in was noisy and jerky."

"It was probably a geared traction elevator," Donnie said matter-of-factly. "They're louder and rougher, but they're robust, too, and cheaper to maintain."

"Are you an engineer?" she asked.

"No. I'm just a car mechanic, but I like all kinds of machines. My name is Donnie Culpepper."

She smiled. "I'm Mindy Chasen."

"Nice to meet you." He gestured to me. "This is my sister, Della."

"We've met," she said coolly.

The elevator door opened and she exited.

Donnie looked at me and I just shrugged. "Come on, my door is this way."

He followed me down the hallway, taking in every detail. I stopped to punch in my access code.

"You don't have a key?"

"No, just a secret code."

"Like the new cars."

"That's right." I opened the door and his eyes widened.

"This is your house?"

I nodded. "Come in."

He walked inside, turning circles in his eagerness to absorb everything. "Wow, this looks like a place a celebrity would live."

I enjoyed seeing my condo through his eyes. The modern finishes and ice cream colors were sleek and soothing—and about as far away from the green clapboard house in Dewdrop as one could imagine.

"You must make a lot of money," he breathed.

That stopped me. "I do okay." But he would be astonished if he knew how much money was required to keep all of this going. When I put a pencil to it, I was a little shocked myself.

He walked to the window. "Wow, look at this view!"

"From there to there," I said, pointing, "is all Triangle Point."

"What's that building?" he asked in awe, pointing to a skyscraper so close it looked as if we could open a window and swing over to it.

"It's called the Battlecoin Building."

"It must be fifty stories tall."

"I think you're right."

"People live there?"

"No. It's an office building."

"I'll bet they have amazing elevators."

"I'll bet they do."

He turned back to me. "You're not mad that I came to see you?"

I touched his arm. "Of course not. Why would you say that?"

He shrugged. "You just seem angry all the time."

"Well, sure, I'm upset over the Gil situation."

"I mean before Gil. You changed after you got that sales job."

I crossed my arms. "Changed?"

"Yeah. And not just the way you look."

"Donnie, I think you might have misunderstood. I'm… fine."

He nodded. "Okay. My doctor says sometimes I make mistakes about people."

"Just know I'm very glad to see you," I assured him. I checked my watch. "Why don't we go walk around Triangle Point? I'll give you a little tour and we can have lunch before you head back."

"That would be great," he said, then he sobered. "I brought you something."

"What?"

He withdrew a piece of paper from his shirt pocket. "It's the information Mom wouldn't give you about Gil. She said you knew

51

a cop who could find him."

I took the paper. "I don't know if he can find Gil, but he can find out things that might help locate him."

"Good. Because what Gil did wasn't right."

"Thank you, Donnie. This really helps."

We spent the next couple of hours window shopping, eating at food trucks, listening to live music, and—much to Donnie's delight—checking out a half dozen concept cars on display in the arcade. He couldn't have been happier.

"This is a great place," he said. "I can see why you like living here." Then he nodded to a knot of young people sitting on a sidewalk nearby. "Are those kids homeless?"

"I don't know," I said. "But it appears they're either homeless or passing through."

"I've seen a lot of kids like that today."

I frowned. "You have?"

"Yeah. Did you see the three girls in front of the music store? They were dirty and looked like they were lost."

"No." I sighed. "I guess I see it so often, I stop seeing it, you know?"

"I guess so," Donnie said, but he seemed worried.

It's the way he gets when he can't reconcile why things are the way they are. And it's one of the reasons why I've sheltered him from the city.

"It's not anything you have to worry about," I assured him.

I turned to throw away my lunch wrapper and noticed Charlie Graham a few feet away surveying one of the futuristic cars. He saw me, too, and when he made a move toward me, I turned and grabbed Donnie's arm. "Come on... let's get a scoop of ice cream before you head home."

"Okay," Donnie said cheerfully.

I glanced back to make sure Charlie wasn't following me. He caught my gaze and gave me a quick head nod. I kept going.

July 17, Monday

"DETECTIVE JACK TERRY."

"Hi, Detective, this is Della Culpepper. We talked last week about a financial predicament my mother is in."

"I'm sorry, ma'am, can you be more specific?"

"Her boyfriend took money out of her bank account without her permission."

"Oh, right. Money you gave her, if I recall."

"Yes, twenty-five thousand to pay off a loan against her house."

"Yeah, I remember. Has the guy turned up?"

"No. You said if I got some personal information, you could see if he's in the system?"

"I can check to see if he has a record, maybe get the names of known associates. Or who knows, he might have done something stupid with the money and be sitting in jail."

I could only hope.

"But you have to promise me something."

I frowned. "What?"

"You seemed pretty angry last week, and don't get me wrong— I totally understand why. But if I help you find this guy and you go all vigilante on me, we're both gonna be in a world of trouble."

I mouthed a string of vile curse words.

"I heard that."

I winced. "Those weren't directed at you, Detective. I hate that I have to get involved in dirty little things like this."

"You're preaching to the choir, ma'am. But that's life. So I have your word you're not going to off anyone?"

I sighed. "Yes, Detective."

"Okay, give me the info."

I read the information Donnie had written in sturdy letters on the piece of paper.

"Last known address?"

I dictated my mother's address.

"And your best contact number?"

I told him.

"Okay. Sit tight, Ms. Culpepper. This could take a few days. But I'll call you to let you know what I find."

"Thanks, Detective."

I disconnected the call and walked to the kitchen for a glass of water to take a Beltina tablet. But while I pushed the tablet out of its blister pack and washed it down, my mind churned over the phone conversation. The detective was the second person in two days to say I'm an angry person.

But didn't I have the right to be angry? I mean, Donnie's life is small and he didn't have too many concerns, so of course he's easygoing. And Detective Terry probably went home every night to a sweet wife who made him dinner and otherwise lubricated his way through life.

The events of the last couple of weeks of my life, though, were piling on, and it was difficult to pretend I was happy in this slippery place. And why should I pretend?

A tide of rage rolled over me. As I placed my empty glass in the kitchen sink, I slammed it down hard. I felt the glass give way under my fingers, felt the sharp zing of pain as blood trickled down the drain.

It felt almost... good.

July 18, Tuesday

"WHAT DID YOU DO TO YOUR HAND?" Anthony asked, pointing to the bandage.

I made a face. "A glass broke in the sink."

"Ugh, I hate when that happens. Did you have to go to the emergency room?"

"No." Thank goodness. Because when I reread the agreement Portia had presented to me, I discovered my health coverage ended when I signed it. I was eligible for COBRA continuation coverage, but at a hefty price. So it behooved me to stay healthy.

It occurred to me I should have consulted an employment attorney before I signed squat, but that was water under the bridge. Now I could only hope my allegiance to the company would mean something when the FDA completed its scrutiny of Beltina. I'd set up online search alerts for the drug and for Traxton, but so far, no information about the situation had been released.

"Well, maybe new living room furniture will cheer you up," Anthony said, steering his compact car into a parking spot in front of Modernity Décor in Buckhead.

I just smiled because I had no intention of buying new furniture today. But I needed to get out of the condo, and browse-shopping would be a fun way to spend the afternoon.

My phone vibrated and when I checked my messages, I was

happy to see someone had bid on my Valentino shooties, and way above the reserve price I'd set. As the book had advised, I'd set up short auctions to experiment and create urgency, but since four of the auctions ended today and as of this morning had no bidders, I'd decided the strategy was flawed. But apparently not.

"That must be from Kyle," Anthony said.

I looked up. "Hm? Oh, no, it's someone else. I mean—it's some*thing* else."

He looked intrigued, but he didn't comment. "When does he come back?"

I looked up. "Who?"

"Kyle."

"Oh." I stowed my phone. "This weekend."

My phone vibrated again, so I checked it. Wow—another bid, this one aggressively more than the first bidder.

"I'm sure that'll be a happy reunion."

"Mm-hm."

With twenty minutes still to go on the auction, there was time for the bidding to go higher. I put my phone away.

"You're going to love this place," Anthony said, as we walked up to the door. "Everything is to-die-for. I've heard Libby Lakes shops here."

Kyle's patient, the reality show star. She must be all-that.

It was a gorgeous store. Within seconds of walking in, I found myself pining for the days when I could buy pretty much whatever I wanted. *That* was the life I was meant to have. Hadn't I worked hard to get into a top earning bracket?

My phone vibrated—twice. A quick glance revealed the bidding on the Valentino shooties was approaching what I'd paid for them retail two years ago. And someone had placed a bid on the red cape!

Anthony had found three sets of white living room furniture to show me. The first one was a couch and two side chairs featuring tufted backs and carved black legs.

"Beautiful," I breathed, running a hand over the leather.

The second was two love seats and an ottoman. The seats were overstuffed and the leather was finished with a burnished metallic sheen.

"Lovely," I said, sinking lightly into the comfortable pillows.

And the third was just a couch—but what a couch. It was a white leather island, eighteen feet long and five feet wide, a statement piece that would serve as the only seating in the room.

It was spectacular.

"Wouldn't this look great in your space?" Anthony asked.

I nodded. My living area was a long skinny rectangle, and the reason I'd considered buying new furniture is because the pieces I had simply didn't fit the awkward space. This couch would solve the problem exquisitely.

"And it fits perfectly—I measured," Anthony said, pleased with himself.

"How much is it?" I asked the saleswoman.

"It *was* nineteen thousand," she said, "but it's just been reduced to twelve. I don't think it'll be here long."

No way could I afford twelve grand for a couch right now... but wow, I wanted it *so* much.

"And remember," she said, "this one piece is all you need, so you don't have to buy chairs. And this shelf pulls out from beneath the seat, so you don't need side tables, either."

My phone had been vibrating like crazy every few seconds. "Excuse me," I said, holding up a finger.

When I checked my messages, my pulse picked up. The Valentino shooties had sold for almost twice what I'd paid for them, bidding for the red cape was brisk, and the opening bid for the Chanel bag would yield me a profit, too. And those were only the first few items I'd listed—I had dozens more to go.

"You could sell the furniture you have," Anthony suggested, "and put it toward the couch."

He was right! That would reduce my net cost.

"Twelve months same as cash," the woman sang. "No money down, and no minimum monthly payment."

In twelve months, my situation would right itself—if not with Traxton, then I could work in sales elsewhere after the non-compete clause expired.

Meanwhile, I was a reseller wizard. I could swing this.

"I'll take it."

July 19, Wednesday

ON THE HEELS of my eBay wins, I'd decided to spend the day taking the unworn clothes Anthony had sorted out back to the stores where I'd bought them. So far, though, I'd had limited success in getting cash refunds—most offered a partial chargeback on my card or a gift card for a greatly reduced "return value." Every little bit helped, but I confess I was disappointed in the yield for the effort.

There was, I acknowledged, an upside to Traxton taking a while to process my termination: I still had my company car and gas card, else returning the clothes to seventeen different places would've bordered on impossible.

I was down to my last few stops and Neiman Marcus was next. I was feeling pretty good about the chances of getting a chunk of cash back from Neiman's though, because their customer service is legendary.

"May I help you?" asked a dark-haired woman behind a counter.

I was instantly jealous because she was so effortlessly beautiful and her clothes were so casually chic. Getting ready for the day took me hours, which is why I'd been happy to skip it this morning, opting for bare face and gym togs.

"I'd like to return these items," I said, hefting an armful of bags to the counter.

She nodded. "No problem. If you have receipts, it will speed up the process."

"I don't have receipts, but the tags are still on everything."

"Okay," she said cheerfully. "Let's take a look."

Ugh, when she smiled, the gap between her front teeth was so haute cool, she could start a reverse-braces trend. Her neat metal nametag read "Carlotta W."

Another woman walked up behind Carlotta. "What do we have here?"

From her tone, I sensed the woman held a more senior position.

"Just sorting through a return," Carlotta said, pulling items from the plastic bags I'd brought in.

The woman looked at me with cool eyes. "Did you bring your receipts, ma'am?"

"No," I said, matching her tone. "But as you can see, everything still has its tags. And I bought all of these items this season."

But the woman was shaking her head. "I'm sorry, but these garments aren't in returnable condition."

I frowned. "What do you mean?"

She held up a blouse with makeup stains on the collar.

"That's just from trying it on. I never even wore it!"

"Still, we can't put it back on the floor. Or these," she said, holding up a dress and a skirt with brownish smudges.

I covered my hand bandage. Some of the cuts had reopened and I could've stained some of the items when I'd bagged them.

Or considering my eating habits this week, the stains could be chocolate.

"I'm sorry," the woman said, pushing the items back to me. "I wish we could help you."

She walked away to assist another customer and I could feel my anger morphing into pity. I'd been counting on getting something back.

"May I make some suggestions?" Carlotta asked.

I shrugged, ridiculously close to tears.

"We do have a pretty lenient return policy because we want our customers to be happy and come back to shop with us again. And no one understands better than I do the impulse to buy things that later turn out to be perhaps not the best use of your, um, resources." She gave me a conspiratorial smile. "But if you need to return something for its maximum value to any retail store, there are a few... tricks."

I sniffed. "I'm listening."

"Spot clean the makeup stains, then put everything on hangers and steam them to get out the wrinkles. Iron the tags if they're curled up. And bring everything back on generic hangers. Basically, make everything look as new as possible. If you don't have the exact receipts, bring any Neiman's receipt to show management you shop here. Or you can bring your Neiman's credit card statement and sometimes we can verify purchases that way. And—" She stopped and pressed her lips together.

"What?" I pressed.

She gestured to my outfit. "Look, it shouldn't matter what you wear when you bring in a return, but it kind of does. You obviously have good taste in clothes, and I'll bet you have something in your closet that's nicer than workout gear."

I nodded and fidgeted self-consciously with the brim of my ballcap.

"So if you're in a pinch," she said quietly, "just put in a little effort." She reached down and withdrew a few Neiman's shopping bags from under the counter. "Here—if you decide to try again, use these instead of the plastic grocery bags."

"Okay."

"And one more thing?"

"Yeah?"

She gave me a little smile. "Be nice. It goes a long way in retail."

"Thank you," I murmured, then gathered up my pile of crumpled plastic bags and slunk out of the store.

July 20, Thursday

THE CHATTY CONCIERGE—what was his name?—tried to flag me down when I walked into the lobby, but I waved and kept walking. I was tired from a brutal workout, and I was eager to get back to my place and relax.

I stopped at the mailboxes and checked mine. I was keeping an eye out for an envelope from Traxton, just in case they cut a paper check for my severance pay and bonus instead of wiring it into my account. But it was full of envelopes that put a knot in my stomach—bills, bills, bills. I shoved them all back into the box and closed the little door.

"Hi, there."

Charlie Graham stood a few feet away dressed in street clothes, also checking a mailbox.

"You live here?" he asked.

"Nope," I said cheerfully, then turned toward the elevators.

"Ms. Culpepper," the concierge said, jogging up. "A piece of furniture was delivered for you today."

Great—proof I do live here. "Thanks for letting the delivery people into my unit." I reached into my bag for a tip, hoping I had cash.

"I couldn't let them in, ma'am. It wouldn't fit through the door."

I frowned. "It has to fit. My personal assistant measured."

Charlie came up to stand next to me. "You heard the woman, Henry—her assistant measured."

He was mocking me.

"I'll call tomorrow and have it re-delivered," I said.

"Oh, they left it."

"Left it? Where?"

"In front of your door. I wanted to warn you, your neighbors aren't too happy. And you might have to crawl over it to get inside your unit."

I closed my eyes. This I did not need.

"Sounds like you could use a hand," Charlie said.

"No, I—"

"Wait—think it through before you turn me down. Henry and I are standing here, willing to help, aren't we, Henry?"

Henry nodded enthusiastically.

"Unless one of your boyfriends is coming by to help you?"

"She only has one boyfriend," Henry said. "He's a doctor."

"I've met him," Charlie said. "But he's out of town, so there's another guy—younger, better looking?"

"Oh, that's her brother," Henry supplied.

"Really?" Charlie said. "Good to know."

I pursed my mouth.

"Nice fellow," Henry added. "But he doesn't live close enough to help with this situation."

Charlie looked back to me and shrugged. "So it's me and Henry, or your furniture sits in the hallway."

I wanted to throttle them both, but I knew he was right—this time. "Alright."

"Did I hear a 'please'?" Charlie asked, cocking his head.

I sighed. *"Please."*

"That's better. Lead the way."

Henry jerked his thumb over his shoulder. "I'll grab some gloves and take the freight elevator to meet you up there."

Charlie followed me to the elevator and I stabbed the call button. "I assume you live here, too?"

"Just moved in a couple of days ago. I hear the neighbors can be dicey."

The doors opened and we walked on. I held the door hoping someone else would get on—where was that pug-toting woman when I needed her?—but no one came. When the doors closed, I stood rigidly away from him.

He leaned close to me and sniffed over my gym bag. "Do I smell donuts?"

"No," I said, moving away.

"I definitely smell donuts. Which is funny because, as I recall, you don't eat donuts."

"If you must know," I said, exasperated, "they're for my assistant, as a thank you for helping with the couch."

The door opened on my floor and I walked off, then slowed when I saw my entrance—or rather, when I didn't see it because the crated island couch was blocking it... and most of the hallway.

"Holy cow," Charlie said. "What is it?"

"It's a couch."

"That's not a couch, that's a spare room."

Henry arrived from the other direction. "I brought tools in case we need them."

Charlie clapped his hands. "Okay, let's pull away the crate and see what we got."

The uncrating took a while, but at last they uncovered the island couch, covered in thick plastic. By that time I had clambered over the top and opened the door to my condo.

"It's still going to be close," Charlie said, gauging the size of the opening and the width of the couch. While the men discussed how to turn the piece to get it inside, I pushed my current couch, chair, and table to the far wall to make room.

The men eased the big piece inside slowly, maneuvering and pushing and straining when necessary. When it finally slid through the opening, I cheered and they high-fived. After I directed them where to situate it and pulled away the plastic, I couldn't help but smile—it was perfect in the space.

"That's the biggest damn couch I've ever seen," Charlie pronounced, "but it does look good sitting there."

"It does," Henry agreed. "Say, Ms. Culpepper, what are you going to do with your old furniture?"

I shrugged. "Sell it, or give it to Goodwill."

"I could use the chair in my TV room at home. The table, too."

"And I'll buy the couch," Charlie said. "My place is still empty."

"Take them," I said, feeling magnanimous. "For all your help."

"That's too much," Charlie said, but I waved him off.

"You saved me."

"Just being neighborly."

"Thank you, ma'am," Henry said with a grin. "I'll help you carry the couch to your place, Mr. Graham."

Charlie conceded with a nod, then they carried the couch and the chair to the freight elevator.

"I can get the table on my own," Henry offered.

"I'll meet you at my unit," Charlie said.

Henry left with a wave. When we were alone, I felt Charlie's presence acutely.

"Thanks again," I said to bridge the awkwardness, my hand on the doorknob.

Charlie pressed his mouth together. "I owe you an apology."

"For what?"

"For bringing you to my personal table in the restaurant the other night to prove a point. It was childish."

I shrugged. "It was a nice meal and my friends loved it." I wet my lips. "Thank you, by the way, for going along with the mock celebration."

"Obviously they don't know about… your job situation?"

"Right. But it's fine… I have a plan." I lifted my chin.

He gestured to the couch. "Obviously, if you bought that behemoth."

I managed a tremulous smile. "Right."

He grinned. "So, do *I* get a donut for helping with the couch?"

"My old couch isn't enough?"

"Call me greedy."

"Okay—just one. I only bought two."

I walked over to my gym bag and pulled out a peach-colored wax sack.

"Wow, Chloe's." He reached into the bag and pulled out a cake donut covered with brown sugar and cinnamon. A spicy sweet aroma danced on the air. "No wonder you passed on my donuts—

she makes the best pastries in the tri-state." He took a bite, then his eyes rolled back in pleasure. "Mm. So good." He headed toward the door. "I feel bad that you won't get one."

"You shouldn't," I assured him, "because I don't eat donuts."

He saluted, then left.

When the door closed, I carried the wax sack to my new couch, sat down on the sumptuous expanse of white leather, and pulled out the second donut.

July 21, Friday

"I CAN'T STOP thinking about him," Sabrina said.

"I know," Susan added. "I'm not normally into stocky guys, but Chef Charlie Graham is one sexy man."

We were getting mani-pedi's. I was already feeling a little sick about the money I was spending on this luxury, but it was our regular girl thing, and I needed to keep pretending everything was normal. But I hadn't planned on having to listen to the girls drone on and on about Charlie Graham.

"Did you know he lives in our building, Della?"

I nodded. "I ran into him yesterday by the mailboxes."

"What floor does he live on?"

"I didn't ask."

"Does he live alone?"

"I didn't ask."

"Does he rent, or buy?"

"I didn't ask."

Sabrina fanned a hand freshly painted with cotton candy pink polish. "Well, when you see him again, will you put in a good word for me?"

"Or me," Susan said. "He can basically sleep with either one of us, so... find out what he likes."

"I'll ask him the next time I see him getting mail," I said drily.

"Have you ever had sex with a big guy?" Sabrina asked us.

"I don't think so," Susan said.

I shrugged. "What do you mean by big?"

"More than two fifty."

"God, no," Susan said.

"I'll bet Charlie is two seventy-five," I offered.

"What? No way."

"Way," I said, nodding.

"I guess you'd know all about weight issues."

I yanked my head up. "What do you mean?"

Susan squinted. "Since you sell a weight loss drug?"

"Oh." I relaxed. "Right."

"Wow, two seventy-five," Sabrina said. "What position do you think big men like to have sex in?"

"If the guy's heavy, I think the girl should decide," Susan offered.

"That makes sense," Sabrina said, nodding. "I should definitely be on top."

"Doggy-style would work, too."

"Or froggy," Sabrina added.

"I always forget about that one," Susan said. "I should write it down."

"Hey, Della, do you think Charlie has a big schlong?"

"Whoa, I'm out of this discussion," I said.

"Are you so hung up on Kyle you can't discuss other men's hoses?" Sabrina taunted.

I arched an eyebrow. "You didn't just say "hoses"?"

They both laughed.

"We're only teasing," Susan said. "When does Kyle get back?"

"Tomorrow."

"Ooh, someone will have a UTI by Monday."

"How often do you and Kyle do it?" Sabrina asked.

I shrugged. "Enough."

"Enough for what?" Sabrina pressed.

"Enough to know we're compatible."

Susan made a face. "What kind of answer is that?"

"The sex is good," I clarified. "Very good."

"Did you dirty Skype while he was gone?"

"No," I said pointedly. "And if we did, I wouldn't tell you."

"I want a long-distance boyfriend just so we can dirty Skype," Susan offered.

"Wait—I've got it," Sabrina said to Susan. "You and I could have a threesome with Charlie!"

Susan looked thoughtful. "Yeah, that might work."

I gaped. "Please tell me you aren't serious."

"What?" Sabrina said. "I'm sure it wouldn't be his first. Chefs are notoriously randy."

I looked at Susan. "Is that true?"

"Yeah. They're surrounded by women all day, so you can bet they're doing the underchefs, the hostesses, the waitresses, the bartenders—"

"And the customers," Sabrina added.

"Right. It's an ego thing. He's probably having sex right now."

Hm. Charlie was flirtatious, and he definitely had an ego, but he didn't seem like a ladykiller. He hadn't tried to put the moves on me last night.

Not that I'd wanted him to.

And ew—if he was having sex right now, it was probably on my couch.

July 22, Saturday

"DO YOU HAVE a few minutes to take a survey about adult incontinence products?"

The person hung up.

I sighed, struck a line through the phone number, then dialed the next number on my list.

"Hello, sir, do you have a few minutes to—"

The person hung up.

"Dammit!"

Eighty-three effing phone calls and not a single person had taken the survey. At this rate it would take me three years to find my quota of a hundred people to take the survey in order for me to earn a lousy five hundred dollars.

I massaged my aching temples, then pushed to my feet. I needed a break—and I needed to think of some other way to make money between now and December. The eBay auctions were still doing well, but after paying commission, then subtracting shipping and insurance for the items—most of which were bulky and/or heavy—and tipping Joon-woo to do the modeling, I hadn't come out with as much cash as I'd hoped. Still, I was learning.

I walked into the hallway toward the kitchen and looked around to see how far Joon-woo had gotten in her cleaning. I followed a strange, low noise into the living room.

Joon-woo was asleep on my brand new couch, snoring lightly, still holding a cleaning cloth in one hand, and a spray bottle of cleaner in the other hand, which had God-knew-what in it that could stain the leather. Or what if something on her grubby clothes rubbed off? Bottom line, I wasn't going to pay a housekeeper to nap.

My anger runneth over. "Joon-woo!"

She startled, then bolted upright.

"Is this what you do when people aren't home—sleep on their brand new furniture?"

She shook her head, then held up a king-sized candy bar wrapper—my snack last night. She was implying she'd been cleaning up after me when she'd sat down and fallen asleep.

I snatched the wrapper out of her hand. "Get back to work!"

She scurried off to the kitchen where I heard the sound of water running. I placed a hand over my racing heart, trying to push down the panic mounting in my chest. I would figure out something to tide me over financially. I hadn't gotten this far in life without being resourceful.

The doorbell rang and my first thought was Kyle had stopped by to surprise me instead of waiting until tomorrow like we'd planned. But when I opened the door, Anthony stood there grinning.

"Hi, Della."

"Were you in the neighborhood? This is a nice surprise."

He raised his eyebrows. "We texted this morning and you said I could come by to see the couch."

I bit into my lip. "We did?"

He held up his phone to show me our conversation.

"Oh... I guess we did."

He squinted. "Are you okay?"

"Fine. Come in. My housecleaner is here."

He walked in and as he passed the kitchen, waved to Joon-woo. She looked up, but didn't wave back.

"She's not very friendly," Anthony whispered.

"I caught her sleeping on the new couch," I whispered back.

"Oh, yikes." Then he caught sight of the leather island and

gasped. "Oh. My. God. It's *beyond*."

"It does look amazing," I agreed.

"I'm glad you think it's worth what you paid me to find it."

"Mm-hm."

"Okay, I have errands and you're busy, so I won't stay," he said. "Do you mind if I use your bathroom before I leave?"

"Sure, go ahead."

When he was out of sight, I picked up my phone to prove to myself he and I had texted. It was there, all right, but I didn't remember doing it. Luckily, there were no other text conversations I'd forgotten.

It wasn't a big deal because Anthony and I texted so often, I had probably compartmentalized it into the automatic part of my brain.

But I couldn't shake the feeling I wasn't operating on all cylinders. I was letting the stress shut me down, and that hadn't happened before.

I needed to get a grip.

July 23, Sunday

I WATCHED KYLE play ping pong with Libby Lakes, his star client and apparent addition to his weekend crowd, trying not to feel jealous. I had hoped he and I would have some couple time today, but someone in his circle of friends had suggested an impromptu cookout and the backyard of Kyle's palatial home had become the gathering spot. Libby was the guest star and putting on a great performance in short skirt and hooker-heels.

Kyle's sister Helen walked up to me, holding a plate of finger food. "Don't worry. Kyle adores you."

I tried to play cool around Kyle's super chic sister who had managed to marry a man who made even more money than her father, but in truth, she made me nervous—it was as if she could see me for the fraud I was, could smell the country on me, and was waiting for me to falter.

"Libby's beautiful," I said. "I could understand if his head was turned."

Helen scoffed. "She's too chunky, too crass, and too accommodating for Kyle. He likes skinny, balls-to-the-wall, stylish bitches—always has."

I blinked.

"It's a compliment," Helen said with a laugh. "Speaking of skinny, I'm out of Beltina and my doctor says there's a manufacturing shortage so it might be a while before he can get more. Can you hook me up?"

So Traxton was disguising the FDA pullback as a surge in demand, creating a sense of scarcity to drive the demand for Beltina even higher. Brilliant.

"I could probably float you a couple of samples," I said, "but my company has pulled way back on my sample allocation." Not a lie.

"Great," she said. "I love it. This is the first time in my life I've actually been able to *eat* and keep my weight down."

She popped a meatball into her mouth and chewed with abandon. When she offered me one, though, I declined. I could only push one finger between my belly and the waistline of my shorts this morning, and that was less breathing room than I liked.

But her comment did trigger an idea. I was eating more lately because of the stress, but I hadn't adjusted my dosage. If I added a half-pill a day, I'd still have enough samples to get me through the end of the year.

The revelation gave me a lift.

And license to stop at the grocery on the way home to buy snacks. Sitting on my new couch and eating no-no food had become a strange ritual I looked forward to.

July 24, Monday

"SO I'M THINKING we should put the pots and pans in this cabinet," Anthony said. "And the lids in that one. What do you think?"

I sat at the breakfast bar nursing a green smoothie that tasted like dirt and staring at my ominous checkbook. "Sounds good."

He held up a large pot. "This still has the sticker inside."

"So?"

"So, do you want Kyle to think you don't cook?"

"I *don't* cook."

"But it's important to give the impression if you *wanted* to cook, you could. That's what modern kitchens are all about. Do you think anyone actually uses a fifth burner or a second oven? Heck, no. But it makes people look like they have their own cooking blog."

"Actually, why don't you set that pot aside. I might take it to Goodwill." Code, of course, for returning it for a refund.

"No one cooks anymore," Anthony mused. "It's too easy to eat out. Speaking of which, have you been to Graham's Eatery?"

"I have."

"Isn't it fabulous?"

I took another drink of the smoothie and winced. "Anthony, do you think I'm bitchy?"

He laughed. "Well, yeah—it's kind of your thing, Della."

I blinked. "My thing?"

"Yeah. Some girls are just born with an attitude."

That wasn't me at all. In fact—

"Hey, what's all this?" Anthony reached into a drawer and pulled out a bag of chips and a box of Fiddle-Faddle. "Is this your junk food stash?"

Damn, I thought I'd locked that drawer. "That's... for my brother when he comes."

"You have a brother? Where's he?"

"South of the city."

"You don't talk about your family much. If you like, after I get the kitchen organized, I can go through your family photos and put them in order. I did that for Kyle's mother and it turned out so nice."

Yeah—that would never happen.

"Oh, Joe-Joe's. My favorite," he said of the sandwich cookies. He brought the crack of the box lid to this nose and inhaled. "This must be what heaven smells like."

"You look like you've lost weight," I offered.

He grinned. "I have. My willpower has been amazing lately. Ordinarily, I would've torn into these cookies, but look—" He put them back and closed the drawer. "I'm fine."

I reached down and pushed my fingers into my waistband. No give. Hopefully my increased dosage of Beltina would kick in soon.

"Except my landlord raised my rent again," Anthony said, "so I'm looking for a new apartment." He stacked plates and hummed to himself.

I glanced back to my checkbook and my stomach rolled. Anthony might have to find a new job, soon, too. I couldn't continue to pay him to move things around.

I forced down another mouthful of the bitter-tasting smoothie.

July 25, Tuesday

WHEN I SAW THE WORDS "Atlanta Police Department" come up on my phone screen, my pulse skipped higher. I crossed my fingers, then connected the call.

"Della Culpepper."

"Ms. Culpepper, this is Detective Terry at the APD."

"Hi, Detective. Did you find out anything useful on Gil Malone?"

"How are those anger management classes going?" he asked mildly.

"Relax, Detective. I'm not going to murder Gil." Probably.

"Okay, well... turns out he does have a record."

"I knew it!"

"For bigamy."

"Wait—what?"

"He apparently married two women without divorcing the first one."

I was in shock that two women would agree to marry the man.

"He served a little time in the state pen about ten years ago, and looks like he's been clean ever since."

"And the women?"

"Both divorced him. Well, actually the second marriage was annulled."

"So they're not in the picture anymore?"

"One of the women passed away. The other woman lives here in Atlanta."

"Do you have an address?"

"Look, all I can give you is what's in the public record. The woman's name is Lucy Bellweather."

"Spell that, please."

He did. "Ms. Culpepper, I don't want to get a call that you've been involved in an altercation where someone got hurt."

"Don't worry, Detective. I won't involve the police. Thank you." I ended the call.

Because if I found Gil Malone and had to murder his thieving ass, they'd never find his body.

July 26, Wednesday

"SO LUCY BELLWEATHER moved out last fall? And would you happen to know where she moved to? Okay, thanks anyway."

I disconnected the call and cursed, then steered the SUV into my assigned parking place. One of the advantages of buying a nicer unit was getting a spot near the elevator. I turned off the engine and climbed out, then circled around to get my groceries out of the back. I weighed the trouble of juggling two bags and my purse with having to make a second trip, and opted for the juggling routine.

I clicked a button on my keyless remote to close the hatch, and when I turned around, a scary looking guy was standing close—too close. My breath caught in my throat. My mace was buried in the bottom of my purse. By the time I found it, he would have grown a beard.

"I'm sorry, ma'am. I'm going to need those keys."

Oh, God... I was being carjacked.

"I need my car," I said. "Surely we can work something out. I have some cash." It was a roll of quarters, but still.

"What's going on here?"

I never thought I'd be so happy to hear Charlie Graham's voice. When I turned, he was walking toward us, carrying a sack with baguettes sticking out the top.

"Help me! He's stealing my car!"

The robber scoffed. "I'm not stealing your car, lady. I'm retrieving it for Traxton Pharmaceuticals."

"Oh." My outraged shoulders fell. "No one called me."

"You should've received something in the mail."

"Oh." It was probably in my mailbox, with all the bills.

"Do you have any personal belongings you'd like to remove from the vehicle?"

"My Starbucks travel mug," I mumbled.

"I'll hold your bags," Charlie offered.

I wanted to disappear, but I handed him my bags and retrieved my beloved coffee mug from the console, along with a lipstick, a tin of mints, and a travel-size bottle of Poo-Pourri (look it up).

"Okay, now I just need for you to sign here," the guy said. "And the keys."

I signed, then opened my purse to dive for the keys, which were apparently at the bottom, cavorting with my mace. I removed a makeup bag, two magazines, a bottle of coconut water, a jump rope, my emergency flats—

"Jesus," the guy muttered.

"Found them," I announced, then unhooked the Audi keys, and handed them over.

The guy nodded his thanks, then climbed into my SUV, and drove away. It was like watching my career being repossessed.

"Sorry about that," Charlie said finally.

I was quiet. My humiliation was complete.

"I'll carry your groceries up for you," he offered.

I just moved numbly toward the elevator.

"At least we live in a place where you don't need a car," he added cheerfully.

Unfortunately, it was also a place where I needed to have a job to stay there.

We rode up in silence, and when we got off on my floor, he walked with me to my door. "I can take these in for you."

I punched in my code. "That's okay, I'll take them."

After the girls' unabashed discussion around his purported prowess, I was suddenly nervous about being alone with him. I took my bags. "Thanks for trying to come to my rescue back there."

"You're welcome."

"But what were you planning to do, stab him with a baguette?"

He laughed. "I have other life skills besides cooking."

"Oh, right—the boxing."

He smiled. "You've been reading up on me?"

"Absolutely not. Goodbye, Charlie."

When I closed the door, I leaned against it for a few seconds, my skin tingling with embarrassment. The next thing I knew, my cheeks were wet. The man must think I'm a complete loser.

Not that I cared what he thought.

After a few more minutes of self-pity and when my groceries grew heavy, I carried them into the kitchen, feet dragging.

That's when I realized Charlie had put a loaf of the homemade bread in one of my bags. I pulled the baguette out of its cloth sleeve and inhaled the yeasty scent. It was still warm.

I pulled out a cutting board, located a bread knife and cut it into thick slices. From the fridge I retrieved a wedge of butter, and smeared it on. When it had melted into the air pockets, I sank my teeth into it.

I had been rescued.

July 27, Thursday

I SLID THE WEIGHTED needle across the numbers on the top of the scale, down, then back up... up... up.

127.

I stared at the number in disbelief, then quickly jumped off the scale. I'd gained six pounds in three weeks?

"Oooh!" Charlie Graham had started the avalanche with his damn donuts... and cheesecake... and bread.

I slammed my locker door and once again, looked up to see everyone staring at me warily.

"What?" I asked, then turned and walked out.

On the way home, I tossed back another Beltina—I'd have to increase my dosage to three pills a day until the scale started moving in the right direction again. Portia would never hire me back if I ballooned up.

For comfort's sake, I replayed the voice message she'd left on my phone this morning.

Hi, Della, it's Portia. I wanted to give you a quick update. Although I can't give you any details, let me just say that things are looking good for us being where we want to be by the end of the year. I hope you know what that means, and will hang in there. Take care.

So all I had to do was figure out a way to get by temporarily.

I could do this.

I walked the long way back to the condo for extra exercise. It was actually good that my car was gone, I reasoned. With no transportation crutch, I'd have those six pounds walked off in no time.

As long as I avoided Charlie Graham.

When I walked through the lobby, I scanned for the big man in case I needed to make a run for it. I decided it was time to tackle the monster in my mailbox, so I dragged out the piled up envelopes and carried the armful of doom upstairs. When I spread them over the breakfast bar, my heart began to race. How much financial trouble had I let myself get into?

Quite a lot, it seemed. I opened them one at a time and as the stack grew higher, my mood sank lower.

When I opened the bill from the furniture company, I frowned. "This can't be right."

Almost thirteen thousand dollars due within thirty days? This, at least, I could straighten out now. I phoned the furniture company and asked to speak with the billing department. I provided to the customer service representative the name of the saleswoman I'd worked with.

"She said the amount could be financed at twelve months, same as cash, with no money down and no minimum monthly payment."

"That's right, ma'am," the guy on the phone said.

I relaxed.

"If you qualify," he continued. "But there's a note on your account that says your employment didn't check out."

I'd forgotten—of course they would do a credit check and verify employment, the latter of which I had none.

"I was laid off just a few days ago," I explained.

"And do you have another job?"

"No."

"Okay, how about a credit card you can put the amount on?"

I swallowed. "No. Will you take the couch back?"

"We can take it back," he said.

I relaxed.

"But we charge a forty percent restocking fee, which is payable on pickup."

I did the math, but my brain seemed sluggish today, so it took me longer than I would've liked. "I'm supposed to pay you over five thousand dollars to take back the couch?"

"I can see how it would seem that way," the man said agreeably. "But look at it from our point of view."

I opened my mouth and a torrent of vile words flew out.

He hung up on me.

I pulled my arm back to throw my phone, then caught myself. That was an expense I couldn't afford right now. I tossed my phone on the counter and brought my hand to my temple, trying to still the alarm that sounded in my head. I needed... I needed... I needed... something.

My gaze landed on another piece of mail. I pulled it closer, then picked up my phone and dialed.

"Delivery, please. Yes, one large pizza, with the works..."

July 28, Friday

"HELLO, SIR. Do you have a few minutes to take a survey about adult incontinence products?"

He hung up.

I sighed, struck a line through the phone number, then moved the ruler down to the next number on my unending bleeping list.

My phone rang and it was Anthony calling. I needed a break, so I connected the call. "Hi, Anthony."

"Hi, Della."

I could tell by his voice something was wrong. My glute muscles tensed. "What's up?"

"The cleaning company called. They said your card was declined for payment."

I winced. "Oh... sorry about that. I was late sending in my credit card payment is all. Give me their number and I'll take care of it."

"Actually, they said they've been using a temp agency, and it would be faster if you pay the agency directly." He gave me the name of the place.

"Okay, I'll handle it. Meanwhile, will you call the cleaning company back and cancel the service? I'm just not happy with the quality of work from this new maid, Joon-woo."

Not exactly true, but I wasn't about to tell Anthony I couldn't afford it anymore.

"Will do," he said. "Later."

I considered putting off the bill, but it was small in the scheme of things, and I didn't want Anthony to get another call from them. I phoned the temp agency twice, but it rolled to voice mail. When I realized the name of the company seemed familiar, I looked it up and learned it was just a couple of blocks away, inside Triangle Point. I'd probably walked by it a thousand times.

Since it was a good time to go to the gym—my membership was still paid for through the end of the month—I decided to stop by the temp agency on the way. Two more eBay auctions had ended this morning on an upnote, so I could pay the agency and be done with it.

The Anita Temp Agency was located in a narrow storefront next to other service businesses—drycleaners, phone repair, and pet grooming, among others. Since it was along the route I normally took to the gym, I *had* walked by it a thousand times, yet never looked twice. Another example of something I looked at all the time, yet didn't see... like the homeless teenagers Donnie had been so concerned about.

When the question floated into my mind of what else I might be missing, I pushed it away. I was too busy to notice every little thing.

I pushed open the door to the agency and walked in. The front counter was unmanned, but I could hear movement in the back, so I waited and glanced around. The lobby was neat and bright, populated with lots of posters and placards about how the agency could fill almost any job imaginable.

"Hello, sorry for the wait," a woman's voice said. "How can I help you?"

I turned and gasped at the chic, professional woman in front of me. "Joon-woo?"

She grimaced, then recovered. "Hi, Della."

"Oh. My. God. You can speak English." Perfectly, with no accent.

"I'm American. I was born and raised here."

"Then why the act? And what are you doing here?"

"This is my place," she said, gesturing to the office. "And sometimes I take jobs that are hard to fill, especially on the weekends. It's extra money for the agency, and it allows me to interact with customers."

I narrowed my eyes. "You lied."

"No," she said, lifting her finger. "You assumed I didn't speak English—I never told you." She crossed her arms. "Which is a little racist, by the way."

I bristled. "You lied by omission."

She held up her hands. "Okay… you're right. I'm sorry. It was just easier to pretend. How can I help you?"

Despite the apology, I felt totally duped. "I came to settle my bill. Apparently, there was some misunderstanding and my card was declined. The cleaning company asked me to stop by and handle it directly."

She inclined her head. "They give me a lot of business, so thank you." She looked up the account, gave me the amount, and I used my debit card.

"How are the eBay auctions going?" she asked.

"Fine," I chirped.

"Here's your card back," she said with a smile. "Thanks for stopping by, and again, I'm sorry for the subterfuge."

"That's a mighty big word for a housecleaner," I snapped, then turned and marched out.

Honestly, you couldn't trust anyone these days!

July 29, Saturday

"KYLE, I WISH I could come up, but my car is in the shop."

"Oh, I didn't know. Then I'll come pick you up, and we'll drive to the lake from there."

I smiled into the phone. "That would be nice."

"Okay, see you soon."

I was so happy to be going out on the lake today—I needed to relax, and Kyle and I needed some alone time. It would be nice to get away from the condo for a little while, and those endless calling lists—ugh.

I took special care picking out the right swimwear and matching outfits. Kyle appreciated it when I dressed nice, and it made me feel like I belonged in his crowd. I think a couple of the women in his circle were actually a little jealous of me—something I couldn't have imagined growing up. Now my looks and my figure were my competitive edge, both in my personal and my professional life.

I smiled down at the orange pill in my hand. Beltina had given me that edge, and I would forever be loyal to it. I downed it with a glass of water, then checked my waistband. Definitely roomier than yesterday.

When the doorbell rang, I grabbed my overnight bag and turned off lights as I strode to the door. I swung open the door, expecting to see Kyle. Instead Joon-woo stood there, her face screwed up in anger.

"You complained to the cleaning company about my work?"

I crossed my arms. "I might have said I wasn't a hundred percent pleased."

"I worked my ass off for you!"

"I caught you asleep on my couch!"

"One time," she said, lifting her finger. "Because I pulled an all-nighter on another job before I came to your place. And besides, I didn't hurt your precious couch."

"But you could have."

Her mouth tightened. "Do you know why I worked for you? Because no one else would, that's why. Elena was the only person who could stand you, and when she disappeared, I had to step in to keep the cleaning company happy. And now, because you complained, I lost their account."

I blinked. "I... didn't mean for that to happen."

"Because you don't think about anyone but yourself," she spat out. "I'm sorry that my work wasn't up to your high standard, but I really tried. I even let you take those pictures of me for your stupid eBay auctions!"

"Hey, I tipped you extra for that." I bit into my lip. "Look, I wasn't totally unhappy with your work. Actually, you did a good job."

That took some of the wind out of her sails. "Then why did you give me a bad report?"

"Because... I can't afford the service anymore. My financial situation has changed, and I was too embarrassed to say so."

Joon-woo sighed. "Della, if you need some extra cash to get you through a tough spot, I could really use someone like you in my employee stable."

I guffawed. "Temp work? No way."

I heard the elevator door open and Kyle came around the corner.

"Now get lost," I hissed.

Joon-woo frowned, but thankfully she wheeled off just as Kyle walked up. "Ready, doll?"

I recovered and smiled. "Absolutely."

July 30, Sunday

"THANKS FOR A great weekend," I said to Kyle, and meant it. Spending time on his boat with like-minded people was the escape I needed from my own life at the moment.

"I'm so proud of you," he said, leaning over the console of his convertible to touch my arm. "Proud of the way you take care of yourself, and proud of what you've accomplished. I love having you by my side."

I leaned in for a nice goodbye kiss. The sex had been surprisingly good last night—and this morning. Good and *different*. As if we'd entered some new phase in our relationship.

"Bye," I said, then climbed out of his car and waved.

I floated through the lobby and stopped to check my mailbox in case my check from Traxton had arrived in yesterday's mail. Once I received my bonus money, my problems would be solved for a while.

But darn, it wasn't among the envelopes I flipped through.

"Bad news?" Charlie asked, walking behind me to get to his mailbox.

I turned my head, but was determined not to engage. "Nope, everything's swell."

He looked me up and down. "Been to the lake, huh?"

"Yes."

"With your boyfriend?"

"Yes."

"I hear it's nice up there."

"It is." I turned and walked to the elevator, stabbing the button several times, willing the elevator car to get there. When the doors opened, I jumped inside and pressed the "close door" button.

"Hold the door," Charlie called.

But it was closing just as he walked up. "Sorry," I called.

"Not sorry," I muttered when the door closed.

Too late, I realized I wasn't alone. Mindy Chasen stood there holding Howard.

"Hi," I said with a little wave.

But she just stepped farther away.

"Bye," I called when we walked off the elevator. Again, no response.

But I wasn't going to let anyone or anything wreck my mood. I'd had a wonderful weekend with Kyle, and I could limp along financially until my bonus check arrived.

Assuming I had no big unexpected expenses.

In keeping with my pledge to open every bill as soon as it arrived, I walked toward my desk, loosening the flaps and peeking inside, relieved each time a statement revealed I was no worse off than before. No better, but no worse.

The last envelope was from the Fulton County Tax Assessor's Office. I was familiar with property tax statements, so it didn't concern me. My condo taxes were escrowed with my mortgage payment, and I received regular updates as assurance they were being paid as scheduled.

"Blah, blah," I said, skimming. "Blah—"

I stopped. A quick comparison of Previous Year's Fair Market Value and Current Year Fair Market Value showed my property value had... *doubled*?

That was the good news. The bad news was so had my property taxes, which were already hefty. The net-net was I needed to come up with another six grand between now and year end.

I lifted my skirt, shimmied out of my panties, and looked them over, gauging their worth to an incarcerated man. I could sell my dirty underwear.

Or....

July 31, Monday

I'D REHEARSED a few things to say on my behalf, but when I walked into the Anita Temp Agency and Joon-woo came out to greet me, my confidence waned.

"Hi, Joon-woo."

"Hello, Della. I got a call from the cleaning company this morning. They said you'd contacted them and reversed your review. Thank you for that."

"You're welcome."

"What can I do for you?"

"I need a job," I blurted. "Just for six months until my former boss rehires me." I extended a folder. "Here's my resume. I've been working since I was a teenager and I have experience doing a lot of things. And I'm teachable."

She took the folder warily, but opened it and skimmed the papers inside.

"Look, Joon-woo... I treated you abominably, and I wouldn't blame you if you told *me* to get lost. But if you'll hire me, I promise I'll show up every day and do anything you ask."

She raised her eyebrows.

"I don't do sex work," I amended, "and I'm not great with kids. But everything else—yeah. Wait—I draw the line at cutting people's toenails. But everything else—"

"Okay," she said.

"Okay what?"

"Okay," Joon-woo said, sticking out her hand, "you're hired. Welcome to the Anita Temp Agency."

I grinned and shook her hand. "Great. When do I start?"

"Tomorrow."

"Ooh, that soon?" Then I recovered and made my head bounce up and down. "Okay... I can make that work."

So for now, just call me Temp Girl.

This should be interesting.

AUGUST

August 1, Tuesday

I'VE BEEN ONE OF THE TOP sales reps for Traxton Pharmaceuticals for a while now, but that wasn't always the case. Before Beltina was a dieting sensation, it was considered just another pill among countless others that promised weight loss, but delivered a plethora of unpleasant side effects like spontaneous diarrhea and homicidal urges. No one wanted it. I schlepped samples from practice to practice, using deli sandwiches and glazed donuts to entice medical personnel to listen to my sales pitch. (Hypocritical, I admit, but food does have a way of lubricating relationships.) Anyway, what I'm getting at is I'm not afraid of hard work—I put myself through college with a series of odd jobs I wouldn't dream of listing on my LinkedIn profile. But standing in front of the Anita Temp Agency, I was seized with a bout of panic mixed with anger.

I was so above this, dammit.

I stamped my foot on the sidewalk and my ankle wrenched sideways. I yelped in pain and when I stood, realized the heel of my Gucci sandal had snapped off. Double dammit.

Although maybe it was a sign I should go home and figure out another way to stay afloat until Portia rehired me.

I'd turned to limp back to my condo when I heard the door to the agency open and Joon-woo call, "Della?"

I winced, then turned back. "Hi."

She smiled. "Good morning. We were just about to get started."

"We?"

"I have two other employees starting today. I thought we'd do orientation together."

I held up my broken heel. "I need to postpone. Maybe we can do this tomorrow?"

"That's not necessary—I have extra shoes here." She waved for me to come inside. "We wear the same size, remember?"

I remembered. Fighting a sigh, I trudged inside and followed her through the lobby down a hallway to a closet she'd turned into an office. She opened a desk drawer and pulled out the ugly beige lace-up shoes she wore when she cleaned my place. "Here you go."

I shook my head. "I don't think so."

"I have socks."

"Even worse," I said.

She shrugged. "Okay, go barefoot for all I care."

I frowned and reached for the fugly shoes. "Just until I can go back to my condo."

"You're welcome," she mocked. "Come to the back room when you're ready."

I kicked off my sandals and hopped on one foot to put on the white socks and lace-up shoes. To my dismay, the shoes did fit. And I conceded they felt like foot pillows. But they didn't do much for my chic white capri pants and fitted navy tunic. I jammed my sandals into my Louis Vuitton bag and plowed ahead.

The room in the back was windowless and lined with several cubby workstations, some of which contained personal items, but none were occupied. In the center sat a white table with simple chairs around it. Two other people sat there—a man in his forties and a woman who was a well-preserved fifty, if I had to guess.

God, if I were a temp girl at their age, I'd kill myself.

"This is Tyler and Ellen," Joon-woo said to me.

I nodded a greeting and they smiled, all chipper.

Joon-woo gestured to me. "And this is—"

"Mae," I cut in. "You can call me Mae."

Joon-woo squinted, then nodded. "Okay... Mae. Have a seat."

I took the seat at the opposite end of the table, already over the whole experience. I did not belong here.

"Welcome to the Anita Temp Agency," Joon-woo said, smiling wide. "Since opening a year ago, I've acquired a list of clients who need temporary employees for various reasons, and the list continues to grow. So you can see why I'm in constant need of good people who are well-rounded. I hired each of you because I believe you possess the skills necessary to accommodate a wide range of situations."

Her gaze paused on me. "Mae, is it too bright in here?"

She was referring to my oversized dark sunglasses and black hat. I didn't want any of these temp people to be able to recognize me on the street.

"No," I said cheerfully.

"Wouldn't you be more comfortable without the sunglasses?"

"Eye infection," I said without missing a beat.

"And the hat?"

"Lice. I'm on my last treatment."

Tyler and Ellen squirmed in their seats.

Joon-woo smirked at me, then passed around thick ivory-colored folders with the name of the agency printed on the front. "We'll be going over the employment agreement and general policies. But before we get into the paperwork, do you have any preliminary questions?"

Tyler raised his hand. I rolled my eyes.

"Yes?" Joon-woo asked.

"What kind of time commitment will this entail?"

"You can work as few as ten hours a week, and as many as fifty. All of the assignments are in either four- or eight-hour increments."

Ellen raised her hand.

"You don't have to raise your hand," Joon-woo said cheerfully. "Just ask."

"How are assignments made?"

"That's my job. I will make a best effort to match you with the skills you listed on your resumes, but you should know that you could be called on to perform a job that you've never done before or is not your first choice."

"Can you give us an example?" Tyler asked.

"Sure. Most of the businesses that engage my services are within Triangle Point. At first, you'll be floaters, so on any given day, you could be called upon to work in an office building, a retail business, or a service business. The term of the job is typically one or two days to fill in for an employee who might be on vacation or out sick, but some of the jobs could extend for a week or more."

"And how do we receive our assignments?" Ellen asked.

"You'll call in to a message service each evening and enter your personal code to obtain the next day's assignment," Joon-woo said. "I'll let you know the pay rate, start time and the dress code, if any, required at the business, as well as the name of the person you should report to." She pointed to the desks lining the perimeter of the room. "You'll be given the use of one of these personal workstations with a locked cabinet if you'd like to keep a few items here. You'll get a card to key in and out of the office since I'm not always here."

"I'm confused about the benefits," Tyler said.

"You're employed by this agency, not the company where you're assigned, so your paycheck and your benefits, such as health insurance, comes through ATA."

I sat forward. "We get health insurance?"

Joon-woo gave me a slow-blink. "Yes, uh, Mae. But you have to work at least thirty-five hours a week."

How had that tidbit slipped by me? I opened and closed my stiff hand, now healed from the broken glass incident, but a sobering reminder of how quickly things could go sideways without coverage.

My new boss opened the folder in front of her. "Any other questions before we get started?"

"Just one," I said. "What if we don't like our assignment?"

She smiled. "Did I mention you get health insurance if you work at least thirty-five hours a week?"

Translation: This was going to suck.

August 2, Wednesday

IN HINDSIGHT, "suck" was an understatement. At least for my first assignment: gift wrapper at Dorman's department store.

"You left too much overlap when you pulled the two sides together," my prune-faced tutor Peg chastised. "Now you have long corners. Try again."

I could feel my blood starting to bubble, and I had proof when in the process of adjusting my overlap, I gave myself a deep, sizzling papercut. My third one in ten minutes.

"Dammit!" I yelled, then sucked the end of my finger.

"You'll get calluses," Peg offered, as if it were aspirational. "Meanwhile, you got blood on the wrapping paper, so you'll have to start over. And watch your language. When I move you to the counter, you'll be dealing directly with customers."

Ooooh! I bit down on my finger to keep from telling the woman what I was thinking. Knowing she would be reporting back to Joon-woo on my performance was the only thing that kept me from stapling a bow to her forehead. After four hours of cutting, folding, creasing, and taping, I finally got a nod of approval from Pruney Peg.

"Your bows could use some more fluffing," she said, "but you'll do."

I ran out of there, fighting tears—tears of boredom from the mind-numbing tedium of the job and tears of pain because my Miu Miu mules were not meant for hours of standing. I'd thought of Joon-woo's ugly shoes in my bag more than once, but I hadn't succumbed to their marshmallowy unsightliness. I decided before I could be tempted to don those dogs again, I should return them to Joon-woo, and find a subtle way to tell her the gift-wrapping gig sucked.

"The gift-wrapping gig sucks," I announced when I walked into the agency's back room.

A few other temps at their workstations turned to stare at me. Joon-woo, who was refilling a copy machine with printer paper threw a frown in my direction. "Della—"

"Mae," I corrected.

"Mae, why don't we step into my office?"

I followed her back to the cramped closet. We practically had to spoon in order to close the door.

"How's the eye infection?" she asked dryly, referring to the disguise. "And the lice?"

"Bad," I lied.

"I realize this is your first day," she said, "but it's not helpful when you complain about assignments."

"I'm supposed to pretend I liked it? Look at my hands—it looks like I've been juggling scalpels."

"And yet Peg Townsend just called to tell me you did a good job."

That took the wind out of my sails a bit. "A monkey could do that job," I groused.

"No. Peg is hard to please, so—good job."

"Okay, I don't need to be patted on the head," I said tersely.

"But Peg says you have to lose the sunglasses and the hat, and I'm sure my other clients will feel the same."

I made a face, but nodded. "Here are your godawful shoes."

She took the bag and handed me back a key. "And here's the key to your workstation, number nine. Feel free to bring in some personal items to make it your own space."

My look stopped her cold.

"Or not," she said with a shrug. "But most people find it's helpful to keep their timesheets here." She handed me a pad of them, along with a pen.

"Thanks," I said, then shimmied my way out of the closet. "By the way, I don't work Sundays—my religion forbids it."

I ignored her look of skepticism, then stalked to the back room. I studiously avoided the other temps—I had zero intention of getting to know them—and found workstation nine.

It was a simple vertical cabinet with a desk surface and multiple locked drawers. It was IKEA-quality, but serviceable and clean. I unlocked a top drawer and dropped the timesheets inside. When I turned to go, I noticed the workstation next to mine—or rather, the photo in a corner.

Joon-woo walked by with another stack of printer paper. "This is Elena's station?" I asked.

She nodded, then sighed. "She disappeared. I don't know what to do with her stuff."

I thought Elena had decided not to work for me anymore. I didn't realize she'd stopped working altogether. "When was the last time you heard from her?"

Joon-woo looked to the ceiling. "It's been over a month, I suppose."

"Don't you find that strange?"

"Not really. She talked about going back to Mexico all the time, so I just assume that's what happened. And she isn't the first temporary employee who moved on without notice."

She walked on, unconcerned.

I frowned, wondering if my vase-throwing fit had hastened Elena's decision. Then I harumphed. Here I was thinking I might track her down to apologize, yet she didn't have the common courtesy to let anyone know she was leaving.

At least I didn't have to feel guilty anymore.

So why did I?

August 3, Thursday

"HAVE YOU DECIDED what color of bow you'd like?" I asked the woman through gritted teeth. Wrapping gifts, I decided after a second day of it—eight hours this time, eight—was the worst job ever. If this lady ever made up her freaking mind she'd be my last customer. If.

"Not yet," she said, humming. "What do you think?"

"The pink," I said because it was the spool closest to me.

She worked her mouth back and forth. "I'm thinking the blue."

"Perfect," I said, then reached for the angled end of the blue ribbon and gave it a yank to unwind a couple of feet.

"No, maybe you're right," she said. "I'll take the pink."

I was seriously considering stabbing her with my scissors when her expression changed.

"Wait—don't I know you?"

My heart skipped a beat. This was what I feared most—running into someone who knew me. I took in her pale face, dark eyes, and red glasses, my mind racing. "I don't think so." I busied myself with the ribbon.

"Are you a patient of Dr. Hemple in Decatur? I'm his receptionist."

Ah. I'd called on Dr. Hemple more than a few times for my sales job with Traxton. "No," I said, pulling the ribbon up to obscure my face. "I've never even been to Decatur."

"Gosh, you look so familiar," she pressed.

"Is it nice?"

"Is what nice?"

"Decatur."

"Oh, sure," the woman said, then launched into an exuberant description that would make the Chamber of Commerce proud.

"There you go," I said, interrupting her rambling by sliding her wrapped package across the counter. "Have a nice evening."

"You, too," she said, although she was still squinting at me as if she was trying to recall where she knew me from.

I plunked down my "Next window, please" placard and wheeled away, my pulse pounding. If I was going to pull off this temp girl thing, I really needed to think of some way to change my appearance.

But for now, I was exhausted, and I was really looking forward to being horizontal. When I got to my building, I limped through the lobby with a quick wave to what's-his-name the concierge and stabbed the elevator button.

"Hello there."

At the sound of Charlie Graham's voice, I winced, then turned my head a fraction of an inch. "Hi."

The door opened and I jumped on, but he was hip to my quick button-pushing, and was right behind me. Damn, he smelled like bread... warm, crusty bread from a firebrick oven, with those oat-y bits on top.

I pressed the button for my floor and he pressed the button to the floor two down from mine, I noticed—not that I cared.

"How are... things?" he asked, flipping through his mail.

"Fine."

"You're, um, working... things out?"

"I am," I confirmed, irritated he knew my boss had fired me. "In fact... it's better than the situation I had before."

"Good for you." Then he grunted. "What did you do to your hands?"

I glanced down at the SpongeBob Squarepants Band-Aids criss-crossing my fingers, then shoved my hands in my pockets. "I've been... cutting things."

"In the kitchen? Wow, I didn't take you for a cook."

I shrugged.

"Hey, I'm really enjoying the couch."

"Isn't this your floor?"

"So it is." He stepped out. "See you around."

"Uh-huh." I punched the "close door" button to block the scent of bread, although by the time I got to my place, dammit, I was craving carbs. I fell onto my bed face-first and felt around blindly until I found my TV remote control. Charlie Graham's infuriating round face kept coming back to me. I didn't know what all the women were raving about—the man was not hot. At the most extreme stretch of the imagination, he was, at the most, slightly cute. Those dimples were ridiculous, frankly, and not very manly. Combined with the fact that he spent most of his time in the kitchen kissing his own fingers and I couldn't fathom why women thought he was sexy. Sabrina and Susan had suggested a threesome only because they were intrigued by the chubster thing—it was a novelty to them.

I grimaced and pressed the heels of my palms into my eyes to try to block the unpleasant images from my brain.

I was obviously missing Kyle if my mind was going to those places.

I flopped over on my back, then groaned. It had been a while since... you know.

I reached over and opened the drawer in my nightstand to look for my vibrator. When I came up empty, I checked my underwear drawer, then under my bed, but nada. I padded into the bathroom where I checked all the drawers and my makeup bag, but still, nothing. Beyond irritated, I flounced back down on the bed, wracking my brain for when I'd last seen or used it. My memory has been a little spotty lately for stuff like that.

But at least the urge had passed. Which was good because I didn't want to have an orgasm even close to the vicinity of thinking about Charlie Graham.

August 4, Friday

MEET YOU AT the gym for a weigh-in?

I stared at my trainer Jan's text, torn. If Traxton hadn't cancelled her services, then they were still paying for my gym membership and—more importantly—it proved they were still invested in my wellness and intended to rehire me in December.

But a weigh-in? I slipped a finger into my waistband and made a face at the snug fit.

Still, a weigh-in was probably what I needed to get back on track. Since my sucky gift-wrapping stint wasn't until later in the day, I texted back yes, changed into featherweight workout clothes and walked the few blocks to the gym. I passed Anita Temp Agency on the way. Joon-woo waved, but I pretended not to notice. I was trying to keep my distance from all the people at ATA, including Joon-woo. When I got to the gym, I held my membership card up to the scanner and walked on by.

"Wait," the girl at the desk said. "Says your membership has expired."

My pulse blipped in panic, but I feigned nonchalance. "That can't be. I've been a member for years."

"And now you're not," she said flatly.

Okay, so I hadn't been overly nice to the girl, but it was her job to be nice to me. "My employer pays for my membership," I said evenly. "Something must have fallen through the cracks."

"Well, until it's fixed, I can't let you in—liability and stuff." She slow-blinked to let me know she was happy to be putting me in my place.

"More of a liability than having a porky girl work the front counter?"

Her eyes flew wide, but I turned and left before she could respond. On the way out, I squashed a pang of remorse by reasoning in the scheme of fat insults, "porky" wasn't as bad as lardass, blubberbutt, supersized, whaletail, thunderrump—

"Della?"

I looked up to see Jan walking toward me on the sidewalk.

"Sorry I'm late," she said.

"It's fine," I said, improvising. "Actually, I just got a text about work, so unfortunately, I can't stay."

"I just got a text, too," Jan said, holding up her phone. "Traxton let me go."

"Really?" I hedged.

She nodded, then sighed. "Frankly, I think this business of making their Beltina sales reps maintain a certain weight is archaic, and I must've said so one too many times. I guess they're replacing me."

"Oh. That's… too bad."

So Jan didn't know sales of the drug were on hold. According to the silence of the news feeds I'd been checking, no one else did either. I was dying to reach out to fellow sales reps, but the agreement I'd signed forbade it, which was probably why none of them had reached out to me.

"Anyway, Della, I just wanted to say goodbye and good luck."

"Thanks, Jan. You too."

Meanwhile, advertising hadn't ceased—if anything, I was seeing more impressions of Beltina than before across TV and online. The only negative mention I'd found was on a weight-loss forum—patients were not happy about the sudden scarcity, viciously so.

She began to walk away, then turned back. "Listen, Della, I always assumed you were taking Beltina."

But I shook my head. "I don't have a prescription."

She nodded. "I assumed that as well. Just be careful, okay?"

I frowned. "What do you mean?"

She pulled her hand over her mouth in a zipping motion, then walked away.

I stared after her, thinking maybe she did know Beltina was in danger of being pulled from the market. But she obviously thought I didn't know, and was warning me my job was in danger.

Too late for that.

Oh, well, at least I didn't have to worry about her expecting me to keep her on as my trainer. I was going to have enough trouble figuring out how to come up with the hefty monthly fee to rejoin the gym. If I let myself go, Portia would never hire me back, archaic practice or not.

August 5, Saturday

IT HAD BEEN YEARS since I'd ridden the MARTA train. But sans a car, it was the best way to get to Neiman Marcus where I hoped to return enough clothing to restore some much-needed cash flow. I hadn't had any luck yet tracking down my mother's boyfriend to recover the money—my money—he'd taken from her account. And I wouldn't get my first paycheck from ATA for another week. So I'd taken the salesclerk Carlotta's advice and spruced up the return items—and myself—for another shot.

"Looking good," a guy on the train leered.

"Shut your pie hole," I replied, then turned my back. I was standing, hanging on to an overhead rail, not because there weren't any seats, but because I didn't want to risk creasing the garments in the hanging bag I held.

Once I reached the department store, I checked a couple of counters before I found the dark-haired woman. She was finishing ringing up what appeared to be a sizable sale, from the looks of the bulging bags the customer held. When I walked up, she turned a smile toward me and I squinted. Something about her was different.

"Hello," Carlotta said. "May I help you?"

"I'm Della. I was here a couple of weeks ago to return some items and you waited on me."

"Yes, I remember you."

I lifted the hanging bag in one hand, my credit card statements in the other. "I'm back to try again."

She took the bag and nodded in approval. "You look very nice."

"Thanks. Um—didn't you have a gap between your front teeth before... and brown eyes?"

She nodded, then gave me a little smile. "I have a side job that sometimes requires me to change my appearance. I'm going there straight from here."

Ah—she probably did modeling. I watched her while she rang up my return. She obviously had a retainer to fill in the gap, and blue contact lenses.

Then a thought occurred to me—I'd been so spooked by the woman who almost recognized me the other day, I needed to do something to tweak my own appearance, and the sunglasses and hat weren't going to fly. "Do you have any tricks you can share about... changing your look?"

I could tell she instantly found me more interesting. "It's mostly hair and eyes," she said casually. "Wigs or spray-in color are quick and effective. Colored contacts or fake glasses work, too, and changing your eyebrows can make a big difference." She nodded to my skirt and silk tee. "And clothing. You can camouflage yourself if you… don't want to be noticed."

Hm—why would a model dress to not be noticed? "Thanks."

"You did a good job with the garments," she said. "I need to ring a supervisor for a return of this amount, so it might be a few minutes."

I didn't have to be at the dreaded gift-wrapping job at Dorman's for a few hours. "No problem."

She made the call, then set down the receiver. "Returns are usually less of a hassle, but there's a shoplifting ring moving around the city, and all the stores in the mall are taking a big hit. What do you do, Della?"

"Pharmaceutical sales."

She smiled. "That's job security in this country."

I managed a smile in return. "Uh-huh."

The same supervisor who had rejected my return last month appeared and scanned me with a critical eye, then gave the garments a cursory glance, punched in something on the register terminal, and left.

"Would you like the refund back on your Neiman's card, or cash?" Carlotta asked.

My neck warmed. "Cash."

She nodded, then opened her cash register and counted out the bills. "Here you go."

"Thanks," I murmured. "And thanks for the tips on… the other thing."

"You're welcome," she said. "It's a woman's prerogative to change as the situation requires."

I said goodbye and walked back to the train thinking how right she was. Being a chameleon had served me well in the past. I just needed to take it to the next level. A few half-truths here, an outright lie there, and I could get through the next six months. At least that's what I kept telling myself during the ride back on the train and the short walk to my building.

I ignored the panic licking at me, the whisper that I was in more trouble than I realized. As I walked off the elevator toward my condo, I told myself I just needed to keep acting like everything was normal.

"There you are."

Anthony stood in front of my door, his face creased in concern. "I've been calling."

"You have?" I reached into my bag to get my phone.

"It's going straight to voice mail."

My stomach dropped when I saw the red line through my screen along with a message to contact the billing department of my service provider. Traxton had obviously suspended my service.

"My battery is dead," I said, then returned the phone, hoping Anthony didn't notice my hand was shaking.

"You've been riding MARTA?" he asked, pointing to the fare card in my hand.

"My SUV is in the shop," I lied. "Didn't I mention it?"

"No. But don't you Uber?"

"Sure. But I was just going to the mall, and the train seemed quicker." And cheaper.

"I bought the towels you asked me to get," he said, holding up a shopping bag. "And I bought a spice rack for your pantry."

"Okay," I said punching in the entry code. I didn't remember asking him to get towels, but it sounded like something I would do. And I wanted to chastise him for stopping by unannounced, but he'd probably texted me and I hadn't received it.

He followed me inside, then glanced around at the clutter and groaned. "I'm so sorry—I forgot to call the cleaning company to arrange for someone else to come by."

"Don't do that," I said quickly. A maid was no longer in my budget. At Anthony's confused frown, I tried to recover. "A neighbor is giving me a referral to someone she uses."

"Ah. Okay, let me know if I can help." He went to the pantry to situate the spice rack and after admiring his handiwork, leaned over to open the cabinet where I stashed junk food. His face fell in disappointment. "I was going to sniff the box of Joe-Joe's, but I see your brother has been here."

"Right," I said, nodding.

He closed the drawer with a sigh. "Does he visit often?"

"Not very."

Anthony pointed. "I'll put away your towels."

When he was out of sight, I grimaced. I was going to have to address keeping him on—I couldn't afford him, but neither could I afford for him to find out I'd been let go.

He came back, folding the shopping bag. "So are you officially taking over your new position this week? Any appointments I need to schedule?"

"Um, not yet," I hedged. "In fact, it might be a couple more weeks. I decided to take some vacation days."

"Where are you going?" he asked excitedly.

"I might just hang around here."

"Can't blame you—being at the lake on Kyle's boat is like being on a private cruise."

I nodded.

Anthony shifted. "So I was wondering if you could pay me before I leave?" From his messenger bag, he pulled out a sheet of paper with his hours on it.

"Sure," I said, although it would take a chunk of what I'd just collected at the department store. "Is cash okay?"

"Even better."

I counted out the bills with a sinking feeling in my gut, but smiled when I handed them to him.

"Thanks," he said happily. "Don't forget to charge your phone."

"I won't," I said, then walked him to the door.

When the door closed, I sighed. The rest of my cash would undoubtedly be going to my cell phone provider. I walked to my couch and sat down, fighting a feeling of powerlessness. I reached behind a fat down cushion, pulled out the box of Joe-Joe's, and opened it.

August 6, Sunday

ANTHONY WAS RIGHT about one thing: Being at the lake on Kyle's boat was indeed like being on a private cruise.

I was lying on a chaise lounge on the lower deck, lightly buzzed on a watermelon cosmopolitan and enjoying the honeyed haze of doing absolutely nothing. This was a job I could get used to—being Dr. Kyle Covey's wife. It wasn't lost on me that with the stroke of a pen, Kyle could make all my financial problems go away. But his recent acquisition of a half million dollars' worth of Traxton stock meant I couldn't tell him about losing my job. I couldn't risk him panicking and selling his shares, exposing me and him to insider trading charges. And if I broke the exit agreement I'd signed, I'd never get my bonus. Plus I'd have to admit to Kyle what had happened to my rainy day money, exposing him to the complete underbelly of my life, i.e., my mother's redneck bigamist thief boyfriend and a slew of white trash relatives.

I excluded my sweet brother Donnie from that heap. But revealing Donnie and Kyle to each other was another risk—and not just for me. I didn't want Donnie to feel snubbed, especially now when he was beginning to be more perceptive within his limitations of autism.

I felt torn—the world I'd come from was pulling at me from behind, and the world I wanted was tugging me forward.

Shade fell over my eyes. "You're being anti-social," Kyle said.

I smiled up at him. "Sorry, I had a rough week, and this feels so good."

"You look sexy lying there."

I preened. "So join me."

He extended his hand. "I can't abandon my guests, and people are asking for you. Besides, you don't want to get too much sun—you'll freckle."

Duty called. "Okay. Will you hand me my coverup?"

"No way you're covering up that gorgeous bod. I want to show you off."

How could any woman resist that? I put my free hand in his, allowing him to pull me up.

He frowned. "What happened to your hands?"

The old paper cuts had dried to maroon, scabby slits—the new ones were bright pink.

"Oh, just dealing with a lot of paperwork lately."

"For the new position?"

"Mm-hm."

"I'll get you some ointment. You don't want to scar."

We climbed to the upper deck and he handed me off to his sister Helen. She was talking to two other women who were squeezed into shapewear disguised as one-piece bathing suits.

"Della, you know Trish and Julie from the club."

"Hi," I said. "Good to see you again."

"We were talking about your amazing drug," Helen said, then whispered, "Thanks for the samples."

I was glad she appreciated them—sharing meant less for me to last until December.

"Della just got a promotion because her sales have been so fantastic."

I squirmed, remembering Portia's implication that my stellar sales had put a spotlight on Traxton's star product.

"Congratulations," the women chorused in harmony.

"Beltina is better than cocaine," Julie said. "I've dropped fifteen pounds in a month."

"Twenty for me," Trish said, holding up a pink frozen drink. "And I get to enjoy alcohol."

"Right—no more seltzer water," Julie added, clinking her frosty glass with Trish's.

Trish stared at my body unabashedly. "You've probably always been thin, like Helen, so you don't know what we're talking about."

I smiled and took another drink of my cosmopolitan.

Julie sighed. "I didn't win the skinny genes lottery."

"Me either," Trish said. "I've been hungry since sixth grade trying to keep my weight in check—until now." She squinted at my crotch. "Oh, my God—you have a thigh gap. I thought they were an urban legend." She pulled out her camera and took a picture.

I dearly hoped she planned to post it on social media.

"We could hate you, Della," Helen said, "except Kyle adores you."

"And we all adore Kyle," Julie added.

"Some more than others," Trish observed over her glass.

We all turned to look. Libby Lakes had snagged Kyle to open a bottle of champagne, and he was struggling. The image of Charlie Graham opening a bottle so expertly at his chef's table flashed back to me, but I pushed it away. After all, Charlie probably couldn't perform a facial chemical peel.

When the cork popped, people nearby cheered and dodged the

flying foam. Libby held up a glass for Kyle to fill and made a joke about how well he'd popped her cork. Kyle laughed nervously then handed the bottle to someone else and walked toward me, holding up the small tube of ointment for my hands.

I smiled back, but a woman knows when her relationship is being threatened. So for now, I'd keep acting as if I was the successful pharmaceutical sales manager Kyle and everyone else thought I was.

Sigh… instead of the Temp Girl I really am.

August 7, Monday

"MOVE ALL THE CDs in slots one through ten to slots eleven through twenty," my stoner fifteen-year-old boss Blowz said. "Gotta make room for this week's top ten." He reeked of stale pot.

"Okay," I said. "What should I do with the CDs already in slots eleven through twenty?"

"Put them out in their obspective areas all over the store."

I gave Blowz a flat smile. "I think you mean in their *re*spective areas all over the store."

He gave me a solemn look. "I respect everyone, no matter what their sexual orientation."

He wheeled off in a self-righteous huff leaving me wondering what was going to become of the planet Earth in my lifetime.

Past then, I didn't much care.

I glanced around the store and took in the dozen or so teenagers browsing the racks or listening to tracks at a kiosk. Most of them looked as if they'd worn the same clothes for a week and had no use for combs. Grunge was in again.

Even without Blowz telling me, I knew step one was moving the CDs in the lower slots to empty them. So I used a shopping basket to begin schlepping them to their respective areas of Hip Hop, Pop, Alternative, Country, blah, blah, and filing them alphabetically.

Phil's Music Emporium was my assignment for two days. I had yet to meet Phil, but if I did, I would tell him he needed to raise his hiring standards a smidge. I lifted my foot and a stringy wad of green chewing gum followed it. Ugh—and the tile floor needed to be pressure-washed.

At least I was allowed to wear tennis shoes. And jeans. The only dress code requirement was a music-related T-shirt, so I'd unlocked the storage closet in my extra bedroom and stepped inside long enough to find an oversized black Elvis T-shirt. I resisted tying it on the side to look cute. Instead I let it swallow me. It matched the rest of my camouflage getup—horn-rimmed glasses and a bandanna tied around my hair, outlaw style.

No one would recognize me.

"Excuse me," a man said behind me.

I closed my eyes—I knew that voice. For someone who owned a restaurant, Charlie Graham seemed to have plenty of free freaking time.

"Can't help you," I mumbled in a low voice over my shoulder.

"I just need to be pointed in the right direction," he said. "Is Yonder Mountain String Band shelved in Alternative or Bluegrass?"

I blindly pointed left, then dipped my chin, picked up my basket and moved away.

And promptly slipped in something on the floor which I suspected wasn't Lysol. Down I went, up flew the basket, then the CDs came raining down in a clatter.

"Are you okay?" Charlie asked, leaning over me.

I was still trying to get my breath and my fake glasses were askew, but I could see the moment he recognized me.

"Della?"

"No," I managed to get out.

He scoffed. "Did you break anything?"

I shook my head.

"Can you get up?"

I nodded. But truthfully, I wasn't sure, so I let him help me since he was so… sturdy. But between the slippery floor and me trying not to lean into him, it was awkward and we wound up practically bear-hugging.

"Alright, alright," I said, pushing away from him. He was wearing a plaid shirt, and I don't mean Burberry—ugh.

"What are you doing in here?"

I pulled myself up. "I'm a customer, like you."

Blowz appeared at my elbow. "Hey, Mae, if you broke any of

those CD cases, they're coming out of your check."

I wanted to punch the world in the face.

"Blowz," I said through gritted teeth, "can you help this man find something called Yonder String Bikini?"

"Yonder Mountain String Band," Charlie corrected.

"Over in Bluegrass, dude."

"Thanks," he said, then Blowz blew away. Charlie looked back to me. "Did he call you Mae?"

I gave a little wave. "Bye now." Then I stooped to pick up the scattered CD cases, noticing that dammit, yes, some of them were broken. Perfect.

Charlie squatted down and retrieved some of the CDs, straightening them and putting them back in the basket. "What's going on? What's with the..." He gestured to my glasses and bandana.

I kept picking up CDs. "It's not obvious by now that I'm working here?"

"This is the situation you told me is better than you had before?"

"It's temporary," I hissed. "Now get out of here. You're going to get me fired from the worst job in the world." I felt dangerously close to tears.

He looked at me. "Della—"

"Please," I choked out. "Please leave."

He hesitated, then gave a curt nod, pushed to his feet and walked out of the store.

I exhaled, mortified down to my marrow, then I was immediately furious that I cared what Charlie Graham thought. The man listened to banjo music, for heaven's sake.

I put myself on autopilot and resumed picking up the CDs. Some of them were wet from whatever was on the floor. I lifted one for a sniff, then retched.

Oh, yeah—it was urine.

August 8, Tuesday

"GIL HASN'T BEEN back?" I asked.

"No," Donnie said. "I've checked with all his buddies in the last few days, and no one's seen him."

But Donnie took people at their word—he could be lied to easily. I should've driven back to Dewdrop to look for Gil Malone when I still had a car. "Do you think Mom knows where he is?"

"I don't think so. She cries all the time like she misses him."

I rolled my eyes, but bit my tongue. "Will you ask her to come to the phone?"

"When she saw it was you calling, she left."

Because she probably had an inkling I'd uncovered something unsavory about Gil Malone, and she didn't want to hear it. I wondered if she'd be so supportive if she knew he might've run to his ex-wife who lived somewhere in Atlanta.

"What can I do to help?" Donnie asked, sounding anxious.

"Do you know what kind of car he's driving?"

"A 1997 Ford F150 truck—yellow."

At least it shouldn't be hard to spot.

"Is your cop friend going to look for him?"

"Um... yeah."

"Tell him it has Cook County tags."

"I will. Let me know if Gil shows up, or if the bank starts leaning on Mom again about the loan."

"Okay."

"And Donnie... what the heck is Trap music?" My brother's love for all things repetitious, like a drumbeat, have made him a bit of a music aficionado.

"That's easy," he said. "Trap music is a mix of hip-hop, dance music, and dubbing. It's called Trap because musicians use the same type of drum machine to create the sound."

I squinted. "But how is it different than just a plain old song?"

He laughed. "The beat is the same for the entire song. There aren't any drum solos like in rock music."

Repetitive and droning—comforting to someone like Donnie. "I think I understand."

"Why are you listening to Trap music?"

"You think I'm not cool enough to listen to Trap music?"

"No," he said bluntly.

I laughed. "Just trying to expand my knowledge base, Professor. Thanks for the explanation. I'll talk to you soon, okay?"

"Okay. Bye, Sis."

I ended the call with a sigh, then used my phone to get directions to the address I'd found that might be linked to a Lucy Bellweather, the name of Gil's ex-wife I'd gotten from Detective Terry in the APD. The address was for Eve Bellweather, who had been listed as a relative of Lucy's—a sister, I presumed, since they were close in age. I frowned at the location balloon on my phone—it was at least a mile from the nearest train station, and not in a sweet part of town.

On the other hand, I had to get my exercise somewhere since my access to the gym had been ripped away. There were still a few hours of daylight left. And I was still wearing jeans and tennis shoes from my agonizing second stint at the music store. Blowz had taken it upon himself to try to educate me on "modern" music. I'm not sure which was more excruciating—trying to follow his pot-fueled byzantine explanations, or listening to the tracks he forced on me that all sounded the same in their shrill weirdness.

But at least Charlie Graham hadn't come back to mock me. I had, in a moment of utter boredom, loaded a Yonder Mountain String Band CD into the listening kiosk and sampled the songs. I'm still not sold on the frantic group-yodeling style of Bluegrass, but I can see where someone as folksy and plain as Charlie would gravitate to it.

I swallowed my evening dose of Beltina. Then without changing out of my "Mae" outfit, I armed myself with mace, power-walked to the nearest train station, and managed to keep from touching other passengers while I rode to the stop closest to the Bellweather address. When I exited the station and found my bearings, a cloudy sky was bringing on dusk a little too quickly, so I decided to jog. I was in a shabby part of town, and even the nicer areas could be dangerous after dark. In hindsight, I probably should have brought someone with me, but none of my friends would even want to know about this, much less participate.

As I neared the address, I scanned for a yellow truck. In this neighborhood, people parked on the street, which was unfortunate for them, but a lucky break for me. I didn't see it, but I located the address I was looking for. Unfortunately, it was an apartment building, which complicated things a bit. I walked up to the concrete breezeway and searched through two dozen call buttons.

Bellweather—bingo.

I pushed the button and a dial tone sounded, then the beeps of a number being dialed. After the second ring, a woman's voice came on the line.

"Hello?"

"Hi. Is this Eve?"

"Yes. Who's this?"

"I'm looking for Lucy. Is she there?"

I could hear whispering in the background, and one of the voices was definitely male. "Who's asking?" She sounded wary.

"A friend of Gil Malone's."

More whispering. "What's your name?"

"My name is MaeDella Culpepper."

And yet more whispering, including, "Holy shit." Gil Malone, the slimy weasel, was so there.

"What do you want with Gil?" Eve asked in a nervous voice.

"I have something for him." A kick in the groin, for starters. Then I was going to mace the effer.

"Gil's not here."

I had to keep the conversation going. "Have you seen him lately?"

"Uh, no. No, I have not seen Gil lately."

"Maybe I could talk to you in person?" I got out my mace.

"I don't think that's a good idea," she said. "I'm hanging up now."

From the other side of the building I heard a heavy door open and slam shut, then the sound of booted feet running away.

I ran out of the breezeway in time to see Gil bobbing down the sidewalk, running like he was on fire.

Which he was going to be if I caught up with him. "Gil!" I screamed, then tore off after him. "Stop running, you coward!"

But he didn't, of course, and he had a head start. A couple of blocks later, I heard an engine roar to life, then a yellow truck veered out into the street ahead of me and peeled away.

I stopped to pick up a rock and threw it after him on principle. But it fell uselessly onto the street, a reminder that I'd fallen short again. White hot anger whipped through me. I pulled my foot back and kicked an ancient tree uprooting the sidewalk. Pain ricocheted through my toes. I threw my head back and screamed in frustration until my ears rang. A sudden piercing pain in my temples stopped me. My heart was pounding so hard, it lifted my shirt.

Across the street, two men who looked like trouble turned and went the other way. The words "crazy" and "mental-case" floated back to me.

I leaned over and massaged my temples until the pain eased, then I limped back to the train station, marinating in disbelief.

Last month my life had been glossy and perfect. And now I was in a shady part of town, scaring the locals.

How had things gone so bad, so quickly?

August 9, Wednesday

"I'M AFRAID THERE'S nothing I can do," Detective Terry said over the phone. "Your mother has to press charges."

"She refused. And besides, I talked to the bank this morning—the thirty-day window has closed for her to file a police report."

"Then legally, you're out of options."

I groaned. "Could you send someone over to rough him up a little?"

Silence sounded, then, "The APD doesn't do that, Ms. Culpepper. And I strongly urge you to stay away from him, too. Else he could file harassment or assault charges, and I'd really hate to have to arrest you."

My anger exploded. "I'm the victim here!"

"I understand how you must feel, but chances are, this guy's already spent your money. And if he has any sense at all, when he got in his truck, he kept driving."

I snorted—Gil Malone had as much sense as a toothbrush.

"Just chalk it up to experience," the detective said, "and hope he stays out of your mother's life. I have to take another call. Don't do anything foolish, Ms. Culpepper."

"I'm not making any promises," I yelled into the phone, then ended the call. "Ooooh!"

While Gil Malone was across town spending my hard-earned money, I was on my way to ATA to get a last-minute assignment I dearly hoped wasn't gift-wrapping or CD-shuffling. I'd been looking forward to having the day to stalk Gil, but Joon-woo had called with the promise of a job at a higher pay rate than I'd worked before. And since my bonus hadn't landed and my debts hadn't evaporated, I'd decided to take her up on it.

I pushed open the door and she was standing at the counter, working on a laptop.

"Who's Anita?" I asked.

She squinted. "Excuse me?"

"The name of your company—Anita Temp Agency?"

"Oh." She grinned. "I-need-a, like I need a dog walker—Anita. Get it?"

I stared. "That's terrible. Who would get that?"

She frowned and handed me slip of paper. "This gym needs a cleaner. The pay-rate is above average."

I looked at the sheet of paper and my eyes widened. It was my gym. Porky at the check-in counter would be delighted if I showed up with a mop in my hand.

"I've done it before," Joon-woo said. "If you're efficient, you can get the cleaning done in two hours, even though your timesheet will show six hours. If you do a good job and are willing, they need someone every Wednesday and Saturday."

My mind churned and I pushed up my fake glasses. On the other hand, what if Porky didn't recognize me? "I'll give it a shot. I just need to run home first to get a couple of things."

"Great," Joon-woo said, as if she'd expected me to resist. She handed me a plastic bag. "Here's the smock their janitors wear."

Janitor? Wow.

"They'll have all the equipment and supplies you'll need. And the cleaning checklist is in the supply closet."

"Okay. Um, speaking of cleaning," I said, glancing around to make sure we weren't overheard, "I'm missing something from my condo."

She glared. "I didn't steal anything."

"It's my vibrator."

She pulled back. "Well, I certainly didn't steal that."

"I didn't think you stole it—I was wondering if you remember seeing it. I... misplaced it."

"What does it look like?"

"Like a penis," I said, exasperated. "It's pink, about five inches long, and it vibrates."

"Have you checked your vagina?"

I frowned. "You could've just said no."

I left and hurried back to my condo to get a few things and to fuddy-up my already duddy outfit. But I still wasn't sure I'd get past the front counter without being recognized. When I walked into the gym, Porky was there.

"I'm the cleaner," I said, keeping my gaze down and fussing with my large canvas tote.

The girl barely looked up, jerked her thumb over her shoulder. "The janitor's closet is between the women's and men's locker room." She slid a key across the counter. "You can put your purse in a locker in the women's room. When you're ready to clean the men's room, just make sure no one's inside, will ya?"

I nodded, then swept by the desk and went to the women's locker room to drop off my bag. The Zumba class was just getting out, so the women were loud and exuberant. No one even looked at me. I spotted the woman who'd asked me about taking Beltina and wondered if she'd gotten a prescription before cut-off. She looked slimmer.

Suddenly a sweaty woman shoved a towel into my hands. "The hamper is full," she said.

And before I could respond, a dozen other women had piled their dirty towels on top of hers, filling my arms to my forehead. The stench was nauseating. I walked out and made it to the janitor's closet where I found a rolling hamper to dump them. A few women from the high intensity interval training class I took walked by me as if I were invisible. I was overcome with a sense of déjà vu—high school... and college. I'd been invisible then, too.

I found the cleaning checklist and did a mental run-through to plan the most efficient use of my time, then I set to work.

It was not pretty, or fun. Cleaning a facility where a large number of people sweated and stank and generally created a funk was hard enough, but doing it while maneuvering around them was really challenging. Too late, I realized I should've worn rubber gloves—my manicure was a wreck. But I finished in less than three hours, so not bad for my first time through. Before I cleaned the last bathroom stall, I stopped by the locker to get my bag and took it inside the stall with me. Once the stall was clean, I pulled my gym bag from the canvas bag, changed into workout clothes, then stuffed all remnants of Cleaning Woman inside, including my bandana and glasses. When I emerged, one of the women from the HIIT class who'd ignored me earlier was coming out of the sauna.

"Hi, Della. Where've you been?"

"Oh, around," I said.

"Better grab you a towel now—they're going fast. The people who work here are sloths."

"Yeah." I took a towel, then dropped my gym bag in the locker and walked out to the workout area. I half expected someone to stop me, to question if I'd carded in, but no one did. After a few minutes, I relaxed—the girl at the counter obviously never wandered back here.

After performing my regular cardio workout, I took the bag into the shower with me, and after a few minutes under the warm spray, redressed in my Cleaning Woman garb. I emerged, wiping down the walls, as if I were just finishing my shift.

When I passed the counter on my way out, I gave the girl a little wave, but I needn't have bothered—she was glued to her Candy Crush game.

When I walked outside, I punched in a number on my phone. "Joon-woo, it's Della—I mean, it's Mae. I'll take the gym cleaning assignment. Yes, every Wednesday and Saturday."

August 10, Thursday

"WOW, your place is so clean," Anthony said when he walked into the condo, then he inhaled. "And it smells great. Guess your neighbor got you that housecleaning referral?"

"Right," I said, nodding.

In truth, I didn't have a job assignment, so I'd spent the day cleaning to distract me from thinking about going back for Gil, or rather—for his truck. It had occurred to me a dumbass like him might think the best place to hide twenty-five thousand in cash would be somewhere in his ugly ride.

"Ugh, the leather couch is so gorgeous. Don't you love it?"

"I do." But I didn't love the late charges accruing until I could produce a paystub from ATA and reapply for credit at the furniture store. I'd forgotten how much work it was to be poor.

"I'm going to get your dry cleaning," Anthony said, pointing toward the bedroom.

I nodded. It was a simple enough chore for him to do until I figured out how to end our arrangement.

"You don't have very many items," Anthony called.

"I haven't been wearing as many work clothes," I called back.

"I'll say." When he came back to the living area, he was holding my dry cleaner's bag—and my gym cleaning smock. "What's this? And this?" He waved my bandana.

"Oh... those. I was in a doctor's lab a couple of weeks ago, and I had to cover my clothing—and my hair. Just leave them. I'll probably throw them out."

"Okay, well, I'm out of here, unless I can do something else for you?"

I bit into my lip. If I knew Gil was still hanging out at Eve Bellweather's apartment, I could go back after dark and break into his truck.

Hey—it's not stealing if you're stealing something back that was stolen from you.

But I needed a vehicle to canvass the adjacent blocks. "Could you give me a ride?"

"Sure. Is your SUV still in the shop?"

"Yeah, something about the universal joint." An easy lie because practically no one knew the part's function, but it sounded super serious. Admittedly, I knew only because Donnie was a car genius.

"I hope you need a ride to a manicurist." He picked up one of my hands and tsked, tsked at the red, rough skin and my botched polish. "What have you been doing?"

"It's um... a new retinoid hand lotion I'm trying. For sun spots."

"I hope it's worth it. Where do you need to go?"

"My brother is thinking about buying a house. He asked me to check out the neighborhood."

"Where is it?"

I gave him the address.

"Ooh—we don't have to drive over there. I can tell you, it's rough."

"It's a house he's flipping," I ad-libbed. "Would you mind?"

He shrugged. "I don't mind living dangerously if you don't."

During the drive, Anthony chatted about television shows and—his favorite topic—celebrities. "I heard Libby Lakes was on Kyle's boat Sunday."

"She was," I confirmed.

"Did you talk to her? What's she like?"

"I didn't talk to her, but she seems... nice."

He seemed disappointed. "Really? On her reality show, she's so evil."

"I'm sure that's an act."

"Maybe. Or maybe being nice is an act."

I laughed. "Okay."

He coughed. "I heard she was pretty friendly with Kyle."

"She was friendly to everyone," I murmured.

"Just be careful," he said. "She has a reputation for getting what she wants."

I frowned. "So do I."

That made him laugh. "Yes, you do."

I pointed. "Turn here." We were close to the apartment building. "And slow down a little."

"Lock your door," he said, clearly on edge to be trolling the questionable neighborhood.

I scanned both sides of the street for the tacky truck, then asked Anthony to turn at the next corner. We systematically covered five square blocks, but I didn't find what I was looking for. Defeated, I sat back and told Anthony we could go.

I churned most of the way back. If Gil had taken off, like the detective had suggested, who knew where he'd go next. I was pretty sure he wouldn't run back to my mother until he was broke again.

"Thanks for doing that," I said to Anthony when he pulled up to my building to drop me off.

He looked troubled. "Della... I think I know what's going on here."

My pulse blipped. "What do you mean?"

"You've been acting strange lately, out of character... wearing a bandana." He put his hand over his heart. "And I pride myself on being perceptive."

I sat and waited.

"You're a drug addict, aren't you?"

My eyes flew wide. "What?"

"That's why we were driving around in that terrible part of town—you were looking for your dealer, weren't you?"

I gulped air.

"I've heard this happens to a lot of pharmaceutical sales reps—you have access, it's irresistible."

I pinched the bridge of my nose. This wasn't happening.

"Is it coke? Meth? Heroin? Please tell me it's not heroin."

"It's not heroin," I said emphatically, then cut the air with my hand. "It's not anything—I'm not a drug addict!"

He sighed. "Okay. I'll accept your answer for now. But just know that I care about you and I'm here when you're ready to talk. Meanwhile, your secret is safe with me."

I frowned, then climbed out of the car and slammed the door closed.

Anthony gave me a mournful wave, then blew me a kiss and drove off.

August 11, Friday

I DECIDED once my stint with ATA was up, I would never wrap another package. From now on, anyone who received a present from me would receive it in a nice, shiny gift bag.

I slid the beribboned package of plastic kitchen utensils across the counter to the customer, along with the receipt she'd given me as proof of purchase for free wrapping. It had cost the store more to giftwrap the large box than it made on the sale of the inexpensive item.

"Have a nice day," I said, then sagged into the counter when she turned away. At least no customers were waiting—I could take a breather.

"Long day," the woman at the next counter said. She was dimply and pretty—and under the bright pink dress, I guessed she was pushing at least two hundred fifty pounds.

"Uh-hm," I agreed, not eager to make small talk.

"You work for Anita Temp Agency, don't you?"

I nodded.

She smiled. "Me, too. I'm Casey. I've been with Joon-woo practically from the beginning."

I gave a dry laugh. "And you still get the gift-wrapping assignments? I thought this job was for newbie floaters."

"I don't mind it," she said. "People who shop for gifts are generally pretty happy. Besides, Joon-woo knows I'll work wherever she needs for me to go."

I closed my hands into fists, then splayed them wide to dispel the soreness. My interval workouts at the gym apparently were not working the tiny muscles in my hands.

Casey came out from behind her counter and walked to mine, holding up a small wedge of hard, contoured plastic. "It's a food scraper, but it works great to put a sharp edge on the paper folds. No paper cuts." She handed it to me. "Keep it. I have another."

"Thanks," I said, feeling contrite for being standoffish. "I'm Mae."

"I know," she said. "I've seen you around the office. You keep to yourself."

"Only because I don't plan to be working for the agency long."

Casey laughed. "That's what I said. But when I got a permanent job doing the same thing every day, I got bored." She gestured to my headwrap. "I like your scarf."

I stabbed at my fake glasses. "Thanks."

"Women should wear scarves and hats more often, I think."

I didn't want to say I was wearing it only to hide my telltale blond hair.

"You should wear brighter colors. You're a Spring."

"Spring?"

"Based on your skin and eye color, and the bits of blond I see under the scarf—you're a Light Spring, so you should wear orange, medium blue, and pale green."

I wanted to tell her those were most of the colors hanging in my closet, but then how would I explain the drab olive smock? I'd learned the janitorial garment would stifle any other garment, so I wore it often. "Uh, thanks." Then a thought occurred to me. "Did you know Elena?"

"Elena Padilla? Sure."

So that was her last name. "Do you know where she went?"

Casey shook her head. "No. One day I realized she hadn't been around the office in a while. I asked Joon-woo about her and she said she'd probably gone back to Mexico. She had a daughter there in college. She sent her money regularly."

She seemed young to have a college-aged daughter, but she'd never talked about her family or where she was from. And I hadn't asked.

"But how would anyone know if she went back to Mexico? She didn't take her personal things from her desk."

Casey shrugged. "She's probably planning to come back. Elena was working toward U.S. citizenship, and I know it meant a lot to her."

I hadn't known, but that was… impressive.

"Here comes the boss lady," Casey murmured. "I'd better get back to my station."

Pruney Peg rounded the corner. "Ladies, please be diligent about removing security tags. We've had reports of wrapped packages setting off the door alarms, and we know whose fault that is." She gave us a disapproving look, then turned and strode out.

Casey looked at me and shook her head. I smiled. After years of territory sales, I'd gotten used to working alone. But it was kind of nice to have an ally in this dreadful job.

August 12, Saturday

I TAPPED THE CAMERA button on the screen to take a picture, then lowered my phone. "Thanks for doing this."

Joon-woo gave me a deadpan look as she struck another pose. "You didn't give me much of a choice."

I frowned. "It's not like I kidnapped you and brought you here under duress."

"No, but in case no one's ever told you, Della—you can be pushy."

I snapped another photo. "I think you enjoy this." She was modeling my "D" outfits now that the E-level duds were all gone.

"It beats cleaning your condo. You're kind of a slob, although it looks nice today," she said grudgingly. "Did you ever get the broken mirror fixed in the bathroom?"

"No," I muttered.

"How'd that happen?"

"None of your business."

She smirked. "That's what I thought. How did the cleaning go at the gym today?"

"Fine." Afterward I'd changed into workout gear to take a spin class and enjoy the sauna before switching back to Cleaning Lady. "So far it's the best worst assignment I've had. Turn your head a little to left. Good. This is the last one. Okay, we're done."

"You're holding up better than I thought you would," she admitted, shrugging out of a Halston long denim jacket. "I'll try to divert some better assignments to you. Meanwhile, hang in there."

I set down my phone and pressed my lips together. "When will I see my first paycheck?"

"At the end of this week. If you need an advance—"

"No, I'm good," I cut in.

She let it drop, then gently removed my Gucci embroidered silk platform pumps and put on her worn Keds sneakers. She picked up her backpack and swung it to her shoulder.

I followed her to the door, picking up my wallet along the way. I fished out two twenties and tried to put them in her hand, but she shook her head.

"Joon-woo, I want to pay you for your trouble. You've been here all evening."

"It was no trouble," she said with a little smile. "That's what friends are for. Later."

I stood staring after her, a little flat-footed at her pronouncement that we were friends. We were?

When she disappeared around the corner, I closed the door and pursed my mouth.

I was halfway to the bedroom when the doorbell rang. I smirked. She must've changed her mind about the money, and I couldn't blame her. I picked up the two twenties from the breakfast bar and opened the door.

To Charlie Graham.

"Hi," he said.

"Hi," I returned, wary. I hadn't seen him since our encounter in the music store.

"Did you order takeout?" he asked.

"Hm?"

He pointed to the money I held.

"Oh... no." I folded the bills into my pocket and straightened. "Did you need something?"

"Actually, I'm returning something."

I squinted, then he held up a brown paper sack, its top neatly folded over.

"I found something in your couch I thought you might want back."

I couldn't imagine what it would be, but I dearly hoped it was a wad of money. When I took the bag, though, it felt more like a roll of quarters—which I would gladly take.

"Goodnight," he said with a smile and a wave, then strode away.

I opened the bag and looked inside. Mortification shot through me.

My vibrator.

I crunched the bag closed.

Around the corner I heard the elevator doors open, then the sound of feet walking on. "Have fun," Charlie called, then the doors closed.

I stood there for a few seconds, mouthing every vile word I could think of, then turned and dragged myself back inside. The man was probably having a big belly laugh at my expense.

I pulled out the pink vibrator and carried it to the bathroom. It would be getting a thorough cleaning before being put back on active duty.

Something rattled in the bag and I realized there was another item inside. My pulse blipped higher, wondering what other embarrassing souvenir of my life he'd unearthed.

I reached in and withdrew a dangly silver earring.

Not mine.

I smirked. One of Charlie Graham's conquests had obviously lost it in the couch since he'd taken ownership.

August 13, Sunday

KYLE LOWERED HIMSELF to the end of my chaise. "You're being anti-social again."

I looked up from the book I was reading and gave him a pout. "I was hoping it would be just the two of us around the pool today."

The usual twenty or so suspects were hanging around, and a few new faces.

He shrugged. "What can I say? Everyone migrates here." Then he rubbed my leg. "But next Sunday, I promise, it'll be just the two of us."

"Is it me, or does everyone seem more rowdy today than usual?"

He nodded. "It's getting close to the end of summer, I think everyone just wants to pack in as much fun as they can before Labor Day. And everyone seems to be enjoying the frozen drinks machine Libby brought."

I looked over to where Libby Lakes stood at the bar in a minuscule white bikini, dispensing enormous drinks from what looked like a commercial-grade frozen drinks maker, with three separate chambers.

"That must have cost a pretty penny. And when did Libby become such a fixture here?" I asked lightly.

"She's happy to have people to do things with. It must be lonely to be away from LA where all her friends are." But Kyle's neck was red and I could tell he was nervous.

"Should I be jealous?" I asked, trying to inject a playful note into my voice.

He scoffed. "Of course not. Lib is just a client."

"Lib?"

His color deepened. "I need a small favor."

I was instantly wary. "What?"

"Well, business has been a little... slow. The new dermatology spa in Alpharetta wooed away a lot of my clients from that area. But having Libby as a client has really helped bring attention to my practice, and she's already sent some of her celebrity friends my way."

"What's the favor, Kyle?"

"There you are," Libby said, walking toward us, teetering on five-inch heels, holding a huge glass of something that resembled frozen Windex. "I brought you a drink, Della, to thank you."

I had to take the glass with both hands. "Thank me?"

"For supplying me with enough Beltina to get me in shape for my movie audition. Apparently there's a shortage, and none of my doctors can get their hands on any pills, but Kyle says you can hook me up?"

I looked at Kyle and he pleaded with his eyes. In my mind, my supply of samples was dwindling to the point that I wouldn't have enough for myself—and that simply could not happen. I was not going back to being MaeDella, the fattest girl in the room... the girl no boy would look at, the girl Dr. Kyle Covey would find utterly repulsive.

My mind churned, looking for a way out... but I didn't see an option that would make everyone happy.

"Sure," I said.

Kyle beamed.

Libby beamed.

But I felt my own light dim.

August 14, Monday

"IS CHEF GRAHAM available?" I asked.

The hostess at Graham's Eatery made a rueful noise. "Chef Graham is off tonight. Can I help you with something?"

In my pocket I fingered the silver earring I'd placed in a tiny plastic bag. I didn't want to leave it and give the impression something was going on between us. "No, thanks, I'll come back another time."

I walked back to the condo building, my shoulders achy after a day of filing for the autospa. Another less than great job assignment, but at least it was behind the scenes and I didn't have to worry about being recognized. I looked down at my hands. But more paper cuts. I wondered if OSHA was hip to the hazards of paper cuts in the workplace.

When I walked into the lobby, the familiar concierge was on

his way out.

"Hi, Ms. Culpepper."

"Hi… there." Why couldn't I remember the man's name? "I was hoping you could deliver something to Charlie Graham for me."

He grimaced. "My shift just ended and my ride is waiting. But Mr. Graham is in—I saw him walk in less than an hour ago."

"I don't even know which unit is his."

"Seventeen twelve," he said congenially, walking backward. "Goodnight, Ms. Culpepper."

I debated whether to take it to his place—what if he were entertaining a woman? On the other hand, it would be satisfying to see him squirm when I handed over a piece of jewelry someone had left at his place.

I rode to his floor and found his unit. I heard music playing inside and smiled to myself, then rang his doorbell.

The door opened and Charlie stood there wearing a stained apron and a smile. "Hi, Della."

"Hi." I craned my neck to see around him. Fragrant food aromas floated out. "You probably have company."

"No. Come in."

"I don't—"

"I have something on the stove I need to stir."

He disappeared and I stepped inside, closing the door behind me. Classic country even I recognized—Glen Campbell's By the Time I Get to Phoenix—came from hidden speakers. His condo had a great view—maybe even better than mine, and from what I could see, a similar layout. I peeked around the breakfast bar. But his kitchen was way more tricked out than mine. Charlie stood at the stove, holding a lid over a pot, stirring something with a wooden spoon.

"You cook on your day off?" I asked.

"How did you know it was my day off?"

"I stopped at the restaurant first."

"Ah. Was it busy?"

"Very."

He smiled. "Good." Then he gestured to the stove. "Just experimenting with a new sauce. Want to try?"

My mouth watered. I hadn't eaten all day—my stomach had

been too tied up in knots over the thought of giving away my Beltina samples. "I can't stay. I just wanted to drop this off." I pulled the earring from my pocket and held it up. "It's not mine."

"No?" Then he grinned. "But the other item was yours?"

I frowned and decided to ignore him—and his stupid grin. "The earring must belong to one of your... visitors."

He shook his head. "That's not possible. I haven't had any visitors."

I gave a short laugh. "Right."

He ladled some of the red sauce into a shallow bowl and brought it back to the counter. "What's that supposed to mean?"

"Your reputation precedes you."

"What reputation?" He sliced a fat loaf of brown bread on a cutting board and handed me a wedge.

I took it, then followed his lead, dipping the bread into the sauce. "My girlfriends say no one gets more tail than chefs." I bit into the bread and hummed in appreciation.

"Not this chef," he said, then tasted the sauce and nodded. "What do you think?"

"It's... great."

He smiled. "I agree."

I laughed. "Aren't you supposed to be objective about your own cooking?"

"Absolutely not." He removed two stemless wine glasses from a cabinet. "I just opened a nice syrah."

"None for me," I said, holding up my hand.

He ignored me, poured two inches of red wine into each glass, then slid one in front of me. He drank, then grunted with pleasure and reached for more bread. "Are you talking about your girlfriends who ate with you in my kitchen?"

I nodded, lifting my glass for a sip. The wine was so smooth, I took a bigger drink. "Sabrina and Susan. Now that I think about it, the earring probably belongs to one of them."

"They seemed like nice girls."

I laughed.

"What?"

"They want to have a threesome with you."

His eyes bugged. "A threesome?"

I nodded and followed another bite of bread with a mouthful

of wine. "I told them I would let you know."

He laughed, then shook his head. "Sorry to disappoint, but that's not my thing."

"No? What is your thing?"

As soon as I said the words, I wanted them back. The air was suddenly supercharged.

"This," he said finally, gesturing to the bread and the sauce and the wine. "Enjoying good food and good music with one interesting woman, who has laugh lines."

I lifted a cloth napkin off the counter and wiped at the corners of my mouth self-consciously. "I'm not that interesting."

"I disagree."

I swallowed hard, panicked. I had way too many problems in my life right now—most of which this man knew about—to add more to the heap.

"I have to go," I said, setting down my napkin and moving toward the door.

"At least finish your wine."

My hand was on the doorknob before he could walk around the bar. "Thanks for the bread and the wine and the... information." I was babbling.

I opened the door, then I was out of there like a rocket.

August 15, Tuesday

"ARE YOU SURE THIS is the one you want?" the guy at Home Depot asked me.

I glanced at the flatbed pickup truck with "Rent Me Starting at $19" written on the side and nodded. "I'm sure."

He scratched his head and looked me over. But to his credit, he didn't ask any questions.

Smart man.

I plunked down nineteen bucks for seventy-five minutes of drive-time, and a fifty dollar deposit, then climbed into the truck and familiarized myself with the controls. Then I set off in the direction of the apartment building, hoping to find Gil's truck somewhere in the vicinity. In my bag was a slim-jimmy tool, the one Donnie had given me when I'd moved to the city, bless him, in case I ever locked myself out of my car. It had come in handy once or twice.

Newer cars had made the tool obsolete, but it would work just fine on Gil Malone's old jalopy.

The Home Depot truck was, I'd determined, simply the cheapest rental car in town. I garnered a few looks on the drive, and more than a couple of honks, but I was focused on my mission. Once I reached the area, I followed the same pattern Anthony and I had used to systematically search the five blocks around the apartment building. Unfortunately, I didn't see his truck.

But since I had time left on my contract, I slowly drove an ever-widening perimeter. Seven blocks out from the center, I spotted the piece-of-shit yellow truck with Cook County tags.

I pulled the Home Depot truck into a wide spot in front of the pickup, and glanced around to make sure the coast was clear. But it was an August afternoon in Atlanta—fortunately for me, everyone was indoors in air-conditioning or next to fans.

I climbed down with my bag, then used it to conceal my slim tool as I worked it into the door panel. I was rusty, but I had the driver side door open within a minute. Still, I was sweating when I swung inside and closed the door behind me—the flatbed had to be back in forty minutes.

If I'd had any doubts the truck belong to Gil Malone, they were erased by the clutter of crushed beer cans in the floor, and the picture of my mother hanging from his rear view mirror, the louse.

I began searching for the cash, starting in the obvious places, then moving to the more obscure areas of the ceiling panels, door panels, and floor panels. Every few seconds I checked to see if anyone had noticed me. At the end of the search, I had only food wrappers and bent pages torn out of porn magazines to show for my efforts. I had admitted defeat when I opened the driver side door to climb out, and the interior dome light came on. My eye went to the light cover and I could see something was inside. I used the slim tool to pry it loose and my heart jumped when I saw the money envelope for the People's Bank of Dewdrop wedged inside. I pulled it loose, but I could tell it didn't contain twenty-five grand. It was empty, except for a withdrawal receipt in the amount of twenty-four thousand nine hundred dollars stamped the day after I'd given Mom the check.

The redneck had left one hundred dollars for groceries.

Anger welled up in my chest and bubbled over. I wanted to destroy his truck—at least break out a window, but I didn't have time. So I took the envelope, the receipt, and the picture of my mother, and left the light cover hanging.

And I turned on the headlights—at least Gil would have a dead battery when he came back.

But I was still shaking with fury when I climbed back into the flatbed truck and started it. I considered ramming the front of the flatbed into the pickup, but I was worried the airbag would deploy, and a collision would damage the grill. I needed my fifty dollar deposit back. I sighed, put the big truck into gear and pulled out onto the street.

Then I gritted my teeth, put it into reverse, turned the wheel hard, and hit the gas. The back of the flatbed swung around and caved in the driver side door of Gil's pickup with a satisfying crunch. No one gave a flip about the back of a work truck.

I put the Home Depot truck in drive and pulled away smiling.

August 16, Wednesday

I SLID THE WEIGHTED needle across the numbers on the top of the scale, down, then back up... up... up.

129.

I jumped off as if I'd been bitten. I'd gained two more pounds? Even after a five-mile run and a good sweat in the sauna?

Of course I knew why—because I'd scaled back to one and a half Beltina tablets a day to see if I could stretch my supply of samples enough to shave off one hundred twenty tablets for Libby Lakes. But when I'd gone back through my inventory, I realized I'd made a mistake—I didn't have as many samples as I thought. The only way I'd have enough to spare was if I dropped back to one tablet a day.

Which meant the scale would keep going up.

Especially if I kept succumbing to carbs.

During my shower, my mind kept bouncing back to stopping by Charlie's condo and how skillfully he'd drawn me in to ply me with bread and wine. I frowned—the man had made no secret of the fact that he thought I needed plumping up. That alone was reason enough to avoid him.

As far as the physical chemistry that had materialized that night...

I turned the shower to a blast of cold water, then toweled off and changed back into Cleaning Woman. On the way out, I waved to the girl at the check-in counter.

"Have a good one," she droned without looking up.

When I was walking home, Kyle called. I winced, then answered, hoping he'd tell me Libby had changed her mind, or he'd changed his mind about asking for a favor.

No such luck.

"Hi, doll. I was thinking maybe I'd come down for dinner and pick up those samples for Libby."

"Dinner sounds nice, but I won't have the samples ready."

"Is there a problem?"

"Uh, no. No problem, I've just been really busy." Drinking wine with other men... playing demolition derby with my mother's boyfriend's truck... and generally lying my ass off—or, as the scale would attest, lying my ass on.

"I'm sure your new job is keeping you hopping," Kyle said. "By the way, when do I get your new business card?"

"Soon," I said. As soon as I got them... as soon as I got the promotion... as soon as I was rehired.

"Okay, well, since you're so busy, let's skip dinner. Can I tell Libby you'll give me the tablets Sunday?"

"I'll do my best," I promised.

"I know you'll come through," he said. "Thanks, doll."

I stood and looked at my phone, then it hit me—there was one person who could help. I pulled up my boss Portia's number, then tapped the connect button. The phone rang twice and I fully expected to get her voice mail, especially since it was still early on the West Coast. So when her voice came on the line, I was surprised—and encouraged.

"Della? How are you?"

At least I was still in her contacts list. "I'm fine, Portia. Just wondering if you can give me an update on... anything."

"So far, so good," she said cryptically.

"I haven't seen anything negative come out about Beltina," I said, fishing.

"Fortunately, we've been able to control the message, but that hinges on total secrecy from people like you."

"I haven't said a word to anyone." It was true—the only person who knew I'd been fired was Charlie, and only because he'd been in a position to witness it, not because I'd told him.

"Good. Keep honoring your agreement. If you look out for Traxton, Traxton will look out for you."

"Do you know when I might get my bonus?"

She made a rueful noise. "I'm afraid that's in the hands of HR. They're meticulous about the paperwork in a situation like this to avoid lawsuits—on both sides. Is there anything outside of the red tape I can do for you, Della?"

"Actually, I was wondering if I could get more Beltina samples, say, a hundred tablets?" I crossed my fingers.

"Well, that doesn't sound like it would be a problem..."

I gave a fist-pump.

"Unfortunately, it is a problem."

I turned my fist over and stabbed an imaginary dagger into my chest.

"Since you're not currently employed by Traxton, I couldn't send them if we had them, but the truth is, we just don't have them."

"I understand."

"We'll talk again soon. You hang in there, Della."

The call ended.

I was hanging, all right. But the noose around my neck was getting tighter.

August 17, Thursday

I'M IN HELL.

"Welcome to Triangle Diet Center," I said to the young woman who made her way slowly to the counter. Her weight was affecting her mobility. "How can I help you?"

The girl's gaze swept over me with a mixture of envy and distrust. "Is there someone else I can talk to?"

I handed her a clipboard. "Have a seat, and fill out this form.

A counselor will be with you soon."

She took the form and found an empty chair in the waiting area that was bedazzled with displays of colored vitamins and supplements and special meal powders. The women sitting there ranged in size from curvy to record-setting. In my mind, I calculated where I would've fit in the spectrum at my highest weight. Somewhere between the girl in red who kept pulling at her tight clothes and the girl in brown who sat listlessly, sipping on a diet soda. I pictured myself sitting in the empty chair between them, trapped in a body so big, it rendered me invisible.

The timing of the assignment seemed especially cruel, when I was terrified that external forces were pushing me back to that place.

I realized the women were looking at me and fidgeting. They thought I was staring at them, judging them. They didn't realize I saw myself in them.

I felt the urge to run out of there. Instead I picked up my water bottle and walked back to the water fountain to empty it, and refill it.

A door opened and I looked up, pleasantly surprised to see Casey from ATA standing there, with bags of brightly-colored pills stacked in her plump arms. She smiled. "Hi, Mae. You're here today, too?"

I nodded. "Reception. What are you doing?"

"All the window and waiting room displays have to be changed out."

I wet my lips. "Would you be willing to swap jobs with me?"

Casey grinned. "What's the matter—does dealing with all those fat girls make you uncomfortable?"

I squirmed. "Don't say that."

"Okay, I won't. Sure, I'll trade with you."

"Tell me what to do."

"Simple—empty the containers of the old pills and fill them with new ones—blue for blue, purple for purple, etc."

"Why are we doing it?"

"The gel coatings fade after a while sitting in the sun and under those lights. The Center likes to keep everything bright and cheery."

I nodded. "Okay. What do I do with the old pills?"

She held up a trash bag. "Dump them."

"Dump them?"

"Yeah, they're all empty, it's just for show—see?"

I read the label on the unopened bag of orange capsules she extended. Empty gel capsules, made of beef gelatin and water— kosher, gluten-free, preservative-free.

But it was the next word on the label that caught my eye. Placebos.

My mind began to race with a plan, weighing the possibilities, risks, and outcomes.

"Got it?" Casey asked, transferring the bags of capsules to me.

"Got it."

This could work.

August 18, Friday

"HERE YOU ARE, ladies," the hostess said. "Table for three. Enjoy."

"Guess the chef's table was reserved tonight," Sabrina teased me.

"We don't have anything to celebrate tonight," I muttered. Although we hadn't that night either. Charlie had just played along when the girls said we were celebrating my promotion.

"How's your new job going?" Susan asked.

"It's... varied," I said, hedging. "Some days are more interesting than others."

"I never see your SUV parked in your spot," Sabrina said. "You must be traveling all the time."

"Yes, I'm all over," I confirmed.

But it felt good to be out as Della instead of being worried someone would recognize me. I'd taken pains with my hair and makeup, and, as Casey had suggested for my coloring, pulled a pale green wrap dress from my closet. That said, I was going to have to mind my budget tonight.

So when the girls ordered drinks, I stuck with water and endured their protests. "I'm watching my sugar intake."

That, at least, wasn't a lie. I had to get the scale going back down. Two days of working in the diet center had scared me straight.

The girls chattered about their jobs and the guys they'd met on dating sites.

"You're so lucky you have Kyle," Susan said.

"Amen," Sabrina said. "Hey, did you ever tell Chef Charlie about our offer of a three-way?"

"As a matter of fact, I did."

They guffawed. "What did he say?" Susan demanded.

"I said I prefer one woman at a time," Charlie said.

I turned to see him standing next to our table in his chef's attire. He was looking at me, but he encompassed the girls with his amused smile.

"We could take turns," Sabrina said, only half-joking as she sucked on a straw.

Susan kicked her under the table, then nodded subtle agreement.

"Girls," I chided.

"Oh, hush, Della, we don't have a Kyle."

"Right," Susan added. "Someone who keeps us so satisfied, we don't need anything else."

I felt Charlie's gaze on me, saw his mouth twitch.

I cleared my throat pointedly. "Chef, do you have any recommendations for dinner?"

His eyes twinkled. "I do." He rattled off his top three choices, then nodded to my water. "Would you like some of the wine we had the other night?"

"She's watching her sugar intake," Sabrina said.

"Ah. Well, I'll leave you ladies to enjoy your evening. I hope to see you again very soon." But again, he was looking at me.

I dropped my gaze until he left.

Susan poked me. "I think he has a crush on you."

I gave a dismissive wave. "No, he doesn't, and besides, I'm not available." To change the subject, I reached into my purse and pulled out the silver earring Charlie had found in my old couch. "Does this belong to either one of you?"

They each looked at it, then shook their heads.

"No."

"It's not mine, either."

A waiter arrived to take our orders, so I slipped the earring back into my bag. To save money, I ordered a salad and an appetizer as an entrée. When Portia rehired me, I would never again take my expense account for granted.

The food was delicious, and the mood was festive. But the more the girls drank, the more I was glad I'd stayed with water. In my purse my phone vibrated, signaling the end of my eBay auctions for the week. I was eager to see what the bids were. I signaled the waiter to bring our checks. As I turned, I caught a familiar flash of color across the room. It was Casey, talking to another woman, laughing over a drink. I jerked back and held my hand in front of my face. The last thing I needed was for her to recognize me and start talking about the temp agency.

Sabrina, now a bottle of wine into the evening, glanced around the room, then turned back to us. "Get a load of that hippo over there in the bright yellow dress."

Susan looked, then winced. "Oh, my God. You'd think she'd be wearing camouflage instead of drawing attention to herself like that."

When I realized they were talking about Casey, I sank low in my seat.

"Can you see her, Della?" Sabrina asked, expecting me to chime in.

"Come on, girls, cool it. She's minding her own business."

"That dress is a frontal assault," Susan said, and Sabrina cracked up.

I looked through my fingers to see if Casey had noticed we were talking about her.

She'd noticed. I knew that body language. Then she squinted at me, craned her head, and mouthed, "Mae?"

Oh, God. I twisted in my seat to turn away from her.

The waiter came back with our checks—and three pieces of cheesecake. "Compliments of the house. Chef sends his regards."

The girls dove in, but I didn't touch mine, although it smelled heavenly.

"I'll bet the hippo would eat it," Susan said loudly, and they laughed, rocking together.

"I need to take off, girls," I said, standing. "I have to work tomorrow."

They pouted, but said goodnight with sloppy hugs. I had a

feeling they would be out for several more hours. As I strode through the restaurant back to the entrance, I kept my head bowed and my hand up to avoid looking at Casey.

When I reached the sidewalk, I exhaled into the muggy night air, then muttered a curse aimed toward Charlie Graham and walked toward my condo. He knew I was trying to watch my sugar intake, yet he'd deliberately tried to sabotage my diet by sending out the cheesecake.

It was disrespectful. And sneaky.

On the way, I remembered I needed eggs, so I stopped by the supermarket. But to get to the eggs, I had to walk past the bakery case. I stopped for a quick look, then wavered... then surrendered.

The woman behind the counter wordlessly reached into the case and boxed an entire cheesecake, then handed it to me.

August 19, Saturday

WHEN I FINALLY DRAGGED myself out of bed and walked into the kitchen, the empty cheesecake container sat there, like a reminder of a sordid affair. Disgusted, I stuffed it deep into the garbage can.

I closed my eyes and groaned, feeling heavy with guilt for eating too much last night, and for dissing Casey at the restaurant.

And for thinking way too much about Charlie Graham.

The man was like a burr in my brain, and I couldn't fathom why. He wasn't my type, we had nothing in common, and... he wasn't my type.

My phone vibrated with a text. It was from Joon-woo.

I have your paycheck, can drop it by in 30 min

I cheered. A paycheck to deposit, and a paystub to re-apply for credit to pay off my couch over time.

Yes, I'll be here

The day was looking up. I tossed back a Beltina tablet, then stepped into the shower for a quick rinse. I dressed in my Cleaning Lady garb and mentally checked off the things I needed to do today, including ship the clothes and shoes from yesterday's eBay auctions.

The doorbell rang. I looked out my peephole to see Joon-woo

wave. When I opened the door, she stood there in a khaki dress and bucket of cleaning supplies.

"I have a job here today," she said by way of explanation.

"Come in."

She stepped inside and set down her bucket. From a pocket in her dress, she withdrew an envelope. "Your first Anita Temp Agency paycheck."

"Thank you," I said, feeling a rush of relief. "Direct deposit just isn't the same as holding a check with your name on it."

"I agree." Then she picked up her bucket. "I'd better get to work. Hey, how did the eBay auctions go yesterday?"

"Great. Thanks so much for your help."

"You're welcome."

Just as I reached for the doorknob, the doorbell rang.

I frowned. "Who could that be?" I looked out the peephole to see Anthony standing there. "Oh, it's my personal assistant. I believe you met him once."

She arched an eyebrow. "You still have an assistant? What does he assist?"

I smirked. "He doesn't know about my job situation—it's complicated." I opened the door. "Hi, Anthony. You remember my housekeeper, Joon-woo. She was just leaving."

"You!" Anthony said, pointing to Joon-woo. "You're a thief!"

She looked at me, eyes wide.

I was equally puzzled. "Anthony, what are you talking about?"

He held up his phone. "I have proof that this woman stole some of the clothes and shoes that I catalogued for you for insurance purposes, then she had the audacity to take pictures of herself wearing the clothes and sell them on eBay as—" He checked the screen. "—TomatoGirl29!"

I looked at Joon-woo and she looked at me. I weighed the cost of telling Anthony the truth about my situation against my friendship with Joon-woo, and I knew what I had to do.

I turned to Joon-woo. "I can't believe you betrayed my trust like that. If you don't leave right now, I'm going to call the police!"

She glared at me, then opened the door and left.

I looked at Anthony and shook my head. "You can't trust

anyone."

"Don't I know it." He released a theatrical sigh. "You can be honest with me, Della." He gestured to my temp girl smock and bandana, looking almost teary-eyed. "That woman is the one who got you hooked on heroin, isn't she?"

August 20, Sunday

"DID YOU REMEMBER to bring them?" Kyle asked when I swung into his car.

"Hello to you, too," I said with a little frown.

He looked contrite, then leaned across the console of his convertible to give me a kiss. "I'm sorry, but Libby is so eager to get started on the Beltina."

I reached into my bag and pulled out a plain vitamin-sized bottle, then handed it to him. "One hundred twenty capsules." Of empty gelatin placebos.

"She should take two a day?"

"Right. One in the morning, one in the evening. That bottle should last for two months."

"Perfect. Her audition is the first of November."

I maintained my smile.

He unscrewed the lid, reached in, then held up one of the orange capsules. "I thought Beltina came in tablets."

If he broke open a capsule, I was screwed. "Normally. But these are... new."

"They're not coded?"

"The codes are on the samples packaging." True. "These capsules aren't in packaging because I don't want them to be traced back to me." Also true.

He smiled. "You're smart. And pretty. And sexy." He leaned over and gave me another kiss, then pulled back. "I hopes it's okay if Libby stops by the house this afternoon."

I frowned. "You said it would be just the two of us."

"Most of the time," he said, nodding. "She'll just stay long enough to pick up the capsules."

That wasn't so bad.

"And maybe have a drink with us."

"Kyle!"

"And to thank you for doing this, I have a gift for you." He opened the console, then pulled out a ring box.

My heart jumped to my throat. I felt so petty. All this time I'd felt jealous of the time he was spending with Libby Lakes, and now he was proposing!

"I hope you like it," he said earnestly.

With trembling hands, I opened the hinged box... then squinted at the small glass bottle filled with white fluid. "What is it?

"The injectable I trained on when I was in Sacramento. I'm giving you an entire vial, and I'll inject it anywhere you want— your laugh lines, crow's feet, forehead wrinkles—"

"I get the gist," I cut in. My smile was frozen. "Thank you."

"You're welcome, doll."

As we pulled through the turnaround I saw the chatty concierge talking to another man. The concierge waved. I waved back. Too late, I realized the man he was talking to was Charlie Graham. He, too, gave me a little wave.

August 21, Monday

I SLID THE wrapped package across the counter to the customer. "Have a nice day."

At another wrapping counter, Casey was also finishing with a customer, but she seemed to actually enjoy the interaction whereas I just wanted to get it over with. She'd been ignoring me all morning—not in a hostile way, but in a way that conveyed things between us had changed. I knew it was going to be up to me to reach out, but honestly, I was a little confused as to why I even wanted to. I'd never particularly cared about what people thought of me.

Still, when her customer left and we had a lull, I held up the food scraper she'd given me. "You were right—this thing is saving my hands."

"Good," she said congenially, then returned to straightening her work area.

I sighed. "Look, Casey, if your feelings were hurt the other night at the restaurant—"

"Stop," she cut in with a hand gesture. "You see what you did just now—you said 'if my feelings were hurt,' like it's my fault. That's very passive-aggressive."

I frowned. "I'm normally very aggressive-aggressive. You're seeing the softer side."

She snorted, then shook her head. "You don't have to apologize to me." She made a vague gesture to my outfit. "I don't even know what's going on with the glasses and scarves and the gunny sack you wear for a top, but all I know is I don't trust you. What, are you in the CIA or something?"

I laughed. "Nothing so glamorous. The friends I was with Friday evening don't know about the temp work. And I wear this getup because I don't want people in my real life to recognize me."

"In your real life?" She gestured vaguely between our two wrapping stations. "So this is fake?"

"No," I said sourly. "But it's temporary. And I don't want it to wreck my permanent life."

She looked at me as if I were speaking a foreign language. "Okay, whatever. All I know is what I saw Friday night was just grown-up mean girls."

A customer walked in and Casey dazzled them with a smile. "How can I help you?"

Another customer walked in and I lifted my hand. "Next."

August 22, Tuesday

"SO DID YOU ACTUALLY meet Elvis?" Blowz asked, gesturing to my T-shirt.

I pushed my tongue into my cheek. "Uh, no, because Elvis Presley died a dozen years before I was born."

"Ah," he said, nodding and pulling on his chin as if he were The Great Pontificator. "Yeah, you would've been too young."

I pinched the bridge of my nose. "Dude, you reek."

He smiled. "Thanks, Dude."

"That's not a compliment! And I'm not a dude! Are you just going to float around on a cloud of pot the rest of your life?"

He lifted one shoulder. "Poss."

I lifted my hands. "Poss? What does 'poss' mean?"

"Short for 'possibly.'"

I blinked. "'Possibly' is short for possibly. It's a three-syllable word."

"Dude, you need to chill. You brought some killer organization to the racks, but there's a bal, you know?"

"'Balance' is a two-syllable word!"

The front door opened and a young guy stuck his head in. "Soup's on."

Blowz and I watched while several teenagers dropped what they'd been listening to and rushed to exit.

"What's that about?" I asked.

"Guy walks around the park giving out sandwiches to anyone who wants them."

"For free? Is it a religious thing?"

"I don't think so. I think it's just a ni thing."

I glared. "Don't ever shorten one-syllable words in front of me."

I moved to the window and looked out onto the park where Donnie and I had walked through the concept car exhibit. A clump of two dozen or more young people moved around the man as if they were all one unit. Slowly the teenagers veered off with a wrapped sandwich, until the man was revealed.

Charlie Graham.

My mouth tightened, remembering the snarky little wave he'd given me when Kyle and I had driven past Sunday. The man was so… superior.

As I watched, he lowered himself to the grass to sit cross-legged in the middle of small group, eating his own sandwich and talking. They leaned toward him and nodded. At one point, he casually broke his sandwich in half and handed it to a boy sitting near him. The boy devoured it in three enormous bites. Charlie looked relaxed, just as if he didn't have a restaurant and as if it wasn't the busiest time of the day for customers to be there.

I pressed my lips together in a frown. Superior.

August 23, Wednesday

AFTER A SLEW Of sucky assignments, when I'd picked up the voice message from Joon-woo to be at the Battlecoin Building this morning in smart casual business attire, I thought she was setting me up to get back at me for throwing her under the bus with Anthony. Although, honestly, what choice did I have? And it wasn't as if they'd ever cross paths again.

Anyway, I had resigned myself to showing up in nice outfit only to be sent to the cafeteria. Instead, when I reported in to Constance Hanlon, CEO of a tech-centered venture capitalist group, she shook my hand and said, "Nice to meet you, Mae. Let's walk and talk."

I was several inches taller, but I fairly trotted to keep up with her as she strode through the expansive office.

"My personal assistant is out sick today. I basically need for you to follow me around and take notes on a laptop. Joon-woo assured me you'd be up to the task."

"I'll do my best," I said, surprised at how nervous I felt.

She went from meeting to meeting with such energy and clarity, I found myself sometimes so mesmerized by her style that I forgot to write things down. It was clear she was a woman of great intellect, but she was also warm and she had a dry sense of humor. But she didn't let meetings get bogged down—she ran a tight ship. The startups who came through her office left either smarter or richer—or both.

If I thought I would get a break for lunch, I was wrong. She had a coffee meeting before lunch, a lunch meeting, and another coffee meeting afterward. The afternoon was taken up with internal meetings with R&D incubators working to get more advanced startups married to the market.

Over the course of the day, the amount of money bandied about for this project or that one was staggering. I barely had time to proof my notes between her obligations. She was a one-woman band who didn't stop until six-thirty. At the end of the day, we rode down in the elevator together.

"What was your previous job, Mae?"

"Pharmaceutical sales."

"Did you love it?"

"I was good at it."

She smiled. "It's not the same thing, but it's great when it is."

The door opened to the first floor and I stepped off. "Thank you for the opportunity, Ms. Hanlon. It's been a pleasure."

"We'll see each other again sometime," she said, then added, "if we're meant to."

When the doors closed, I was left with one of those "What just happened?" moments. I had vastly underrated temp work if Constance Hanlon was an example of the kind of people I could have access to. By the time I got home, I collapsed on my couch, utterly exhausted, yet strangely exhilarated.

Verdict: Best temp job ever.

August 24, Thursday

THE GREAT MUSIC philosophers Metallica sing "The higher you are, the farther you fall." (I can't believe I'm quoting Blowz.) Just when working with Constance Hanlon had given me hope there might be some temp jobs I would enjoy, jobs that would challenge me intellectually and help me grow my skillset, I got the assignment I'd been dreading most: The. Pet. Store.

And if the location of the assignment wasn't harrowing enough, consider the dress code I was given: Wear clothes and shoes you don't care to throw away.

I believe I mentioned before I'm not a dog person? Let me take a few moments now to add I'm not a cat person, a hamster person, a gerbil person, a guinea pig person, a ferret person, a lizard person, a snake person, a turtle person, a mouse person, a bird person, or a fish person.

I don't do pets.

So to say I walked into the place with some trepidation would be accurate. I found the man I was supposed to report to, and he looked just as I expected—like a bird, with a long neck and a beaky nose. But he seemed happy to see me. I quickly discovered why.

"Today is our annual members-only sale and we expect a lot of customers to bring in their animals. And even though we stress pets must be housebroken, with so many little personalities running around, there are bound to be accidents." He smiled as if spontaneous pooping and peeing were endearing qualities. Then he handed me a bucket of red sawdust, a broom, a dustpan, and rubber gloves.

"When you hear over the intercom 'code Happy, aisle one, channel one,'" he explained with great precision and expressive hand movements, "that means there's been a piddle in aisle one. Channel two means there's been a BM. Do you know what that means?"

"I think I cracked that code," I said, nodding.

"Good," he said solemnly. "Then this should be a very good day."

"Yes," I agreed. For everyone but me. This, I realized was my payback from Joon-woo.

Things started out reasonably well—for the first two hours, there were only two channel ones and one channel two. Not pleasant, but manageable.

Then a German shepherd male started marking every endcap, and all hell broke loose as other dogs rushed to follow the leader. At one point the store was cleared until I could get it all cleaned up, then the rest of the shift passed with relative channel calm.

I'd staked out a spot at the end of a middle aisle to stand inconspicuously for another seven minutes, forty-six seconds until my shift ended when I saw a too-familiar form walking toward me, seeming intent on the colossal dog biscuit selection.

I closed my eyes. Charlie Graham must have cloned himself—how else was he able to be in so many places? I stood still and prayed he didn't recognize me.

"You know, even if you close your eyes, I can still see you," he said.

I opened my eyes. "Drat."

"Uh-hm." He gestured to my outfit and props, then crossed his arms. "First the job in the music store, and now this. Are you a criminal, sentenced to community service?"

"The truth is… I'm undercover."

A smile lifted the corners of his mouth. "That I could almost believe."

My birdy supervisor appeared. "You can go home, Mae. And I'm going to give a real good report to the agency. Can't remember when we've had a better poo picker-upper."

"Could you say that just a little louder?" I asked.

Charlie snorted with laughter.

I handed the manager back his equipment and stripped off the gloves. Then I bid both men goodbye and turned toward the exit.

"Let me pay for this," Charlie said, lifting the box he held, "and I'll walk out with you. In fact, I'm going home if you need a ride."

I looked down at my stained, smelly outfit. "Are you sure you want this in your vehicle?"

"It's not a fancy ride like your boyfriend's."

I let that comment slide and pointed to the jumbo box of dog biscuits he was buying. "I didn't see a dog when I was at your condo."

"I don't have one."

"What, so now you're feeding homeless dogs, too?"

He gave me a surprised look.

"I saw you in the park the other day with the sandwiches."

"Ah. No, the biscuits are for the restaurant. I don't have a patio where customers can bring their dogs, so I figure the least I can do is send something home for their dog."

"A doggy bag?"

He laughed. "Yeah."

I waited while he paid for his purchase, then walked with him to the parking lot. He stopped next to a white cargo van and unlocked the doors.

"Uh-oh," I said. "My mom warned me about getting into vans with guys."

He grinned. "Smart mom."

I shook my head. "Not really, but thanks."

I climbed into the passenger seat and looked in the back. When he was in the driver's seat, I asked, "What do you use this for?"

"When I pick up produce."

"There's a lot to running a restaurant, isn't there?"

"Sure, but I love it." He started the engine. "So... from the manager's comment, I gather you're working for a temp agency?"

I nodded. "My former boss is going to rehire me in December, so this is just a filler."

"But… no one is supposed to know, so you cover your hair and wear those big glasses?"

I nodded. "It's complicated, but believe me, it's for the best."

"You don't have to explain. Your secret's safe with me." Then he made a face. "You must be the low person on the agency totem pole to draw this gig."

I laughed. "It's penance."

"For?"

"I did something crappy to a friend."

"And now all is right with the world?"

I scoffed. "When are things ever right with the world?"

"Sometimes," he said. "The other night at my place."

I looked at my hands.

"I guess you left your ring at home?"

"Ring?"

"I saw your boyfriend give you a ring box when you got into his car. Are you engaged?"

"No. It… wasn't a ring."

"Ah… earrings? Bracelet? A watch?" He slowed to pull into the parking garage for our building.

"You can let me out here."

"I'll walk you up."

But I already had my seatbelt off and the door open. I jumped to the ground. "Thanks for the ride!"

"I—"

I closed the door on whatever he was saying, then jogged toward the elevator and stabbed the call button in succession. This prickly, coming-out-of-my-skin feeling had little to do with the nasty clothes I was wearing, but they didn't help. When I got off the elevator on my floor, I walked to the garbage chute and stripped off my shoes and clothes down to my underwear, then shoved them all inside. When I turned around, Mindy Chasen was standing there, holding her ever-present pug, staring at me as if I'd lost my mind.

I lifted my hand in greeting. "Hi."

She didn't say a word, just turned and stalked away. A few seconds later, I heard the door to her unit open, then slam closed.

I sighed. Perfect.

August 25, Friday

NEW WORST JOB: Working at the dry cleaners. Performing any task there, really, because the interior temperature was the same as the surface of the sun, but add to it the funky chemical smells, the close proximity of everyone working there, and the frequent tantrums thrown by customers, and it was definitely a new low. At least when I was cleaning up dog poop, it had been at a comfortable temperature.

I was working the mechanical spin rack, just out of sight from the front counter, although I could hear the interactions. The customer would hand their ticket to the person working the cash register, then they would hand the ticket to me and I would play "find the right clothes" by spinning through the numbers until I found a match, then remove the clothes from the rack and hand them to the person at the counter.

It wasn't difficult, just tedious, and is the kind of job someday a robot will do. And it was isolating, left me too much time to think. The sticky topic of the day was Charlie Graham because bits and pieces of impressions of him would find their way into my brain, like plaque.

It unnerved me that he knew so much about me, knew things even my boyfriend didn't know. It left him with a false sense of intimacy with me, I think, and that proprietary bullshit men think women love.

I'm not a romantic person. I learned a long time ago that passion is fickle and if you give it too much credence, once it's gone, you'll be left staring at someone over the dinner table you don't have much in common with except maybe a last name and—in my mother's case—children. I have no memories of my father, but I well remember my mother's life after he left, a miserable trapeze act of swinging from one man who made her feel special for a while to the next, and so on, and so on, with Gil Malone as the final prize. Ugh.

I'd rather have a life with someone who shared my interests and goals for a certain lifestyle so when passion inevitably faded, the underlying threads of connectiveness would be enough to bond the marriage.

Charlie Graham and his dimples and do-gooder warm fuzzies

were upsetting my life plan, and I didn't like it one bit.

"Ticket," the guy at the counter said. "Last name Culp."

He handed back the ticket and I ran the machine quickly until the numbers were close, then slowed it down. When I found the items, I smiled. I had a dress like that. What are the chances? And a jacket like that—

Wait. These were my clothes. Which meant...

I leaned back on the stool until I caught sight of Anthony standing at the counter. I jerked back.

Crap. Now what? I had to get the clothes to the guy at the counter without Anthony spotting me. While my mind spun, I lost my balance and after a few seconds of futile flailing, toppled myself and the stool backward. I landed with an oomph, then skidded. When I stopped I was on my back, still seated on the stool, with Anthony and the guy at the counter staring down at me in shock.

My hope that Anthony wouldn't recognize me was dashed when he screamed, "Della?"

The man at the counter was totally confused, but shaken enough to help me up and right my fake glasses.

"What is going on?" Anthony demanded. Then he planted his hands on his hips. "Joon-woo has something to do with this, doesn't she? Is she making you work slave labor for heroin?"

I closed my eyes. "No."

"Then what? I feel like I'm in some alternate universe where you're your own twin."

I inhaled. "I wasn't promoted in July—I was fired, but my boss said she'd bring me back on in December, so I'm working for Joon-woo's temp agency for money because I'm broke because I gave my savings to my mother to pay off a house loan and her redneck boyfriend stole it, and I bought a big ass couch I can't afford, and my property taxes just doubled, and Kyle can't know any of this or the SEC will lock us both up." I stopped for a breath. "And I can't afford you anymore, Anthony. I'm sorry."

Anthony seemed nonplussed. "Well, since we're confessing, I haven't been making the best choices lately, either. I'm days away from being evicted from my apartment and living in my car. I don't know what the hell I'm going to do."

"I'm having an affair with my wife's sister," said the guy at the counter.

I smirked in his direction. "Hey, cheater man, this is a private conversation." I looked back to Anthony. "You can stay in my spare bedroom if you get a job and help with expenses—and keep my secret. Deal?"

"Deal." He hugged me, then pulled back. "So you're not a drug addict?"

"No!"

"Okay—phew."

August 26, Saturday

I USED MY KEYCARD to open the door to ATA, then secured it behind me. It was a quiet afternoon and the office was deserted. I'd decided to fill out my timesheet now since I'd be at the lake tomorrow with Kyle. I was going to try to put distractions out of my head and focus on our relationship. And maybe the next time he handed me a ring box, it would have a ring in it.

I unlocked the top drawer in my work area and pulled out a timesheet. What an eventful week. I'd put in a lot of hours at some eclectic places. I'd done things I thought I'd never have to do—or want to do. And while these jobs weren't positions I'd list on my resume—or admit to on Facebook—something akin to pride settled in my chest that I'd surprised myself.

After double-checking the form, I made a copy of it and slid one under Joon-woo's office door. When I went back to turn off the lights, my gaze landed on Elena's desk next to mine. I picked up the picture of her and wondered where it had been taken. She looked pretty in the photo, smiling and happy. But the background was indistinct and fuzzy.

I set the small photo frame back and scanned the other items on the top of the desk—a few pencils and some rubber bands, just general office supplies, now dusty from weeks of idleness. I tried to open other drawers, but they were locked. Still, when I jostled the drawers, I could tell they contained items.

I tried my key in the locks, but it didn't work. Then I picked up a paper clip and inserted one end, bending and twisting to send it deeper into the lock. I jiggled and jiggled until at last it popped open. Then I slid out the drawer and looked over the contents.

There were baby pictures of a girl—her daughter, I suspected. There was a lock of fine dark hair clasped in a faded ribbon. And a family Bible in Spanish. The leather binding was old, but lustrous, and the interior was rich with colored art and intricate fonts. I rooted around more to find military medals in a cigar box, with more pictures, most of them black and white.

I bit into my lip. These weren't items Elena would have abandoned—no woman would.

So where was she?

August 27, Sunday

"IT'S REALLY great of you to let Anthony move in," Kyle said. "He's a good guy, even if he hasn't made the best financial choices."

We were lying on floats in the pool, finally getting some quiet time together. "It'll work out well for me, too."

"Yeah, when you're on the road, someone will be at the condo to look out for things."

"Um-hm. How is Libby doing on the capsules?"

He grinned. "Great. She's already lost three pounds."

I bit back a smile. "Three pounds in one week, that's super." The placebo effect—tell someone to take a pill that will make them lose weight, and they lose weight.

Kyle was frowning at me.

"Is something wrong?"

He gave a little laugh. "It's probably just the way you're angled, but it looks like your stomach is sticking out."

I sucked in my abdominal muscles. "Probably just the angle."

"Right," Kyle said, laying his head back. "You've never had a stomach."

Lardass, blubberbutt, supersized, whaletail, thunderrump...

I cracked open an eye and glanced down at my midsection. Were the extra pounds showing? Maybe I was bloated... I rarely had periods anymore, but one could be brewing. I needed to add more sit-ups to my gym routine—

My phone rang, and Joon-woo's name came up.

"I need to take this," I murmured, then connected the call.

"Hello?"

"Della, I'm sorry to bother you on Sunday, but Casey had a family emergency and she can't open the Diet Center—is there any way you could do it? No one else at ATA has worked there."

Ugh—the Triangle Diet Center was one of my least favorite places to be. But I owed Casey for the hurtful snub, even if it hadn't been for the reason she'd thought.

"What time would I need to be there?"

"By noon, if possible."

I checked the time and did some mental calculations. If I left now, I might make it. "Okay, I'll be there."

Joon-woo sighed in relief. "Great. Thanks, Della. I won't forget this."

"I'm counting on it." I disconnected the call, then sighed. "I'm sorry, Kyle, I have to go."

"Now? What's so important to Traxton on a Sunday?"

"Reports," I lied. "Senior management needs a number right away."

He groaned, then reached over to squeeze my hand. "You're in management now. That's what you get paid the big bucks for."

I gave him a flat smile. "Yep."

"I'll drive you back," he said with a yawn. "Just let me lie here for five more minutes."

"I'll call Uber or Lyft, see which one has a car nearby."

"Don't do that," he said without opening his eyes. "People in those jobs are… transitory. Most of them are losers who can't get a real job."

I frowned. "I don't think that's true."

"I don't trust them," he mumbled, then a small snore sounded.

I quietly climbed out of the pool, then dialed a drive-share service. By the time I'd packed my bag to go, the car was pulling up in front of the house.

August 28, Monday

"HELLO, MS. CULPEPPER." Detective Terry sounded amused. "What can I do for you?"

It had taken me a while to work up my nerve to call, and now I was second-guessing myself again.

"Ma'am, are you there?"

"Yes. I'd like to file a missing persons' report."

He sighed. "You can't file a missing person's report on your mother's boyfriend. The man wants to be missing."

I scoffed. "Not on Gil Malone. This is a completely different matter."

"Okay." His demeanor changed and I heard papers shuffle in the background. "Who is the missing person?"

"My housekeeper."

"And how long has she been missing?"

"About eight weeks."

"Did she live with you?"

"No."

"Where did she live?"

"I... don't know. The only address I have is a P.O. Box."

"Okay. What's her name?"

"Elena Padilla." I spelled it.

"Age?"

"I... don't know."

"Is she Hispanic?"

"She's from Mexico, but was pursuing citizenship."

"Is she a minor or an adult?"

"Adult. I'm told she has a teenage daughter Nia, who lives in Mexico City."

"And what makes you think Ms. Padilla is missing?"

"Because she hasn't shown up for work."

"Have you checked with her relatives?"

"I don't know how to do that."

"So for all you know, she could've moved back to Mexico City."

"I hope so. But I found some items in her work area that seem too personal for her to simply abandon. It just doesn't seem like something a woman would do."

"What kind of items?"

"Baby pictures, a family Bible, other things."

He sighed. "I'm not convinced, Ms. Culpepper, that there's a case here. Regardless, you'll have to come down to the precinct to file an official missing persons' report."

I grimaced. When would I have time to do that?

"Meanwhile, I'll run her name through the system and see if anything falls out."

"Okay. Thanks, Detective."

"Before I let you go, a recent report of an abandoned vehicle on a residential street in Fuller Heights caught my eye—a '97 Yellow Ford F150, missing tags, but the VIN number tracks back to a Gilbert Malone in Cook County, specifically Dewdrop, Georgia, who can't seem to be located. You wouldn't know anything about that hit and run, would you?"

"Nope." And I hung up.

August 29, Tuesday

I'D THOUGHT THE gift-wrapping gig was the worst job ever—until I worked at the music store under Blowz. And THAT worst job ever was topped by the pet store assignment. But the pet store was downright captivating next to working at the dry cleaners, which truly was the worst job ever.

Until today.

Today I can confirm the worst job ever in the history of worst jobs is… parking lot attendant for the public retail parking garage.

Picture this: Sitting in a concrete and glass booth, in a concrete and asphalt parking garage, in Atlanta, in August. Got that in your mind's eye? Heat undulating off surfaces that are so hot, you could literally fry an egg on them.

Now toss in gasoline vapors, exhaust fumes, and motor oil spills.

And for the pièce de résistance, add proximity to two enormous dumpsters full of swampy trash, food, and flies, complete with scurrying rodents.

And now you have an idea of the worst job ever.

Plus it's a boring job—most people have parking passes and will zip right through the gates. But occasionally a card reader will fail, or the mechanical arm won't raise, or someone loses their parking ticket, or needs change for the pay kiosk. That's when I have to get involved, which is maybe twenty-five times in a four-hour shift.

Did I mention it's hot as Hades? And that I get to do this all week?

Another part of the job is walking around occasionally and being visible so people don't feel bold enough to have sex in their car. And thieves don't feel bold enough to walk in with a shopping cart and go from car to car, taking whatever they want.

If I do see someone naked or trying to steal, I can't do anything about it, except yell at them to stop. If something bad happened, I'd have to call 9-1-1, like everyone else.

But while walking around the garage, I'd stumbled upon a cool spot. It's near an enormous exhaust fan that's meant to keep an entire floor of the parking garage fume-free. So the area under the fan is dead still and about twenty degrees cooler than any other part of the garage. When the heat in the booth gets unbearable, I walk there and stand for a few seconds to cool off. Other people know about it, too.

Some smart person who drives a beat up Toyota parks there and puts a cardboard accordion screen in their windshield. I'm sure when they come back, it's nice and cool inside.

The upside of doing the garage attendant gig are the bonus hours. Because people aren't standing in line to do this job, ATA fills it often, and the four-hour shift counts for six hours, which really helps if you're trying to get in your minimum hours to qualify for health insurance.

The other upside is it's okay to use your phone. So when my phone vibrated with a new text message, I picked it up. I didn't recognize the number.

Thx for covering for me Sun at Diet Ctr. Casey

I smiled, but because a car was pulling up, I stowed my phone.

I hummed in appreciation. It was a nice car—a new red Mercedes convertible, caramel leather interior—gorgeous. And the man must like red because the girl in the passenger seat was a ginger and from the looks of her, she was either a model or a professional cheerleader—or both.

The driver was rummaging in the console—the sure sign of a lost parking ticket.

He lifted his head. "Excuse me—" His eyes widened.

My eyes widened.

It was Charlie Graham.

"Yes?" I prompted.

"Uh…uh… I seem to have lost my ticket."

"No problem, but I'll have to charge you the maximum of ten dollars."

"Okay," he said. He withdrew his wallet and pulled out a ten, then stiffly handed it to me.

"Thank you. Do you need a receipt?"

"No," he said, then hesitated. "I… hope you're having a good day."

I gave him a little smile. "Everything's right with the world." Then I stepped back into the booth and closed the window.

August 30, Wednesday

AFTER CLEANING THE gym and getting in one hundred sit-ups, I was doing another stint in the parking garage.

And I was still shaking my head over Charlie Graham's appearance yesterday. To think I'd fallen for the "no one's been on my couch" and the "one interesting woman" and the "I don't have a fancy ride like your boyfriend's" spiel. What a crock of shit.

But it was what I needed to see to stop thinking about him, to stop spinning fantasies about him. To focus on Kyle.

A car was pulling up to the booth, but I balked when I recognized it. It was Sabrina's—and she was driving.

I swallowed hard, wondering how I would explain this away if she recognized me.

I tried to make by voice lower. "Can I—?"

"What the hell is wrong with this place?" she yelled, then threw her ticket at me. "Every time I come here, it's a problem!"

"Sorry—"

"Who the fuck is running this outfit, a bunch of monkeys?"

"Uh—no."

"That was a rhetorical question, you idiot!"

I blinked. "Ten dollars."

She threw the money at me. "Fucking let me out of here!"

I activated the arm and she squealed tires going up the ramp.

Wow… she'd had no idea it was me. Was Sabrina like that all the time?

Then I grunted. Was I?

Mulling the unsettling question, I escaped the tortuous heat of the booth and walked to the cool spot in the garage. Reveling in the momentary relief, I took off my costume glasses to dab the perspiration from my forehead.

The Toyota was parked there again today. I squinted at it—it looked as if it hadn't been moved. On the other hand, I hadn't been paying much attention yesterday.

From my smock pocket, I pulled out a piece of chalk. We were supposed to mark the tires of cars we suspected were squatting overnight. I drew a line on the rear tires where they met the concrete. Tomorrow I would be able to tell if the car had moved.

August 31, Thursday

THE CAR HADN'T MOVED.

I frowned and walked all around the Toyota to see if any of the tires were flat—no. But it could have a dead battery. Or, remembering Anthony's worry he might have to live in his car, it struck me that maybe someone was doing just that—working or doing whatever during the day, then coming back here at night to sleep in a place that offered less visibility than a parking lot.

The windows were tinted, so I couldn't see much inside other than vague shapes. And the cardboard accordion screen made it impossible to see in the windshield. I put my weight on the hood and bounced the car to see if the screen would shift, and it did, enough to give me encouragement to bounce harder.

Little by little, the cardboard screen shifted until I could make out something in the front seat. I leaned in more, but I slipped and fell face down on the windshield just as the screen fell away. I winced at the pain in my cheek—that was going to leave a mark— then I focused to make sense of what I was seeing.

At first I thought I was right about someone sleeping in the car—a woman was slumped in the driver's seat, head lolling back. Then I realized with horror the woman wasn't sleeping... and I recognized the still face.

My housekeeper Elena Padilla wasn't missing. She was dead.

SEPTEMBER

September 1, Friday

"YOU'RE STILL HERE, Ms. Culpepper?" Detective Jack Terry asked. "I thought you left with your boss."

I tore my gaze from the beater car where Elena Padilla's body was still entombed. The detective stood on the inside of the police tape and I stood on the outside. I bristled at the reference to my former housekeeper Joon-woo as my boss—that was so temporary. But considering my *other* former housekeeper was dead, now wasn't the time to pick nits about my various relationships.

"I wasn't sure if you needed anything else from me," I offered.

He glanced at his watch. "It's past midnight. Go home. I'll call you to come to the station to review your statement."

I glanced around the parking garage, blazing with illumination from silent pulsing colored lights atop official vehicles, and hugged myself. "It seems strange just to... leave."

The detective nodded, his expression grim. "I know. But they'll be moving the body soon, and you shouldn't be here for that."

I nodded in concession.

"Is your car close by?"

"I live here in Triangle Point, so I'm on foot."

He frowned. "It's too late for you to be walking. I'll get a uniform to drop you off. Go stand over there. I'll be in touch, Ms. Culpepper."

I marveled how the man could give orders rolled up in concern. Handsome *and* chivalrous. Woe to the woman who fell for Detective Jack Terry.

I turned to leave when someone next to the white morgue van caught my eye. I squinted at the dark-haired woman while thinking I couldn't possibly know someone who worked for the morgue. But then recognition dawned—Carlotta from Neiman Marcus? That seemed so preposterous, I decided she must have a twin. But as I walked closer, I saw it was her. I must have been staring because she was looking back and it was apparent she didn't recognize me.

"Hi," I said. "I'm Della—you waited on me recently, and gave me some good advice." I touched the glasses and gestured to the scarf that helped to obscure my identity while I worked the somewhat demeaning temporary jobs to get me through a financial rough patch.

She blinked. "Oh... hi."

"You work for the morgue?" I asked.

"Sometimes. What are you doing here?"

"I found the... body," I managed to get out.

"I'm sorry," she murmured.

The fierce-looking, tatted woman next to her touched her arm. "They're ready for us."

Carlotta gave me a rueful look, then began to don scrubs.

Detective Terry was right—I didn't want to see the body being moved, so I lifted my hand in a wave to Carlotta and walked to the spot he'd directed me. I kept my back to the scene and a few minutes later, a congenial officer loped over to claim me. He tried to make small talk on the short drive to my building, but I was numb from the night's events. Outside of the Floyd Funeral Home in Dewdrop, Georgia, I'd never seen a dead person. And the way Elena had looked in the front seat of the car was a far cry from the spit-shined, pink-cheeked departed souls lying in rest at Floyd's.

Elena was dead. Gone. She had been deleted, edited out of life. It was jarring and made me feel as if life was more precarious than I'd ever realized.

When he pulled the squad car up to the door of my high-rise condo building, I thanked my uniformed escort and hurried to card into the entrance. My hand shook, and I suddenly felt vulnerable in the dark, thick summer air, like someone might attack me from behind.

"Hey."

I screamed, then realized the voice belong to Charlie Graham. But when the door buzzed open, I clambered inside and walked fast. I hadn't seen Charlie since he'd driven through my pay line at the parking garage in a smoking hot convertible with a smoking hot redhead.

"Della, wait!" He caught up with me at the elevator and snagged my arm.

I shook him off. "Don't man-handle me!"

He was still wearing his chef's smock, so apparently, he'd just gotten off work. He held up his hands. "Sorry. I didn't mean to scare you." Then he jerked his thumb toward the entrance. "But what's up with the police car? Are you okay?"

"I'm fine." I said, jabbing the call button several times. "The officer was just giving me a safe ride home."

He straightened. "Oh. Good." Then he paused and I knew he was remembering the last time we'd seen each other—me in servitude and him being served. "How are you?"

The elevator doors opened. "Tired," I said. "And if you don't mind, I'd like to be by myself." I stepped inside and the fact that he didn't follow told me everything I needed to know about the situation with the redhead—he didn't press me because he didn't want to be pressed, either.

When the elevator door closed and the creepy feeling descended again, though, I almost wished I'd let him ride with me. The feeling persisted when I alighted onto my floor. I jogged to my door and fumbled with the entry code, my heart pounding. When the lock finally opened, I swung inside the dark interior and slammed the door behind me, leaning into it in relief.

But my relief was short-lived when I heard a noise in the hallway and realized someone was in my condo. My heart vaulted to my throat as I clawed for the light switch in the entryway. When light flooded the room, Anthony Wazniak stood there in tidy whities, a pink sleep mask pushed high on his forehead.

"Hi, roomie. You're home late."

I sagged. In all the commotion over finding Elena's body, I'd forgotten my former personal assistant was moving in.

He winced. "Rough day?"

September 2, Saturday

"THANKS FOR COMING DOWN," Detective Terry said.

I shifted in the uncomfortable guest chair in his sad office. "I expected you to call yesterday."

"Yeah, sorry. I got pulled in on another case."

That explained his bloodshot eyes, I reasoned. The man looked as if he was carrying the weight of the world on his big shoulders. He picked up a giant mug of coffee and took a sip, then glanced at me sideways.

"Who are you, Ms. Culpepper?"

I frowned. "What do you mean?"

"You came to see me, what—six weeks ago because your mother's bank account was looted. Since then you've been connected to a hit and run, a missing person, and now, a body."

I lifted my chin. "I told you I don't know anything about the hit and run to Gil Malone's truck. He left that jalopy parked on the street—anyone could've bashed into it." With a flatbed truck from Home Depot.

He peered at me over his mug. "How did you know his truck was parked on the street?"

I pressed my lips together. "I... guessed?"

"Uh-huh."

"And for the record," I added, "the missing person and the body were the same woman, so that's really only one thing."

He sat back in his chair. "I see you're back to looking like you did when I first met you. Yesterday you looked... different."

I shifted in the chair again. "It's a woman's prerogative to change her appearance, isn't it?"

His eyes narrowed. "You remind me of someone else I know."

I brightened. "Is that a good thing?"

"It depends on what day you ask me," he said drily. He took another drink of coffee, then came back from wherever his mind had taken him and opened a file. "So, I'm confused, Ms. Culpepper. How can a woman who works as a parking attendant afford a housekeeper?"

I shifted again. "I… can't. Until recently I was employed in sales and Elena Padilla worked for me then."

"And that changed?" His desk phone rang. He picked up the receiver, then set it back down.

"I was… laid off. But my manager is going to rehire me in December, so in the meantime, I'm working for the Anita Temp Agency."

"For Joon-woo Park?"

"Yes, she's the owner."

"And that's where Elena Padilla worked as well?"

"Yes." I swallowed. "What happened to her? Was she shot? Stabbed?"

He looked grim. "I really shouldn't say, but there were no outward signs of foul play."

"Are you saying she died of natural causes?"

"I'm not saying anything until the autopsy is complete."

"How long will that take?"

"Could be a few days, could be a couple of weeks, depending on the work load at the morgue and the tests the medical examiner decides to run." He took another drink of coffee. "You didn't file the missing person's report on Ms. Padilla."

"I didn't have time," I said flatly. "Before I could get a chance to file the report, I found her body."

He nodded. "I looked back over my notes the day you called and you said she'd been missing for about eight weeks?"

"I can't be sure, but that's when she didn't show up to clean my place."

His desk phone rang. Again, he picked up the receiver, then set it down. "And that wasn't like her?"

"No. And she didn't return my calls."

"That corresponds with the information Ms. Park gave us on her last contact with Ms. Padilla. So, let's talk about the car Ms. Padilla's body was found in. When did you first notice it parked in the public garage?"

I squinted. "That would be Tuesday, four days ago."

"And what made you take note of it?"

"It was parked in the coolest part of the garage, under a fan. The booth where I worked was so hot, I walked to that area of the garage a couple of times a day for relief. I remember thinking someone had figured out where to park their car to keep it cool. Then the next day I noticed it again."

"Did you notify anyone?"

"No. We're supposed to use chalk to mark the tires of cars we suspect are being left overnight, so that's what I did."

"You didn't look inside the car?"

"I couldn't see inside. The windows were tinted and a sun shade was in the windshield."

He stopped writing. "So the next day the sun shade had fallen and that's how you were able to see inside?"

I swallowed. "Well, if you want the truth…"

He gave me a deadpan look. "That's kind of a given around here, ma'am."

I sighed. "Okay, well, the next day when I realized the car hadn't moved, I tried to look inside and I… bounced on the hood until the shade fell. That's when I saw Elena—er, I mean, her body."

He frowned. "That wasn't smart."

"If I hadn't done it, that car might still be sitting there with her inside. So, you're welcome, Detective."

"I just mean you should've alerted someone. Now your fingerprints are on the hood."

I coughed. "And my, uh, faceprint on the windshield. I kind of fell on it."

He sighed.

Then I straightened. "Wait—if you don't suspect foul play, why are you taking prints?"

"We aren't—yet. The car was impounded pending cause of death."

"Was it her car?"

"You don't know?"

I shook my head. "I never saw the car she drove. Joon-woo would know."

"She didn't, although she assumed Ms. Padilla had a car. We're trying to find out if the Toyota was hers."

"Have you located her family, her daughter?"

"Still working on it." He put down his pen, then stood. "Thanks for your help, Ms. Culpepper."

I'd dreaded the interview, but I wasn't ready for it to be over. I reluctantly pushed to my feet. "So what happens now?"

"We wait for the autopsy, then go from there."

My face must've reflected my misgivings, because his expression gentled. "Don't worry, Ms. Culpepper. We'll sort through it. I'll show you out."

September 3, Sunday

"I'VE ALWAYS FOUND Labor Day weekend so depressing," Libby Lakes said with a pout.

I'd held my tongue all day while the actress had sashayed around Kyle's boat in a teeny metallic bikini, finding ways to bend and stretch in my boyfriend's line of sight, and I was feeling testy.

"I suspect the working class wouldn't agree," I said. "Isn't it their holiday and we all simply get to enjoy it?"

My comment brought sharp glances from Kyle and his sister Helen. "Della," Kyle chided. "We work, too."

"Some of us," I said lightly, taking a sip from a gargantuan frozen drink generated by Libby's ridiculous machine.

For a second I detected a flash of anger in Libby's eyes, but she must have remembered I was the person supplying her with the weight loss drug Beltina for her upcoming audition because she recovered with a laugh. "That didn't come out right. I just meant that Labor Day signals the end of summer, and that makes me sad. My show wraps this week, and I only have a few weeks left before I go back to L.A."

Was it my imagination, or did she give Kyle a wistful glance? "So you'll be back on the set tomorrow?" I asked.

"No. The set is closed for the holiday. I'm actually free until Tuesday."

"You can spend the night in one my guest rooms," Kyle offered. "And come back out with us on the boat tomorrow."

"I'd love that," Libby said, then checked herself. "If Della doesn't mind, of course."

I smiled. "I don't mind. The guest rooms are located away from the master suite. You won't bother me and Kyle." Meow.

"What part of town do you live in again?" Libby asked, as if to remind me I didn't live with Kyle full time.

"Della has a condo in Triangle Point," Kyle offered helpfully.

"Is that near your home?" Libby asked lightly.

"Yes," I said.

"Not really," Kyle said at the same time.

I pivoted my head to look at him. He at least had the good sense to flush.

"Triangle Point," Helen interjected, no doubt to diffuse the tension, "is a live-work-play development near midtown. Great shopping and restaurants, all within walking distance—it's the 'it' place to be."

Helen's friend Julie made a rueful noise. "Except I heard on the news a woman was found dead in her car in a parking garage there."

My pulse blipped.

"I heard that, too," Trish said. "It happened just a few days ago."

Kyle frowned at me. "Is that true?"

I squirmed. "I did hear something about it."

"I heard she was an illegal immigrant," Trish said.

"Oh, well, then," Libby said.

The dismissive tone she used went all over me. "What's that supposed to mean?"

Libby blinked. "Hm?"

"You said that like she had it coming because she wasn't a U.S. citizen."

The actress balked, then glanced around for support. "That's not what I meant at all."

"Della," Kyle said in a cajoling voice, "you're making too much of this."

It's true that my heart was racing and I felt hot enough to combust. That sharp pain was back in my temple.

"Let's change the subject to something more cheerful," Helen suggested. "Della, Kyle tells me Traxton stock price is way up. It must feel good to be a sales manager for a company that's booming."

I nodded, breathing deeply to force my vitals to slow while I conjured up a smile. "Yes. I've never felt better."

September 4, Monday

"WHEN WILL YOUR car be out of the shop?" Kyle asked as he eased onto the interstate to take me home. After another day of boating, he looked tanned and tousled and so handsome.

"Didn't I tell you? The company decided to take back the SUV and give me a new one."

"That's great—to go with your new position, of course."

"Uh-hm. But it might be a while before it arrives."

"I know you're traveling less since you don't have to make sales calls, but what are you doing for transportation?"

I shrugged. "Uber or Lyft... or MARTA."

Kyle frowned. "The train? Isn't that dangerous?"

"It's not bad, and better than sitting in traffic."

"Still, I don't think I want a girlfriend of mine to ride the train with... everyone else."

"A girlfriend of yours?" I gave him a teasing jab. "Do you have more than one?"

"Of course not—you know what I mean."

"And what kind of people do you think ride the train?"

"People who have no other option."

It was hard to chastise him when I'd always felt the same. I'd ridden the train when I was younger and poorer, so not having to had made me feel like I'd come up in the world.

He reached over to clasp my hand. "I just want you to be safe, doll. All that talk about finding a woman dead in her car has me spooked."

He'd have a stroke if he knew I'd been the finder. "I'm fine," I assured him. "And don't forget Anthony moved in."

"Right. How's that going?"

"So far, so good."

"That's a sweet setup, to have your personal assistant living with you. You're going to be the most successful sales manager Traxton has ever had."

"Let's hope so," I said. December couldn't come soon enough.

He wheeled the convertible into the turnaround in front of my building.

"Do you want to come up?" I asked. "It'll just be us—

Anthony has plans."

"Can't," he said. "I have several procedures tomorrow, so I want to get in bed early."

Alone? I wondered. Libby had left mid-afternoon, but for all I knew, she could be waiting at a Pinkberry for him to pick her up.

"Last night was great," he said, as if he'd read my mind.

"I thought so, too," I murmured. "And I'm glad business is good."

He nodded. "Thanks to Lib and her social media stream. Oh, and thanks to you for being nice to her." He winced. "Although you could be nicer."

"I'm sorry—she just rubs me the wrong way."

"She doesn't mean to," he said. "She's not used to being around common people."

"Common people, like me?"

"No—common people like us. Non-actors. She likes you. And she really appreciates the Beltina you were able to get for her."

So she hadn't realized the "samples" I'd given her were empty gelatin capsules—*phew*.

I kissed Kyle goodbye and climbed out. When I walked into the lobby, the chatty concierge—what was his name?—waved.

"Hi, Ms. Culpepper."

"Hello... there."

"How's your brother?"

"He's fine, thanks."

But when I swept by, I felt a pang of guilt because I hadn't checked in with Donnie for a few days. In truth, I didn't want to know if Mom's financial situation was worse, because there wasn't much I could do about it until my Traxton bonus arrived.

I stopped at the mailboxes to check for an envelope. Not only were my hopes dashed, but the stack of bills made my stomach clench. The money I was making with ATA would barely cover my mortgage.

Selling my worn panties was starting to sound less icky, more entrepreneurial. I idly wondered how long I'd have to wear them to get top dollar—two days? Three?

"I've been hoping to run into you."

I closed the door to my mailbox with a bang and turned to give

Charlie Graham a flat smile. "Did you locate the owner of the earring that was lost in your couch?"

He hesitated. "No." Then he sighed. "Look, I want to explain about the day I drove through the parking garage."

I held up my hand. "Please. Don't."

He pursed his mouth. "Okay. Well, the reason I was hoping to run into you is I heard about the woman who was found in the parking garage and I realized it was the same night I saw the police car drop you off. Were you working there at the time?"

I nodded. "Actually, I found the body."

His face blanched. "I'm so sorry that happened to you. Are you okay?"

"Fine as frog hair. See you around." I turned and strode toward the elevator bay, but he was on my heels.

"Wait—don't you want to talk about it?"

"Not to you," I said, beyond irritated that he thought we were besties. The elevator dinged to announce its approach. I glanced toward the stairwell and made a split-second decision. "I'll take the stairs."

"Up thirty floors?" Charlie asked.

I glanced over his stocky figure, then gave a wry shrug. "Some of us work out. Bye now."

The man must know his limits, because when the door to the stairs slammed behind me, he didn't follow.

September 5, Tuesday

I RUMMAGED THROUGH the refrigerator for a carton of Greek yogurt, finally deciding I must be out. I thought I'd bought more the last time I'd stopped at the grocery, but my memory for rote tasks hasn't been great lately. I've been so distracted thinking about Elena... I simply couldn't get the picture of her death-mask out of my mind. Wakefulness is difficult, and sustained sleep, out of the question.

I closed the refrigerator door a little too hard, then frowned at the curled foil lid lying on the counter, dripping blueberry yogurt. I reached for a paper towel to wipe up the mess, but touched an empty cardboard holder.

"Anthony!"

"Ye-es," he said in a happy sing-song, then appeared in front of the breakfast bar, scraping a spoon around an empty yogurt container to get the last drop.

"That was my breakfast," I said.

"Oh... sorry." He licked the spoon. "If it's any consolation, it was good."

I frowned and gestured to his stained robe that barely covered the tidy whities that were becoming way too familiar sights within my four walls. "Are you going to get dressed today?"

"I need to do laundry and I'm still unpacking." He sighed. "I love it here."

"So do I. You need to get a job."

"But I work for you."

"Another job—a job that pays. The deal was you could live here if you help me pay expenses, remember?"

He looked contrite, then nodded. "And keep the secret about your job situation, which I have. I've been looking online for a job, but there aren't many listings for a personal assistant." Then he brightened. "Hey, do you think Libby Lakes would hire me?"

"Possibly—but you'd have to be careful not to let it slip you're not working for me anymore, say you're looking for extra hours or whatever."

He nodded. "So no one else knows about this temp gig of yours?"

"Except for the people at ATA."

"I can't believe your housekeeper owns the temp agency."

"I know—right?"

"I feel bad about accusing her of stealing your clothes to sell on eBay."

"Don't worry about it. Joon-woo is cool. She understands why I need to keep a low profile until Traxton rehires me."

"Why couldn't your boss keep you on while the company was being reorganized?"

I'd had to lie to Anthony about the reason for my layoff—I couldn't afford for him to inadvertently start a rumor about Beltina being under scrutiny that would boomerang back to me.

"It wasn't her decision," I hedged. Then I winced. "I just remembered—someone else does know about my situation—

Charlie Graham."

"Who's that? His name sounds familiar."

"He's the chef at Graham's Eatery, and he lives in this building."

Anthony snapped his fingers. "Wait—wasn't he named one of Atlanta's most eligible bachelors with Kyle?"

I nodded.

"I remember him—he's cute."

"Some people might think so."

Anthony squinted. "How does he know about your job situation?"

I gave a dismissive wave. "It's a long story, but basically, my boss and I had lunch at his restaurant when she... let me go, and Charlie overheard. Then he bumped into me a couple of times when I was temping and I had to come clean to keep him from spilling the beans to Sabrina and Susan—or Kyle, for that matter. For some reason, Kyle loves Charlie's restaurant."

"So if Charlie saw through your disguise, aren't you worried you'll run into Sabrina or Susan?"

"I already have," I admitted, remembering the day Sabrina had blown through my line in the parking garage in an expletive-laced tirade. "I don't think I have to worry about them recognizing me, probably because I'm so out of context, they don't make the connection."

"I don't know if I would've recognized you at the drycleaners if you hadn't made a spectacle of yourself."

"Thanks."

"Are all the jobs that sucky?"

"Most of them, yeah."

"I can't believe you found your other housekeeper dead in her car. I mean, what are the chances?"

"Remote," I agreed. "On the other hand, since ATA has a lot of clients in Triangle Point, it makes sense that we temps would cover the same ground."

He looked grave. "Are you okay? I've heard traumatic events like this can trigger PTSD, or send an addict back into a spiral."

I frowned. "I'm *not* a drug addict."

"Just checking. I can't imagine finding someone dead—ew." He did a heebie-jeebies dance. "But if you ever want to talk about it, I would absolutely pretend to listen."

"I'll pass," I said drily.

"Okay. So, do you think Kyle would talk to Libby Lakes about hiring me?"

My smile flattened. "I'm sure he'd be happy for a reason to talk to Libby Lakes."

"Uh-oh. Maybe I should forget it."

"No—I'll give Kyle a call." I gave Anthony a weak smile. "I wasn't kidding when I said I needed for you to help with expenses. I'm strapped until my bonus arrives."

"I'll figure out something," he said. "If all else fails, I'll sell my worn underwear. I've heard there's a real market for it in the prison system."

September 6, Wednesday

WHEN I ARRIVED at the gym in my cleaning garb and glasses, I experienced a blip of panic because the disinterested girl at the desk actually glanced up at me.

If she realized I was the one who'd called her porky after she bounced me when my Traxton membership expired, she might keep an eye on me—which would prevent me from working out after I cleaned and did a switcheroo to gym togs in a shower stall. And I really needed to keep working out if I expected my boss Portia to rehire me in December.

"Hey, wait," she said.

Oh, crap. I stopped.

"The women's room is completely out of TP and I can't leave the desk."

Her argument would have been more convincing if gaming noises weren't coming from the phone she held.

"Okay," I muttered, then swept on by.

As I passed the water fountain, I noticed the girl who'd asked me about Beltina a couple of months ago put a familiar orange tablet in her mouth and lean down to get a drink. So she'd managed to get her hands on some of the drug before quantities had grown scarce. It must be working for her because she was noticeably slimmer in her body-con workout wear. As I removed an armful of toilet tissue from the supplies closet, she wiped her mouth and headed toward the weight machines, looking springy and energetic.

I smiled to myself. It was the kind of Beltina success story I liked to see—weight loss, with improved energy and confidence. It had been my experience as well, and why I'd been happy to represent a product I believed in.

I refilled all the tissue holders and left extras in case Porky couldn't be lured away from her gaming the rest of the day. I cleaned the men's locker room first, then backtracked to clean the women's locker room last so I could change in the shower stall to do my own workout. It was a physical, dirty job, but I was getting more efficient, and I appeased myself by reasoning it was a good warmup to the cardio and weights I'd do later.

After wiping down the last shower, I closed the curtain and swapped my cleaning outfit for gym clothes, stuffing the former into a bag I would stow in a locker. In the stall next to me the water came on and steam filled the air, making me already anticipate the hot shower waiting for me afterward.

When I stepped out of the shower stall, I heard sounds coming from the adjacent shower that stopped me, sounds of... pain? At first I thought the woman might have fallen, so I moved a step closer. The curtain was parted just enough for me to see it was the woman I'd noticed earlier at the water fountain. Her back was to me and she was standing upright. Thinking I'd been mistaken, I turned to go but saw her—I blinked—punch herself in the ribs? My initial thought that she was trying to massage a kink out of a muscle evaporated when she wound up and punched herself again—hard. I could make out a series of colorful bruises on her torso. I stepped back, my heart pounding. What the—?

"Everything okay in there?" I yelled.

The curtain moved, then the gap closed. "Everything's fine," she called.

I frowned, not sure what to make of what I'd seen, but not inclined to get involved. So I put in my ear buds and turned up The Black Eyed Peas. I had enough on my plate.

September 7, Thursday

WHEN I WALKED into the Anita Temp Agency, another temp, Casey, stood behind the counter. She was dressed as vibrantly as always, but her normal wide smile was tempered with sadness. She had known Elena, and I hadn't seen Casey since finding Elena's body.

"Hi, Mae."

"Hi, Casey."

"Are you doing okay?"

I nodded, not quite sure how else to respond. No one really wanted to know I'd started sleeping with the light on because Elena came to me in nightmares pleading with me to find her before it was too late. "Is Joon-woo around?"

"She's talking to a police detective in her office. She asked me to man the front desk."

I frowned. "Big guy, cowboy swagger?"

"That's him."

I started down the hall toward the office.

"She asked not to be disturbed," Casey called.

I stopped at the closed door, rapped once, then pushed it open. Joon-woo and Detective Jack Terry swung their heads to look up at me. I feigned surprised. "Oh, hi, Detective. Any news on Elena's case?"

"Still gathering information," he said.

"Ah, that's why you've been dodging my calls. Have you located her family?"

"Not yet."

"Did you find out if the Toyota belongs to her?"

"Uh... not yet."

"It seems as though that would be an easy detail to track down."

"We're doing our best, Ms. Culpepper."

Joon-woo cleared her throat. "Detective Terry was just telling me about the conversation you had describing things Elena left in her desk?"

I squirmed. "That's right."

"Do you want to tell me how you got into her locked desk?"

"No."

The detective's mouth twitched.

Joon-woo sighed. "Do you need something?"

"Yes."

"Can it wait?"

"Not really."

The detective stood. "If you could point me to Ms. Padilla's desk, I'll give you two some privacy."

"Down the hall to the back room," Joon-woo said. "Desk nine."

"Eight," I corrected.

She pursed her mouth, then said, "I'll be right there, Detective."

When he strode away, Joon-woo crossed her arms. "What?"

I held up my paycheck. "I was overpaid for last week."

She didn't react. "You can't use the extra money?"

"Of course I can, that's not the point."

She gave a little shrug. "I thought you deserved something extra for what happened with... Elena."

I arched an eyebrow. "You mean, like combat pay?"

"Call it a bonus." She sighed. "You were right to be concerned about Elena. Maybe if I'd listened to you... "

"Ms. Park?" Detective Terry called from the back room.

"Coming," she said. Then she gave me a flat smile. "Look, if it makes you uncomfortable, do something charitable with the money."

"Charitable?"

"Relax," she said. "I won't tell anyone underneath that crusty layer of icy cold indifference is a person who can be nice when she wants to be."

She walked away, leaving me flat-footed and flummoxed. My mouth tightened with indignation. "You'd better not!"

Because it really wasn't true.

September 8, Friday

"AND YOU OUGHT to see the house Libby's renting while she's in town," Anthony said with a squeal.

We were sorting through more of my clothes to sell on eBay.

With my "E" and "D" list duds gone, I was up to items on my "C" list, and they were going to be harder to part with.

Anthony had been talking nonstop for an hour about the amazing Libby Lakes and her amazing Hollywood lifestyle. "And I thought your wardrobe and closet were amazing, Della, but her wardrobe and closet are like something you'd see on TV."

"That's interesting," I offered. "Because every time I've seen her she wasn't wearing more than a few scraps of fabric."

He stopped. "Am I being too much of a fanboy?"

"A little bit."

He sighed. "I'm sorry. I know you don't like her."

"I don't dislike her, I just don't have much in common with her."

"Except Kyle?"

"Except Kyle," I agreed.

"But this is the perfect setup," Anthony said. "I can find out if she's got the hots for Kyle."

I shook my head. "No spying."

He raised his eyebrows.

"Okay, minimal spying. But didn't she make you sign a confidentiality agreement?"

"Yes, but all bets are off if she's messing with your man."

I was ironing a Milly blouse, nursing rumblings of misgivings about Anthony working for the actress until she went back to L.A. for the audition she was slimming down for. After all, if she had Kyle in her sights, she could've given Anthony the job so she could gather intelligence on me to use in her quest. "Just be careful you don't let something slip about my situation."

He smoothed a hand over an exquisite Emilio Pucci tunic. "You know Kyle would help you out with your finances, all you have to do is ask."

I used to think so, until Kyle confessed he was under his own financial pressures. "Kyle can't know I was laid off because he might panic and sell his Traxton stock, remember? Then we could both be charged with insider trading. And I could lose my bonus just for telling you about the layoff, so if the subject of me comes up with Libby, change it."

"Don't worry, I know where my bread is buttered. When are you supposed to get your bonus?"

"Sometime this month, I hope. My boss Portia said it's out of her hands."

"No one in the human resources department can help you?"

I grimaced. "I, uh, kind of pissed off some of the people who work there, so no one will return my calls."

Anthony pressed his lips together.

"What?"

"Nothing."

"Something," I insisted. "What?"

"Have you always been so... easily annoyed?"

I scoffed. "Are you insinuating I have anger issues?"

He gave the hot pointy iron in my hand a worried look. "No. Forget I said anything."

I set down the iron. "No. I want to know why you'd say something like that." I was tired of being judged for having a strong personality that a man would be praised for.

Anthony swept his arm out. "Look around, Della. Every room in the condo has a broken mirror or a dented wall. You're either very clumsy, or you're throwing stuff."

My temper ignited, then flared. "I didn't invite you to move in so you could analyze my life."

He put up his hands. "I shouldn't have said anything. You've been through a lot with your job, and your finances, and I'm sure you're still on edge about finding that woman's body."

Didn't he realize he was confirming all the things I had to be angry about?

"I noticed you've been sleeping with a light on," he ventured. "Are you sure you're okay?" Then he jumped toward me. "Della—the iron!"

I looked down to see I'd burned my hand with the iron. The skin was bright red. I couldn't feel the pain yet, but I knew it was coming. And when it did, it felt raw and punishing. And after the first wave of pain subsided, I realized the relief in comparison to the pain felt almost... good.

I allowed Anthony to rush me to the bathroom faucet to run cold water over the singed skin, all the while wondering:

Was this why the woman at the gym had punched herself?

September 9, Saturday

I DIDN'T SEE the self-injuring woman when I cleaned the gym the next day. Which was a relief because I didn't know what I'd do. I couldn't confront her without blowing my cover, and besides—I glanced at the bandage covering the burn on my hand—how hypocritical would that be?

On Saturdays it took longer to complete the cleaning because there were more people to maneuver around. I still marveled over how people who were friendly and conversational when I was Della in my workout gear barely looked in my direction when I was Mae the cleaning lady. But it left me with a sense of power because I could be invisible when I wanted to be.

I seized an opportunity to jump on the scale to check my weight. I slid the weighted needle across the numbers on the top of the scale, down, then back up... up... up.

126.

I exhaled. Still six pounds over my ideal weight, but three pounds lighter than when I'd last weighed myself. Since I hadn't been forced to share my Beltina stash with Libby Lakes after all, I was able to resume my regular dosage. Finally, the numbers were heading in the right direction.

Since I had only an hour to work out and shower before reporting for duty at Dorman's to gift-wrap—ugh—I decided to take a high intensity interval training class that was starting. As usual, I scanned for the girl who worked the front desk to make sure she hadn't ventured into the area where sweating was required. She hadn't.

I snagged a mat and a towel and claimed a spot, then began to stretch and warmup while the instructor was getting ready.

"Hello."

I froze in a hamstring stretch. *Oh, no.* I slowly stood and turned my head to see Charlie Graham had staked a spot next to me. "You belong to this gym?"

He grinned. "Yeah. Thanks for the suggestion."

"Suggestion?"

"The other night when you took the stairs and made a comment about working out? It was a good reminder that I hadn't yet found a gym."

"But did you have to join this one?"

He surveyed my tights. "I like the scenery here."

I smirked. "Really? I seem to recall you saying my behind needed padding."

He studied my ass like it was of great scientific importance, then worked his mouth side to side. "Call me crazy, but it looks bigger than before."

Damn him. I picked up my mat to move to another spot, but the class had filled and the instructor was taking his place.

"Looks like you're stuck with me," Charlie said with a shrug.

He was dressed in old school workout clothes—running shorts, tall basketball socks, and a ratty University of Tennessee T-shirt. He was thick, but he seemed solid, and I was mildly impressed at the size of his biceps. Still, I felt the need to warn him.

"This is a tough class, so no one will shame you if you have to quit," I said. "Except me."

He gave a little laugh. "Don't be too hard on me. It's been a while since I've done burpees."

I was looking forward to showing him up. But once the music started and the instructor began yelling commands, the man didn't miss a beat. He banged out jump squats, pushups, situps, and even the dreaded burpees as if he'd been attending the class regularly. I was the one whose form suffered because I was suddenly conscious of him watching me bend and twist and squeeze and—

One second I was thinking I wish someone would turn up the ceiling fans and the next, I was on my back with Charlie's face bending over me. "Della? Are you alright? Can you hear me?"

I'd slipped in urine on the floor... no, wait—that had happened at the music store. This was...

"Where am I?" I murmured.

"At the gym," he said gently. "You must've passed out. Let's get you some air. Can you stand?"

I nodded and let him help me up. The class had stopped and people around us looked half-concerned, half-irritated I'd interrupted their cardio. Charlie assured the instructor he would take it from there and led me out of the room to a bench where he plied me with water until I pushed away the cup.

"I'm okay," I insisted.

"When did you last eat?"

"I don't remember," I admitted.

"Ah, well, that's probably it." From the pocket of his running shorts he pulled an energy gel—a gelatinous packet runners use for quick fuel—and opened the top. "Eat this."

"That's full of sugar," I protested.

"And sodium and other electrolytes. Take it."

I was too weak to fight. I tilted my head back and squeezed the berry-flavored gel into my mouth, swallowing until it was gone. "Thanks," I managed.

"You're welcome," he said, then nodded toward the entrance. "Come on—I'll walk you home."

But I was embarrassed and didn't relish a conversation with Charlie that would likely consist of my troubles and his redhead. And more of my troubles. Plus I couldn't risk the girl at the check-in counter recognizing me. I stood and moved toward the women's locker room.

"No, thank you. I'm going to shower."

"So am I—I'll wait for you."

"That's okay. I need to be somewhere. But thanks."

Then I fled.

September 10, Sunday

"SO WHAT DO you think I need?" Kyle's sister Helen asked, peering into a hand mirror.

Kyle stood behind her holding a pencil like a pointer. The usual Sunday crowd had dwindled, leaving just the four of us—including Libby, of course, who sat nursing a cocktail. And somehow, an impromptu dermatological consultation had erupted.

"Maybe a little filler between the eyes, and some around the corners," Kyle said. "And maybe a little here and here to restore the apple in your cheeks."

Helen nodded, using her forefinger to lift and rearrange the skin on her face. "You're right—that'll make me look younger."

Kyle lifted his gaze to mine across the patio table. "Maybe you can come in with Helen and I can take care of your procedure at the same time."

I squirmed, thinking of the vial of milky fluid he'd given me. Was I being stubborn because I thought I was too young to start injectables, or because I wanted to think I didn't need them?

Libby leaned forward as if she was suddenly more interested. "What would you do to improve Della's face?"

Ha—Kyle wouldn't fall into that trap. I smiled up at him, waiting for him to say I was already perfect in his eyes. Instead he angled his head and descended on me with his pencil.

"I'd add a little filler here and here to get rid of these hollows, and I'd fill in her laugh lines a little." He squinted. "Hm."

"What's wrong?" I asked.

"I've never examined your face under a strong light, but…" He pulled the end of the pencil down one side of my mouth. "It almost looks as if you've lost weight in your face at some point."

My pulse bumped higher.

Then he gave a little laugh. "It's probably just the sunlight— the ultraviolet rays are so harsh this time of the year."

"You're so lucky to have someone like Kyle at your disposal," Libby said, although the way she said it, she wasn't talking about his medical aptitude.

"I know," I said. "I'm lucky to have Charlie."

At the confusion on Kyle's face, I realized what I'd said— holy God.

"Who's Charlie?" Libby asked.

"No one," I said in a rush. "I'm tired. I m-meant 'Kyle,' of course. I'm so lucky to have Kyle." I beamed up at him even as my mind reeled. Where had that come from? Eager to change the subject, I looked at Helen. "But my schedule is so hectic these days, maybe you shouldn't wait for me."

Libby cackled. "I think Della's trying to say you need to have something done as soon as possible, Helen."

Helen's face fell. "Do I look that bad?"

I frowned at Libby, then bounced a smile to Helen. "Of course not—you're beautiful." I was a little stunned at Helen's demeanor. I'd never known her to be overly vain or paranoid about her looks.

"You southern girls can carry off that natural look," Libby said with a dismissive wave. "Della, I see you're letting your roots grow out, is that a new thing?"

I gritted my teeth. I hadn't had the time or the money to get my hair done lately. It had fallen lower on the priority list, behind the utilities. "I thought I might give the ombre look a try."

Kyle lifted his empty glass. "I'm going in to get another drink—anyone else?"

I shook my head—my tongue had already lost its mind.

"I'll go with you," Libby gushed.

I watched the two of them walk away, and Helen watched me.

"He loves you, you know."

"I love him, too."

"Good." Then her brow furrowed. "But don't take his love for granted. We women have to be on guard—there's always someone waiting to take our place." Her voice wavered with shaken confidence.

"Helen," I said carefully, "is everything okay at home?"

She looked back to the hand mirror and pulled her skin tight. "Nothing that can't be fixed."

September 11, Monday

"YOU KNOW THE DRILL, Mae," Blowz said, pointing to a rolling cabinet stacked high with CDs and vinyl albums. "Move the older titles down to make way for tomorrow's new releases."

Tedious, but it would pass the hours. I wondered idly if Charlie would stop by to pick up his banjo music, then backspaced and deleted the thought before it could fully form. Yesterday's tongue lapse still haunted me. Kyle hadn't asked me about it when he dropped me off, but I'd felt the awkward tension emanating from him.

"Blowz, is there a reason albums are released on Tuesday?"

My teenaged stoner boss grinned. "I know that one. Shipments of new releases usually arrive over the weekend, but weekends are the high traffic days, so stores don't have time to put them out. Since Mondays are usually slow, it's the best time to restock." He lifted his hands. "Everyone is ready to go on Tuesday, so sales start accumulating on the same day, everywhere."

I blinked. "You're smarter than you smell, Blowz."

His eyebrows went up. "Are you flirting with me?"

"I take back what I just said."

He loped away to help a customer, and I started the mind-numbing task of rotating the CDs and albums. I found a couple of CDs I thought Donnie would enjoy and set them aside to buy later.

As usual, there were a number of grungy teens and young adults in the store browsing through the stock and listening to samples at the kiosks. Occasionally the security guard who dozed in the corner caught someone with a CD down their pants, but for the most part, the kids seemed to appreciate having a place to hang. I had begun to recognize some of them by their appearance—Red Plaid Shirt, Frizzy Man Bun, Neck Tats, Beaded Dreadlocks, Pierced Face.

Today though, two young girls I hadn't seen before came in to browse, and I was immediately suspicious. They were both roughly pretty and painfully young—fourteen?—even more so considering one of them was very pregnant—and dirty. My heart squeezed for her and the unborn child—what chance did they have? Some charming bad-boy had probably said all the right things to make that happen, then disappeared when the stick turned blue.

From the way they kept glancing toward the security guard, I had a feeling they were planning to shoplift. And while part of me wondered if getting caught might be a good thing if it put the young mother-to-be in the system, another part of me acknowledged that could just as easily go sideways.

I remembered what Joon-woo said about doing something charitable with the extra money in my paycheck, and moved in their direction.

"Hi," I offered.

"Hi," they chorused in low voices. I could tell from their body language they were irritated by my appearance.

"Do you guys go to Georgia Tech?" I asked.

They eyed me suspiciously.

"You're wearing black and gold," I said to the pregnant girl.

"Do we look like college material?" the non-pregnant one sneered.

"Actually, yeah," I said.

I was just making conversation, but my comment made the

pregnant girl's head come up.

"Are you girls hungry?" I murmured. "I could buy you lunch." I pulled a folded twenty-dollar bill from my pocket and extended it toward them.

"Are you hitting on us?" the non-pregnant girl asked.

I blinked. "No."

She grabbed the money, then pushed her pregnant friend toward the door.

I watched them leave, feeling defeated except I might have thwarted their shoplifting intentions. At the door, the pregnant girl turned back to look at me with a look of desperation in her eyes. Then she was gone.

September 12, Tuesday

"SO, ARE YOU still loving your new job?" Sabrina asked, pointing to the color polish she wanted the technician to use on her nails.

"It's... better on some days than others," I hedged.

"Are you still traveling a lot?" Susan asked. "Your parking space always looks empty."

I nodded. "I'm in a different place every day."

"I hope you're being careful," Susan said. "I guess you heard about the woman they found dead in her car here a couple of weeks ago."

"Oh. My. God," Sabrina said. "I use that parking garage all the time. That could've been me."

"I don't think they know yet what happened to the woman," I offered.

"I heard she'd been there for *months*," Susan said. "That there was only a skeleton left."

"That's not true," I said, then added, "I don't think so anyway."

Sabrina shuddered. "And to think I probably drove by that body a hundred times. Wonder who was the poor schmuck who found her?"

"I don't know," Susan said. "That would give you nightmares for the rest of your life."

I hoped not. I hid a yawn behind my hand.

"Are we boring you?" Sabrina asked.

"No—sorry. I haven't been getting much sleep lately."

"For good reasons, I hope?"

"Yeah, how are things with Kyle?"

"Fine." I told them about the incident where he'd given me a ring box and it turned out to be a vial of injectable wrinkle filler.

Susan groaned. "But he meant well."

"And that's not a cheap gift," Sabrina said. "You could probably sell that vial on Craigslist for five thousand dollars."

I blinked. "How much?"

"She's right," Susan said. "Doctors who can't get it from the manufacturer will take it off your hands and make twice that when they resell it to their patients."

"You could buy a ring," Sabrina joked.

"Speaking of rings," Susan said. "I went to the jeweler's on the next block to have a link taken out of my watch, and guess who I ran into? Chef Charlie."

My stomach pinched. "Really? He was buying an engagement ring?"

"Guess he found that one woman," Sabrina said with a sigh. "Too bad."

"I kind of thought he had a thing for you," Susan said to me.

"That's silly," I said. "I've seen him around with a woman—a redhead, I think."

"Well, from the size of that diamond, she's one lucky woman."

"Guess Charlie's not going to make next year's most eligible bachelor list," Sabrina said.

Nope, I thought sourly. Would Kyle?

When I said goodbye to the girls, I walked home slowly, taking a circuitous route via the supermarket bakery.

"Long time, no see," said the woman behind the display case.

"Just give it to me."

With Anthony around, though, I was going to have a find a good hiding place for the empty cheesecake container.

September 13, Wednesday

WHEN I ARRIVED AT the gym the next day to clean, the Zumba class was just getting out.

Under my lashes I watched the girl I'd seen punching herself, still sweaty from the exertion, step onto the scale. She looked slender in her form-fitting workout clothes, but as she slid the weighted needle across the top of the scale, I watched her expression go from anxious to frustrated to angry.

Like a snake striking, she lifted her hand to pinch the back of her arm. Three times. If someone didn't know better, they'd think she was simply scratching her arm, or would miss the movement altogether. But from where I stood, I could see the bright red welts turn into bruises, alongside older bruises of the same sort.

When she stepped off the scale, she glanced around, probably to see if anyone had observed her behavior. She locked gazes with me and I telegraphed I'd seen it all. Her eyes flashed with shame, then her gaze turned lethal, as if she dared me, a lowly cleaning woman, to expose her. Then she lifted her chin and headed toward the showers.

I felt as if I'd just witnessed a crime, but had no way to prove it.

In the pocket of my smock my phone vibrated. When I saw it was Detective Terry calling, I connected the call and moved to a quieter area of the locker room. "Hello, Detective."

"Hi, Ms. Culpepper. I thought you'd want to know we located Ms. Padilla's family in Mexico. Her body is already on its way back to them."

I exhaled on happy tears. "That's very good news. What did the coroner rule as the cause of death?"

"We don't have the autopsy results yet."

"But you can release the body?"

"Yes, that's protocol. We don't want to hold up burial services any longer than necessary."

I swallowed. "How did her family take it... her daughter?"

"Not well, as you might expect. They hadn't heard from Ms. Padilla in a while, so I think they were already prepared for bad news. Still, it was a shock."

"Will you be able to return her personal items to them as

well?"

"Yes, they're going with the body."

"Thank you, Detective, for letting me know."

"I should be thanking you, ma'am. If you hadn't reported her missing, connected the dots, we might not have been able to identify the body at all. Ms. Padilla's family sends their gratitude."

"Th-that's not necessary."

"You did a good thing, Ms. Culpepper. Feel good about it."

He hung up, and I sat staring at my phone, feeling everything but good.

September 14, Thursday

I WAS BACK at the drycleaners. It was a thousand degrees, noisy as hell, and smelled like burnt hair.

"Here are all the tickets over six months old," the guy running the counter said. "Pull the clothes and hang them on this rack."

I couldn't look at him without wondering if he was still boinking his wife's sister, but considering he hadn't asked about my confessions the day Anthony had found me out, I figured I should be equally respectful... if disgusted.

"What happens to the clothes?" I asked instead.

He shrugged. "I don't know."

It was par for the course—everyone here seemed to have one little job that was disconnected from everyone else's little job. But the specialization seemed to work—from what I could tell, it was a thriving business with a fleet of vans delivering uniforms and linens to restaurants and hotels.

I sorted the tickets for the unclaimed garments to speed up the retrieval, but it was still a tedious process of spinning through the long hanging rack of plastic-covered clothing and matching numbers. I assumed the garments would be forgettable items—stock dress shirts or frumpy slacks no one wanted enough to schlep back to the cleaners. But most of the clothing I pulled was nice and some of the items so special, I began to make up stories about why the owners hadn't claimed them.

The navy Brooks Brothers suit had been abandoned by a guy who couldn't spend another minute in a cubicle facing the wall.

The green winter coat had been abandoned by someone who'd moved to an even warmer climate. And the white wedding dress had been abandoned by a bride who had already abandoned the marriage.

An hour later, the rack was bulging with disinfected and disenfranchised clothing. When I asked my cheating boss what to do with it, he waved me toward the closed double doors that connected the front operation the customers saw to the, shall I say, *warts* of the business. The large back room was a sweltering, stinky morass of dirty laundry and dirty people jammed together, elbow to elbow over steaming vats of liquid and hissing iron plates. The workers were mostly female, and the few who lifted their heads looked as if they had been crushed by life.

"You can't be back here without the proper clothing," a woman said. She carried a clipboard and wore a paper mask over her mouth, no doubt to filter the fumes.

I pointed to the rolling rack. "These are unclaimed items. I was told to bring them back here."

"Set them over there," the woman said, pointing to a vacant wall. "Then close the doors behind you."

She didn't have to ask me twice—I was happy to get out of there and back to the tedium of the spinner rack. I had dubbed the drycleaning temp work as one of the worst assignments.

But clearly, there were worse jobs to be had.

September 15, Friday

I WAS SURE my bonus check would come today, and when it didn't, I ventured another call to Traxton human resources. In preparation, I wrote "Be Nice" on a sticky note and put it in front of me.

"This is Jessica How may I help you?"

I winced. Jessica and I had history. "Hi, Jessica, this is Della Culpepper calling. How are you?"

"Fine," she said flatly. "What can I help you with, Della?"

I gave a friendly little laugh. "I'm still waiting for my bonus check to arrive and I'm hoping you can check the status for me. My social security number is—"

"I have it memorized," she cut in.

I bit my tongue while clicking keys sounded in the background. "The system still says the payment is 'pending release.'"

"It's been pending for a while now," I said cheerfully. "What does that mean, exactly?"

"It means it's stalled."

I wet my lips. "Right. But why is it stalled?"

"How am I supposed to know?"

I crumpled the "Be Nice" sticky note in my fist. "I don't know, Jessica—maybe because it's your *job*?"

She hung up.

"Ooooh!" I massaged the sudden sharp pain in my temple until it subsided. The quick headaches were becoming more frequent—brought on by stress, no doubt. And lack of sleep... the nightmares continued.

Compelled to get answers to something today, I punched in another number and waited.

"Atlanta PD, Detective Terry."

"Hi, Detective, it's Della Culpepper, calling to see if the results of Elena Padilla's autopsy have been released."

"Hi, Ms. Culpepper—let me check."

Keys clicked in the background—he was a hunter and pecker.

"The system says the autopsy is 'pending release.'"

Of course it did. "Which means it's stalled?"

"Unfortunately, yes."

"Can you tell me anything at all?"

He hesitated, then grunted. "This isn't official, but it looks as though Ms. Padilla was living in the car, and died from heat exhaustion."

I covered my mouth with my hand. "So... it was just a tragic accident."

"It looks that way, but I'll keep you posted."

I thanked him and hung up the phone, feeling sick. Elena had been living in her car and studying to become a citizen between cleaning jobs, cleaning for people like me, who threw vases at her.

The headache was back.

September 16, Saturday

WHEN I WALKED into the gym with my bag o' supplies, I attempted to wave and sail past the check-in counter.

"Hey—wait," the girl said.

Oh, crap. I stopped.

"The men's locker room is out of towels, and I can't leave the desk." *Beep, honk, whrrr.*

I nodded, then kept going.

Servicing the men's locker room took a bit of maneuvering. I first had to shout to see if anyone was inside or round up someone to check for me, then back my way in announcing my presence. It was not ego-boosting.

"Towel lady," I broadcasted. "Coming in."

I was up to my eyeballs with armloads of white towels, so I couldn't see much until I set them on the counter. I straightened the stacks, then turned around and came up so short, my fake glasses nearly fell off.

Charlie Graham was emerging from the shower room, whistling... and naked.

To his credit, he stopped and cupped his hands over his privates. Then he grinned. "If you wanted to see my credentials, Della, all you had to do was ask."

I sputtered and clambered backward, bumping into the counter. "I... we... you could've warned me."

He was enjoying this. "I didn't hear you come in. Besides, you were the last person I expected to see. This is one of your temp gigs?"

"Obviously," I said through gritted teeth.

"Could I get a towel, then? I'd reach for one, but... "

I grabbed a towel off the counter and threw it at him. He caught it with both hands, giving me a money shot.

I squeezed my eyes shut to the tune of his amused chuckle.

"You can open your eyes now," he said.

I did, but I was still grappling for equilibrium. He had wrapped the towel around his waist, shifting the attention to his powerful chest. The man was... abundant.

"If you stick around, I'm going to have to ask to see yours," he said with a shrug.

I turned and scrambled to get out of there, slipping and sliding on the wet tile floor. His laughter boomed behind me.

"Oooh!" The man was insufferable... and unapologetically proud of his unfashionably big body.

I threw myself into cleaning the women's locker room, shot through with mortification that the man had seen me yet again at my worst. Fetching towels and scrubbing toilets—what must he think of me? I fought back tears of frustration and anger, made worse that I cared what he thought. Then I gave myself a mental shake.

I needed to get my groove back.

I needed to stop thinking about Charlie Graham.

And I definitely needed a bigger vibrator.

September 17, Sunday

"YOU SEEM SUBDUED today," Libby declared.

We were on Kyle's patio by the pool. Everyone had assumed the position: prone on chaises, drinks in hands.

"I have to leave early for a memorial service," I said.

Helen turned her head. "Who died?"

It was hard to look at her—Kyle had gone overboard with the filler, in my opinion. Her features looked puffy and her skin had the waxy look of aged Hollywood starlets. Worse, she seemed to know it because she was constantly touching her face and dabbing at her eyes. Whatever demons had driven her to try to look more youthful had now doubled. I was watching her fall apart.

"A coworker," I said, allowing them to believe it was a Traxton employee.

"Oh, that's too bad," Kyle said. "Was it a close friend?"

"Not really. But I feel as if I need to be there."

"Smart," he said, nodding. "Part of being in management is attending those kinds of gatherings outside of work."

He wasn't being unkind—it just came out that way.

"Speaking of work," Libby said, "that Anthony is an organizational whiz. Thank you so much, Della, for lending him to me these last couple of weeks."

"No problem," I said. "Anthony is definitely a find."

Libby smiled. "You and I seem to have similar taste." Her eyes flicked to Kyle, then back. "Maybe there are other things we could share."

I set my jaw. "If you need the name of my gynecologist, let me know."

The woman gave a dismissive wave. "My mother told me my vagina is like a self-cleaning oven. Turn it on, and let it do its job."

She and Helen and Kyle laughed.

"On that note," I said, pushing to my feet. "I need to go. My Uber car will be here in ten minutes." I picked up my bag, then leaned over to give Kyle a lingering kiss.

"I'll walk you out," he offered.

"I'll do it," Libby piped up. "I need to powder my nose anyway."

I sensed an ulterior motive for her to follow me to the front door, but I let it play out.

"Della," she said in a girl-friendly voice, "I'm not seeing the results I'd hoped for with the Beltina. Any advice?"

"Kyle told me you were losing weight."

"I was... in the beginning. Now I've gained back the weight I lost."

So the placebo effect of the placebos had worn off.

"It's important to me and Kyle that I get the role I'm auditioning for."

I frowned. "You and Kyle?"

"For his business, of course," she said smoothly. "The higher my profile, the more clients I can steer his way."

And the sooner she could get him into her oven?

I glanced at the frozen drink that had become the actress's staple. "Okay, I don't tell everyone this, but alcohol and sugar helps with the metabolism effect of the pills I gave you."

Her eyes widened. "Really? That seems so... counterintuitive."

"Doesn't it? But it works." I pointed to her glass. "Keep it up, and don't shy away from Krispy Kreme."

"I'll have Anthony set up home delivery," she said.

"Even better. There's my car. Bye now."

I was probably going to hell for that, I decided on the ride back into midtown. But I could live with it.

The memorial service was a tiny, sad affair Joon-woo had set up at the ATA office. There was punch and cookies and someone had lit a candle. Next to the candle was the picture of Elena from her desk, looking a bit younger, and smiling. It was the face from my nightmares, I acknowledged, studying the picture. Elena wouldn't let me be.

Then a detail I hadn't noticed before leaped out—the earrings she was wearing in the photo. Now that the picture had been enlarged, it was easier to see the detail.

It was the silver dangly earring Charlie had found in my old couch.

September 18, Monday

"THE BANK SAYS they need a thousand dollars paid on the loan before Friday," Donnie said. "I'm sorry, Sis. I spent all my savings on back utility payments. The power company was going to cut off the electricity."

"It's okay, Professor," I said with more composure than I felt. "I guess that means Gil hasn't shown his face?"

"No one's seen him, or his truck."

That almost made me smile. "How is Mom?"

"She's not good," he said. "Some days she won't get out of bed. She's not working very much, which is why we're behind on the bills. And that just makes her more sad."

"Tell her I'll handle the bank. But she has to come to grips with the fact that Gil probably isn't coming back."

"I'll tell her," he said. "Are you doing okay, Sis?"

"Right as rain, Professor."

He laughed. "Tell Henry I said hello."

The concierge—*that* was his name. "I will. He always asks about you. I love you, Donnie."

He hesitated. "Me, too."

It was as good as I would get out of Donnie, who wasn't great at identifying or expressing emotion. But maybe his relative detachment was a blessing—it made him more resistant to the fallout of our dysfunctional family.

The headache was back. I massaged it away while I pondered how I was going to get a thousand dollars to pay the Peoples Bank of Dewdrop when I was already behind the financial eight-ball.

Then I remembered the comments Sabrina and Susan had made about selling the vial of injectable Kyle had given me on Craigslist. It was worth a shot.

September 19, Tuesday

AT LAST—a somewhat normal work assignment in a string of sucky ones: a bookstore.

I was pleasantly excited when I walked through the door to report to the manager. Growing up in Dewdrop, books had been my primary source of entertainment. I felt a kinship with them because they had transported me to places I thought I might never see. Just the scent of paper and binding took me back to lying on my twin bed with a flashlight under the covers.

I kept the fake glasses, but had traded my bandana for a nice scarf and my drab smock for a decent blouse.

"Here's your apron," the manager said, knocking me back down a notch. He took off walking and gestured for me to keep up. "We have a booksigning event to get ready for. I'll need for you to help merchandise the table, and to replenish books as they're sold."

"Got it." I covered my blouse with the big stiff burgundy apron that wrapped around me almost twice, then secured the long ties.

"And it's your job to make sure the author has everything he needs—water, pens, that kind of thing."

"Okay." I was having a little bit of a nerd moment at the thought of meeting a novelist. "Who is the writer?"

"He's a local celebrity," the man said, sweeping his arm toward a festooned table that had been set up in a cleared area. "Chef Charlie Graham."

I stumbled, then caught myself. "I've heard of him."

"He's written a cookbook that's getting raves," the man said, putting a copy of the hardcover book into my hands. "And we were lucky enough to snag him for a signing because his restaurant is just around the corner."

A picture of Charlie graced the cover under the title *Fat and Happy*. I flipped through the pages and took in the high production value of the photographs and the design. It was an appealing book featuring recipes for wholesome, comfort food, peppered with anecdotes from Charlie and his adventurous outlook on life. I could see how it would be a bestseller.

"And here's our guest of honor now," the manager said, walking over to welcome Charlie, who wore his white chef's smock. "We were just getting set up for you."

"I'm a little early, but I thought I might help—I know the books are heavy."

"Oh, we have someone for that," the man said, then glanced at me over his glasses. "I'm sorry—what did you say your name was?"

I felt Charlie's gaze land on me. "Mae," I supplied.

"Well, Mae, get on over here and start stacking books," the man said. "I'll round up a chair for Mr. Graham."

I did as I was told, offering Charlie a smirk and a wave.

"You do get around," he murmured.

"So do you," I replied. "I didn't know you were an author."

"It's one of those things people find out about each other when they have a—what do you call it? Oh, right—a *conversation*."

I reached into one of the open cases of books and began stacking them on the table. "I think we know quite enough about each other."

He reached into the same box to grab a handful of books. "Oh, I see—you think because you've seen me naked, you know everything there is to know about me."

I frowned. "Keep your voice down."

"There are some things about me you should know," Charlie said.

Behind him, the store manager was returning with a chair. "If you mean the engagement ring," I hissed, "I know all about it."

He looked surprised. "How do you know about that?"

"My friend Susan saw you in the jewelry store." I lifted my chin. "So if you think I'll be your last fling before you walk down the aisle, you've got another think coming."

He leaned in, his eyes flashing. "Right back at you."

Oooh!

"Here we are," the manager sang, setting the chair behind the table. "Customers are already heading this way, so let's get you situated, Chef Graham."

I busied myself removing and stacking books while Charlie took his place. Sure enough, customers were soon lining up to get a signed copy of his cookbook. I made myself useful by turning to the title page and inserting a bookmark before handing it to him to sign. He was friendly and gregarious to the (mostly female) customers, and was happy to pose for pictures—most of which I wound up taking. Throughout, I avoided eye contact, and the few times our hands grazed as we passed the books, I could almost feel the electricity.

Toward the end of the signing, a tall, glamorous and familiar redhead walked in and established her place by bypassing the line and walking up to the table to claim a kiss. Charlie seemed genuinely happy to see her, and she was obviously equally enamored of him. I hung back, feeling like a clod in my disguise. After exchanging a few words, she left, and the signing continued for another hour, until the books were gone.

While the manager was glad-handing Charlie and thanking him, I stole away to the bathroom to relieve my swollen bladder and review yet another close encounter with the man.

I had yet to escape unscathed.

September 20, Wednesday

THE NEXT DAY I was a nervous wreck cleaning the gym. Not because I was afraid of being found out by the chunky girl at the counter—she barely looked at me when I rushed by in my cleaning garb. And not because I was afraid of running into Charlie—I saw him in the workout area and managed to avoid him.

I was nervous because of my chore afterward.

When I left the building, I had redressed in disguise, but had traded my fake glasses for sunglasses, and I was wearing my tennis shoes... in case I had to make a run for it.

I walked to the end of the street, checked the time, and scanned for a black Corvette. In my sweaty hand was a small padded envelope containing the vial of injectable fluid. I had lain awake last night ruminating about all the ways this could go bad— what if the buyer was an undercover cop? What if the buyer was a bad guy and I was robbed and got nothing for my trouble? What if the buyer was a *really* bad guy and I was robbed, then *shot* for my trouble?

I had assuaged my guilt and calmed my fears by reminding myself it was wrinkle-filler, for goodness sake, not painkillers or narcotics.

I paced back and forth for a few minutes and when I spotted the car, my pulse vaulted. I considered pulling the plug on the deal then and there, but I was running out of options for cash.

The exchange spot was a one-way street near a traffic light. The plan was for me to walk up to the driver's side of the car and make the swap before the light turned. I got the feeling the buyer had done this kind of thing before. I, on the other hand, was a novice drug dealer.

The car flashed its lights and I walked to the edge of the sidewalk, keeping an eye on the light. The car slowed and came to a stop next to me just as the light turned red.

The window buzzed down. The driver wore sunglasses and a hat. "Let me see it."

On the verge of wetting myself, I handed him the envelope. He withdrew the vial, gave it a shake, then scanned the label and checked the seal.

I swallowed hard, poised to hear sirens any minute, or for the Corvette to peel off and leave me standing. The light turned green. I felt faint.

The guy handed me a roll of bills. "Fifteen hundred," he said. "Nice doing business with you."

Then he pulled away with traffic, as easy as you please.

I was stunned by the relative civility and ease of the transaction. I quickly counted the bills, and it was all there. Feeling jubilant, I stuffed the money into my pocket, then turned in the direction of my bank.

Charlie Graham stood a few feet away carrying his gym bag. And from the look on his face, he'd witnessed the sordid transaction. My feet slowed and my mouth opened. I wanted to explain, but how could I? And did it really matter? Charlie and I were on different life paths.

He turned to walk in the opposite direction... and I let him.

September 21, Thursday

I DECIDED JOON-WOO must still be feeling bad about putting me in an assignment where discovering bodies is a possible outcome, because she had set me up once again to work with Constance Hanlon at the Battlecoin Building.

Working as the administrative assistant of the CEO of a tech-centered venture capitalist group had been the highlight of my temp career so far, and I was excited to be back in my element.

"Hi, Mae," she said, extending a firm handshake. "Good to see you again."

"It's good to be back," I said, and meant it.

"You know the drill," she said, already walking to her first meeting. "Let's do this."

The day was an alternate version of the last day I'd spent shadowing her in meetings, taking notes on a laptop, feeding her documents she needed, and generally keeping her organized and on-time as she moved through conferences with the mayor and with the Girl Scouts with equal gravity and aplomb.

"You must like temping," Constance said at the end of the day as we rode down in the elevator.

"It wasn't exactly a choice."

"Everything is a choice. Even not choosing is a choice."

Everything that came out of the woman's mouth sounded wise and as if it was a message meant especially for me. I got off the elevator on the lobby level and turned to say goodbye.

"The assignments aren't all as good as this one," I said, "but it keeps life interesting."

"If you can take the worst job and make it count for something, that's the very definition of success," she said. "Even the smallest, most demeaning task means something to someone. Do you like clean toilets, Mae?"

"Of course."

She smiled. "So do I. Remember, there are no small jobs, only small people. I hope to see you soon."

Once again, I felt as if the woman was looking straight into my heart. Elena Padilla was a hard-working immigrant who had almost nothing to her name, and I had demeaned and abused her. She wasn't haunting me in my dreams. The memory of the way I'd treated her haunted me.

September 22, Friday

"LAST NAME Jeffers," the guy at the counter of the drycleaners said, then handed the ticket back to me.

I was sitting on a hard stool, operating the spinner rack, trying to remember what Constance Hanlon had said about every job, no matter how small, meaning something to someone. I slowed the rack of swinging garments and matched the numbers.

To Mr. Jeffers the fact that these three ugly shirts were clean and starched meant something. Now he could go out on that first date that might miraculously result in a second. Or he could visit his great-grandmother in the nursing home and make her happy he was wearing a shirt she'd given him. Or he could go to that retro 80s costume party and win first prize.

"Here you go," I said, handing off the clothes. I couldn't resist sneaking a peek at Mr. Jeffers. Although the suspenders were unexpected, the rest of him meshed with the persona I'd built in my mind, down to the blatant wink he gave me before swaggering out.

I was resigned to returning to the spinner rack when a scene out the window caught my eye. The woman with the clipboard from the backroom of the cleaners was standing next to the rack of unclaimed clothing, and she appeared to be giving it out to anyone who wanted it. A knot of people surrounded the rack.

"Is that the owner?" I asked Cheater Boss.

"One of the owners," he said, nodding. "That's Mrs. Gladstone—she and her husband own the place. She does that all the time—gives away the unclaimed clothing to homeless people who hang around the park."

"That's nice of her," I murmured, happy the clothes I'd ferreted out would find a home.

Even the smallest, most demeaning task means something to

someone.

I recognized two people in the crowd vying for the garments—the teenage girls, pregnant and non-pregnant, I'd seen in the music store. The pregnant girl looked ready to pop, and both of them looked even more bedraggled and lost. But they both had smiles on their faces as they held up and assessed the free, clean clothes.

It was something.

September 23, Saturday

AT LEAST I didn't have to worry about avoiding Charlie Graham at the gym, because he seemed intent on avoiding me, too. I supposed seeing me engage in what appeared to be a hard-core drug deal had tainted me in his mind. And I didn't see an advantage in correcting his opinion of me.

After leaving the gym, I reported to one of the assignments I found most difficult—working at the weight-loss center. It dredged up too many sad associations for me. In turn, I sensed the customers misread my standoffishness as being judgmental. It was an uncomfortable cycle I was still trying to break, with Casey's help.

She was working at the center today, too, and I was glad to see her smiling face. The customers adored her and her flamboyant clothing. She always found a way to make people feel welcome.

I was manning the reception desk and things were not going well. Two of the clients I'd checked in were sitting in the waiting area discussing how I couldn't understand what they were going through. They either thought I couldn't hear them, or didn't care.

"Why doesn't she get a job at the anorexia clinic?" one girl said in a loud whisper.

"She looks like a crack in the wall," another girl said. Everyone laughed.

I frowned.

"No, she looks like an exclamation point." More laughter.

That was just plain mean.

"No she looks like one of those dried up pieces of beef jerky on those Beltina commercials."

I scoffed and pushed to my feet, ready to confront them.

"Oh, gosh, whatever you do, stay away from that stuff," the first girl said. "I have a friend who took it and went off the deep end."

I stopped.

"I know someone who took it and killed her boss. I mean, the man needed to be killed, but still."

Huh? I walked around the corner and the women all froze. "What did you just say?"

The girl blanched. "Look, I'm sorry about the exclamation point thing."

I waved it off. "I mean about Beltina. What do you mean 'went off the deep end'?"

"Went crazy," the girl said with a shrug. "She's in a mental hospital in south Georgia, and I heard they have a whole ward for people on that Beltina drug."

I crossed my arms. "Tell me more."

September 24, Sunday

"FALL IS IN THE AIR," Kyle said, breathing in the cool breeze blowing across the lake. "We probably won't have many more nice weekends like this to bring the boat out."

"I won't mind," I said, looking down at the group of people on the lower deck. With every passing weekend, the numbers dwindled as fair-weather boaters hung up their swimsuits until next summer. "It'll be nice to have some alone time."

He nuzzled my ear. "You said it."

I nodded down to Helen, who sat by herself in a corner chair. She looked anxious, and was doing something I'd never seen her do—bite her nails. "I'm worried about Helen. Is she okay?"

Kyle made a rueful noise. "Her husband hired a new secretary—young and pretty, and she's obsessed with the idea they're having an affair."

"Are they?"

"No. Her husband asked me to talk some sense into her. He said he has no interest in his secretary, but this fixation of Helen's is ruining their marriage. If you get a chance, will you see if she'll talk about it?"

"Sure." Then I winced. "I have to tell you something."

He pulled back. "What?"

I sighed. "The vial of the injectable you gave me—I dropped it and broke it. I'm sorry."

"Is that all? I thought this had something to do with Charlie Graham."

Now it was my turn to pull back. "Why would you say that?"

He shrugged. "Since that day you slipped and called me Charlie, I guess I've been a little fixated myself."

I shook my head. "There's no need. Charlie Graham has nothing on you."

He pulled me close for a very nice kiss that was interrupted by a scream from below. Libby was shouting and running from a man chasing her with a water balloon.

"When does Libby leave?" I asked with a groan.

"In a couple of weeks. Did she talk to you about the Beltina samples?"

"Yes. She said she's not losing." I tried to inject innocence into my tone. "I don't know what the problem could be."

"The problem is she's not taking it."

My head came around—had they discovered I'd given her empty placebos? "What do you mean?"

"I mean I don't think she's taking the capsules as regularly as she's supposed to."

"Oh." I exhaled.

"Libby can be a little... difficult."

"I hadn't noticed," I said drily.

"Now, now. Be nice." He pointed to Julie and Trish who were cavorting and laughing at the other end of the deck. "They seem to be doing great on your drug. I've never seen them look better or be more outgoing. They could be poster girls for Beltina."

Suddenly another scream sounded, except this time it wasn't a scream of laughter. Julie and Trish were fighting—fist-fighting, landing punches and grabbing handfuls of hair. Attempts to separate them failed as they fell to the deck and rolled around, kicking and shouting obscenities.

"Break them up!" Kyle shouted, turning to hurry down the

stairs to the lower deck. I followed and by the time we got there, four men were holding the woman apart, but they were far from calm.

"I'll kill you, you bitch!"

"Not if I kill you first, you piece of shit!"

"That's enough!" Kyle shouted. He and Helen converged on the long-time friends to try to calm them. I hung back and reflected on what Kyle had just said.

They could be poster girls for Beltina.

September 25, Monday

"PORTIA," I SAID into the phone, "could you expound on some of the complaints filed against Beltina?"

My former boss gave a little laugh. "What's with all the questions, Della?"

"I've been hearing rumors."

"What rumors?"

"That Beltina is causing personality disorders. Someone told me there's a ward in a psych hospital in South Georgia for Beltina patients. Is that true?"

Portia scoffed. "How ridiculous—of course it isn't true. That's propaganda put out by our competition. Della, you know how this business works. If a company has a drug that's too good to be true, the other guys have to tear it down any way they can. Psychiatric and personality disorders are the easiest side effects to claim because they're the most difficult to prove or disprove."

"True," I agreed. "I guess I'm getting antsy to get back to work. And I still haven't received my bonus."

Portia heaved a sigh. "I'm so sorry, Della. I'm going to make some calls tomorrow and pull some strings to get you your bonus. You've been so loyal and so patient. Meanwhile, it's crucial you uphold your exit agreement. Confidentiality is of the utmost importance. You've seen yourself how quickly rumors can get out of control and bring down a perfectly good product. We're trying to make sure that doesn't happen. Can you stay the course just a little longer?"

I closed my eyes. "Yes."

"Good. I'll be in touch."

I ended the call, then picked up my morning dose of Beltina. I turned the orange pill over in my palm, considering it... weighing the unproven risks against what the pill had empirically already done for me.

I placed the pill on my tongue, then swallowed it with a drink of water.

September 26, Tuesday

"Hi, Ms. Culpepper, it's Detective Terry."

My pulse picked up. "Hi, Detective. Do you have news?"

"No news," he said, his voice grim. "Just confirmation on Elena Padilla's cause of death. The autopsy confirms heat stroke, so she probably died in her car."

"But heat stroke doesn't make sense considering how cool the area in the garage was where the car was parked."

"I hear what you're saying, but you don't know what the conditions were before you worked in the garage. The car might've been sitting there for a week in the heat, then someone turned on the fans."

I bit into my lip. True. "Do you know when she died?"

"No... it's almost impossible to tell in a closed environment like that. The best the M.E. could guess was maybe a month before the body was found."

Tears pricked my eyes. She'd lain in the car for a month, undetected?

"I'm sorry," he said. "I know you feel close to this woman for some reason, but in a case like this, I'm not sure there's any good news."

"Thank you, anyway, Detective."

"You're welcome, Ms. Culpepper. Stay out of trouble."

I ended the call, then reached into my pocket to withdraw the silver earring. Then I held it up and pinged the tip to make it sway and shine.

September 27, Wednesday

I HAD FINISHED cleaning the women's locker room and was changing into my exercise clothes when I received a text from Jan, my former trainer.

Hi, Della. Just checking to see if you're okay?

The last time I'd seen Jan, she'd told me Traxton had let her go. She'd warned me to "be careful," and at the time I'd assumed she was trying to warn me my job was in danger.

But what if she'd been trying to warn me about something else, like reported side effects of Beltina?

I typed in 'Do you know something about Beltina I should know?" My finger hovered over the send button, then I pulled my hand down my face. My conversation with Portia was still fresh in my mind, and I was sensitive to not doing anything to jeopardize my pending bonus. Even if Jan told me yes, what then? Traxton was a huge pharmaceutical machine. There was nothing I could do to affect the outcome of anything.

I used the back-delete button to erase the text, then typed in

All is well. Hope you're good, too.

I hit send.

The high intensity interval training class had already begun. I found a spot in the rear of the room and joined in. A thick figure closer to the front of the class caught my eye—Charlie Graham. My face burned when I remembered the first class we'd taken together and how my plan to show him up had backfired. I had to hand it to him—for a stocky guy, he was agile.

And decently limber.

My endorphin-fueled mind put those facts together with another factoid I remembered from the shower room, and I concluded that Charlie Graham, like Sabrina and Susan had suggested, probably knew his way around the bedroom almost as well as he knew his way around the kitchen.

The instructor called for a water break, and Charlie turned his head in my direction. Our gazes locked for a few seconds, then we each thought better of it, and looked away.

September 28, Thursday

I WAS ON MY WAY to Dorman's for a gift-wrapping stint when my phone rang. I frowned at the local number I didn't recognize, but connected the call.

"This is Della."

"Hi, Della. My name is Rainie Stephens. I'm a reporter for the *Atlanta Journal-Constitution*, and I wondered if you'd be willing to answer some questions."

The reporter probably wanted to tell Elena's story. "Sure. Did Detective Terry give you my number?"

"You know Jack Terry?"

I frowned. "He investigated the death."

"I'm sorry—whose death?"

"Isn't this about Elena Padilla, the woman I found deceased in her car?"

"Um, no. But we can talk about that, too, if you like."

I frowned. "Why did you call?"

"It's a little delicate—part personal, part investigative. I've been taking a weight-loss drug called Beltina. Can you tell me anything about possible hidden side effects the company is aware of but is keeping from the public?"

I stopped, swallowed hard, then said "No," and ended the call.

September 29, Friday

I STUDIED my nibbled nails with dismay. I'd been a bundle of nerves since the call from the *AJC* reporter. I considered phoning Portia to tell her about it, but I was afraid she'd worry I'd talk to the woman.

Although what did I know, really? I had nothing but a few gossipy rumors and some anecdotal stories that a few Buckhead housewives who were taking Beltina were losing their shit—like that didn't happen every damn day anyway.

And the woman who punched herself in the shower? Who knew how her wire had gotten crimped.

As Portia had pointed out—mental issues were notoriously easy to attribute and difficult to prove: Does a woman who takes

Beltina decide to start punching herself, or is a woman prone to self-injury more likely to take a drug like Beltina?

It was the classic chicken and egg conundrum.

The sound of flushing toilets roused me from my musings. Casey had convinced me to sign up for a ladies' restroom attendant during the annual Cirque du Soleil tent show in Triangle Point. She assured me the tips were phenomenal... and since I didn't have any more wrinkle-filler to traffic, I relented.

It was my job to make sure the forty or so bathroom stalls were clean and topped out with one-ply toilet paper, and there was sufficient hand soap, tampons, maxi-pads, and paper towels on hand to keep the female customers of the upscale circus happy and moving through the lines so they could get back to their overpriced seats.

Patrons who appreciated the effort dropped a dollar or a few coins in my tip jar. I was dressed in a black suit with gold epaulets that made me look somewhat official—or like a monkey organ grinder, take your pick. But I was wearing fake glasses and had hidden my hair under a cap. In the relatively low light of the bathroom and the fact that no one really wanted to make eye contact with the woman who stocked the johns, I didn't think I'd have to worry about anyone recognizing me.

And I was right. Before the show started, Sabrina and Susan came in, teetering on high heels. They'd asked me to come with them, but I'd made up an excuse, unwilling to part with my hard-earned temp dollars to see acrobats swing from silk scarves. Not only did the girls not recognize me, they didn't tip me, either.

I was learning a lot about my friends.

And myself.

While what Constance Hanlon said about every little job being important to someone, I'd be lying if I didn't say I think my talents were being wasted spraying Maui Morning air freshener in the ladies' bathroom.

Just before intermission, a statuesque redhead walked in—Charlie Graham's girlfriend. Correction—fiancée. I watched her as I passed out paper towels and gave nods of thanks for tips. She didn't go into a stall, just stood in front of the mirror and redrew her lipstick with stop-motion precision. It wasn't until she walked over to me that I realized a perfect tear had run down her cheek.

She held her face motionless, as if she were afraid if she blinked, the Hoover Dam would break.

I handed her a paper towel and she delicately dabbed at the lone tear and the corner of each eye, then tipped me ten dollars, and walked out.

Curious.

I walked to the door and peeked out to see Charlie waiting for her. He looked handsome, dressed in slacks and a nice dress shirt. She walked up and he smiled, then clasped her hand. As they walked by, I ducked back.

I puffed out my cheeks in a sigh. That woman would probably never be caught tending to a public restroom.

I used to be that woman.

And I wanted to be that woman again.

Intermission was called and for thirty minutes, I was too busy to think about anything as the unending waves of women came and went. When the show resumed, I surveyed the mess left behind— rolls of toilet paper strewn and unrolled, soggy paper towels, clogged toilets. I sighed and tackled each stall one by one. At the end of a row, I pushed on a door and it wouldn't open. I peered under to see it was empty—somehow it had been locked from inside. Which meant I had to crawl under to unlock it—ugh.

I shimmied under and squinted when I saw a basket sitting on the commode. Something green was inside—cloth... no, a coat.

That moved.

I froze, then heard a sound coming from the coat. I pulled it aside and stared down at a face that seemed surprised to see me, too. The baby responded by opening its mouth and howling.

I joined in.

September 30, Saturday

"IT'S UNBELIEVABLE," Kyle said. "Who would abandon a baby?"

I thought I knew because I'd recognized the green winter coat as one of the unclaimed garments from the drycleaners. The newborn baby boy most likely belonged to the pregnant teen I'd seen trying on the clothes. "Someone desperate, obviously." I'd explained away stumbling onto the infant by telling Kyle I'd attended the show with Sabrina and Susan.

Not a lie—all three of us had been there.

"Well, he's in good hands now with Children's Services," Kyle said.

I nodded. I dearly hoped so.

"Are you sure it's okay that we came here for dinner?" He opened the door to Graham's Eatery, but hesitated.

"It's fine," I said. "Charlie and I are... friends."

"Good, because I love this place."

When we walked inside, the restaurant was packed, but we had a reservation and were shown to a table quickly. I didn't see Charlie, and it was likely he'd never know we were there.

"Hello."

I looked up to see him smiling at us. Kyle shook his hand and they made small talk. Charlie and I exchanged curt glances before he moved on to talk to other diners.

Kyle ordered wine, and when the waiter left, he smiled. "One little order of business before our drinks arrive." From his jacket pocket he removed a ring-sized box and pushed it toward me on the table.

I managed a smile—he'd brought me more injectable to replace the bottle I'd "broken." I wasn't going to be able to wiggle out of this procedure gracefully. "Kyle, you shouldn't have."

I opened the box and gasped. It wasn't a vial of filler—it was a diamond ring. I looked up. "I changed my mind—you should have!"

He grinned, then his handsome face grew serious. "I thought it was time. Della Culpepper, will you marry me?"

I realized the restaurant had quieted. The diners at the tables around us looked expectant and wide-eyed. They needn't have worried. There was only one answer to Kyle's question:

"Yes!"

OCTOBER

October 1, Sunday

"A TOAST," Libby Lakes said, holding up a flute of pink champagne, "to Kyle and Della—congratulations on your engagement!"

"Hear, hear!" the crowd of friends gathered on Kyle's patio chorused.

I managed to maintain my smile. Although I wasn't thrilled the flirtatious actress was toasting my future, I ventured she was even less thrilled about doing it. After all, I was the one wearing a sparkling diamond ring on my left hand, so in the sphere of female-cattiness, I'd won.

I lifted my glass for a drink, but Kyle's whispered protest near my ear stopped me. "Not until everyone else has taken a drink," he chided.

An embarrassed flush burned my neck. "Of course," I murmured, as if I'd forgotten toasting protocol, when in truth, the only formal toasts I'd seen had been on TV and in movies. I'd given Kyle the impression my family was worldly and of some means, when in truth, they were barely presentable.

Except my sweet brother Donnie, of course, whom I fondly called Professor. But since I wasn't sure how Kyle would respond to the challenges of Donnie's autism, I'd kept that quiet as well.

It occurred to me now, though, that I'd have to come clean to Kyle about my backward, dysfunctional family before we walked down the aisle.

Unless we eloped—now, there was an idea.

"Now," he prompted out of the side of his mouth.

I lifted my glass dutifully and drank in a mouthful of the cold, fizzy liquid.

"Thank you all," he said, then took the requisite drink.

"Are you pregnant?" Libby asked loudly.

I inhaled and choked on the champagne.

"Of course not," Kyle said with a laugh, then he reached over to pat my stomach. "Della has just put on a few happy pounds."

I had? I mean—I had. I just didn't realize they were so noticeable. I sucked in my stomach and vowed to find a walking route to my condo that circumvented the bakery case at the supermarket. Even Beltina tablets couldn't overcome frequent cheesecake binges.

"But you're going to have kids?" Libby pressed in a sing-song voice.

"Absolutely," Kyle said.

"Maybe," I said at the same time.

Laughter burst out while Kyle and I exchanged glances—I wondered if my surprise at his resoluteness registered on my face.

It must have because he hooked one arm around my shoulder and smiled at everyone. "Della is still reeling over finding that baby in the ladies' lounge during the Cirque du Soleil show she attended Friday night."

I'd lied to Kyle about why I was in the restroom, naturally.

"I heard about it on the news," Libby said. "Except the reporter said it was found by a bathroom attendant."

Was that suspicion in her voice?

"They got it wrong," Kyle said easily. "It was Della. Tell them what happened, hon."

I gave a little shrug. "It was after intermission. I went into the ladies' room and opened a stall door and there was the basket, with the baby inside. I called 9-1-1 and waited until the police arrived."

"Have they found the mother?" Helen asked.

"Not that I've heard."

"Gawd," Trish said, "I wonder if she had the baby right there in the stall."

"I don't think so," I said carefully.

"She had to be some homeless city person," Julie said, her voice ringing with censure.

"Obviously," Trish shot back from the other side of the room. "Because no one in the burbs ever abandons their children."

Julie huffed. "My kids wanted to be with their dad!"

Apparently, the women were still feuding. At least the black eyes and scratched faces had healed. And at least other people were endeavoring to keep distance between them.

"How could anyone just abandon a baby like that?" Helen asked, her voice breaking in a way that made me think her marital problems had not eased.

"Lord," Libby said, fanning herself, "what is going on in that place where you live, Della? First someone finds a dead body, and now a baby?"

"I doubt the two are related," I said in defense of my home base. Then I bit my lip—except through me as the finder of both—ack.

"Hey," Kyle said, "this isn't party talk. We're supposed to be having fun. Now, who needs another drink?"

As he moved away to accept handshakes from some of his buddies, my heart squeezed with admiration... and apprehension. Kyle and I had talked about kids in the abstract, but there had been no serious conversation about a timeline or—*gulp*—how many. Finding the abandoned baby had reinforced all my fears about what a huge responsibility a child was. And what if the child had special needs, like Donnie?

Libby came to stand next to me. "I didn't mean to put you on the spot about children."

Yes, she had. "No worries," I said, holding my ring up to the light.

"When Kyle showed me the ring and said he was going to propose, I told him to make sure the two of you are on the same page about everything."

Wow. She was letting me know she knew about my engagement before I'd known about my engagement. "We are," I assured her.

"Well, that's what an engagement is for," she said brightly, "to decide if you're right for each other before you make a mistake."

I narrowed my eyes at her. "I appreciate the advice of

someone who's been married—I forget, is it two times, or three?"

Her smiled faltered. "Three."

I gave her a bitchy nod, then walked away.

But dammit, she'd gotten to me.

October 2, Monday

"WE HAVE TO STOP meeting like this," Detective Jack Terry said dryly.

I gave him a finger wave as I dropped into the visitor seat in his so-called office. "Hello to you, too, Detective."

"Coffee?" he asked, lifting his cup.

"No, thanks. I've had a long day working at the pet store, so I'd like to give my statement and go home."

"Pet store?" He wrinkled his nose. "Explains the smell."

New worst job assignment: Assistant Dog Groomer. Which basically meant I helped to restrain dogs while the groomer washed them. The dank smell of wet fur had seeped into my pores. If I weren't so tired, I'd be completely pissed off. "Can we get on with it?"

He took a drink from his mug, grimaced, then nodded. "Right. Just give me a minute to locate the right file. Let's see… this isn't about your mother's boyfriend who looted her bank account… and it's not about you finding your housekeeper's body in her car…"

I pursed my mouth while he amused himself.

"Oh, wait—here it is. This is about the baby you found abandoned in a bathroom stall." He grunted. "You do get around, Ms. Culpepper."

"Is that how you charm all the women, Detective?"

"Hardly."

He sobered and for a moment, I wondered if I'd treaded on something serious.

He opened the folder. "Now then… tell me everything you can remember about finding the baby."

I nodded. "It was Friday evening. I was working as an attendant in the bathroom during the Cirque du Soleil tent show."

"As part of your temp work?"

"Yes. Intermission had just ended, and the place was a mess.

I was going from stall to stall straightening things, and one of the stall doors was locked. I crawled under and there was the baby. I could tell it was a newborn because he was still a little bloody. But I knew he was alive because he started crying. I called 9-1-1 and waited until the police arrived."

"What time was that?"

"Maybe eight-thirty."

"Did you see anyone with a baby earlier?"

"No. Lots of little kids, but no babies."

"So you don't know who left the boy?"

"I didn't say that."

His head came up. "You do know who left him?"

"I think so. A young pregnant woman—a teenager, I think—has been hanging around Triangle Point for the past few weeks. I talked to her a couple of times. She seemed like a transient. And I saw her with a green coat, the same green coat the baby was wrapped in."

He was making notes. "Did you get her name?"

"No."

He made a rueful noise. "Even a first name or a nickname would help."

"No, sorry."

"Okay. Can you describe her?"

"Petite, dark blond hair. Tight clothes, bad skin. She was hanging around with a dark-haired girl about the same age."

"Did you see them Friday night?"

"No. And I haven't seen them since I found the baby."

"They're bound to have been caught on a security camera somewhere on the property."

"What happens when you find her?"

He looked grim. "That's up to the D.A.'s office. Abandoning an infant is serious, but there are domestic violence safehouses scattered around Triangle Point, so the girl might've thought it was safe to leave the baby where she did, especially if she saw you working there."

I gave a little laugh. "If the mother thought her baby would be safe with me, she had to be desperate."

He shrugged. "I wouldn't say that, Ms. Culpepper. You strike me as someone with a lot of resolve."

"Raising a child takes more than resolve."

"You can say that again," he murmured.

"You have kids, Detective?"

"Not… yet," he said in a way that made me think he was conflicted about the idea of being a father.

"An unattended birth couldn't have been a walk in the park for the mother," I offered.

"True, although the medical report says the umbilical cord had been tied off properly."

"She or someone with her could've learned how to do that on YouTube."

He grunted in agreement. "All the more reason to find the mother—in case she needs medical attention herself. All the hospital E.R.'s on are alert for a young woman who might've given birth recently, but who doesn't have the baby with her."

"And the baby is in good hands?"

He nodded. "I talked to the case worker this morning and she said a foster family has already been found."

I exhaled.

Detective Terry closed the file. "That's all we can do for now. If you see the girl again, call me."

I stood. "I will. Oh, and Detective…"

"Yes?"

"Is Elena Padilla's car still impounded?"

His expression grew suspicious. "I believe so. Why?"

"Would it be possible for me to search it?"

He frowned. "No. Why?"

"I found one of Elena's earrings she must've lost when she was cleaning my place, and if I can find the match, I'd like to send them to her daughter."

His face softened. "Oh. I'll check to see if an earring or other personal items were recovered."

I inclined my head. "Thank you."

He stood and walked to a file cabinet. "Try to stay out of trouble, Ms. Culpepper. If you keep this up, I'm going to have to clear out an entire drawer for you."

October 3, Tuesday

"AND LIBBY ONCE went skinny-dipping in Colin Derringer's pool," Anthony said, his voice breathless. "Can you imagine?"

We were cleaning my condo. I was elbow deep in the toilet wearing rubber gloves and Anthony was shining the mirror, wearing a ruffled apron.

"Was Colin's wife home?" I asked dryly.

"Libby said she was the one who suggested they all get naked!"

I shook my head—was nothing sacred anymore? "I hope alcohol was involved."

"Cocaine," Anthony confirmed. "She said it was piled up on patio tables like snow." He lifted his hand to talk behind it. "And she mentioned doing something indecent with Colin's Oscar."

"Nice," I said sarcastically. "When is Libby going back to LA and all her friends, human and otherwise?"

"Mid-month she's going back to get ready for the movie audition the first of November."

Good. Although that meant Anthony would be out of a job again—and since my bonus hadn't yet arrived, I was still pinching pennies, and still needed Anthony's contribution to make my pesky mortgage payment.

"Apparently the movie director is Marcus Applegate, and the critics clamor around him," Anthony continued. "Lib says this could be the turning point in her career."

"Does she talk about herself the entire time you're with her?"

"Pretty much. And she asks a lot of questions about you."

My pulse spiked over the fear that Anthony had loose lips. "Like?"

"Like how long you and Kyle have been dating, stuff like that."

"She let me know she knew Kyle was going to propose," I offered. "As if they're besties."

He scoffed. "We all knew it was just a matter of time before Kyle proposed. He's no dummy."

I tossed him an appreciative smile. "Kyle might rescind his offer if he knew what I've been doing the past few weeks." I sniffed my arm. "I still smell like wet dog from yesterday."

"Maybe you're not giving him enough credit. Don't you think he'd appreciate you being resourceful when you could be mooching off him?"

"I have a feeling the embarrassment of a girlfriend who washes dogs will sort of override everything else." I sighed. "Besides, I'm lying to him."

"But you don't have a choice," Anthony said. "You said yourself if he thinks your company is in trouble and sells his stock, you'll both be in bigger trouble."

"True."

"So you're doing the brave thing—you're protecting him."

It was a bona fide reason to keep my unemployed status from Kyle, but honestly, if the stock situation was off the table, I still can't say I'd tell him. Because the truth is, *I'm* embarrassed I have to do crappy temp work, so I'd expect him to be embarrassed, too. I wanted to be with Kyle because he wanted the best life had to offer.

And that meant I had to be the best.

"Libby asked about your job with Traxton," Anthony said. "She wanted to know how successful you are."

I stopped scrubbing the toilet. "What did you tell her?"

He gestured to the toilet and grinned. "That you're good at whatever you decide to do."

I laughed. "Thanks... I think."

"I know you don't like her, but she did tell me she's grateful you gave her the Beltina samples."

I kept scrubbing. The "samples" I'd given Libby were empty gelatin capsules.

"Except she's not losing weight," he continued with a sigh. "Libby admitted she's not diligent about taking them, so I text her when it's time."

"Hopefully that'll do the trick," I said lightly.

"Libby gets and sends lots of texts."

"That's nice."

"From all kinds of people."

"Uh-huh."

"But mostly from people named Kyle Covey."

I stopped scrubbing and glanced up at Anthony. He stood with his back to me, but I caught his apologetic expression of warning reflected in the mirror.

"Duly noted," I murmured. Then I frowned and flushed the commode.

October 4, Wednesday

I SPOTTED CHARLIE GRAHAM at the gym, but thankfully, he was fully clothed and standing near the front of an interval cardio class. I tried not to notice his one-armed pushups, but I confess I was grudgingly impressed—until I imagined him doing pushups on his redheaded girlfriend.

I took my time showering and changing back into my cleaning woman disguise (so the girl at the counter wouldn't recognize me as the member whose pricey membership had expired) in an effort to avoid running into him when I left. But the man must've lingered in the steam room because just as I was ducking out, he strode up behind me, then passed me to hold open the door, dammit.

"Thanks," I muttered.

"You're welcome," he said cheerfully. "Where's your engagement ring? Don't tell me the wedding's already off."

I gave him a flat smile. "Nope. Just didn't want to lose it while scrubbing a gym toilet."

"Ah. That would be hard to explain. I assume he still doesn't know about..." He gestured to my bandanna-covered hair, big glasses and baggy clothes.

I gritted my teeth as we walked out onto the sidewalk. "No, he doesn't."

Charlie looked up and down the street. "Am I keeping you from doing business?"

"What are you talking about?"

"I saw you make a suspicious package-for-money exchange a few days ago. Didn't take you for a drug dealer."

I closed my eyes briefly. "It's not what you think."

"Ah—more secrets."

I walked faster in the direction of our condo building, but so did he.

"Did you need something?" I asked, exasperated.

"Just to say congratulations. And to think, you got engaged in my restaurant." He grinned. "That means every time you look at your fiancé, you'll think of me."

I pushed my tongue into my cheek. "And where did *you* get engaged?"

"About that... I'm not engaged, Della. When your friend saw me in the jewelry store, I was having my mother's ring repaired."

"Your mother's ring?"

"We lost my dad a few years ago, but she never took off her engagement ring. The last time I was home she wasn't wearing it because a prong was loose, but she was afraid to take it to a jeweler, has heard too many stories about stones being swapped." His voice was indulgent. "I'm friends with the jewelers around the corner, so I brought it home with me to have it repaired."

A likely story... dammit. "So who's the redhead?" I blurted.

His mouth quirked. "Megan is an ex-girlfriend from Nashville. I ended things and she married someone else, and now her marriage is ending."

"And you're getting back together?"

"No. We weren't a good couple before, and that hasn't changed, but we're still friends."

That explained the tears.

"Tears?"

I hadn't realized I'd spoken aloud. "I saw you both Friday night at the circus. I was in the women's restroom and she came in. She looked... upset."

"She's having a hard time with the divorce. She's staying here until everything is final."

"Oh. Well, Susan and Sabrina will be happy to know you're not off the market," I said lightly. "I'm sure their offer still stands."

He smiled. "Listen, Della... I'm sorry."

I turned my head to look at him. "For that crack you made about my skinny ass when you first met me?"

He gave a little laugh. "That... and I kind of thought things were... I don't know—going somewhere between us before Megan showed up. If so, I'm sorry."

"I don't know what you're talking about," I lied.

"Right. Since you got engaged, I guess I was wrong about

pretty much everything. Anyway, congratulations. I hope you'll be very happy with Kevin."

"Kyle," I corrected.

"Whatever. And I know this temp agency work you do is temporary, I think it's kind of kooky and cool and it shows a lot of spunk, and... that's kind of rare."

I blinked. And was grateful our arrival at our building kept me from responding.

But I was still thinking about our conversation as we entered and walked across the lobby. Henry the concierge lifted his hand and we waved back, then veered into the mailbox area. My heart lifted in anticipation that today would be the day my Traxton bonus arrived and I could start putting my life back in order.

But my heart sank lower as I flipped through the envelopes. Still nothing.

"Everything okay?" Charlie asked, closing his box.

"Hunky dory." I closed my box with a bang, then walked to the elevator bay.

He flipped through his mail while we waited for a car, apparently less affected by his previous words than I had been. Not that it mattered now—I was an engaged woman.

"Ah, a coupon. But I can't use it. Maybe you'd like it?" He held out a colored flyer for a free appetizer at Graham's Eatery.

I smirked. "Sure. I'm due a night out with the girls." When we walked onto the elevator, a thought struck me. "Charlie, do you remember the earring you found in my couch?"

"You mean in *my* couch. What about it?"

"I discovered it belonged to my former housekeeper."

He squinted. "The woman you found dead in her car?"

I nodded. "She must've lost it when she was cleaning. I'd like to find the mate and send them to her daughter. Would you mind checking the couch again?"

"We can both check." The door opened to his floor.

I hesitated. The one and only time I'd been inside Charlie's condo had been... unsettling. "I can't. I'm... late."

"Okay. I'll let you know if I find anything." He stepped out, then turned back. "Della, did you say you were in the ladies' room the night of the circus?"

I nodded.

"Did you hear an attendant found an abandoned infant?"

"Um, that would be me."

His eyes widened, then he gave a little laugh. "Why am I not surprised? You're amazing."

The doors closed and I found myself smiling and feeling a little... amazing.

October 5, Thursday

DETECTIVE TERRY waved me into a small room with a wall of digital screens. "Thanks for doing this, Ms. Culpepper."

"Glad to help find the mother of the baby, if I can."

"I see you're back in disguise," he murmured, indicating my baggy T-shirt, bandanna, and glasses.

"Right... heading to a temp job after this."

"By the way, I checked the box holding the miscellaneous contents of Ms. Padilla's car. I even checked the car itself one more time... but no earring. Sorry."

"Thanks anyway, Detective."

"This is Evan," he said, gesturing to a wiry man sitting in front of a computer. "He's going to run the security footage for us."

I nodded hello. Evan gestured for me to take the seat next to him. Detective Terry stood behind us.

"Can you remember a specific day and time when you saw the pregnant girl?" the detective asked.

I had consulted my work schedule for the day I'd last seen her—the day I'd worked at the drycleaners and had witnessed the clothing giveaway. I gave the date and approximate time to Evan and observed while he typed in the information. Within a few seconds, the screens on the wall were synched to the time and day he'd entered, displaying black and white pictures from all around Triangle Point.

"The camera across from the drycleaners is number eight," Evan said, pointing to the wall. "Let me switch this monitor to eight. I'll run the tape and you stop me if you see her."

I stared hard at the screen, but the foot traffic was brisk and it was practically impossible to see every person clearly. It wasn't long before my eyeballs hurt from straining.

Then I pointed. "Wait—there's the owner bringing out the racks of giveaway clothing." Unfortunately, when she stopped, only a portion of either rack was visible. "Did another camera capture the area that's just off this screen?"

The man scanned the wall, then shook his head. "No."

"Maybe we'll get lucky," Detective Terry said.

"I'll slow it to half-speed," Evan offered.

Even at half-speed, it was challenging to register every moving form. A crowd moved toward the racks, and some figures went off-screen. I scoured the film, asking the operator to rewind and replay many times, but I didn't see the pregnant girl. The crowd eventually dispersed and at length, the racks were rolled back to the drycleaners.

To my dismay, almost three hours had passed.

"That's enough for now," Detective Terry said. "Would you be willing to come back another time and work with Evan to check other places you think she might have hung out?"

"Of course. How's the baby?"

"The Child Services rep says he's a perfectly healthy baby boy... he just doesn't have a mother."

For a few seconds, the big man seemed to go to a another place in his mind, and I got the feeling he was thinking about another baby without a mother. Then he blinked, and he was back to business.

"But hopefully he'll be placed in a good permanent home."

"Or perhaps the father will come forward," I offered.

He nodded. "That would be a good thing."

"The public seems to have taken an interest in the case," I said. "I hear they're calling him Baby Doe?"

"Right—for John Doe. If the mother is anywhere near a television or radio, she has to know we're looking for her."

"And that the baby is okay."

He nodded. "Let's hope she does the right thing."

I pressed my lips together. From what I'd seen of the bedraggled teen, maybe she *had* done the right thing.

October 6, Friday

DELLA, BUTTER ME.

I was sitting alone at Graham's Eatery waiting for Susan and Sabrina, and the bread in the basket on the table was calling to me.

Butter me real good.

My phone vibrated with a call. Grateful for the distraction, I checked the screen. But my stomach crimped to see the number for the *Atlanta Journal-Constitution* reporter Rainie Stephens, who'd tried to get me to confirm reports of hidden side effects of Beltina. I stowed my phone and winced at the pain in my temple. These sudden stress headaches were becoming more frequent... little wonder considering the way my life had been yanked sideways.

I'm good and warm, Della. And warm. And good.

It looked like the same amazing bread Charlie had shared with me the night I was at his condo, the night when—how had he put it? Things between us had been going somewhere.

I glanced all around. Although the restaurant was crowded, no one seemed to be paying attention to me and my impending carb crisis. I reached for a thick slice, surreptitiously used a knife to spread honey butter on it, then ate it quickly in big bites to get rid of it.

Jesus God, it tasted good. Crusty on the outside, light and chewy on the inside. I felt sad when it was gone.

And since no one seemed to notice my slip, I buttered and ate another piece, this time faster.

I was still chewing the last bite when Charlie's voice sounded next to me.

"I thought that was you."

I held up my napkin to hide my manic chewing.

"Don't rush—it's meant to be savored."

I nodded, regretting cramming that last huge chunk into my mouth all at once.

He grinned. "You don't have to talk. I just stopped by to tell you I didn't find the earring in the couch."

I nodded, disappointed, but not surprised since I hadn't heard from him.

"I did find something else stuck between the back cushions,

though."

My eyes widened, but I still couldn't seem to swallow.

He held up a fork, and I recognized my cutlery pattern. What the—?

Charlie grinned. "It was crusted over with something that smelled suspiciously like cheesecake, but I cleaned it up for you."

My face grew warm, then hot. Busted! Meanwhile, the traitorous bread seemed to be growing in my mouth.

"That couch of yours has seen a lot of fun activity."

My embarrassment and irritation spiked. I snatched the fork out of his hand, and finally succeeded in choking down the last bite. "You're... incorrigible!"

His eyes danced. "Enjoy your meal."

Oooh! Just when I was starting to—wait, no, I wasn't going there.

He passed Susan and Sabrina as they walked toward my table and said hello. They shamelessly pivoted to watch him walk away, then turned to give me big smiles.

"Congratulations on the engagement, about fucking time," Sabrina said, plopping down.

"Let me see that piece of ice," Susan said, sliding onto a chair.

I held out my left hand so the light would catch the ring. It was blinding.

"Wow, that must be what? Two carats?"

Sabrina moaned. "At least three with the circle of stones."

"The certificate said just over three," I confirmed.

"Nice," Susan oozed. "Did you have any idea he was going to propose?"

"Not at all. When he handed me the box, I thought it was another vial of wrinkle filler."

"You lucky dog," Sabrina groused. "The only thing better than snagging a dermatologist would be snagging a plastic surgeon." Then she sighed. "But plastic surgeons would be looking at titties all day, and who needs that pressure?"

"True," Susan said, then arched an eyebrow. "Was Chef Charlie over here checking out your ring?"

"Um, no—he saw it the night Kyle proposed."

"Oh, right." Susan squinted. "Did he say something to upset you? You don't look well."

"Oh, my God, are you pregnant?" Sabrina squealed.

"What? No! Why would you say that?"

"It would explain the sudden engagement."

"Kyle and I have been dating a long time," I reminded her.

"Maybe Kyle was starting to feel as if he had some competition," Susan said, nodding in the direction Charlie had gone.

"It would explain why he proposed here," Sabrina added, nodding.

I tried to laugh, but it came out sounding shrill.

Sabrina squinted. "Seriously, though—do you feel okay? You look... not like yourself."

She had no idea how often I hadn't looked like myself lately. "Just a headache." And an all over ache I couldn't put my finger on. "I've had a lot going on."

Susan squeezed my arm. "Well, tonight we'll celebrate. Maybe we can even get you to eat dessert for once?"

I felt the sharp craving for sugar kick in. "Maybe—for once." Once now, once later, once when I got home...

October 7, Saturday

AFTER CLEANING THE GYM, I stopped by the Triangle Point security office to sit with Evan and watch more footage in search of the baby's mother. For two hours we pored over footage around the music store, the drycleaners, and a couple of clothing stores teens seemed to favor, but came up empty. I left with dry, tired eyes and the promise of returning another time, then hurried to the music store for an afternoon shift.

When I walked into the store, for no particular reason, I moved to the spot where I'd talked to the two girls the day I'd given them cash. On a hunch, I looked up... and smiled at the camera mounted in a far corner.

"Hi, Mae," Blowz said. "We got a new shipment of T-shirts—"

"Blowz," I cut in, pointing to the camera. "How many days of security footage is saved?"

He scratched his balls. "It's supposed to save up to two

weeks, I think."

My hopes rose. "Can I see the footage?"

"Yeah, no. It's not working. But if it *was* working, we could go back two weeks. I think."

I groaned. "How long has it not been working?"

"It's never worked," he said with a shrug. Then he leaned closer. "Are you stoned? Your eyes are all bloodshot."

"What? No, I'm not stoned! Listen, Blowz, I'm trying to track down a teenage girl who's been in a couple of times. She was pregnant."

He lifted a finger. "Yeah, I remember her. She was with another girl."

"Yes! Do you know their names?"

"No." He frowned. "Hey, is she the one who abandoned the kidlet in the crapper?"

Ah, a budding poet. "Maybe. Have you seen her around in the last few days?"

"No."

"How about her friend?"

"Her either." Blowz crossed his arms. "But… "

I waited until it was clear he'd lost his train of thought. "But what?"

He looked at me. "Hm?"

I pinched the bridge of my nose against the pressure there, then rubbed my stabbing temple. "You started to say 'But something' about the pregnant girl."

"Oh—right. *But* I've seen her hanging out in the park across the street. The guy who gives out sandwiches might know her name."

Of course—Charlie might know something. Why hadn't I thought of that? "That's actually… brilliant."

Blowz grinned like a fool. "That's why I'm the boss."

"I'll be back in fifteen minutes, Boss."

"Hey, you just got here."

I ignored him and kept walking, out the door and up two blocks to Graham's Eatery. I glanced down at my uninspiring outfit and weighed the real possibility of running into someone I knew, like Sabrina or Susan… or Kyle, for that matter.

Great—now I didn't have to worry about Elena visiting me in

my nightmares tonight because *that* scenario would keep me up.

I cut down an alley and circled to the rear of the building, past two pungent-smelling dumpsters, then walked up a ramp to a loading dock and pounded on the door.

A few seconds passed before a woman cracked it open. "Yes?"

"I need to see Chef Graham, please."

She frowned. "He's busy, the restaurant is very crowded."

"Tell him Della needs to talk to him."

She closed the door and I waited. A couple of minutes later, the door opened again, and Charlie stood there in a stained chef's jacket, looking concerned. "Della? Are you okay?"

I gave a dismissive wave. "I'm fine, but this is important. When you were giving out sandwiches in the park this summer, do you remember a pregnant girl hanging around?"

He stepped out onto the loading dock. "Yeah, I think so." He squinted. "She was small, and she wore baggy clothes so at first she didn't look pregnant, but at one point I noticed it. I remember thinking she looked so young. Dark blond hair?"

I nodded. "That's her."

"Wait—you think she's the mother of the abandoned baby?"

"It seems so. Do you remember her name?"

He winced, then nodded. "I remember hearing someone else call her by name… it started with an "P" I think…. Peggy? No…"

"Polly?"

"I don't think so."

"Pam? Patty? Penny? Paula?"

He snapped his fingers. "Penny… I think it was Penny."

I grinned. "Are you sure?"

"Yes, that's it—Penny."

I gave a whoop of relief. "Charlie, I could kiss you!"

He smiled. "I wouldn't stop you."

My mouth opened, but not wide enough for me to remove my foot. "I… need to make a phone call." I turned and fled. When I got to the bottom of the ramp, I turned back and waved. "Thanks!"

"Anytime," he called.

October 8, Sunday

"AND THEN HE just left," Helen cried, collapsing against Kyle's chest. "What am I going to do?"

He gave me a worried glance over his sister's head, seeming at a loss.

"Helen," I soothed. "Maybe Reggie was just going out to cool off."

"With three suitcases and his golf clubs?"

Kyle and I exchanged winces.

"He probably went to the corporate apartment," Kyle said.

"Right—to be with his new secretary," she shrieked.

"You're jumping to a conclusion," Kyle said. "Reggie assured me nothing is going on."

"That's what he told me, too," she sobbed. "But he's gaslighting me! He wants people to think I'm crazy."

I was stunned to see this poised, put-together woman reduced to a puddle of emotion. With her red, puffy face and streaked makeup, she was unrecognizable.

When I heard a noise at the door, I hurried to run interference. Libby Lakes was coming out to the patio holding a drink, but I shepherded her back inside.

"What's going on?" she asked sharply, juggling her ridiculous blue frozen drink.

"Helen is going through a rough patch. So it's better if you… don't stay."

She blinked. "You mean leave?"

I pressed my lips together, then nodded.

"But I'm her friend."

I had to bite my tongue on that one. Just because the woman had insinuated herself into Kyle's Sunday social group didn't mean she was his sister's friend—and I was sure Helen would agree. "This is a family matter," I said firmly. "I'm sorry, but we'd like some privacy."

Her mouth tightened and for a moment, I thought she was going to argue, but suddenly she smiled and set down her drink. "Of course. Tell Kyle I'll check in tomorrow."

We both knew I would do no such thing.

She turned and picked up her bag, then walked in the direction of the front door.

I waited until I heard the door open and close, then returned to the patio. "Libby left," I mouthed to Kyle and he gave me a grateful look.

"Will you stay with her?" he asked. "I'm going to get something from the cabinet to help her calm down."

I nodded, and Helen didn't seem to mind being passed from her brother's chest to mine. Her limp body heaved with wracking sobs. When I put my arm to her back, I was alarmed to feel her bones protruding.

"Try to take deep breaths," I murmured. "Helen, dear... when was the last time you ate?"

"No food," she whimpered. "I have to look good for my husband. No food... only Beltina."

I swallowed hard.

October 9, Monday

I WAS STILL mulling Helen's troubling words the next day when I showed up for my work assignment.

It was Columbus Day and you know what that means in America. No, not studying maps and history and how the accidental discovery of the New World by Christopher Columbus way back in 1492 sort of set this entire hemisphere in motion.

It's a day set aside for mattress sales.

So I'm at MTM Mattress, wearing a snazzy blue MTM vest and a paper nametag, standing by for the stampede... and feeling as though I might fly apart.

When I'd told Portia about the conversations with the women at the weight loss center about harmful side effects of Beltina, and their assertion a psychiatric ward had been set aside in a Georgia hospital dedicated to patients with Beltina-associated mental disorders, she'd discounted them as lies and rumors started by competing drug companies. And she'd reiterated my strict adherence to the confidentiality agreement I'd signed was paramount to Beltina getting back on the market and everything getting back to normal.

Better than normal, actually, since she'd all but guaranteed me a promotion to Sales Manager when she hired me back in December.

But it was difficult to ignore the emotional erosion I'd seen in Helen, and the fury that had erupted between Trish and Julie. And the fact that all of them were taking Beltina.

Then again, all the women could be having regular, run-of-the-mill mid-life crises.

"Here comes the first wave of customers," our supervisor said as he walked by a clump of us employees. "Look sharp."

I wanted to point out the blue vest made that impossible, but kept my mouth shut. Instead, I tidied the stack of flyers I held announcing our Columbus Day specials. We had strict orders to force them into the hands of anyone over the age of six as they milled around the seemingly endless selection of mattresses set up in the showroom on box springs and platforms, ready to be lain and bounced on at will.

I was doing my fair share of blanketing the customers with flyers. "Here you go, ma'am. Here you go. Have a flyer, these are our sales. Here you go—" I looked up, hand outstretched, surprised to see Charlie standing there. "Sir."

He grinned. "You again."

"I'm afraid so."

"Nice vest."

"Please take a flyer, else the vest might be my only compensation for the day."

"In that case, I'll take two."

He looked somewhat handsome in jeans and a black T-shirt and slip-on sneakers. The T-shirt did more for his powerful chest than the white chef's jacket. His dark hair looked freshly trimmed and for the first time, I noticed his unusual eye color—they were gray. The new awareness made me nervous, especially considering our last encounter on the loading dock.

"By the way," I said, "I passed the name of the young girl to a detective working the case. He thinks with an unusual name like Penny, they might have a shot at finding her in the system."

"That's good news—I hope."

"Public sentiment seems to be running in her favor, so I think that bodes well for her." I smiled. "So… are you in the market for a mattress?"

"Yeah—I've been sleeping on a futon, and my back can't take it anymore."

"A futon? What grade are you in?"

He laughed. "I know. It was supposed to be temporary, but like I said, I haven't had time to shop."

"Well, you came to the right place."

He glanced around the palatial showroom. "I can see that, but it's a little overwhelming. Where do I start?"

I mentally reviewed the ten-minute spiel we'd all been given before the doors opened.

"What size do you want?"

"Um, what do you suggest?"

"Will you be sharing it?"

He grinned. "Hopefully."

"Then I'd suggest a king."

He nodded. "King it is."

"What firmness do you want?"

He scratched his temple. "What do you suggest?"

"I like a firm surface myself."

"Sounds good."

"That's the orange section," I said, moving in that direction. He followed me and when we reached the correct row, I pointed. "There you go."

"Do I just pick one?"

"Don't you want to try them out first?"

He pursed his mouth. "Sure." He walked to the first one—a top of the line model—and tested it with his hand, then sat on it. "Feels good."

I crossed my arms. "Unless you're buying it to sit on, you really should lie down."

"Okay." He kicked off his sneakers, then scooted back on the mattress and lay sprawled with his hands behind his head.

The unexpected sight of him in a bed did funny things to my stomach that had nothing to do with the empty cheesecake container I'd sent down the trash chute before Anthony got up. "H-How does it feel?"

"Great," he said. "But then anything would feel great after what I've been sleeping on."

"So, you sleep on your back?"

"Actually, now that you mention it, I'm more of a stomach sleeper."

"Me, too," I blurted, as if it mattered.

He flopped over on his stomach and rested his head on his hands. He groaned. "I could go to sleep right now." He extended his hand. "Come on, tell me what you think."

I shook my head. "Oh, no—I can't. Employees aren't supposed to."

"Oh, come on—I want your opinion on whether it's too firm for a woman."

I swallowed nervously, then sat on the edge of the bed. "It feels nice."

"I'm hoping the woman will be doing more than sitting."

I toed off my shoes and slowly scooted back to stretch out, staying as close to the edge as possible. As soon as I relaxed, I groaned. "Oh... this is... nice."

I suddenly realized how few z's I'd gotten last night. Between the nightmares and everything I had on my mind, sleep had been elusive.

The sound of a light snore reached my ears. I turned my head to see that Charlie had dozed off. I smothered a smile—the man must be exhausted if a few minutes of... lying on a... nice mattress... could...

I smothered a yawn. Maybe I'd close my eyes... just for a few seconds.

October 10, Tuesday

ANTHONY'S EYES BUGGED. "You and Charlie Graham fell asleep together on a mattress?"

I grimaced. "It's not as bad as it sounds."

Anthony narrowed his eyes.

"Okay, it was bad," I admitted, pressing my palms into my eyes. "It was very bad."

"How bad?"

"Spooning bad."

He guffawed, then reached for his phone. "Are there pictures on social media? There have to be."

"The owner of the store had the pics sanitized." Thank goodness—else how would I explain that to Kyle?

"Were you fired?"

"No... but that probably had something to do with the fact that Charlie bought a top-of-the line mattress set."

"So, what's the deal with this guy?" Anthony asked. "Do I have to remind you, Della, that you're engaged... to a gorgeous doctor... who just gave you a rock the size of a golf ball?"

I glared. "No. And there's no 'deal' with Charlie. We're just friends. We cross paths often because Triangle Point is such a small world. That'll change when I go back to work for Traxton."

"Okay, if you say so." He waved his keys. "I'm off to Libby's. Fingers crossed that she's lost some weight."

Yeah—that probably was not going to happen. "On the way home, will you get some toilet tissue please? We're down to one roll."

He frowned. "Della, I said I would."

I blinked. "When?"

"When we had this exact conversation fifteen minutes ago." He angled his head. "Are you okay? You've been so forgetful lately."

I waved it off. "I'm not sleeping well."

"Charlie Graham would beg to differ," he called in a sing-song voice on his way out the door. "Bye."

"Bye," I said, mostly to myself.

I padded to the bathroom to get a Beltina tablet from my supplies closet, but while I stood there, I was overcome with a powerful sense of déjà vu—had I already taken one this morning? I couldn't remember. I pressed one of the orange tablets out of its protective packaging into my hand. Better to take an extra than to forget one, especially since I knew I'd gained a few pounds.

I tossed back the pill and washed it down with a drink of water, then decided it was a good time to call Portia on her cell—I might catch her on her commute into the office.

But no such luck. The phone rang a couple of times, then rolled over to voice mail. At the beep, I tried to force cheer into my voice.

"Hi, Portia—it's Della... Culpepper. I hope you've had a chance to pull those strings you mentioned the last time we talked, because I haven't received my bonus yet." I wet my lips. "I'm starting to feel as if the agreement I signed with Traxton is one-sided. Please call me with an update when you get a chance. Thank you."

I ended the call with a growing sense of unease that bordered on panic when I checked my bank account balance. If I didn't have a resolution soon, I might need to enlist the services of an employment attorney to review the agreement and advise me on my next step.

As long as he or she agreed to work on the contingency of me getting my promised bonus because heaven knew I couldn't pay a retainer.

The phone rang and my hopes rose that it was Portia calling me back. Instead it was the reporter Rainie Stephens again.

I hit "decline."

October 11, Wednesday

WHEN I LEFT THE gym, I checked my voice messages, hoping I'd heard from Portia. She hadn't called, but my brother Donnie had, which always left me with mixed feelings of happiness to hear his voice and dread over hearing what new mess my mother had gotten herself into.

I called him back and he answered on the first ring.

"Hi, Sis. How are you?" I assumed he was at work because I could hear the whirr of a power lug wrench in the background.

"I'm good, Professor." A necessary lie. "How are things there? Any news?" I crossed my fingers.

"Some. A guy stopped in earlier and said Gil Malone was back."

My blood pressure immediately shot up. "He's back in Dewdrop?"

"Not now. He was only in town long enough to buy a vehicle from this guy."

Because I'd totaled the last piece of crap he'd driven. "Did you get the make and model?"

"It's a 2006 blue Ford Escape—that's an SUV."

"Okay. Do you have the license plate number?"

"Of course."

He rattled it off and I jotted it on my arm with a pen. "Okay, thanks. Do you know if he visited Mom when he was in town?"

"I don't think so. She's still sad and crying all the time."

I closed my eyes.

"But she's back working at the diner again, at least a few hours a week."

That was something, at least.

"I have to hang up now," he said.

"Okay, thanks for letting me know, Donnie. This helps."

"Good. Bye, Sis."

I ended the call and a bad taste backed up in my throat. Gil Effing Malone, my mother's latest no-good shack-up boyfriend, owed me twenty-five grand that was supposed to keep Mom from losing her house.

And I planned to get it back either in cash, or in satisfaction.

I walked back to the condo, changed into a pair of sandals with thick wooden heels, found my ice pick, and a bar of hotel soap.

Then I called a ride-share service and punched in the address for Gil Malone's ex-wife's sister's place, where the leech had been hiding out. When we neared the address, I batted my eyelashes and convinced the driver to unwittingly canvas the area with the explanation I needed to leave a gift in my uncle's car. Thankfully a couple of blocks over I spotted the battered blue SUV and matched the license plate.

"Let me out here," I said. "And since there's traffic behind you, why don't you circle the block and I'll be done by the time you come back."

The driver was agreeable. I jumped out and walked to the SUV, head on a pivot. I waited until an older woman walking a little dog passed by, then I removed a sandal, crouched down, and used the wooden heel to drive the ice pick into a tire. I pulled it out quickly to the gratifying hiss of leaking air. After quickly deflating the rest of the tires, I toed my foot back into my sandal, then used the bar of soap to write "25k?" on the windshield.

By the time the driver pulled up, everything was stowed and I was ready to go with a smile.

I hoped Gil Malone got the message: *Don't mess with*

MaeDella Culpepper.

October 12, Thursday

"NO BOOKSIGNING TODAY. We're doing inventory!"

The bookstore manager handed me a stiff burgundy apron and I dutifully tied it on.

I didn't know what that "doing inventory" entailed, but I was pretty sure unless it's gold bars, doing inventory of just about anything is not fun.

I was right again. I was banished to the dusty stockroom where I spent hours climbing up and down a rolling metal ladder logging titles, ISBNs, then counting and recounting books in stacks, books in boxes, and books in bags, separating the damaged ones and marking them accordingly. I got as many papercuts as when I did the gift-wrapping gig, with the bonus of an aching hunchback.

Working in a bookstore is not for wimps.

And at the end of that punishing job, I rounded out my shift performing the most cruel, the most heartbreaking, the most barbaric act I've ever witnessed: stripping books.

I stared at the manager in horrified disbelief. "You want me to do what?"

"Strip off the cover and put it in that pile, then throw the carcass over there."

Yes, he said "carcass," my friend. Apparently, this is what happens when a paperback book doesn't sell—the cover is stripped and returned to the publisher or distributor for a full credit, then the carcass of the book is recycled.

I would've lifted my fist to the sky in outrage if I could've straightened my spine.

Instead I carried out the job with tears brimming in my eyes. Kyle once took me to an "art burning" where a local watercolorist auctioned off her accumulated pieces for charity. She would set a minimum reserve, and if no one bid—you know what comes next, right? Bic lighter, metal garbage can. It was traumatizing, and after the first piece went up in flames, people flung open their wallets so they didn't have to witness it again. I think that's what should happen with books because trust me, no one could bear watching this carnage. I rescued a couple myself, setting them aside to purchase later.

By the end of the day, I had accrued a stack of books to lug to the checkout counter. I realized ruefully I was spending more than I'd make for my day's labor. On a front table, I spotted a copy of Charlie's book, *Fat and Happy*, with a gold "autographed by the author" sticker on the front cover.

I added the book to my stash.

October 13, Friday

ANTHONY WAS SCANNING the titles I'd hauled home. *"How to Negotiate to Get Anything You Want. Win at Life. Why People Lie."* He made a face. "What's with all the starchy stuff?"

"Maybe I'm trying to better myself."

He reached over and tipped up the book I was reading. *"Fat and Happy by Chef Charlie Graham?"* He sent an arching eyebrow my way.

I shrugged guiltily. "I'm getting married—I need to learn to cook."

"Okay, can we just diagram that sentence? You're learning how to cook for your soon-to-be-husband from a guy who has the hots for you?"

"You're making way too much of it. I told you—Charlie and I are just friends."

"I'm the only guy in your life who wants to be just friends with you, Della, and that's because I'm saving myself for someone super special. No offense."

"None taken. And I'm learning how to cook from Charlie's book, not from Charlie."

He sighed. "Just be careful with that one. He seems dangerous."

I laughed. "Charlie wouldn't hurt a fly."

"I mean the other kind of dangerous," he said lightly.

I swallowed, then snapped the book closed and pushed it away.

Anthony stood and picked up his messenger bag. "It's my last day working with Libby. I'm going to miss all of her excess."

"Speaking of which, how's her weight loss going?"

"She's gained almost ten pounds."

A pang of remorse stabbed my chest. No wait—it was only the underwire in my bra.

"You should tell her to do whatever you're doing," I said. "You're looking svelte."

"Meanwhile, I'm hungry all the time," he said, rubbing his stomach. "And I still have a lot more to lose."

I felt for him—I remembered that feeling too well.

"But at least my job doesn't depend on it," Anthony said. "Libby's worried the extra pounds will knock her out of contention for the movie. But if she doesn't get the role, that's good for me because it means she'll come back to Atlanta." Then he winced. "But that won't be good for you, will it?"

Dammit, Anthony was right. What if my strategy where Libby was concerned backfired?

October 14, Saturday

"THAT WAS A GOOD WORKOUT," Charlie said.

We had both showered, I was back in my cleaning woman garb, and walking toward the exit.

"Deena is one of the best instructors," I agreed. "I always feel energized afterward instead of exhausted."

He grinned. "Well, I'm feeling energized because I'm finally getting a good night's sleep on my new mattress."

My face tingled at the memory of waking up next to him on the mattress display at the store.

"Hey, Janitor Lady!"

I recognized the voice of the girl at the counter, and she was obviously talking to me. I turned back. "Yes?"

"Women's john needs toilet paper, a-sap!"

Now my face was tingling for a different reason. "Duty calls," I muttered.

"Hang in there," he said.

I walked back toward the counter, my head bowed and rummaging in my big bag as per usual to avoid being recognized on my way to the supply closet.

"Hey," the girl said.

I glanced up. "Yeah?"

"Don't talk to our members. You're here to clean, not to socialize."

A hot retort leapt to my tongue, but I swallowed it. I couldn't lose this gig, not until I could afford to rejoin as a member myself. So I gave her a curt nod, and kept going. At the supply closet, I pulled down thirty-six jumbo rolls of toilet paper and headed back to the ladies' locker room to work my magic.

Once inside, I politely waited until each stall was vacated before heading into battle. When each dispenser had been refilled and extras stored discreetly, I carried the bag of empties and plastic wrap back through, dodging bouncing bodies along the way. I hadn't seen the young woman who punched herself in several days. But I spotted one of her Zumba buddies at a locker, and decided to ask about her.

"Excuse me. I haven't seen your friend in a while, the pretty one with short braids."

"Fiona?" The girl's face clouded. "She's... ill."

"I'm sorry to hear that. Will she be okay?"

"I don't know. She had a breakdown of some kind. She's in the hospital."

I inhaled sharply. "Oh, that's... terrible."

She nodded. "Her friends, we're all shocked. Fiona's the most driven, most upbeat person we know. She got us all involved in Zumba, kept us all going."

"I'll keep her in my thoughts," I murmured.

"Thanks." She closed her locker door, then strode away.

I tried to reconcile the outgoing woman who'd first asked me about Beltina and the fit woman I'd seen taking an orange tablet at the water fountain with the woman who'd flogged herself in the shower and now, had suffered a meltdown.

My headache was back, and with a vengeance.

October 15, Sunday

KYLE SET DOWN his phone.

"How's Helen?" I asked.

He shook his head. "Not good. Reggie is at his wits' end. He came home for a change of clothes and found her curled up on the floor of their closet."

Their closet was a thirty-foot by forty-foot room with a skylight and heated floors, but still.

"He took her to the emergency room," Kyle continued. "They want to admit her for a psych evaluation."

I nodded. "I think that's best, don't you?"

He sighed. "I suppose. I just can't believe it. Helen has always been the rock of our family. She's the strong one. This behavior is just so out of character for her."

"You don't think she could be doing any kind of drugs, do you?"

"Della, have you *met* Helen? She's a total straight arrow. She doesn't even like taking aspirin."

"And this thing with Reggie and his secretary—you're sure nothing's going on?"

"I believe Reggie. And he said he was going to help the secretary find another job because the strain to his marriage isn't worth it. He loves Helen, is devastated that she's deteriorating right before his eyes."

"Is there any history of mental illness in your family tree?"

He looked at me and frowned. "No, of course not. And if there were any skeletons in my family closet, I would've told you about them before I asked you to marry me."

I swallowed guiltily. Unlike me. *This would be a good time to tell him about yourself, MaeDella. About your less-than-upstanding lineage, and the fact that they will probably always be a financial drain.*

"I'm sorry," Kyle said, then pulled me into his arms. "I didn't mean to be sharp with you. Everything is just so unsettling right now. First my practice, and now Helen."

I pulled back. "But business is picking up, right?"

He nodded. "Some. Libby's helping, and if she gets the part she's auditioning for, it could be good for her and for me... for us."

Dammit.

"And even if it takes a couple of years to rebuild my patient list, we'll be fine because the Traxton stock I bought is doing great, off the charts." He lifted my hand and kissed it. "We owe a lot to Beltina. So smile."

I forced the corners of my mouth upward.

October 16, Monday

"WHEN YOU SAID the tips for working the Cirque du Soleil show were good," I said to Casey, "I didn't know someone was going to leave a baby behind."

She laughed merrily, an all-body shimmie. Casey was beautiful and she dressed flamboyantly to show off her full figure. I envied her moxie a little. We were standing at the counter of Anita Temp Agency with the owner, Joon-woo Park.

"They still haven't located the mother?" Joon-woo asked.

"Not that I know of. We think her name is Penny. I've been going through security footage trying to find a shot of her that can be publicized, but so far, nothing."

The door opened and I was surprised to see Anthony walk in, dressed in a dark green suit and brown shoes—very dapper. "Hi, Della."

"I'm *Mae*," I corrected with pointed eyeball language.

"Oh, right—sorry." Suddenly he caught sight of Casey and I watched as his face transformed to pure awe. "Who are *you*?"

Casey smiled and stuck out her hand. "I'm Casey."

"Hello, Casey." He took her hand and pumped it slowly, still transfixed.

"This is Anthony," I offered. "He's my roommate. But why are you here, roomie?"

Casey rescued her hand, and Anthony pulled out of his reverie long enough to say, "I'm here about a job. I want to work here." He pulled a folder from his messenger bag and handed it to Joon-woo. "Hi. Remember me?"

Joon-woo frowned. "Yes. You accused me of stealing clothes and selling them on eBay."

He winced. "Sorry about that. But Mae thought you couldn't speak English, and you still hired her."

I looked at Joon-woo. "He has a point. And the man can do a

lot of different things."

She was still scowling. "Give a few minutes to read your resume and think about it." She headed to her office and I followed her, leaving the besotted Anthony to fawn over Casey.

"Joon-woo, can I get the key to Elena's former desk?"

She rolled her eyes up to look at me. "Why?"

"I'm trying to find the mate to the earring she lost at my place. It's so small, I'm wondering if it could've fallen into a crevice and we overlooked it."

"You've already broken into her desk at least twice that I know of, and now you want the key?"

I lifted my hands. "I'm turning over a new leaf."

She rummaged in her desk drawer, then handed me the key. "Should I hire your roommate?"

"Yes, please, so he can pay me rent so I can pay my mortgage."

I carried the key to the rear room where the workstations were located. Joon-woo still hadn't reassigned Elena's desk, and I was glad. She'd been gone so long before anyone had noticed, and her death seemed so unnecessary, leaving her desk empty was a small modicum of respect.

I unlocked the doors and drawers, then carefully searched each one with a flashlight and with my hands, looking and feeling for the missing earring. I told myself if I found it and returned the pair to her daughter, maybe I would feel some sense of atonement for the way I'd treated Elena, and the nightmares would stop.

But, I finally conceded after a fruitless forty minutes, the earring would have to be found another day, another place. For now, the nightmares would endure.

October 17, Tuesday

THE STINK AT THE drycleaners just didn't get better, but I amused myself by trying to describe it like fine wine.

The putrid fumes of scorched fiber and flammable chemicals roll through the respiratory system like a fragrant, yet tornadic wind, with notes of battery acid and fusty mold lingering in the lungs until the next toxic whiff.

"More tickets over six months old," the guy running the counter said in a bored voice, handing them back to me. "You know the drill."

He'd been more morose lately, so I had a feeling either his sister-in-law had cut him off, or his wife had gotten hip to his philandering.

I sorted the messy stack of tickets, then perched on my stool and spun through the hanging rack. I was getting better at it, so I ran the machine faster and faster, sending the plastic-covered garments fluttering and flying when they rounded corners.

At the drycleaners, you get your entertainment where you can.

One by one I retrieved the unclaimed items, once again marveling over the range of the clothing and the sheer volume. It wasn't long before I'd filled two rolling racks. I asked Cheater, Cheater, Pumpkin Eater what to do with them and once again he waved me to the closed double doors that connected the front operation to the even less appetizing rear operation.

It was as bad as I remembered. The heat alone was like working in a pressure cooker, let alone the caustic emissions. And the noise was deafening. I rolled the racks inside and was intercepted by the same stoic woman as before—one of the owners, I was told. Mrs. Gladstone.

"More unclaimed clothing," I shouted.

She lifted the paper dust mask that covered her mouth. "Over there," she said, pointing, then returned to her clipboard. She was the only person wearing a mask, and appeared to hold herself as far from the muggy, malodorous operations as possible.

I set the racks in place and when I turned back toward the doors, I caught sight of a familiar face—it was Penny's friend, the dark-haired girl who'd taken the cash I'd offered. She glanced up and I waved. I could tell she recognized me, but she didn't respond.

"Close the door behind you," Mrs. Gladstone bellowed to me.

The girl bent back to her job, and I left. But on the way back to the spinner rack, I pulled out my phone and called Detective Terry.

"You're sure it's her?" he asked.

"Yes, I'm sure. Have you located Penny?"

"Not yet. I hate to keep asking you to watch surveillance, but we need a photo, if only to match it to the girl if we do locate her."

"Okay. Are you going to talk to the friend?"

"I can't get away today, but I'll try to send a uniform so you can point her out. Could be a while, though—we have a hostage situation in midtown that's taking all our resources."

I thanked him and disconnected the call. I understood—finding the mother of the abandoned baby had fallen out of the media and off the priority list.

"Hey," the guy at the counter said, waving his arms. "I need your help up here."

"What time does the shift change in the back?"

He checked his watch. "In about fifteen minutes. Why?"

"What door do the workers leave by?"

"In the back, on the loading dock. Are you going to help me or what?"

"Or what," I said.

I exited the front door and walked all the way around the building until I found a row of vans with the drycleaner's name on them. The doors on the loading dock were closed, which explained the extreme heat inside. A couple of guys stood on the loading dock smoking—drivers, I guessed. They kept checking their watches, so I assumed they were either on break or were waiting for the shift change, like me.

One of them spotted me and got the attention of the other guy, who walked to the end of the dock. "Can I help you?"

"Just waiting for a friend," I said, gesturing to the doors.

"You can't wait here," he said. "We got rules."

I nodded and gave him a friendly wave, then went around the corner to wait, hoping Penny's friend came in my direction when she left.

In a few minutes, a stream of soggy, pungent workers walked by me, some talking amongst themselves, but most of them quietly trudging to their destinations. I scanned for Penny's friend, but it was hard to see every face that went by. When the flow of people ended, I reasoned she could've simply exited in another direction. I backtracked to the front of the building, on alert for her petite figure, but I didn't see her.

The door to the drycleaners burst open. "Hey!" Cheater Boss screamed. "We have customers stacked up in here!"

I sighed. "Coming."

October 18, Wednesday

"I COULD DO THIS EVERY DAY," Anthony declared from his gift-wrapping station at Dorman's. He looked over at me. "You made it sound positively awful."

"Mae is a diva temp," Casey said, curling a ribbon with a pair of scissors.

I scoffed. "That is such a lie."

She lifted a perfect dark brow.

"Okay, maybe it was true in the beginning. But I've changed. I can blend with the little people."

Casey and Anthony exchanged glances.

"What?" I demanded.

They straightened as a customer appeared. Three open windows and of course the guy picked mine.

"Hi," I said, offering a half-smile. Then I squinted. "Hey... Frizzy Man Bun."

He frowned. "Huh?"

"I've seen you in the music shop. I have pet names for all you guys. How's Neck Tats?"

His eyes narrowed. "He's gone." He lifted a shopping bag to the counter. "I need to get this gift-wrapped."

Funny, but he didn't seem like the kind of guy to be buying—I pulled a box from the bag—a six piece set of rubber spatulas. But hey, for all I knew, it could be an art project... or used for making meth... or for spanking.

"Receipt?"

"Huh?" He seemed nervous, kept looking up at the surveillance camera above my head.

"I need to see your receipt to be eligible for free gift-wrapping."

"Oh." He fumbled in his front shirt pocket. "Here you go."

I checked it, and handed it back. "Thanks. Do you happen to know a girl named Penny?"

"I don't think so."

"Petite blonde, pregnant?"

He shook his head. "Don't know her."

"Do you know anything about the baby abandoned in a bathroom a couple of weeks ago?"

"Lady," he said, wiping his forehead, "can I just get the package wrapped?"

"Sure." The guy was sweating like someone in detox. "What kind of paper do you want?"

He sighed. "Whatever is fastest already."

"Okay, I hear you." I picked up the box to unroll the wrapping paper closest to the counter. But when I set the box on the paper, I misjudged and it fell to the floor. "I'm sorry," I said, stooping to pick it up. "Then I held it up for him to inspect. See? It's not damaged."

But when I set the box back on the counter, I heard a clinking noise. I frowned. Rubber spatulas don't clink.

"I'm just going to open the box to make sure I didn't dislodge anything," I said.

He lunged for the box, but I yanked it back. Then he spun and sprinted away.

"What the heck was that all about?" Anthony asked.

I opened the box, reached inside, then held up a diamond tennis bracelet. "Call security. And Pruney Peg. I'll bet this is how the shoplifters have been smuggling so much stuff out of here."

October 19, Thursday

"YOU KEEP THIS UP," Detective Terry said. "And I'm going to have to deputize you."

"How much does it pay?" I asked.

"Not nearly enough." He returned a small notebook to an inside jacket pocket. "You did good. We're going to send notices to every retailer in the metro area warning them about the gift-wrapping scheme."

"Good. Any developments on finding Penny?"

He shook his head. "But I know it's important to you, so I'm putting it back on the top of my pile. Do you have time to go with me to the drycleaners where you say you spotted her friend?"

"Sure. It's right around the corner." I led the way, but was thinking ahead. "How will you handle this? I don't want to get her in trouble. She looks like she needs the job."

"She's not in any trouble. I just want to talk to her."

When we walked in, Cheater Boss squinted. "Are you working today?"

"Not here, thank God. This is a police detective, he needs to talk to one of the employees working in the back room."

The man frowned. "What about?"

"We're trying to locate a friend of hers," Jack said. "I just want to ask her some questions."

"Wait here."

Jack looked around the bleak room. "So you work here, too?"

"Yeah. And this isn't the worst place."

"Damn."

We heard footsteps and saw the counter guy coming toward us with the woman I'd encountered yesterday in the back room.

Jack flashed his badge. "Atlanta PD, ma'am."

"Lela Gladstone," she said with an easy smile. "What's this about?"

I marveled over the difference in her countenance.

"This woman says she saw someone who works here who might be able to give us some information in an ongoing investigation. I'd just like to ask the employee a few questions. She's not in trouble."

Lela Gladstone flicked her gaze over me. "Don't you work here?"

"I'm a temp," I said with a smile.

"What's your name?"

"Um... Mae... Culpepper."

"You were here yesterday, weren't you?"

"The day before. I brought a couple of racks of unclaimed clothing to the back. That's when I saw the young woman who knows the girl the police are looking for."

"Yes, I remember now. Are you talking about the woman with dark hair? You waved to her, I believe?"

"That's right."

"She doesn't work here anymore. As it turns out, she's underage and she lied about it on the application. I had to let her go—for safety's sake."

"What was her name?" Jack asked, withdrawing his notebook.

The woman sighed. "I don't know. She lied about that too, gave a fake social security number."

"Can I see that application?"

"I'm sorry, Detective, but I threw it away. The information on it was bogus, so I didn't see a reason for keeping it."

He nodded and stored his notebook. "Okay. Thanks, ma'am. If she comes around again, I'd appreciate it if you'd give the police a call."

"I will."

"Another dead end," I said when we walked back outside.

"We're not giving up. Got time to watch more surveillance footage?"

"Sure."

"I'll go with you." We turned in the direction of the security office, also nearby. I had to practically jog to keep up with his long stride.

"By the way," he said, "did you ever find your mother's boyfriend?"

"Let's just say I know where he is."

"Don't say anymore."

"Okay." I wet my lips. "Detective, do you know a reporter named Rainie Stephens?"

"Rainie? Yeah, sure. How do you know her?"

"I don't. But she's been calling me about... something, and I'm wondering if I can trust her."

"I would say yes. Rainie's a good one. Does this 'something' have anything to do with one of the cases you're involved in?"

"Uh... no. It's another... thing... entirely."

He sighed. "Are you sure you don't know Carlotta?"

I blinked. "Carlotta, the sales associate at Neiman Marcus?"

He looked incredulous. "Yeah."

"And who works for the morgue?"

"That's right. Are you a friend of hers?"

"No, we've just met in passing. But she gave me some great tips on disguises."

The detective pinched the bridge of his nose. "Why am I not surprised?"

"How do you know her?"

"It's a long story," he said, opening the door to the security office.

"With a happy ending?"

"I don't know yet." He nodded for me to go in ahead of him. "Let's concentrate on finding Penny."

October 20, Friday

"HELLO," I said, walking up to a group of six teens standing around a music listening kiosk, sharing headphones.

They all looked at me as if I were an alien. An old alien.

"What do you want?" a surly dark-haired boy asked. He was a good-looking kid, but he had a too-wise edge about him.

"Information."

They all glazed over and dismissed me, turning back to their conversations.

"Did I mention I pay for information?"

They all turned back.

"How much?" the surly kid asked.

"That depends on how much information you give me."

"About what?" a girl asked.

"About a girl named Penny who was pregnant."

A few of them exchanged glances, so I knew they knew something.

"Who wants to know?" another boy asked.

"Ah, hi, Pierced Face," I said, using my pet name for the kid. "Haven't seen you in here for a while."

He frowned. "Are you crazy?"

"Maybe," I conceded. "So, the police would like to know where Penny is."

They all scoffed and disengaged again.

"But since I'm not the police, I'd like to find her first, and help her."

The girl looked suspicious. "Help her how?"

"Whatever she needs. First we need to make sure she doesn't have any medical issues, and that she's safe."

"Nobody's safe," the dark-haired kid said. "Everyone has to

fend for himself."

"Or herself," the girl said.

"Okay, that's fair," I agreed. "But Penny just had a baby, so she needs extra help." I looked all around their faces, then pulled out a stack of ten dollar bills and held up one. "Who knows where she is? Or how to reach her?"

They were fixated on the ten, and so was I—I really needed it to pay bills. Reluctantly, I held up a second ten. "Anybody? Nobody wants cash?"

"We don't know where Penny is," the girl blurted. "We've been looking for her, too."

"How about her friend, the dark-haired girl?"

"Amy?" the dark-haired boy asked. "She's gone, too."

"What do you mean, gone?"

He shrugged. "Moved on, I guess. Like Nick and Trace."

"And Mika and Renni."

"They told us they were offered good jobs, and they were going away."

I frowned. "What kind of jobs?"

"It was one of those magazine subscription jobs, you know where you go to a certain area and go door to door?"

Ugh. Those were usually pretty scammy operations... but it was a better alternative to imagining Penny lying in a ditch somewhere.

I sighed. "Okay, here's a ten for each of you." There went my grocery money for the week. "If you get any information about Penny, promise me you'll come in here and walk over to that guy and tell him... and he'll tell me."

They all turned to look at Blowz, who was trying to balance a pencil on his nose.

"That guy's a loser," one the kids said.

I sighed. "I know. But he's a nice loser and he lets you kids hang out in here."

"Yeah," the girl said to the guys. "And he lets us use the bathroom."

They all nodded, relenting.

"So we have a deal?" I made eye contact with each one until they nodded or blinked or grunted.

It wasn't exactly promising.

October 21, Saturday

I STOOD AND STARED at the entrance to my new job assignment: Graham's Eatery.

"This won't be awkward at all," I muttered.

I took a deep breath and walked inside. The place was relatively quiet. A waiter clearing a table smiled. "We're open, but we're closing in one hour for a private party."

I nodded. "I'm supposed to work the party."

"Okay. Go through those doors and ask for Megan."

I followed his directions and walked into a room where a half dozen other women had gathered around a tall, statuesque redhead.

Charlie's ex-girlfriend Megan.

The women exited through another door behind her. She turned and waved me forward. "You're late."

"I'm sorry. I only just received the assignment."

She glanced over my baggy work "uniform." "It's hard to tell what size you wear, but this should fit you." She handed me a hanging dress bag. "You need to get changed into your outfit right away."

I blinked. "Outfit?"

"It's an Octoberfest party." She unzipped the bag. "It's a traditional Bavarian dirndl dress."

"With a corset," I said through my frozen smile.

"Show as much cleavage as makes you comfortable. I'm sure the boys won't object."

"Boys?"

"I'm throwing a party for the owner. His brothers will be here and all his guy friends."

"Oh." I did remember reading something in Charlie's book about his German heritage.

"And lots of beer, of course. That's why we need servers."

"I should warn you, I don't have much experience."

She leaned in. "Then show more cleavage."

I gave her a tight smile, then walked through the door the other women had gone through and followed the noise to the women's bathroom. The other servers seemed bubbly and fun, and they were all helpful to each other and to me as we changed into our "outfits."

In case you're not familiar with the traditional Bavarian dirndl dress and how it gets translated to waitressing, think "Heidi makes a porno."

And yes, we all had wigs with blond braids.

For the next hour the head waiter and the bartender schooled us on how to order and serve drinks, gave us a tutoring session on the beer list and the custom menu, and told us, yes, we could accept tips. The official duration of the party was four hours, but we were told it could stretch to six.

As we made our way out to the main seating area and bar, my nerves were jumping. We were assigned specific tables and given trays, notepads, and pens. It was clear everyone there had more experience than I did. And more cleavage. I felt so exposed, I decided to leave my big glasses on, which contributed even more to the game of "Which waitress is different from all the others?"

My feet were already hurting; in hindsight, I should've worn different shoes. And different underwear considering how much of my bra showed through the low-cut blouse. Because my mother was a waitress her entire life, had bounced from one diner to the next greasy spoon and back, I had fastidiously avoided waitressing when I was young.

But I took a deep breath and rallied my resources. How hard could it be? After all, my mother could do it.

Famous last words, I realized quickly enough. The crowd arrived seemingly all at once—about thirty guys who all appeared acquainted considering the decibels of the laughter and raucous storytelling. I saw Charlie arrive—Megan met him at the door. He kissed her on the cheek, but I noticed her movement at the last second to offer her lips instead, and the way she clung to his arm.

Perhaps Charlie believed they weren't getting back together. But Megan seemed to be of a different mindset.

He stayed at the door for a while, greeting guests. It was clear when his brothers arrived—the bearhugs were boisterous and the affection was genuine. They all wore sweaters with the same Bavarian crest, so I assumed it was particular to his family.

It was so different from my "family" experience, it was jarring.

I was envious.

But I didn't have time to wax nostalgic because the party went from neutral to wide open in a matter of minutes. I took orders and moved as fast as I could to serve my tables, but it was a steep learning curve. And throughout, I was waiting for the moment Charlie recognized me.

It was from across the room. Megan stood next to him, clasping his arm. They appeared to be surveying the party like any good host and hostess—a couple. I saw him look at her fondly many times and I could tell he was appreciative of her efforts. At some point, she gestured to the servers, and I saw her single me out. She winced and shrugged. My face burned when I realized she was apologizing for me.

I caught his gaze and saw his expression and body language change. He appeared to make excuses to the people nearby, then made a beeline for me. I was carrying a tray of three enormous beers back to a table when he intercepted me.

"What are you doing here?"

"I'm working," I said cheerfully.

"Della, I don't want you serving my friends."

I pulled back. "I know I'm not good at this, so if I'm embarrassing you—"

"You're not embarrassing me. I just don't...."

I waited. "What?"

"I don't like it," he finished, wiping his hand over his mouth.

"It's fine," I assured him. "And besides, I can use the money."

His mouth tightened, then he relented. "But if anyone gets out of line, tell me."

"Charlie, go enjoy your party." I walked around him and delivered the heavy tray, offering up a smile to the men. Then I took more orders and did it all over again.

And again. For six and a half hours. I was too busy to keep tabs on Charlie, but our gazes locked a few times over the course of the evening. He seemed to be having a great time, and Megan was always close by.

When I left the restaurant, my feet hurt so bad, I took off my shoes and carried them as I walked toward my building. I ached all over, and I was exhausted from swatting away flirtatious hands and fending off innuendoes. I'd made good tips, but God

Almighty, it was hard-earned.

A horn sounded from the sidewalk. I looked up to see Charlie and Megan in the sexy red convertible. "Get in, we'll give you a ride. We can squeeze together for a few blocks."

But Megan's expression was less welcoming, and I didn't want to intrude. "Thanks, but I'd rather walk. And I need to make a phone call."

"Okay," he said, sounding disappointed. He waved, then they sped away.

I pulled out my phone and even though it was late, punched through a call.

"Hello," a sleepy voice sounded.

"Hi, Mom, it's MaeDella."

"MaeDella, is everything okay? Are you alright?"

"I'm fine, Mom." I fought back sudden emotion. My mother's life hadn't been easy, and I'd judged her harshly. I was ashamed. "I was just thinking about you... and I wanted to hear your voice. I'm sorry it's late."

"It's okay," she said. "I haven't been sleeping so well lately anyway."

"I have some good news."

"What?"

"I'm engaged."

Silence rang over the line and I held my breath, unsure what to expect from her. Resentment? Censure? Bitterness?

"To that nice doctor you said you've been dating for a while?"

I exhaled. "That's right..."

October 22, Sunday

KYLE SET DOWN his phone.

"How is Helen?" I asked.

"Better," he said, sounding relieved. "The doctors have her on some sort of detox program, and she seems to be improving."

I frowned. "Detox? From what, exactly?"

"Everything, I think, since they're not sure what's wrong. Reggie said something about an accumulation of heavy metals in the brain."

"That sounds dangerous."

He nodded. "When I get to LA tomorrow, I'm going to call her doctors and find out more. Sometimes they're more forthcoming with another physician."

"Good idea." Then I blinked. "Wait—did you say you're going to LA tomorrow?"

He gave a little laugh. "Yes. I told you—Libby asked me to come out and give her some treatments leading up to the audition."

I squinted. "You did?"

"Yes." He angled his head. "Are you okay?"

I nodded. "I've been a little forgetful lately."

"Entire conversations?"

"I... suppose so. When did we talk about this?"

"Last Tuesday, and again Thursday after I made my travel arrangements."

I rubbed my temple. I'd forgotten two conversations?

"Della, should I be worried about you? This thing with Helen could be environmental, you know. And the two of you have spent a lot of time together the last couple of years." He lifted his hands and gestured vaguely. "Hell, it could be something in my house."

Panic licked at me. I didn't want to give voice to my dark thoughts and suspicions, not yet. If I did, so many things would be destroyed—my career, the company, jobs, investments, research... all on conjecture. But if I waited and Helen's doctors proved her problem was something other than the Beltina samples I'd given her, then I could relax.

I decided it was worth waiting.

October 23, Monday

"YOU LOOK STRESSED."

I looked up from my desk at ATA to see Joon-woo standing there, and sighed. "I am. I signed an agreement with my former company back in July, and now I'm having second thoughts."

"Have you consulted an attorney?"

I gave a little laugh. "No. Because I can't afford one."

She shrugged. "Maybe I can help."

"Oh, really? Do you know an attorney who's willing to work

for free?"

"Me."

My eyes bugged. "You? You're an attorney?"

She nodded. "Emory Law. When I graduated, I specialized in employment law. That's why I became interested in opening the temp business. So if you want me to, I'm happy to take a look at the agreement."

I closed the file folder I'd been reading and handed it to her, limp with relief.

October 24, Tuesday

"ARE YOU SURE ABOUT THIS?"

Anthony stood behind my chair in the bathroom, holding up a bottle of hair dye. He wore a cucumber mask on his face, and his favorite ruffled apron.

I nodded. "I've been blond long enough. I'm feeling the need for a change."

He snorted. "That's such bullshit. Just admit your roots are so grown out, you might as well go darker, and it'll be cheaper to maintain."

I sighed. "That, too."

"Okay, so here we go with Creamy Ash number twelve."

I leaned my head back in the sink and he applied the thick goo, massaging it through with gloved hands, before wrapping a plastic turban over my hair and sitting me up.

"We'll check it after forty-five minutes," he said. "You know who has beautiful hair?"

"Casey?"

"Casey." He sighed. "Isn't she just the most perfect woman?"

I smiled. "She's terrific, alright."

He squealed. "I'm just going to say it. I'm totally head over heels in love with her, and I don't know what I'll do if she doesn't come to feel the same way about me."

I squinted. "When you say 'in love with her,' what do you mean exactly?"

He frowned, cracking the green mask. "What do you mean, what do I mean? In love, as in can't live without her."

I tried another tack. "So are we talking a long-term platonic relationship?"

Another frown, more cracking. "Platonic? No! I can't wait to get in her pants."

I pressed my lips together, not sure where to go next.

He crossed his arms. "Whatever you're thinking, just come out and say it."

"Okay." I chose my words carefully. "How do you think Casey is going to feel about the fact that you're..."

"Fat? Cause I'm losing this weight."

"No."

"Short? I'm well aware that she's taller than I am."

"No."

"Jewish?"

"I didn't know you were Jewish."

"Jewish-light, I'd say. I've strayed from my heritage, but that will probably change when I have a family."

I gave a dismissive wave. "None of those things matter anyway. Anthony, how do you think Casey is going to feel about the fact that you're... gay?"

His mouth gaped. "Gay? I'm not gay! What in the world ever made you think that?"

I lifted a hand to his cucumber-masked, ruffled apron reflection. "All of... that."

His mouth tightened like a little butthole. "I don't even know what to say. I can't believe you. How can we have been friends all this time and you be so wrong about me?"

I pursed my mouth. "I'm sorry. You're right—I jumped to a conclusion because you went to art school and you like decorating and shopping and fashionable clothes and pop culture... and I've never seen you with a woman."

"Okay, okay, I get what you're saying. If you can make that mistake about me, Casey might, too. So I need to butch it up a little if I'm going to win her over."

I bit into my lip.

"Butch it up a lot?" he asked.

I nodded.

October 25, Wednesday

TODAY WAS the first day I'd spent as an attendant in the retail parking garage since I'd found Elena in her car the last day of August. I suspected Joon-Woo had been handing off those assignments to other people to spare me, but it was time for me to face my fears.

It was jarring, but not as bad as I thought it would be. For one thing, the garage was much cooler now, so the stifling feeling of being suffocated was gone.

I found the job to be much the same—still boring and unvaried. I did walk down to the spot where I'd found Elena's car, under the huge fan, which had since been quieted. The space was occupied by a beautiful Audi and I wondered if it would bother the owner to know a dead woman had once been parked in the same spot for days.

I walked all around the spot and into nearby corners on the slim chance the mate to the silver earring had fallen out of the car and had been blown or kicked aside. It was a farfetched idea, but it gave me something useful to do. I didn't find it, though.

While I was walking back to the attendant's booth, I happened to glance up and see a security camera tucked into the concrete eaves.

And it gave me an idea.

After I finished the shift, I walked across the park to the Triangle Point security office and knocked on the door frame.

Evan glanced up from his computer. "Oh, hi, Ms. Culpepper. Do you want to go through some more surveillance footage?"

"Do you have time?"

"Sure. Come on in and have a seat."

He made room for me in front of the monitor and I settled into the chair.

"Do you want to pick up where we left off?"

"I don't think so. Actually, there's another time and place I'd like to search."

"Okay."

"The retail parking garage, the last week of August."

He frowned. "Back that far?"

"Can you find it?"

"Sure. Are we still looking for the little pregnant lady?"

"Not really… but it's just as important." I turned pleading eyes toward him.

He shrugged. "Okay."

October 26, Thursday

WE HADN'T located the footage I was looking for—the point when Elena's car had been parked in the ill-fated spot. The police were convinced she'd been living in her car, that she had parked there alone and perished alone, case closed. So of course they wouldn't bother with looking through hours of surveillance tapes.

But I wanted the peace of mind. I wanted the nightmares to stop.

So I would keep looking as long as Evan indulged me.

It was a busier day than usual in the parking attendant booth. Some of the pay stations had malfunctioned, so more people had to come through my lane and pay manually, and they were all ticked off. I put in earbuds and listened to music so I was only subjected to contorted faces and the occasional lip-read expletive. Mostly I just smiled and nodded and moved people through. I still wore my frumpy disguise in case someone came through who knew me, but that hadn't happened since Sabrina had torn through in a rage, and Charlie and Megan had driven by.

Normally, I did little more than glance up when cars came by, just to stay focused on the driver. But mid-afternoon a vehicle came through the pay lane that brought my head around. My body recognized it before my mind fully processed the implication.

A battered blue Ford Escape SUV. I turned my head to see the driver—Gil Goddamn Malone. He was slung low in his seat, bobbing his stupid head to some redneck song on the radio. But when he glanced up, he instantly recognized me. "MaeDella?"

I dove out of the booth into the open window to get my hands around his scrawny neck. "You lying, cheating piece of shit, where's my money?"

He was screaming like a little girl, but managed to push me away and gun his engine. I fell back into the booth and by the time

I scrambled to my feet, his car was fishtailing up the ramp and out of sight.

I was happy to put some scare in him, but dammit, Gil Malone was one person I didn't particularly want to know about the dive I'd taken in my career.

October 27, Friday

"WAIT—CAN YOU rewind the tape?"

"Sure," Evan said, ever patient.

My heartrate picked up. "I think this might be what we're looking for."

I sat forward in the chair, focusing hard on the computer monitor. The footage was black and white, but decently clear. Around the corner came Elena's Toyota.

"Can you slow it down? I'm trying to see the driver's face." I wanted to see myself if Elena had driven the car and parked it there, or if someone else had.

"Here's half-speed."

While the frames clicked through and the car moved forward, there was one spot where the driver's face was clear. I held my breath. As the car passed the camera, the driver looked right into the lens.

It was Elena.

I exhaled slowly and sat back in the chair, relieved she hadn't met a violent end, but shot through with sadness that her death probably was preventable if anyone had given a damn.

If *I* had given a damn.

"Is that what you needed to see, ma'am?"

I nodded.

"I'm sorry—it wasn't what you expected?"

"Actually, it was. Thank you, Evan, for your time and patience."

"Happy to help ma'am. Did you know that lady?"

"Not well, but yes."

I pushed to my feet, still heavy with the knowledge that Elena had been alive when she'd parked there, and then... not. She'd asphyxiated in the heat, suffocated in the car where she might have been living.

"Let me know if you need to see anything else," the man said with a smile. "It helps to pass the time."

"Okay, thanks again—" Something on the monitor caught my eye. I came back. "I'm sorry, Evan, could you rewind this piece a few seconds, and play it on half-speed?"

"Sure thing. Here you go."

I watched, my pulse pounding in my ears wondering if I'd seen what I thought I'd seen.

Then there it was: A figure climbed out of the passenger side of Elena's parked car, closed the door, wiped the door handle, then strode away, as cool as you please.

I gasped.

"Is that important?" Evan asked.

I nodded, unable to find my voice.

October 28, Saturday

IT WAS DIFFICULT TO concentrate the next day. The footage of the person emerging from Elena's car had been turned over to Detective Terry, and Elena's case officially reopened.

But bills had to be paid, at least until Joon-woo got the letter written to Traxton that would hopefully force them to cough up my bonus.

Still, as far as assignments went, working at a party store the weekend before Halloween was a decent gig.

Since we had to dress in costume, I'd appropriated the Heidi porno outfit from the Octoberfest party we'd been allowed to keep, but made it PG-13 with the addition of a T-shirt under the peep-show blouse. And generally had an enjoyable day of helping people pick out costumes. The kids were the most fun, of course, but plenty of adults came in, too.

Although I wasn't expecting to see Charlie Graham walk through the door... with Megan at his side. They made a striking couple, I conceded, and seemed to move in the kind of choreographed comfort couples that have been together for years tend to.

I wondered if Kyle and I moved like that, and suspected not.

They walked to the customer service counter, which typically meant they'd ordered costumes to pick up. I was contemplating saying hello when Charlie turned his head and saw me. He lifted his hand, then waved me over. The short walk gave me time to conjure up a smile.

"Hi, there," he said. "Megan, you remember Della."

She squinted. "I thought your name was Mae?"

"I go by both names," I said easily.

"I see you kept your costume," Megan said.

"Seemed a shame for it to go to waste. Are you two picking up costumes?"

"Yeah. I'm glad we ran into you. We're having a costume party at the restaurant Halloween night. Come and bring some friends."

I noticed he'd used the word "we." Were they a couple now? "Okay. Thanks for the invitation."

Two costume boxes appeared on the counter. "What are you two going as?"

"It's not—" Charlie began.

"Romeo and Juliet," Megan said.

"Oh. Nice." And impossibly romantic.

Charlie gave me a little smile. Megan beamed.

He picked up the boxes. "I hope to see you at the party."

I watched them dance away.

October 29, Sunday

"HOW'S THE WEATHER?" I asked.

"Perfect," Kyle said. "And Libby's place is unbelievable."

"Oh? You're at her house?"

"Just during the days. She's introducing me to all her friends. I go back to the hotel at night, of course."

Why did he feel as if he had to add that tidbit? "Of course. How is Helen?"

"She's getting better every day, thank goodness."

"Do the doctors know yet what caused her problems?"

"It keeps coming back to the metals accumulated in her brain. They're analyzing hair samples now to find out when she was first exposed."

"How accurate are those tests?"

"Very. They think they can pinpoint the time within a few days of when she started being poisoned."

"Poisoned?"

"In a clinical sense, of course, but yes—poisoned."

"When will they know?"

"Hopefully in a week or so." A scream of laughter sounded in the background. "Oh, sweetheart, I need to go. I'll call you later... or tomorrow."

"O—" But he'd already ended the call.

October 30, Monday

MY PHONE RANG and as usual, I picked it up to check the screen, hoping it was Portia. Instead, it was Rainie Stephens calling again. I toyed with blocking her number, but in a burst of frustration, I connected the call.

"Please stop this," I said.

"I'm sorry to bother you, Ms. Culpepper, but I ran into Jack Terry yesterday and he mentioned a conversation the two of you'd had about... trust?"

"It wasn't an invitation for you to call me, Ms. Stephens."

"Call me Rainie. And I sense you wouldn't have brought it up to Jack unless you were conflicted about telling me something important."

I pressed my lips together and massaged at the needling pain in my temple. Could I share my suspicions about Beltina? Should I? If I did, there was no going back.

"Look, Ms. Culpepper, I can appreciate the sensitive position you're in. But there might be another way we can help each other."

I frowned. "What do you mean?"

"I suspect you have some sort of non-disclosure agreement hanging over your head. So what if you don't actually share information with me, but instead, you point me to someone who might not be operating under the same constraints."

"I don't know who that would be."

"Think for a moment. Someone who's associated with Traxton, but perhaps isn't an employee of Traxton."

"I don't—" I stopped when someone's face popped into my head.

"You thought of someone, didn't you?"

Jan, my former trainer. Looking back on our conversations, I think she suspected something was wrong with Beltina, was trying to warn me.

"The person won't know you gave me their name," Rainie said. "I protect my sources."

I felt as if I might explode from the pressure of the information I was sitting on, and I desperately needed some relief.

I puffed out my cheeks in a cleansing exhale. "Do you have a pen?"

October 31, Tuesday

"THIS IS FANTASTIC!" Anthony said, of the happy, dancing, costumed crowd at Graham's Eatery. He was dressed as Elton John, complete with heart-shaped rhinestone glasses.

Apparently, he hadn't started the "butching up" program yet.

Casey grinned and nodded. "Thanks for inviting us."

She was dressed as Marilyn Monroe, and she was glorious in her white filmy dress and 60s hair. Anthony couldn't take his eyes off her.

"Are you Heidi?" Anthony asked.

"Yes," I said, holding up my stuffed goat. I was getting a lot of mileage out the Octoberfest costume.

Across the room, I spotted Charlie and Megan. They were resplendent in their period costumes, and reigned over the room as the most beautiful couple. He waved and I went over to say hello.

"Great crowd!" I shouted over the melee.

"Thanks!" Charlie said. "Glad you could come."

"You must love that costume," Megan remarked.

"Not everyone can be Juliet," I said brightly. "You two make an impressive looking couple."

"I agree," Megan said.

I angled my head. "But didn't they both die in the end?"

Charlie laughed, but Megan wasn't amused. "I'm going to get a drink, darling."

"Okay," Charlie said agreeably. "I'll wait here with Della."

When she walked away, I said, "I didn't mean to make her angry."

"Don't worry about it. She's in a sensitive place." He surveyed my costume. "Nice goat."

I surveyed his. "Nice tights."

He laughed again, something he did easily, I realized.

"Did you bring Susan and Sabrina?" he asked, glancing around.

"No. I decided to bring my other friends, Anthony and Casey, over there—Elton and Marilyn."

I was glad they had come and were having fun, Anthony in particular. He was dancing spasmodically, bumping into people.

Then I realized something was wrong—he wasn't dancing. Anthony careened forward, then backward, then dropped to the floor.

I grabbed Charlie's hand. "Call 9-1-1!"

By the time I reached Anthony, Casey was kneeling over him. The crowd moved back to give him room and a few seconds later, the music stopped and the lights came up.

Anthony was deathly pale, and lifeless. I choked back tears, trying to stay calm.

"I don't know what happened," Casey cried.

"I saw him fall," I said. "It was sudden. An ambulance is on the way."

"Is he breathing?" she asked.

I watched his chest. "I think so." But I wasn't sure.

The sound of a siren was music to my ears. Two paramedics—one male, one female—rushed in and we stepped back to give them space.

"What happened?" the male paramedic asked.

"He was dancing and just fell to the floor," I supplied.

"Is he taking any medication?"

"I don't know… I don't think so." I put a hand to my temple. "Wait—we were talking about insurance once and he said he didn't take any daily medications."

"What about tonight?" While the female paramedic took

Anthony's vitals, the male paramedic was patting him down. "Be honest—any recreational drugs?"

"No," I insisted. "And Anthony wouldn't anyway," I added to Casey. She was crying. I pressed my fist to my mouth, terrified he hadn't yet opened his eyes.

"Wait, what's this?"

The paramedic was pulling something out of Anthony's pocket—a pill.

An orange-colored pill.

My knees grew weak, and I swayed. Charlie was next to me, steadying me. "Easy. I've got you."

"What is this?" the paramedic asked his partner. She shook her head.

He held up the tablet. "Does anyone know what this is?"

I exhaled. "I do. It's called Beltina."

NOVEMBER

November 1, Wednesday

I WAS LEAVING the gym having successfully scurried past the girl at the counter in my cleaning woman garb without being recognized when I heard Charlie Graham's voice behind me.

"Hey, Della—wait up."

It wasn't that I didn't want to talk to him, but I was in a hurry, had skipped my own workout so I could get to the hospital. And I really didn't feel like talking, had been in a state of near-tears since the previous evening.

"Hey," he said, jogging up next to me. "Are you ignoring me?"

I glanced over my shoulder to see the girl at the counter eyeing us, then kept walking. "Sort of. I was told not to fraternize with members."

He made a face. "Screw that."

"I know, but I need this gig. And on my temp jobs, I go by 'Mae.' You're going to get me in trouble."

He winced. "Sorry."

"Let's just get out of here."

When we reached the sidewalk, I slowed my pace. Charlie wore dark jeans and a plaid shirt, and smelled of some earthy scented soap. I was dressed for a late-night comedy skit and reeked of toilet water—and not the bottled kind my grandmother used.

"You look tired," he offered.

"Thanks for the confirmation. I was at Piedmont hospital all night." Dressed as Heidi, braids and all. Casey, aka Marilyn Monroe, had clambered with me alongside Anthony, a pale and listless Elton John on a rolling gurney. Halloween night at the E.R. was an interesting place.

"How's your friend Anthony doing?"

Charlie had a vested interest, considering Anthony had collapsed at a costume party at his restaurant. "He's conscious. And stable, last I heard. I'm on my way back there now."

"Can I give you a ride?"

I remembered him steadying me the night before when my legs had threatened to give way. I appreciated the support, but I didn't want to get used to it... not from this man. "That's okay. I'll take the train."

"You can take the train back. Let me drop you off before I go to the restaurant. It'll save you some time... and it'll make me feel better."

To my mortification, tears welled in my eyes at the unexpected gesture. My fiancé Kyle was still in Los Angeles and I was feeling very alone in the wake of Anthony's medical crisis. "That would be... nice."

"Hey, hey," Charlie murmured, reaching over to squeeze my hand. "Everything will be okay."

I nodded, then sniffed and pulled my hand away to wipe at my eyes. "Sorry... I'm just..."

"I get it."

Thankfully he didn't push me for conversation the rest of the short walk back to the condo building where we both lived, but I felt his gaze on me, as if he was afraid I might have a meltdown on the spot. I was afraid of the same thing.

When we reached the condo building, I asked, "Can you give me a few minutes to change clothes?"

"Sure. I'll bring the van around. Come down when you're ready."

I hurried into the building and gave myself a mental shake while I waited for the elevator. I had too much on my plate to dissolve into tears like some damsel in distress. In addition to Anthony's collapse at the Halloween party, I was still reeling over discovering the security footage showing a man climbing out of Elena Padilla's parked car, and wiping the handle clean before he walked away.

And although less dire, my own dismal employment and financial situation had to be dealt with sooner rather than later. And then there were the secrets I was keeping from Kyle.

I touched my temple. No wonder my headache was back.

But since none of those issues could be solved at the moment, I tried to push them away when I walked inside my condo. I quickly disrobed, took a one-minute shower, then changed into jeans and a long-sleeve blouse. To add insult to injury, I could barely button my pants, and had to lie down on the unmade bed to get them zipped. My late night cheesecake trysts were catching up with me. Yet one more thing that wasn't going to get better soon because for the first time since I could remember, I'd skipped my morning dose of Beltina, on purpose.

The image of the paramedic pulling the orange tablet out of Anthony's pocket was seared into my brain. When had he started taking it?

I untied the bandanna that helped to disguise my appearance when I worked temp jobs, then leaned over at the waist to brush and fluff my flattened hair. I was still getting used to the darker shade of blond that would require less maintenance. I hoped Kyle wouldn't mind—he'd only known me as a platinum blonde.

But as soon as my coffers were restored, I could go back to being high-maintenance me.

I didn't have time to apply full-face makeup, but I ran a washcloth over my eyebrows I'd darkened and reshaped with an eye pencil as part of my disguise—Carlotta, the sales associate at Neiman's, had taught me that trick—then brushed on powder blush and grabbed a stick of lip gloss to smooth on in the elevator. I wasn't primping for Charlie. He was, after all, one of the few people who knew me in my dreadful disguise.

So why did it give me a little flush of pleasure when I swung up into his van and he gave me an approving smile?

"Your hair is darker," he said.

I buckled my seatbelt. "That's right."

"It suits you."

"Thanks," I murmured. "I'm sorry about your party last night.

I know Anthony would say the same if he could." Charlie had been an impressive Romeo next to his "friend" Megan's radiant Juliet.

"That's the last thing either of you should be worried about." Charlie pulled onto the street that led to Peachtree, which led to Piedmont Hospital. "How do you know Anthony?"

"He's my roommate, actually. He was my personal assistant when I worked for Traxton."

"So when you lost your job, he did, too."

"Right. We decided to combine resources." I swallowed a lump of emotion. "He's such a good guy."

"Do the doctors know what happened?"

"Not really. They're calling it a 'neurological incident.'"

"What does that mean?"

"Kyle says it can be anything from passing out to a stroke."

"But you said he's conscious?"

"And responsive, as of this morning when I left. Hopefully we'll get more answers today."

"He's young, so that has to be in his favor."

I nodded, then pressed my lips together.

Charlie frowned. "Is there something you're not telling me?"

"Maybe."

His lifted dark eyebrows and waited.

I sighed. "It could be nothing."

"Or?"

"Or... it could be something." I bit into my lip. "Can you keep a confidence?"

He made the turn onto Peachtree Street to travel the last mile or so. "You mean like you losing your job and working at the temp agency?"

The man had a point. I wet my lips. "The drug I used to sell was a prescription weight-loss medication called Beltina."

"Never heard of it." Then he smiled, patting his stomach. "But then I've never been the type to watch my weight, if you couldn't tell."

I frowned. "Are you fishing for a compliment, or an insult?"

"Compliments only, please."

I swept my glance over his sturdy frame, but the image of him naked in the men's locker room overrode the clothed version.

"You're... not repulsive."

Charlie grinned. "See? You used to hate me. We've made progress."

"*Anyway*, since I stopped working for Traxton, I've heard rumors that Beltina might have some unreported side effects. And turns out, Anthony was taking it."

"And you think the drug might have something to do with his collapse?"

"Like I said, it could be nothing."

"But you told his doctors, right?"

"They know he's taking it. I told one of the paramedics who tended to him."

"But you told them about the side effects?"

"It's only rumor."

He frowned. "Don't you think you should raise an alarm?"

"I don't have any proof. Besides, I signed a non-disclosure agreement with Traxton."

"And if you blow it, they'll never hire you back."

I nodded.

"So how many other people are taking this drug? Thousands?"

"More like millions."

He emitted a low whistle, then flipped on his signal to turn into the hospital entrance.

"I don't know what to do," I murmured.

He was quiet as he steered the van into a fifteen-minute parking spot, then put the vehicle in park. "Yes, you do, Della. You just don't want to do it."

I turned my head. "It's not that simple."

"You could do it anonymously."

"Not really. The FDA has a protocol for reporting problems with prescription drugs online, but it's a trackable form."

"So let someone else do it for you—how about your doctor fiancé?"

"I can't involve Kyle, for several reasons, plus it would be traced back to me immediately."

"Then hell, I'll do it if you want me to."

Suddenly I felt crowded. He was injecting himself into my decision... into my life.

I unbuckled my seatbelt and opened the door. "No, thanks. Besides, I'm working that angle already." I lowered myself to the ground.

"The angle where you pass the buck?"

At his challenging look, white-hot anger shot through me. He had no right to judge me. I should never have confided in him. "I take back that compliment. Thanks for the ride."

I slammed the door and stalked toward the hospital entrance.

November 2, Thursday

"THE DOCTOR SAYS if I keep improving and my tests come back clean, I should be released in a few days." From his hospital bed, Anthony gave me a regal smile.

I released a pent-up sigh. "That's great news. You certainly look better than the last time I saw you."

Although I suspected the color in his cheeks had something to do with the fact that Casey, our co-worker at the Anita Temp Agency, was playing nursemaid.

She leaned over to tap his nose with the tip of her finger. "Doesn't he?" Then she held up a plastic pitcher. "I'm going to get some ice and let you and Mae visit."

He watched her until the door closed behind her. "I know this is going to sound crazy, but I seriously can't stop thinking about that woman. It's like my mind is on a loop."

Another side effect of Beltina? I dearly hoped he wasn't going to get his heart broken, but for now, I was happy he was on the road to recovery.

"How much do you remember about your collapse?"

"Not much. I hear you were the one to come to my aid."

"Casey was there, too. And the paramedics arrived quickly. Have the doctors given you any idea of what could've happened?"

He shrugged. "I don't think they know really. And I get the feeling they suspect I was mixing alcohol and drugs."

I swallowed. "Were you?"

"No! And I don't take any medication."

"Except Beltina?" I prompted.

He flushed guiltily. "Oh... you know about that?"

"The paramedic found a tablet in your pocket."

His face crumpled. "I'm sorry. I've been taking samples from your bathroom storage closet, which you probably figured out."

I hadn't, but I nodded, stunned. "For how long?"

"For a while. I lifted them when I picked up your drycleaning. I was desperate to lose weight and a prescription was so expensive. Can you forgive me?"

I sighed and nodded. "But don't do it again. And be sure to tell the doctors how long you've been taking it."

He frowned. "Why?"

I scrambled. "Because... they should know everything you've been ingesting."

"Okay," he said, but in a voice that made me think he might not tell them he'd been taking a prescription drug he didn't have a prescription for. "Hey, is Kyle back from LA?"

"Not yet. Saturday, unless his plans change."

"Did he say if Libby had her audition?"

Libby Lakes, Kyle's actress "benefactor," and Anthony's sometime-employer. "He didn't say... and I didn't ask." I pushed to my feet. "I have to go to work. With you and Casey out, Joon-woo is short-handed."

"Where are you working today?"

"The pet store. You're welcome."

He laughed. "Bye."

I left the hospital and walked to the Marta Arts Center Station to catch a shuttle back to Triangle Point. Throughout, my mind churned over Anthony's confession that he'd been taking Beltina for a while. And I scrolled back over all the little comments people had made about me over the past few months... that I was different... angry... forgetful.

And the headaches had gotten progressively worse.

Of course, any doctor or layperson would say the headaches were more easily explained by the mounting stress in my life. The pressure of keeping my background and family skeletons from Kyle, and now the double-life I was leading to maintain the façade of successful pharma sales manager until Traxton hired me back.

But the conditions I'd seen manifested in the close circle of people I knew who took Beltina—the aggression between Kyle's female friends, the bizarre self-abuse of the young woman at the gym, Helen's complete emotional meltdown, and now Anthony's unexplained collapse—drove me to the storage closet in my bathroom. I gathered up my remaining samples and pushed the orange tablets from the blister packs into the toilet bowl. By the time I finished, they had clumped and dissolved into a carrot-colored mess. I flushed the commode and watched it heave and swirl down with a sucking sound.

My phone rang and reporter Rainie Stephens's name came up. Hoping she'd tell me my trainer Jan had been a font of information, I connected the call.

"Hi, Rainie."

"Hi, Della. Is this a bad time?"

"I'm getting ready for work. What's up?"

"I talked to our mutual friend, and she had some good anecdotal information I'm still checking into. But I need more proof that something is wrong with Beltina—internal documents from the company, or some of the pills to send to an independent lab. Can you get me some?"

I stared at the orange stain in my toilet bowl. "No. I don't have any left. And I wasn't privy to any documents about unreported side effects when I worked for the company—I certainly don't have access now."

"Did you keep any correspondence from when you worked for Traxton?"

"They let me keep my laptop, but my email account and correspondence files disappeared."

She made a thoughtful noise. "Most companies control employee data from the cloud now. Instead of confiscating a machine, they simply retrieve the files. Did you print out anything?"

"A few things," I said, walking into my office and opening a drawer in my desk. "But only emails that pertained to accounts of mine."

"Can you send me a list of your accounts? I've been cold-calling physicians to ask if they prescribe Beltina, but I haven't found anyone who'll talk to me."

"But if you start calling my accounts, Traxton will know I've talked to you."

"So get the names of other sales reps' accounts, and I'll call those. Or mix it up. I told you, I protect my sources."

When I didn't respond, she sighed.

"Why don't you go back through your files and see if you can find anything about side effects, something that didn't seem relevant at the time. You never know what one little detail can lead to."

"I have to go," I said, then ended the call and closed the file drawer.

November 3, Friday

"SO HAVE YOU identified the man in the security video?"

Detective Jack Terry was mid-drink into his coffee mug. "Hello to you, too, Ms. Culpepper."

I rolled my hand. "I'm in a hurry here."

He looked over my work disguise. "On your lunch hour?"

"You could say that. I plan to grab something from your vending machine before I head back to my crappy temp job."

His nose wrinkled. "Pet store this morning?"

"And this afternoon. So... the guy on the video?"

"Right." He straightened. "Nothing to report yet." He lifted the top of a manila file folder on his desk to reveal a stack of black and white photographs printed from a still of the video. "We're doing a face recognition comparison against mug shots, and we're circulating the photo to various departments to see if anyone can identify him. If that doesn't produce results, then I think this case would be a good candidate for the Crime Stoppers show."

"How long will all that take?"

"As long as it takes. Could be today, could be a while."

"So that's it? More waiting?"

He set down his mug. I suddenly noticed his tie was hanging low, his shirt was wrinkled, and his jaw was shadowed. It occurred to me he'd pulled an all-nighter.

"I understand why you're antsy for us to find this man," he said. "If he didn't murder Ms. Padilla, he's probably the last person to see her alive. Ms. Padilla's family and the police department owe you for being persistent when we weren't." He gave me a little smile. "When *I* wasn't. I should've listened to you, Carlotta, and I'm sorry. I'll try to make it up to you."

I lifted an eyebrow. "Carlotta?"

He blinked. "I mean, Della… I mean, Ms. Culpepper." He pulled a hand down his face. "I'm sorry—I'm running on fumes here. I'll call you when I have something concrete, okay?"

"Can I have a copy of the photo?"

"No."

I frowned. "Why not?"

"Because this guy could be dangerous. We'll take it from here." Then he brightened. "But that reminds me." He rummaged for another file. "Yesterday we got a hit in the system for someone who could be the mother of the abandoned baby." He opened the file. "Penelope Essex, runaway from Jupiter, Florida, age sixteen. Was in foster care. This is the only photo available." He turned it toward me. "Do you think it's the same girl?"

I squinted at the fuzzy photo, then shook my head. "It could be her, but I can't say for sure."

"Okay. Maybe she'll turn up. You haven't seen her friend around?"

"No. Some of the kids hanging around Triangle Point mentioned other kids leaving to take jobs selling magazine subscriptions."

He nodded. "That happens. The people who do it are usually transient themselves, gather up a bunch of kids to work for them, haul them around in vans or buses to go door to door in neighborhoods, pay them with cheap room and board, and to the kids it's a big adventure."

"It's not illegal?"

"Not if the kids are doing it voluntarily." His mouth turned down. "And if kids are being made to do things against their will, it usually involves something a lot more sordid than selling magazines."

"Forced prostitution? In Atlanta?"

"I'm afraid so. The warm weather attracts runaways, and the airport and interstates make it easy for perverts to get in and out quickly."

I prayed the baby's mother was at this moment ringing someone's bell to sell them a subscription to *Reader's Digest*. "What happened to the kid who tried to shoplift the diamond bracelet through Dorman's giftwrap department?"

"Roy Lipton." He grimaced. "Unfortunately, since he hadn't left the premises with the merchandise, he couldn't be charged."

"So the next time it happens, I should let the person walk out with the diamond bracelet?"

"It would seem so. But promise me you'll call security instead of trying to apprehend them yourself."

I smirked—and made no such promise.

He crossed his arms. "Hey, did you ever get your money back from your mother's boyfriend?"

"No. But he's still in town. I saw him the other day."

His mouth quirked. "And he's still alive?"

The memory of diving through the window of Gil Malone's car and wrapping my hands around his scrawny throat made me smile. "He might be a little sore."

He chuckled. "And did you ever connect with Rainie Stephens?"

"Yes. She and I… are talking."

He nodded. "You have a lot on your plate."

I yanked my thumb toward the door. "Speaking of which, I should go. Those dogs aren't going to wash themselves."

"Wait." He opened his bottom desk drawer and pulled a protein bar out of an open box. "Here—there's nothing healthy in the vending machine."

I took it. "Thanks. Get some rest, Detective."

But he was already reaching for his ringing phone. The man had a lot on his plate, too. I walked away, tearing open the protein bar and smiling over the earlier slip of his tongue.

The detective had a thing for the Carlotta chick. And apparently, he'd done something to her he felt he needed to make up for.

November 4, Saturday

"I SHOULD LAND about four this afternoon," Kyle said, sounding more distant than the two thousand miles between us.

"Okay," I said. "Text me to let me know you've landed safely. I'll see you tomorrow."

"Actually, I thought I might stop and spend the night at your place, if that's okay."

"Oh." My mind reeled for an excuse. My brother Donnie was coming up to spend the afternoon, and I wasn't ready for the two of them to meet, not when so many other areas of my life were in flux. "I'm sorry, Kyle. I'm bogged down in work I have to finish today. Visiting Anthony in the hospital has thrown me off schedule."

Since the first part was a lie and the second part was true, they cancelled each other out, didn't they?

He made a rueful noise. "How is Anthony?"

"Much better. The doctor said he might be released tomorrow."

"That's good. Gee, with your personal assistant laid up, no wonder you're behind."

"Right," I said, squirming. "How's Helen?"

"She's better too, thank goodness. She's not ready to go home, but she was moved to a step-down unit."

"So she can have visitors now?"

"Reggie says she's still not up to seeing anyone. I'm sure neither one of them want people to see her in the state she's in."

"That's understandable," I murmured. "And they need this time for each other."

"Right. There's my boarding call. I'll let you know when I land. I'm looking forward to seeing you tomorrow."

"Same here," I said, and meant it. I needed a break from my life at Triangle Point.

I ended the call, then hurried toward my condo building. Even with skipping my workout, cleaning the gym had taken longer than I'd planned because the locker rooms had been so crowded. I'd maneuvered through the bodies like a ghost, even among the people who took the interval cardio class I liked. They didn't see through my disguise because they weren't the kind of people who made eye contact with the hired help. I knew because I used to be the same way.

My feet grew lighter as I approached the entrance to my building. Spending time with my younger brother Donnie always made me happy. I rushed into the lobby, then balked. Donnie had arrived early—why did that surprise me?—and was standing next to the concierge desk, talking to Henry and my sour neighbor Mindy Chasen. Donnie was tall and handsome, and his job as a mechanic had honed his shoulders and arms. At the moment, he was using those strong arms to hold and stroke Mindy's pug.

Since I was still in disguise, I hoped to slink past them and get to the elevator unnoticed, change, then call Donnie to come up. I turned my head away and picked up my pace.

"Hey, Sis!"

Darn. Of course he'd seen right through my disguise. Donnie's autism allowed him to dismiss details that distracted the rest of us. I turned my head and acted surprised to see him, then walked toward him. "Hi."

Mindy Chasen squinted at my appearance, but her dog saw right through my disguise, too, and began to snarl as if he was going to attack, as per usual.

"Is that a Halloween costume?" she asked, taking the dog and turning it away from me to quiet its yapping.

"Ms. Culpepper is in a play," Henry supplied. The excuse I'd given him for the disguise when he'd stopped me once thinking I was a visitor.

"Really?" Donnie asked. "Are you the star?"

I conjured up a smile. "Of course." Hey, why not?

Donnie grinned. "That's cool. Maybe I can see it sometime."

"Maybe," I said, then nodded toward the elevator. "Let's go up and I'll change."

He said goodbye to his friends. On the ride up in the elevator, Donnie once again commented on the robust mechanics of the elevator—he was obsessed with machinery. Later when he stood at my living room window and pointed out the towering Battlecoin Building near mine, an idea struck me.

After I changed and gave Donnie the stack of CDs I'd bought for him at the music store, we walked through the park toward the building. It was a beautiful fall day and the greenspace was crowded with people.

"This is where the cars were before," Donnie said.

"That's right."

"Those kids are still here," Donnie said, pointing guilelessly toward a clump of transient teens. Then he frowned. "Some of them."

I frowned. "What do you mean, some of them?"

"A few are the same as before, but most of the faces are new."

Donnie never ceased to amaze me. "Probably so. Some of them are just traveling through."

"Is that guy selling sandwiches? I'm hungry."

I looked over to see Charlie walking around the fringes of the crowd, handing out sandwiches to the same group of teens who had caught Donnie's eye. Among them I noticed some of the kids who came into the music shop, the ones I'd asked for information on Penny and her friend Amy.

"No. He's giving them away."

"Can I have one?"

I smiled. "I'll buy you a sandwich. Those are for the people who can't afford them. Let's keep moving." I tried to urge him forward, but Charlie had noticed us and walked over.

"Hi, Della," he said, offering a smile. I hadn't seen him since I'd slammed the door of his van.

I wet my lips. "Hi, Charlie."

"How's your friend Anthony?"

"Much better, thanks. Charlie, this is my brother Donnie. Donnie, this is Charlie Graham. He's a... friend of mine."

Donnie shook Charlie's extended hand with enough power to make Charlie wince. I hid a smile—Donnie didn't know his own strength.

"Nice to meet you, Donnie."

"Nice to meet you," Donnie said, then swung his head toward me. "Mom said you're engaged. Is this the guy you're going to marry?"

I blinked. "No."

"He has a good handshake," Donnie said, as if to endorse Charlie. "And he must be rich since he's giving away sandwiches."

I opened my mouth to change the subject, but I was so exasperated, nothing came out.

"I wish," Charlie said with a little laugh. "But no, I'm not rich, and I'm not marrying your sister."

"So you're just a nice guy?"

Oh, brother. As if Charlie's ego needed a boost.

He laughed again. "I try to be a nice guy, although I'm not

sure your sister would agree. I have a restaurant, so I sell food there, and make sandwiches from the leftovers to give away."

"Do you have beef jerky at your restaurant?"

Charlie made a thoughtful noise. "It's not on the menu, but that's an interesting idea."

Donnie turned to me. "Can we go to Charlie's restaurant for lunch?"

"Another time," I promised. "We'll get something to eat in a bit. There's someplace I want to take you first."

His eyes widened. "Where do you want to take me?"

"You'll see. Say goodbye to Charlie."

"Goodbye, Charlie."

"Goodbye, Donnie. I hope to see you again. Bye, Della."

I locked gazes with him for a few seconds. I expected to see pity for Donnie, had come to expect it from people who met him for the first time. Instead I saw amusement at my expense... nothing new. "Bye."

"I like Charlie," Donnie offered as we walked away. "What's the name of the guy you're going to marry?"

"Kyle."

"When do I get to meet Kyle?"

"Soon," I murmured, then led Donnie to the Battlecoin Building.

"Wow, this is the building I saw from your window. It's really tall."

"The tallest building around," I confirmed. "Let's go in and see if they'll let us ride the elevator."

He grinned. "For real?"

"We can ask."

Donnie scrambled ahead and held open the door that led us into a set of sealed doors. From there, security buzzed us in and we walked to the front desk.

"Yes?" the male security guard asked.

"Hi," I said, offering a smile. "This might be an unusual request, but would it be possible to ride the elevator to the top floor?"

"Are you a tenant or employee?"

"No. But I've worked here for temporary assignments."

"Do you have a security badge?"

"No."

He shook his head. "I'm sorry, ma'am, but unless you have a badge, someone has to meet you and sign you in."

I sighed, but I understood the man had rules to abide by, especially in this day and age.

"Mae?"

I turned to see Constance Hanlon walking toward the desk, dressed down slightly, but still a commanding figure and carrying her briefcase.

"Hi, Ms. Hanlon."

"What are you doing here on a Saturday?"

I gestured to Donnie. "My brother is a bit of an elevator aficionado. I was hoping he could take a ride."

She glanced at the security guard. "Is that okay?"

"She doesn't have a badge, ma'am."

"I'll sign them in with my badge."

"That's so nice of you," I said, then wrote our names on the guest log.

She smiled. "Come on—I'll ride with you."

"But you were on your way out."

"Nonsense—it'll be fun."

When the three of us stepped on the elevator, Donnie's enthusiasm was contagious. Constance established an easy rapport with him, listened raptly as he described the type of elevator system the building had and pointed out where decorative features hid important inner workings. Our climb to the top actually required riding three different elevators. Donnie's excitement escalated each time we scaled another section of the building. By the time we got to the observatory level, he was in awe of the panoramic view. He pulled out his phone to take pictures.

"The guys back at home won't believe this," he said.

Seeing him happy filled me to the brim. Behind his back, I mouthed "thank you" to Constance and she gave me a little nod.

I thanked her again when we got back to the ground floor. Donnie—who rarely touched anyone—gave her a hug. I tensed, but she was gracious and warm, then smiled and waved goodbye.

Donnie was still bouncing when we got back to the food truck area. "This is the best day ever, Sis."

My heart tugged at how easy he was to please. I vowed to try to do it more often. "Do you want a burger or barbecue for lunch?"

"A burger sounds good."

"I agree."

We got burgers and sodas and found a place to sit. Fall was in full swing and the leaf blowers couldn't keep up with the attrition. Red and orange leaves blanketed the grass.

"You've gained some weight," Donnie said bluntly. "You look good. You were getting too skinny."

I stopped mid-chew. "That's not really a compliment, Professor."

"It's not? Sorry. The men where I work like round girls, and so do I."

That made me laugh. "Okay, but please don't tell a girl she looks round."

"Okay, I won't."

"Have you heard anything new about Gil?"

"No. But Mom got another letter from the bank. They want five thousand dollars by the first of next month."

My intestines cramped. It might as well be fifty thousand. "Don't worry about it," I said with as much confidence as I could gather. "I'll handle it."

"Okay," he said, then took another bite of his burger.

I kept eating, too—it made things just a little better.

November 5, Sunday

"THAT WAS NICE," Kyle said, lying back on his pillow. He was still breathing hard from some really decent sex.

"Yes," I murmured, also recovering. It had been a while since we'd hit the sheets in the middle of the afternoon. But it had been a while since we'd been alone, without someone from his social circle hanging around, including Libby Lakes, his actress client who had managed to insinuate herself into Kyle's upscale clique.

From the nightstand, Kyle's phone beeped. He checked it, then set it down.

"Do you need to get that?"

"No—it's just Lib. I'll call her later."

Right on cue. "Did she get the part she auditioned for?"

"She won't know for a while, but she doesn't think so."

"The audition didn't go well?"

"She said she felt like a cow." He winced. "I don't think she'll be endorsing Beltina anytime soon."

I doodled on his arm with my finger. "Will she be endorsing your practice?"

"I don't know," he said, his voice a little high and tight. "She introduced me to a lot of her friends." He laughed. "I gave a lot of free facials."

I wondered what he'd gotten in return.

"And she seemed happy with the way her face looked for the audition—she said the makeup artist raved about her skin."

"That's good."

"Uh-huh. Hey, what happened to your hair?" He was frowning.

I reached up to touch it. "I decided to go a little darker."

"Oh, for your sales manager position—to make you look smarter, I guess?"

It was my turn to frown. "*No.* For less maintenance."

"Oh… right."

So much for afterglow. I raised up on my elbow. "Speaking of hair, did the results come back from testing Helen's hair for toxins?"

"Yes. I talked to Reggie this morning. Bizarrely, it shows an influx of copper into her system."

I squinted. "Copper?"

He nodded. "And the doctors think that's what was causing her problems."

"Where do they think the copper came from?"

"No one knows. Reggie said the doctors asked him to round up all her cosmetics and over-the-counter treatments and bring them in. Copper is a trendy ingredient now, and it could be that she was accidentally overdosing on something otherwise harmless. Good news, huh?"

I exhaled in abject relief. "You have no idea."

"Anyway, they asked him to bring in receipts, too, so they can sync what she was using, when."

"Do they know when it started?"

"About six months ago."

My relief had been short-lived. Six months ago was when I'd given Helen samples of Beltina.

November 6, Monday

"BE HONEST," Anthony said. "Are you pregnant?"

I scoffed. "No, I'm not pregnant."

"Did Kyle give you an STD?"

"No."

"Did my illness send you into relapse on your drug addiction recovery?"

I turned my head to look at him driving. "I don't think this was a good idea on your first full day back."

"Don't be silly, I feel great. And I need to run about a hundred errands, so this was on the way." He flipped on his turn signal, then wheeled into the parking lot of the strip mall. On the far end was a sign for a walk-in lab clinic. When he slowed in front of the entrance, I climbed out and shut the door.

The window zoomed down. "Are you sure you don't want me to stay until you're finished?"

"I'm sure. But thanks. I'll Uber back."

"Okay. Later."

Lady Gaga music blared as he drove away. I shook my head, but smiled after him. It was such a relief to see him out of the hospital and getting back to normal. The doctors hadn't pinpointed the cause of his collapse, and since Anthony seemed fully recovered, I suspected there would never be an exact determination. And because Anthony was taking Beltina without a prescription, there were no 'before' blood tests to compare to the 'after.' In the world of prescribed medicine, he was off the grid.

And so was I. I'd been taking Beltina for years without a prescription.

I walked into the lab clinic and was handed an iPad to check in and select the type of lab test I needed—due to the sensitive nature of some tests, very few words were exchanged. That said, it was a busy little place. While I waited for my number to be called, I surveyed the cross-section of people and knew if I tried to distinguish the customers having diabetes, allergy, or thyroid testing from the customers having paternity, gonorrhea, or opioid testing, I'd probably be wrong.

"Number five sixty-three," a bored-looking woman wearing blue scrubs called.

I stood and followed her down a long hallway with doors on either side into a small room with an exam table, storage cabinet, and chair.

"Hi," she said in a monotone voice, then directed me to sit in the chair. "You're here for a hair metals test, is that correct?"

"Yes."

"Okay, I'll need to collect a sample." She reached into a cabinet drawer and withdrew a small envelope with a form printed on one side. Then she pulled rubber gloves from a dispenser and snapped them on. From the cabinet she assembled a tray with various combs and small tools. "Will this be from the head or the pubic area?"

I blinked. "The head."

"Is your hair treated with chemicals?"

"Yes."

"And have you washed it in the last forty-eight hours?"

"Yes."

"Then I'd recommend using pubic hair instead."

I hesitated.

"If you have any," she added.

"I do," I said quickly. Well, I'd had a bunch of it lasered off, but for my age, I was old-school—I'd left a landing strip.

"Has it been chemically treated?"

I laughed. "No."

"Hey, it's a thing. Pink, blue, striped—I've seen it all." She gave a little shrug. "You can always wait a couple of days and come back for a head sample."

"No. It's okay." I stood and unbuttoned my jeans. The woman glanced at the angry red marks the too-tight waistband had left in my skin. I was going to have to bump up a size if I gained another ounce.

I pulled down my underwear to expose my bushlet. She used a comb to tease up a patch of hair, then used shears to clip it into the envelope.

"All done," she said, then sealed the envelope and asked me to sign it. "The sample will be tested for a range of metals. The results will be mailed to you in about two weeks. If you have any questions about the results, call us or stop by and someone will help you."

"Is this a rare test?" I asked, refastening my pants.

"Used to be… and still is for this place. But I work for a big lab company and I've noticed a spike in hair metal tests from doctors and hospitals the past year or so."

"Must be something environmental," I offered.

"Must be," she agreed absently.

"If you don't mind me asking, what's the most popular metal detected?"

She scratched her temple. "That's the strange thing—you'd think it would be all over the board, and historically, it is. But lately, nine times out of ten, it's copper."

November 7, Tuesday

"HERE YOU GO," Joon-woo said, handing me a single sheet of professional stationery. She had called me to her tiny office at the Anita Temp Agency to review the letter she'd written to Traxton on my behalf regarding my unpaid bonus check.

I squinted at the two brief paragraphs.

"What?" she demanded.

I shrugged. "It's been a few days—I guess I just expected something a little… longer?"

She frowned. "I haven't practiced employment law for a few years, I had to bone up a little. Besides, when you threaten a big company like Traxton, it's best to keep it short and sweet."

"You threatened them?"

"*You* are threatening them," she corrected. "On my legal letterhead."

I scanned the paragraphs that basically said I (the client) had signed an agreement with Traxton concerning my termination and had fulfilled my requirements, but they hadn't done jack squat, i.e., were hanging on to my last quarterly bonus of thirty-two grand. But the letter ended on a softer tone indicating I was eager to get this matter behind me and return to full employment at Traxton in a position that would utilize my skills to their utmost.

I lifted my gaze to hers. "Not bad."

She gave me a wry smile. "Not bad for someone who used to be your housekeeper and you assumed didn't speak English?"

I sighed. "I'm sorry about that. I'm trying to be a better person."

She pressed her lips together. "I know. What you did for Elena—getting her case reopened—that took guts."

I wanted to smile, but I didn't feel heroic. "Thanks."

"Sign the letter and make a copy, then post the original by certified mail—it's more friendly than a courier service. Here's a matching envelope."

"Okay... thanks."

Joon-woo held out her hand. "And I need a dollar for a retainer."

I reached into my purse and pulled out my wallet. Since the bill side was empty, I proceeded to count change into her hand—dimes, nickels, and pennies—in the amount of one hundred cents.

She looked at the pile of change. "Seriously?"

"It spends!"

She rolled her eyes, but turned to dump it in a Styrofoam cup on her desk.

I signed the letter. "Is it alright if I use the copier?"

She gave me a deadpan look, and I skedaddled to the backroom to mooch a copy before things got ugly.

With the sealed envelope in-hand, I walked to the post office to mail it as Joon-woo had instructed. If something was about to happen with Beltina and the Traxton stock, hopefully I'd get my bonus before the ship started to sink.

When I left the post office, I reflected on what Joon-woo had said about me getting Elena's case reopened. What she didn't know—although she probably suspected—was how badly I'd treated Elena. Once I'd thrown a vase at her. She'd ducked, but had cut herself cleaning up the broken glass. I didn't feel bad about it at the time, but now I was shot through with remorse, knowing how even a small cut would've been a lot for her to treat while living in her car.

Pinging with shame, I stopped by the security office and

looked up Evan, the guy who'd sat with me sifting through hours of surveillance film.

He waved. "Hi, Della."

"Hi, Evan. Listen, remember that piece of video you pinpointed from the parking garage that was so important?"

"The closeup of the guy walking away from the car? Sure. What about it?"

I crossed my fingers behind my back to purchase a lie. "Detective Terry said you could print me a copy."

He nodded. "No problem, I got it saved on my desktop." He turned to his computer and after a series of clicks and drags, a copy spooled off the printer on photographic paper.

"Thank you, Evan." I stared at the slightly blurred photo of the man with short dark hair, a hooked nose, and block jaw.

"He's looks like a bad guy," Evan offered.

I murmured my agreement. A bad guy... who looked familiar. I cursed my recent swiss-cheese memory lapses. Where had I seen him before?

November 8, Wednesday

"MY BROTHER really enjoyed the trap music CDs," I said to Blowz, my teenage stoner boss at the music store.

"He seemed like a cool guy," he replied. "I'm glad you brought him in Saturday, I could've talked with him about music all day."

"Donnie is super intelligent about the things he's interested in. His autism makes him laser-focused on one thing at a time."

Blowz nodded. "Autism—I've heard of that. It's like when people are geniuses or something, right?"

I pursed my lips. "I guess you could say that, yeah. Donnie is a genius when it comes to cars and mechanical stuff."

"I wish I was autistic," Blowz said with a sigh.

I smiled to myself. I guess life was all about how you perceived things. Some people found Donnie lacking, other people believed he was gifted.

The door opened, and to my surprise, Charlie's tall redheaded "friend" Megan walked in. Blowz was immediately at attention, but I held up my hand. "I got this." He frowned, but relented and wheeled off to do something lame until it was time for his smoke break.

I walked up to Megan and offered a smile. "Can I help you?"

I didn't expect her to recognize me in my oversized Train T-shirt, plus my bandana and glasses—and she didn't. "Yes. I'm looking for a gift, some music for my boyfriend."

So she was calling Charlie her boyfriend now? "What kind of music does he like?"

"He likes bluegrass—I think."

I smiled. "You don't know what kind of music he likes? He must be a new boyfriend."

She smiled back. "Sort of. He's an old boyfriend, but now we're back together again."

I winced. "Ooh, are you sure that's wise?"

She frowned. "What do you mean?"

"I mean, whatever was wrong in the relationship before could still be there." I leaned on a nearby counter. "So... what *was* wrong in the relationship before?"

"We were younger then... we were both immature."

"And now you're both mature?"

"Well, I certainly am—I married someone else and grew up fast. That's over, though."

"Ah. And did your boyfriend also marry someone else?"

"No."

I winced again. "So he's still immature?"

She frowned. "I don't believe so."

"But you don't know," I pointed out. "You don't even know what kind of music he likes now." I lowered my voice to a conspiratorial whisper. "What else don't you know about him? I mean, is sex the same as it was before?"

She drew back a little. "Well, we haven't... that is, he wants to wait until my divorce is final."

"A likely excuse. He could be hiding a problem, like erectile dysfunction."

She gave a little laugh. "I don't think so, not Charlie."

I angled my head. "So he was good in the sack when you dated before?"

She flushed prettily and almost giggled. "Charlie was the best lover *ever*."

I frowned. "Ever?"

She nodded, then moaned, as if she were remembering. "He used to... no, sorry that's TMI."

"No, it isn't," I assured her, stabbing at my big glasses. "What did he used to do?"

Megan leaned in. "Well, he had his thing he did with his tongue—"

She broke off when the bell on the door chimed. A clump of kids fell inside, noisy and shivering.

"You were saying," I urged her, rolling my hand. "Something about his tongue?"

She straightened and sighed. "You're right. I guess I should pass on the music until I find out what he likes now." Then she perked up. "I know—I'll take a peek at his CD collection tonight."

"Tonight?"

"He invited me over for dinner." She grinned. "Who knows? Maybe we'll get tipsy and one thing will lead to another. He told me he bought a new bed."

"King-size," I confirmed.

She frowned. "Hm?"

I recovered. "Is it king-size?"

"I... don't know."

I narrowed my eyes. "If it is, you should ask yourself what kind of kinky group stuff he might be into these days."

Her eyes flew wide. "Charlie? He'd never do that."

"Maybe... maybe not. Ask him if he's ever been propositioned for a threesome, and see if he gets nervous."

"O...kay. Thanks for the tip."

She looked so concerned when she left, I almost felt guilty.... but not quite.

November 9, Thursday

I WAS EATING a bag lunch in the park, studying the picture of the man leaving Elena's car. I planned to show the photo all over Triangle Point if I had to, but I was hoping something would jog my holey memory and I'd remember where I'd seen him without getting anyone else involved or inadvertently tipping him off. Detective Terry's warning he could be a dangerous man wasn't lost on me. I wasn't trying to be a hero.

I chewed, trying not to look at the front of Charlie's restaurant and think about his private dinner date last night with Megan. Tried not to wonder if it had morphed into a sleepover, and sleeping in.

A few yards away, a group of kids gathered around a picnic table with a pizza box, and opened the lid to share. They were the same kids I'd given money to in the music store the day I'd asked questions about Penny and Amy. One girl, the rest boys. I dearly hoped she had someone in the group looking out for her. Then I noticed the dark-haired boy, the handsome street-wise kid, hovering close to her. I hoped that was good.

I wadded up my lunch bag, tossed the trash, and walked over to them. "Hi. Remember me?"

"Yeah," a couple of them said, their eyes wary.

"I was just wondering if you've seen Penny or Amy around?"

They all shook their heads. "They're not coming back," the girl said.

"Coming back from where?"

She shrugged. "Wherever they went."

"The same place your other friends went?"

More shrugs. "We don't know—they just disappeared."

"Do you know if Penny's real name was Penelope?"

"I think it was," the girl said. "She had a bracelet with the name Penelope on it." The dark-haired boy elbowed her, then gave her a pointed look.

"Penelope Essex?" I pressed.

"She never said her last name," she mumbled.

"Do you guys know Roy Lipton?"

"You're asking a lot of questions," the girl's boyfriend said. "Are you paying for answers today?"

I checked my wallet. "I don't have any cash... but here's a book of stamps." I pulled it out and set it on the table. "Why don't you each write a letter home?"

"Ain't got no home," the boy said, his expression challenging.

I inclined my head.

"Roy's gone, too," one boy piped up.

"You mean, left town?"

"I guess. He bounced as soon as he got out of jail."

"Okay, one more question," I said, then pulled out the photo of the man from the video. "Have you ever seen this man?"

They looked, then they each shook their head.

"What did he do?" the girl asked.

"Maybe something bad," I said.

"Lady, that's everyone walking around," the dark-haired kid said, and the other kids laughed.

My phone rang and when I pulled it out, my heartrate picked up to see my former boss Portia's name come up. "Okay, thanks," I called to the kids, then walked away to connect the call.

"This is Della."

"Della, hi—this is Portia."

"Hi, Portia. How are you?"

"Confused. I told you I was working behind the scenes to make things happen. And now I have this letter in my hand that reads like some kind of veiled threat."

I sighed. "Portia, I don't want to threaten you or the company, but I'm strapped for cash and I have bills to pay. I haven't taken another full-time job because I believed what you told me about being hired back. But I need my bonus check to live on until that happens."

"I hear you. Things are a little hectic here. Please just give me a few more days to make something happen."

"How long?"

"Until the end of the month."

I hesitated, but what choice did I have? I could sue, but that would take forever and if I did receive my bonus, it would be eaten up in legal fees. "Okay, but just until the end of the month. Then I… will have to regroup."

"Thank you, Della. I know you're a woman of your word. And so am I."

I disconnected the call, feeling powerless. Was it too much to ask that something in my life go the way it was supposed to?

On the other side of the park, a red flash caught my eye. Megan's luscious red Mercedes convertible—she was driving, and Charlie was in the passenger seat. She pulled up in front of his restaurant and he climbed out, waved, and went inside.

My mouth moved into a wry frown. I wondered how Charlie's tongue was feeling today.

Oooh! Just one more not-supposed-to-be-happening thing: jealousy over a chubby chef.

November 10, Friday

KNOWING MY BONUS check would not be coming for at least three more weeks, and with the payment from the Dewdrop bank looming large, I decided to double-down on work assignments. This morning I'd worked in the office at the autospa—ack, more papercuts—and tonight I was once again working as an attendant in the ladies' bathroom, this time for a big-tent charity event for military families to celebrate Veterans Day weekend. Everyone seemed to be a celebratory mood, so I knew the tips would be good.

I just hoped this time no one abandoned a baby in a stall.

The memory kept me alert, checking that women who went into a stall pregnant, came out of a stall still pregnant. It also crossed my mind that Penny might come back if she thought I was working, might want to know if her baby was okay.

Fundraisers typically featured lots of cash bars, and the more alcohol ingested, the more trips to the bathroom. I was in constant motion keeping the toilet tissue, feminine hygiene products, hand soap, and paper towels stocked. The women who came in were dressed up and having fun and it was generally a happy group, if a little loud. Toward the end of the evening, though, Sabrina and Susan walked in. They hadn't recognized me at the Cirque du Soleil show and I was wearing the same black outfit and cap, so I assumed tonight would be the same. But my pulse still clicked higher when they came to the sink next to me to wash their hands.

"Tamara knew I was going to wear this dress tonight," Sabrina seethed, "and she wore the same one anyway. I hate her!"

"Relax," Susan soothed. "You look better in it anyway."

Sabrina pumped the lever for the soap dispenser, then cursed when nothing came out. "Hey, Toilet Lady," she said to me, snapping her fingers. "Bring some fucking soap over here."

"Just use the other one," Susan said, nodding to the next sink.

But Sabrina's eyes blazed. "I want to use *this* sink." She glared at me. "What's the matter, can't you understand English?"

Everyone was staring. My face burned with humiliation. Was this how I'd made Elena feel, and Joon-woo?

I felt compelled to do what Elena and Joon-woo hadn't done to me—push back. I peeled off my glasses and my hat. "I speak English fine... Sabrina."

She shrank back and stared at me, horrified. "Della?"

Susan looked equally appalled. "What's this all about?"

I held up my hands. "I'm Toilet Lady."

Sabrina barked out a laugh. "This is a joke... you two are punking me, right?"

"No," I assured her. "I didn't get a promotion in July—I was fired. Since then I've been doing temp jobs to get by."

Susan gasped. "Then why did you tell us you'd been promoted?"

"I didn't—all of you just assumed I had, and I went along. I told myself it was okay because my boss promised to hire me back in December."

Sabrina gestured to my outfit. "But surely there's something better than... this?"

"The tips aren't bad," I said. "Except when it's people like you, who don't tip at all."

Sabrina narrowed her eyes. "Oh, no, don't try to put this back on us. It's not our fault you decided to slum instead of getting a real job."

Susan, too, looked mortified—for me or for herself, I wasn't sure. "You've been lying to us all this time?"

I realized they were both standing there with dripping wet hands. I pick up two paper towels and extended them. "Yes."

They took the towels and wiped their hands, staring at me with contempt throughout. Then they wadded up the used towels and tossed them in the trash on their way out, as if they'd washed their hands of me, too.

November 11, Saturday

"THAT WAS A GOOD class," Charlie said, walking next to me

toward the locker rooms.

"Uh-hm." Although I was unsettled by all the extra jiggling I'd felt today.

"It was nice to meet your brother last weekend," he offered.

"Uh-hm."

"Where does he live?"

"South of here," I said vaguely. "Charlie, when you mingle with the teenagers in the park, do they ever say anything about their friends disappearing?"

He frowned. "I assume most of the kids are transient. And as it gets colder, they probably head south—is that what you mean?"

"I suppose so. Have you ever seen anyone approach the kids about selling magazines door to door?"

"No, but I've heard that's a thing."

"Can I show you something?"

He grinned and swept his glance over my workout gear. "I thought you'd never ask."

I smirked, then dashed into the locker room, removed the picture of the man in the video from my bag and jogged back out. "Have you ever seen this guy?"

He studied the picture. "I don't believe so. Who is he?"

"He's connected to the woman I found in her car."

He took the picture and looked again, then shook his head. "No. But I'll keep an eye out."

"Okay, thanks."

He handed back the picture, then wiped his mouth with his towel. "What?"

"What... what?"

"You keep staring at my mouth. Do I have something on it?"

"How's Megan?" I blurted.

"She's... fine, last I checked."

"Good." I pointed to the door of the locker room. "I have to go do my switcheroo thing. Later." I escaped and stowed the photo in my bag. I caught sight of myself in a mirror and turned to look at my backside. There was definitely more *there* there.

I eyed the scale with trepidation, but made my way over and stepped up, then slid the weighted needle across the numbers on the top of the scale, down, then back up... up... up... up.

137.

I stared, incredulous. I was sixteen pounds over what I considered my ideal weight. My trainer Jan's words from early July came back to me.

At your height, you'd have to gain fifteen pounds before Traxton put you on notice.

I wasn't subject to periodic weigh-ins anymore, but would Portia hire me back if I didn't look the part of a fit pharma employee?

I staggered off the scale. If I wasn't careful, my life was going to slide from Della Land back into MaeDella Territory.

November 12, Sunday

"THANKS FOR AGREEING to do this," Kyle said, his hand at my back.

We were one of at least two hundred couples at the Junior League gala to raise money for children of veterans. "I'm happy to stand in for Helen and Reggie." Once I'd found a dress in my closet that fit. I took a deep drink from my wine glass.

"This is sis's pet charity," Kyle said. "It speaks volumes that she doesn't feel well enough to attend."

"How is the detox treatment going?"

"Slow. As you can imagine, once you have an accumulation of a metal in your body, it's dense, and it takes a while to rid your organs of it."

"Have you heard of other, uh, people or patients with the same problem?"

"Copper poisoning?" He made a thoughtful noise. "Now that you mention it, I was talking to a colleague the other day who said he'd had two diagnoses of Wilson's Disease in the past month."

"Wilson's Disease?"

"Very rare. It's genetic, and it's basically an accumulation of copper in the body over a long period of time."

I frowned. "So Helen has Wilson's Disease?"

"No, the doctors ruled it out—she doesn't have the genetic markers. It's almost as if she has an acquired version of Wilson's... maybe it's a new disease." Then he smiled. "And maybe Traxton will come up with a cure. The stock is killing it."

I took another deep drink from my wine glass.

Kyle's phone vibrated. He checked it discreetly, then smiled.

"Good news?" I asked.

"Lib is back in town."

"Super," I said, then snagged a mini quiche from a passing tray.

"Do you think that's a good idea?" Kyle murmured, then lowered his hand from my waist to the new curve of my hip and gave a tiny squeeze.

I folded the quiche into my napkin and placed it discreetly on a tray of discards.

November 13, Monday

"LIBBY WANTS me to work for her every day this week," Anthony said from the doorway of my office. "But that means I won't get to see Casey hardly at all."

I lifted my head from the stack of printed emails I was reading. "So, tell Libby you can come every other day, unless she wants to offer you health insurance like ATA."

He nodded. "That seems fair. What are you so deep into?"

"Just going through some old work files, cleaning things out."

"Do you think Portia is going to come through for you?"

"I hope so. But just in case, I'm going to sell another round of clothes on eBay."

He frowned. "Oh, I'm sorry."

"It's okay." They wouldn't fit anymore anyway. I glanced at the locked storage closet and wondered how soon I'd have to open it.

"Alright, I'm calling Libby now," he said, his voice fading as he walked away.

"Tell her to leave my fiancé alone," I muttered, for my ears only.

I'd been going through my old emails for Traxton, looking for any mention of side effects from accounts or discussed internally. So far, nothing had stood out.

Suddenly my eyes stopped on the word "Wilson." I backtracked to read more closely, and my pulse ratcheted higher.

It was a one-line bulleted point in a regional report that had been circulated for editing before being finalized for presentation. Portia had copied me to comment on a separate item.

One physician reported a patient with Wilson's Disease deteriorated more rapidly when taking Beltina.

I flipped forward in my file to scan the final version of the report.

The bullet point had been removed.

I broke into an instant sweat and reached for my phone. I pulled up Rainie Stephens's number and punched in a text message.

Check into Beltina-copper link, esp Wilson's Disease

My hand hovered over the Send button, but at the last second, I selected Save Draft.

If it was a good idea today, I reasoned, it would still be a good idea tomorrow.

November 14, Tuesday

I WALKED INTO the living room and was shocked to see Elena Padilla vacuuming my couch.

"Don't worry about the couch," I said with a dismissive wave. "It doesn't need to be cleaned."

Her expression was wry as she pulled multiple items from behind the pillows—a favorite book from my childhood, a grilled cheese sandwich, a bowl of macaroni and cheese, a cheese pizza, a crock of queso dip, an entire cheesecake, and Mindy Chasen's pug, which snarled at me.

I jarred awake. It was one of the more innocuous dreams I'd had about Elena—this time instead of condemning me for her death, she was condemning me for my cheese addiction. And it didn't take a psychologist to figure out the implied link between a lonely childhood, comfort food, and the security of a couch.

But it did give me an idea for another place to check for Elena's missing earring—my vacuum. Maybe she'd dropped the other one, too, and had inadvertently sucked it up in the sweeper.

I jumped out of bed, padded to the hallway closet and pulled out my vacuum cleaner. It took me a while to figure out how to release the dust bin, and when I did, I managed to send a cloud of filth into my face and mouth. Always a nice way to start the day.

I carried it to the kitchen, coughing. After wiping my face, I emptied the bin into a colander and shook it, hoping when all the dust had fallen through the holes, the lost earring would be revealed. Unfortunately, the only thing revealed was a safety pin and two paper clips.

Foiled again.

But the dream had given me another idea. If the man in the video was someone Elena had known, maybe she'd met him on one of her temp cleaning jobs.

I was scheduled to work in the bookstore today—not a bad gig, except for the book mutilation part. On the way, I stopped at ATA. When I opened the door, Casey was working the counter, talking on the phone to what sounded like a potential client. She waved.

I waved and mouthed, "Joon-woo?"

She pointed down the hall toward the office and I nodded thanks. The door was ajar and when I walked up, I could hear Joon-woo's voice.

"I need another line of credit... I know, but my overhead costs keep climbing.... In another three or four months the business should break even, then I can get caught up..."

I frowned—was Joon-woo's business in trouble?

"Okay, I appreciate your help," she said. "Thanks anyway." I heard the sound of the receiver being banged down.

I cleared my throat, then rapped on the door.

"Come in," Joon-woo called.

I stuck my head inside. "Good morning."

She smiled. "Yes, it is. What's up?"

"Do you have a list of all the places Elena worked?"

"Why?'

I crossed my fingers behind my back. "The police need it, and I told Detective Terry I'd get it for him."

"Okay, sure, I can run a report." She used a mouse to click onto an application, pulled down a menu, entered a few pieces of information, then hit Enter. "Done. Looks like a couple dozen places. It's printing now."

"Great—thanks. By the way, the letter you composed for

me?"

"Yes?"

"My former boss called."

"And?"

"And she asked me to give her until the end of the month to make things right. I said I would."

Joon-woo smiled. "Good. I hope it works out."

"You mean you'll be glad to get rid of me."

She laughed. "That, too."

When I turned to walk to the printer, I sighed. The woman was putting on a brave face.

But then, isn't that what women did every day?

November 15, Wednesday

I WAS LEAVING the gym, hurrying past the girl at the counter in my cleaning woman garb when I heard her say, "Della?"

Out of instinct, I turned, then realized my mistake. "Were you talking to me?"

"Yes, you—Della Culpepper." She was holding up a piece of paper that showed a copy of my picture from my membership ID.

The membership that had been revoked.

"You have me mistaken with someone else," I said, then started to walk away.

"Don't make me call security—or the police."

The only thing that made me turn back was the thought of Detective Terry showing up. I closed my eyes briefly and sighed. "Okay, you got me."

Her mouth tightened in fury. "You have a lot of nerve to be stealing gym services."

I scoffed. "It wasn't as if I broke in. So I squeezed in a little workout after I cleaned the nasty locker rooms, so sue me."

She smirked. "That's a possibility."

"Okay, I take that back." I held up my hands. "Look, how about I promise not to do it again?"

"Okay."

I blinked. "Really?"

"No!" she shouted. "Do I look like an idiot?"

"Well, for three months I've been walking past you twice a week in disguise and you didn't notice, so…"

Her eyes narrowed.

"Scratch that," I said, backing away. "I'm sorry, and I'm leaving now."

"Good idea. Maybe next time you'll think before calling someone 'porky'!"

Touché.

November 16, Thursday

"YOU CAN'T EVER go back," Joon-woo said.

"But I did a good job as a cleaner—you said yourself they were happy with my work."

"That was before you smuggled yourself in to steal workouts."

I scoffed. "How did I steal anything? No one was hurt."

Her eyes went wide. "I'm not going to argue semantics with you, Della. You stole from the gym just like the people who were stealing from Dorman's through the gift-wrapping department— that *you* helped to catch!"

I frowned. "Well, when you put it like that…"

She pulled her hand over her mouth. "This is the second account you almost cost me in a month, and I can't afford to lose any business."

Remorse billowed in my chest. "I'm sorry, Joon-woo. Wait—what was the first account?"

"The drycleaners. Something about you bringing a cop around to harass employees?"

I wondered why I hadn't been assigned to work there lately. "Not harass. To question the friend of a missing teenager, the teenager who abandoned the baby."

She held up her hand. "I told the owner of the drycleaners you have good intentions. She agreed to keep doing business with me, but if you go back there, you have to do your job, and that's it, understand?"

"Yes… boss."

She pursed her mouth. "You're expected at Dorman's—go."

I went.

Gift-wrapping has never been my favorite gig, but today I wasn't going to complain. But it sincerely sucked being alone. I missed Casey's and Anthony's company and their good humor. The day slogged by, but I maintained a smiling front in deference to Joon-woo.

Until Libby Lakes walked in.

She was dressed to the nines in a revealing outfit, reeking of perfume. Her one nod to keeping a low profile was a pair of enormous sunglasses.

I almost panicked and ran… until I realized she was so busy trying too hard, she didn't recognize me.

"Hello," I offered, lowering the pitch of my voice.

"Hello," she chirped. "I have a gift that needs wrapping." She set the shopping bag on the counter with a thunk.

I wondered why she hadn't sent Anthony out on this menial chore, until I reached in and withdrew the item. A very pricey bottle of men's cologne—like, a mortgage payment pricey. And I had a feeling I knew who she'd bought it for.

My fiancé.

"Oh, how nice," I said. "What's the occasion?"

"A thank you gift."

I smiled. "He must have done something special."

She nodded, then glanced at her watch. "If you don't mind, I'm in a hurry."

"Of course." I wrapped the cologne in the paper and bow she chose—Kyle's favorite blue and silver, I noticed. No wonder she hadn't sent Anthony on this chore—she didn't want him to know she'd set her sights on my man.

"Would you like to fill out a gift card?"

"Yes, but you write it for me," she said, with a flip of her hand.

"Okay," I said, pen poised.

"A small token of my undying thanks and affection. Love, Lib."

"Is that 'love,' or should I write 'fondly' or maybe 'best wishes'?"

She frowned. "No—*love*. And add a couple of x's and o's."

I gritted my teeth, but added them. "Here you are," I said, pushing the package across the counter.

"Thank you," she said, then fished into her purse and tossed a twenty on the counter. "For you." Then she sashayed away.

I stared at the bill. I'd just been tipped for wrapping a gift another woman was giving to my fiancé.

I folded the twenty into my pocket.

November 17, Friday

THE WEIGHT-LOSS clinic was one of my least favorite assignments because it dredged up so many bad memories for me, but since the numbers on my scale were climbing at an alarming rate, I decided it might be good motivation for me to be more diligent about my food choices. The fact that Casey was working today, too, was a bonus.

"Do you want to man the reception desk, or help with the round room?" she asked.

The "round room" was the place where clients met as a group with a counselor and talked about their dysfunctional push-pull with food. I had no intention of going within ten feet of that room. My sado masochistic relationship with sugar, fat, and salt was private, and I believed others' should be, too.

"I'll take the reception desk."

"Okay."

"Although… if by chance anyone mentions something about a weight loss drug called Beltina, will you let me know?"

She frowned. "Why?"

"I've heard some rumors about it, that it might have some ill side effects."

"Have you checked the web?"

"Yeah, but there's no mention of anything negative."

"None at all?"

"Not that I can find."

"Okay, if there are no negative posts at all, that means the info has been scraped by the manufacturer. Did you check the deep web?"

"You mean the dark web?"

"The dark web is a subsection of the deep web. Did you check there?"

"No."

"Allow me." She pulled an electronic tablet from her bag.

"Can't you get in trouble for this?"

"No. Anyone can download and use the browser for the deep web. It's what you do while you're there that can get you in trouble, but most of the illegal stuff's on the *dark* web. The area outside the dark web is typically stuff that's not illegal, but maybe controversial, or stuff you wouldn't necessarily want anyone to know you do, like read dinosaur porn."

I squinted. "That's a thing?"

"Yep."

"Okay, that's for another day. For now, can you search for any mentions of Beltina?" I spelled it for her.

A few clicks later, she nodded. "I'm getting some hits. Want me to email you screenshots?"

"That would be a *yes*. Is there anything you can't do?"

Casey grinned. "That would be a *no*."

November 18, Saturday

RUNNING IN COLD weather reminded me why I'd joined a gym in the first place. Every breath I drew into my lungs felt like inhaling little needles, and my lips were already chapped. I tried to pass the time by ruminating over the things Casey had found on the deep web about Beltina—the negative comments there were more telling than the rumors related by clients of the weight-loss clinic, but the side effects reported seemed random and sometimes contradictory: lethargy, hyperactivity; forgetfulness, improved cognitive ability; low blood pressure, high blood pressure; depression; exhilaration.

And all of it anecdotal, i.e., easy to disprove. I hadn't yet sent the text to Rainie about a possible link between Beltina and copper accumulation. I'd decided to wait until I got my own hair metals test results back.

I stopped at a red light to remove my mittens, wipe my runny nose and check my pedometer.

I cursed. How was it possible I'd only gone one lousy mile?

A horn sounded. I looked around to see a familiar van pull

into a parking lot behind me. The driver side window zoomed down to reveal Charlie's face—he was growing a beard.

Good—I hated beards.

"Hi," he said. "I didn't see you in the gym this morning. Have you ditched the class for running?"

"No. I was found out, then thrown out."

"Ah—sorry."

I shrugged. "Running is the fastest way to burn calories." The light turned green. "Gotta go."

He nodded, then his gaze swept me up and down. "Don't burn too many calories... you're looking good."

The middle finger I gave him was somewhat mitigated by the mittens. His laughter floated behind me.

November 19, Sunday

"THANKS FOR UNDERSTANDING about the hunting trip," Kyle said. "It's tradition that my dad and I go dove hunting on Thanksgiving, and we have our family celebration on Sunday."

We were standing in his kitchen, making brunch and waiting for a few guests to stop by, including Libby. "It's fine," I assured him, then sniffed at his collar.

"What are you doing?" he asked with a laugh.

"Is that a new cologne?"

"No. I'm not wearing cologne."

"Hm. Must be the bacon," I said, snagging a piece from a platter and taking a bite.

"You've had quite an appetite lately."

I stopped chewing and swallowed the bite painfully. "It must be all the running."

"Hm. Are you still taking your Beltina?"

I went to the refrigerator for a bottle of water to buy time to respond. "What kind of sales manager would I be if I didn't use my own product?"

"Good point. So will you go see your family on Thanksgiving?"

I took a long drink. "Maybe."

He sighed. "I feel doubly bad—it would've been a good time

to meet them."

I offered him a supportive smile. "But you shouldn't break tradition, especially since we're not married yet."

"And the hunting trip will give me a chance to talk to my dad about investing in the practice."

I looked up. "You want your dad as a partner?"

He winced. "Not really, but the business needs a cash inflow."

Panic blipped in my stomach. "Things aren't any better?"

"Marginally, but not enough. I might have to sell some Traxton stock after all."

"Don't do that," I said in a rush.

His head came around. "Why not?"

I backpedaled. "Because... every investor you talk to says to keep your money in the stock market for the long term. I don't plan to touch my Traxton stock for quite a while." Because I'd rather not turn the big three-oh in prison for insider trading.

"So you think I should ask for my dad's help?"

"Yes. When things get back on track, you can pay him back, without disturbing your portfolio."

He winked. "I think that new hair color *has* made you smarter."

November 20, Monday

"HELLO, there."

I was fishing for my post office box key and hadn't noticed Charlie standing next to his box. Although in that terrible buffalo plaid shirt, I don't know how. And his beard was getting lumberjack thick—ugh.

"Hello."

"Hey, you asked about those kids who are always hanging out in the park."

He had my attention. "Yes."

"I think they're afraid of something."

I frowned. "Of what?"

"I don't know, but I mentioned something to one of the guys about working on my loading dock, and he said he couldn't without the others, said they'd taken a pledge to stay together because there was safety in numbers. So I told him they could all work, but they'd have to split the money."

"And did they?"

"Yeah. Did a good job, too." Then he shrugged. "Maybe it's just street protocol, but I thought it was worth mentioning. There's a meeting of the Triangle Point business coalition tomorrow. I'm going to suggest we figure out a way to put these kids to work."

I smiled. "That would be nice."

"But I'm in the minority. Most of the business owners are trying to figure out a way to clear them out."

I understood that side of the equation as well. Customers wouldn't come to shop and eat in a place that looked unsafe. He waved, then left, seeming to be in a hurry. I wondered briefly if Megan was waiting for him upstairs on his king-size bed.

I put the key into my box and opened the little door. Among the stack of bills was an envelope from the lab company. I ripped open the flap, pulled out the letter and scanned the results.

All levels within the range of normal, see diagram below for specific results.

I double-checked the detailed reading for my copper levels, and was satisfied they were within the normal range provided. My spirits lifted—maybe Portia was right. Maybe the chatter about Beltina side effects was just that—baseless rumor propped up and amplified by Traxton competitors.

Kyle admitted Helen could've gotten the copper from a cosmetic or lotion—maybe even from samples of skin care products he'd given her.

Julie and Trish had often joked about the medication cocktails they were on to ward off aging, depression, and a myriad of other maladies.

The friend of Fiona, the self-abusing girl at the gym, admitted she was an over-achiever. Had Fiona been on a self-destructive path before she'd started taking Beltina?

And Anthony could've been taking other things—speed, or other medications "lifted" from the homes of the people he and his parents knew. He had access to just about anything he wanted.

I exhaled, appalled at how easily I'd been pulled into the propaganda. Fake news was a self-fulfilling prophecy that could be applied to elevate or destroy people, products, or ideas. I felt a little ashamed of myself for being duped in this case.

But relieved to have pulled myself back from the brink before I'd torpedoed my chances of going back to work for Traxton.

November 21, Tuesday

I WAS OUT RUNNING AGAIN, in the cold. Ack. Every time my feet hit the sidewalk, I could feel new gelatinous tissue bouncing and sliding, like little avalanches all over my body. In the wake of my revelations, I was kicking myself for flushing all that wonderful Beltina down the toilet. I was barely eating—was hungry all the damn time—yet the pounds were climbing back on.

My phone rang. When I checked it, the sight of Rainie Stephens's name soured my mood further. I answered, partly to settle this once and for all, and partly for an excuse to stop running.

"Hello, Rainie."

"Hi, Della. I'm just checking in to see if you've had a chance to go through the business correspondence you kept from when you worked for Traxton."

The email with the mention of Wilson's Disease flashed in my mind, but I pushed it away. "Actually, I have, but I didn't find anything of interest. And to be honest, I'm starting to think this was all a big mistake, a wild goose chase."

"That's possible," she conceded. "But we won't know unless we follow every lead." She sighed. "I'm getting the feeling a lot of different people know one little piece of the puzzle. Seen alone, it's easy to convince yourself that one piece doesn't mean anything. It's my job to pull all those disparate pieces together. I need whatever pieces you have, Della, because you might be the only one who has them."

Doubts started pinging in my brain like popcorn kernels exploding. *What if she's right? What if something bad happens, and you could've stopped it?*

I squeezed my eyes closed to blot out the what-ifs. "I can't help you. Please don't call me anymore."

I disconnected the call and resumed running, but veered toward the grocery. If I were gaining weight anyway, the least I deserved was a slice of cheesecake.

Or four.

November 22, Wednesday

"HOW MANY POUNDS?" the guy behind the meat counter asked.

I consulted the book I held. "There will be six of us, and this says one pound of meat per person, so I need a six-pound turkey."

"I got a five-pound turkey breast, or a twelve-pound full bird."

I frowned. "I don't want a breast, I want legs and stuff. Besides, six pounds isn't enough."

"So the full bird?"

"Isn't that too much? Will it fit in my oven?"

He pinched the bridge of his nose. "Lady, I have no idea what kind of oven you have."

"I think I might be able to help."

I turned my head to see Charlie standing next to me. "Where did you come from?"

"The cabbage patch, according to my mom." He looked at the guy behind the meat counter. "The full bird will be perfect." Then he looked back to me. "And yes, it will fit in your oven."

The guy handed the wrapped bird to Charlie, who put it in my cart.

I frowned. "I was handling it."

"Badly," he said, then he grinned. "But hey, you're making Thanksgiving dinner—I'm impressed. I'll bet Kevin is, too."

"His name is *Kyle*, and not that it's any of your business, but he won't be coming. He's going hunting."

"Really? I didn't take the doc for an outdoorsman. What's he hunting? Deer? Bear?"

"Doves."

"Ah… that makes sense. Well, I hate to be the one to tell you, but the day before Thanksgiving isn't the best time to shop for your ingredients."

"I… didn't know that."

He pointed to the book I held—*Fat & Happy*, with his big face on the cover. "Page eighty-two."

My mouth tightened. "I haven't gotten that far."

"Wow, you got an autographed copy. I'm flattered."

"Don't be. It was on clearance."

"Ouch. Well, since I'm here, I can point you in the right direction on some other things if you like."

"Such as?"

"Got your yams yet?"

"No." Then I sighed. "I'm a little confused about the difference between yams and sweet potatoes."

He smiled. "Let's go to the produce section."

He was in his element in the grocery, and I let him lead me from section to section to pick the best values in each department. He was an efficient shopper, and a good tutor, and I confess, by the time my cart was full, his beard was growing on me. He had steered my cart toward the checkout counter when someone touched my sleeve.

I turned to find the lady from the bakery case standing there with a big smile, and a big ole boxed cheesecake. "I saw you walk by and since you're one of our best customers in the bakery, I wanted you to have this. I know it's your favorite, and it's complimentary. Happy holidays."

I managed a shaky smile as she placed the huge box in my hands. "Thanks."

When I turned back to Charlie, he looked thoroughly amused.

"Don't say a word," I warned.

"I wouldn't dream of it. Can I help you home with the groceries?"

"Anthony's coming back to pick me up, but thank you. I guess you'll be spending Thanksgiving with Megan?"

"Megan went back to Nashville."

"Oh? For the holiday?"

"For good. Her divorce is over, so it was time."

"Oh." Why did that news cheer me so much? "Well, if you don't have plans tomorrow and you'd like to stop by, it'll be me and my brother and some friends."

"Sabrina and Susan?"

"Uh, no... those friendships have, shall we say, unraveled. These are other friends—I think you'll like them."

"I appreciate the invitation, but I'm working in a soup kitchen tomorrow."

Of course he was. "That's nice. Well, thanks for the help with my menu. Have a good holiday, Charlie."

He smiled. "You, too, Della."

November 23, Thursday

"OPEN A WINDOW!" I shouted over the piercing sound of the smoke alarm.

My hair was on fire. Well, not literally, but my kitchen was. Well, not literally, but my oven was.

"Jesus, Della," Anthony said, "you've never taken the dang paper out of the oven?" He used a pair of tongs to carry the flaming cardboard to the sink and turned on the water.

"I didn't know it was in there. Why would a manufacturer leave something flammable inside an oven?"

Anthony nodded. "It's totally their fault."

"Folks, it's going to be a little bit of delay while I clean up the kitchen," I announced to the motley crew gathered: Anthony, Casey, Joon-woo, Donnie, Blowz, and the last-minute addition of Mindy Chasen—minus the pug—whom Donnie had snagged in the lobby. The men were gathered around my TV, watching football. "But that's okay, it'll give the turkey time to thaw out."

Silence fell over the room... except for the chirping sound of the fatigued smoke alarm.

"You haven't thawed the turkey?" Casey asked.

"Not... completely," I fudged, realizing I probably shouldn't have put it in the freezer yesterday when I got home from the grocery. "Does that take a while?"

"Drink up, everyone," Anthony said, lifting a bottle of wine. "Who needs a refill?"

I did. I drank from my glass and surveyed the mess. I had driven everyone to the living room with utmost confidence I could pull this off. Chopped food, spices, and containers covered the counters. Every piece of cookware was stacked on top of the oven, but I had no idea what to put in what. Joon-woo had brought a cheese platter, which I desperately hoped would tide everyone over for, like, hours. I walked over to the picture on the *Fat & Happy* cookbook and stuck my tongue out at Charlie. "This is all your fault," I hissed.

The doorbell rang, and since I was pretty sure it was the building safety officer checking to see why the smoke alarm had sounded, I said I'd get it and made my way to the door, wine glass in hand.

When I opened the door, I blinked in surprise to see Charlie standing there, a bottle of wine in one hand and a long baguette in the other.

"Hi," I said.

"Hi. I finished at the soup kitchen and thought I'd stop by." He sniffed. "Is something on fire?"

I kind of liked the beard, I decided. "Thank God you're here."

November 24, Friday

WHAT KIND OF SADO MASOCHIST agrees to work in a toy store the day after Thanksgiving?

That would be me.

I assumed I'd be working the checkout, but as soon as the manager heard I had experience working in a book store, he stuck me in that department in the rear of the store with instructions to keep the kids entertained while their parents spent obscene amounts of money.

It had been my job to look after Donnie when we were growing up, and our resources were few. Donnie wasn't a great reader, but he loved being read to, so, falling back on my experience, I plucked a copy of *Harry Potter & the Sorcerer's Stone* off the shelf, stood in the front of the sitting area, and began to read in a loud, theatrical voice.

One by one, children peered around bookshelves and abandoned noisy toys to come and explore, then sit. By the time I finished reading the first section, the entire area was packed shoulder to shoulder with rapt, quiet kids, and even a few adults.

I paused and looked up. "Should I go on?"

"Yes, please," they chorused, and I continued. From the back of the crowd, the store manager gave me a thumb's up.

I confess I was still revving on the energy of the previous day.

Charlie had saved Thanksgiving, with me as his helper. And in no time, he had everyone eating out of his hand—literally, as he passed around dates stuffed with smoked almonds and parmesan cheese, and chunks of bread dripping with brie and cranberries. It was a heady experience, seeing food through his eyes—a first for me. I'd never been comfortable consuming food in front of people. To me, food was something you consumed mostly in secret, where quantity trumped quality.

At the end of the evening, he had helped to divvy up leftovers, taking a few home for himself. He had lingered at the door, but we were both conscious of the curious eyes of my guests, not to mention the engagement ring on my left hand. So he'd left with a wave and I'd closed the door, wondering what had just happened.

And if it could always be that way.

When I left the toy store, I was tired from standing most of the day, but antsy, too, for a reason I couldn't put my finger on. The condo was dark when I arrived home—Anthony was no doubt out with Casey. I took a shower and dropped my engagement ring into cleaning solution, then padded around the condo picking up items overlooked from the night before—a glass here, a saucer there. I walked into the kitchen and opened the refrigerator, but nothing looked as good as it had tasted last night. I found an open bottle of wine and poured a glass, and crunched on a handful of almonds for a makeshift dinner.

When I moved a kitchen towel, I found a wooden box that contained a chef's knife. Even my untrained eye could see it was something special—and needed to be returned. I realized I didn't have Charlie's number, so I pushed my feet into sandals and walked down the stairs two floors to his unit.

I paused in front of his door. From inside I could hear music, and I wondered if I were interrupting something special. Vowing to hand over the knife and vamoose, I rang his doorbell, then waited nervously until he answered.

He, too, wasn't long from the shower, I realized, since his hair was barely dry and he was still buttoning his shirt. "Hi. This is a nice surprise."

"Hi." I held up the knife box. "You forgot something."

"Oh. Yeah, I would've missed my favorite knife sooner or later." He opened the door. "Come in."

"I can't stay."

"Big plans tonight?"

"Not really. I worked all day."

"Where today?"

"At a toy store."

"Jesus, you deserve a drink for that. I just opened a nice bottle of barbera."

I nodded, and stepped inside. "Okay... maybe half a glass."

I knew as soon as the door closed, though, what I was in for.

"Charlie—"

"Della—"

I went to him and he kissed me, a full-body kiss that felt sweet and desperate at the same time. As soon as he touched me, I was electrified. Clothes fell off—his and mine. We made it as far as the breakfast bar. I leaned into it and he kissed his way down the front of me, stopping at all the good places along the way. Then he knelt in front of me and dipped his head to my core, bringing a banked fire to life.

"Ah... ahhhhh...."

The hum of an orgasm thrummed higher and higher in my midsection.

"That's what she... was talking... about."

He lifted his mouth. "Hm?"

I drove my fingers into his hair, wild for him to resume. I *loved* the beard.

He didn't disappoint, laving me until I climaxed, catching me when my legs threatened to collapse. Then he propped me up with his big body, and lifted me onto his erection.

It was sensory overload as my sex consumed his. I wrapped my arms around his powerful shoulders and held on for dear life. He kissed my neck and thrust hard, capturing me against the counter and his hips. His breath came faster as he stroked deeper. When I thought I might fall apart from the sheer intensity of his lovemaking, I felt him explode inside me. I captured his groans in my mouth and pulled him closer until his pulses quieted.

We recovered slowly, taking our time disentangling. Neither one of us spoke—I assumed he was trying to assimilate what had happened, same as I was. He lowered a kiss to my shoulder, then knelt to scoop up our clothing. "I guess that needed to happen."

I was still reeling. "I guess so." I pulled my blouse over my head and stepped into my underwear.

"The question is, do you want it to happen again?"

I blinked. "Now?"

He smiled. "And later."

I pulled on my jeans and decided not to subject him to me trying to get them buttoned and zipped, just pulled my blouse over the waistband. "Can I think about that?"

"Sure," he said, pulling on his own pants and buttoning them without contortions. "How about that glass of wine?"

"Um, I'm going to pass." I walked to the door, carrying my sandals. "I need to... think."

"Okay. Let me know what you decide."

I opened the door and stepped out, closing it behind me.

Having sex is like eating food, right—it doesn't count if you do it standing up?

November 25, Saturday

I GAVE A COMMAND performance the next day at the toy store, picking up where I'd left off the day before. I saw many of the same faces, and lots of new ones as word had spread that parents could leave their kids in a safe, supervised place while they shopped. Most gratifying to me was that books were flying off the shelves and into shopping carts.

I was glad to have something to so thoroughly occupy my mind because Charlie was waiting in every corner, and I didn't want to go there.

At the end of the day, I walked home slowly, enjoying the crisp air and the holiday lights. But if I thought I'd have things sorted out by the time I walked into my building I was wrong. I checked my mail, then rode up the elevator, still a little numb over how easily I had walked into Charlie's arms. I was glad Anthony wasn't home because I was sure "I cheated on Kyle" was written all over my face. I slipped on my engagement ring, hoping it would make me feel more connected to him.

My phone buzzed with a text—from Kyle.

I am thinking about you.

It was as if he had a sixth sense. Or had he—like me—recently had a fling, then realized how much I meant to him?

I am thinking about you, too.

Don't ever doubt how much I love you.

I smiled, then texted back, *I won't.*

My doorbell rang, and my stomach pitched. I knew it was Charlie before I looked through the peephole. Yep—all I could see was beard.

I opened the door. "Hi."

He straightened. "Hi." He held up a sticky note. "I was going to leave this in case you weren't home. I thought maybe it's time we exchange phone numbers."

Since we'd exchanged DNA? "Okay."

He handed me the note. "So there's my number, you can call or text me... if you like."

"Okay."

I realized he was staring at my engagement ring. He pressed his lips together, then sighed. "Look, Della... I want to be with you... but I'm not going to be another secret you keep from your boyfriend."

"I wouldn't want that either."

"I know you're dealing with a lot right now, with your job and the dilemma over the drug you sold, and your family, and a lot of things I don't even know about. I don't want to be another problem for you. If this other guy makes you happy, then I won't like it, but I'll deal with it. But I can't do the halfway, casual hookup situation. Just so we're clear: I want all of you, or none of you, and I want it soon."

Then he turned and stalked away, leaving things in my mind exceedingly *un*clear.

November 26, Sunday

THE COVEY FAMILY Thanksgiving get-together was a lavish party at Kyle's parents' mansion in Buckhead, and everyone was encouraged to bring friends.

I didn't expect to see Libby Lakes there, however. Especially not skulking around the patio with my fiancé, alone. When I realized I'd walked up on a conversation, I stopped behind a pillar to listen, my heart pounding.

Kyle made a rueful noise. "Look, Libby, I'm so flattered by your attention, but I'm going to marry Della, as soon as she'll have me."

My heart gave a little squeeze. He did love me. Guilt barbed through my chest for cheating on him. We could build a wonderful life together, if I didn't ruin things. I needed to get myself back in check—stop eating like two people and stop letting Charlie Graham put his shlong in me.

Libby heaved a dramatic sigh. "I understand—your heart was already taken. But I still want to be the face of your practice, Kyle. I really believe in what you're doing. Let me help—please."

He inclined his head. "I think Della and I both would like that. I hope the two of you will become good friends."

"I'd like that, too," she said.

"Hello," I said loudly, walking toward them. "Can I join this party?"

"Of course," Kyle said, turning a wide smile in my direction. He lowered a loving kiss next to my ear. I sensed he'd turned a corner of some kind.

"Kyle was just saying the two of you should set a date for the wedding," Libby said.

I smiled. "I've been thinking the same thing."

"When?" Kyle asked, squeezing my hand.

"The sooner, the better."

"How about Christmas?"

He gave me another kiss, and I saw my future in his eyes: stature, prestige, power… security. All the things I'd dreamed of one day having growing up in Dewdrop, all the things that endured way beyond physical chemistry. "Sounds perfect."

November 27, Monday

FROM A PALATIAL Buckhead mansion to the choking confines of the drycleaners in mere hours.

It was, I decided, an example of my superb flexibility: I could exist in either world.

And I chose palatial over peon.

I sat on the stool, zipping through the spinner rack, sorting out more unclaimed clothing. When I had filled a rack, I shouted to my boss (I couldn't call him Cheater anymore without feeling like a hypocrite), then rolled the rack to the double doors in the back. I knocked loudly, and when no one answered, I knocked again. After a couple of minutes, I opened one of the doors and peeked inside.

The backroom was just as stifling in the cold weather, perhaps more so because heaters were running in some areas. Beneath my sensible shoes, the floor felt slick with condensation.

The unfortunate workers were jampacked in, elbow to elbow, and no one even looked up as I wheeled the rack inside. Mrs. Gladstone was nowhere in sight, but mindful of Joon-woo's warning to behave, I pushed the rack to the place against the wall where I'd parked the previous racks.

When I turned to walk back, a shiny object on the floor caught my attention. When I crouched down, I gasped—it was Elena's missing earring! Caught under a door, mashed against the concrete floor. I recalled the drycleaners was on the list of places Elena had worked. She must have lost it when she was cleaning, probably on the same day she'd lost the other one at my condo.

I didn't know where the door led, so I tried to pull the earring loose without opening it. But when it wouldn't budge, I reached up and quietly turned the knob, opening the door just enough to release the piece of jewelry.

Suddenly the door flew open, sending me back on my rear. I looked up to see Lela Gladstone standing over me. The door appeared to open into her private office. "What are *you* doing here?"

"I'm sorry—this earring... it belongs to a friend of mine. I just want to get it back to her."

She made a frustrated noise. "Get it, then get out of here. And I don't want to see you back."

I picked up the earring, then picked up myself. "Okay."

I said goodbye to the guy working the counter, then remembered a piece of country relationship advice that seemed a fitting parting gift. "And when it comes to women, remember— you should dance with the one that brung you."

He squinted. "Huh?"

I sighed. "Never mind."

I left the smelly drycleaners behind. Joon-woo would probably be upset with me, but hopefully would be happy I'd found something of Elena's to return to her daughter.

I decided to take my medicine now and walked to ATA. Joon-woo was just hanging up the phone and I could tell by her expression, she'd been talking to Mrs. Gladstone.

"I just lost the drycleaner's account," she said, her voice tearful.

"I'm sorry... but look." I held up the mashed but intact piece of jewelry. "I found Elena's missing earring under the door to Mrs. Gladstone's office! Now we can send the pair back to her daughter."

She sighed. "Della..."

"I'll make it up to you, Joon-woo. And the toy store loves me—that has to count for something."

She nodded and smiled. "Let's just get through the holidays, okay?"

November 28, Tuesday

"DO YOU RECOGNIZE this guy?"

Blowz squinted at the photo of the man in the video, then froze.

My heart rate picked up. "You do know him?"

He turned his head slowly to look me over. "Are you sure you're not a cop?"

I scoffed. "I'm sure. Do you know him? It's really important, Blowz."

He scratched his head, suddenly nervous. "So... I might've bought weed from him a couple of times."

"Where?"

"Uh... around."

"In Triangle Point?"

"Yeah... out in the park."

I inhaled sharply. "Do you know how to get in touch with him?"

"No… it's not like that. He's not my dealer, we just crossed paths. And I haven't seen him in months."

"What's his name."

"Z, something. Zeeker… Zero, something like that."

I pulled out my phone, called Detective Terry, and relayed the information.

"We're one step ahead of you, Ms. Culpepper. Vice identified the guy as Zenith Vargo. He's a known human trafficker. We think he might've tried to recruit Elena, or kidnap her, and she put up a fight."

I covered my mouth. "Oh, no. Poor Elena."

"Poor you if you don't stop flashing this guy's picture around, Ms. Culpepper. He's a dangerous character. For the last time, let the police handle it, okay?"

"Okay," I murmured. "Please keep me—"

But he'd already disconnected the call. I sighed, shaking. No wonder Elena was haunting me in my nightmares. Her death must have been awful.

November 29, Wednesday

"LOOK WHAT LIBBY GAVE ME!" Anthony squealed.

I turned my head from my desk to see him holding up the bottle of pricey cologne I'd wrapped for Libby. "Oh, nice."

"And listen to the card."

As he read the words I'd written, I followed along in my head. So either she'd been planning to give the cologne to Anthony all along, or she'd changed her mind and given it to him after Kyle rejected her.

"And she signed x's and o's—isn't that cute?"

"Uh-huh." All's well that ends well.

"Libby said she's decided to move here permanently, and she wants me to work for her full-time."

My head came around again—crap. "She's moving to Atlanta?"

He grimaced and nodded. "Sorry."

My phone rang and when Portia's name came across the screen, my pulse blipped higher. "I need to take this, Anthony." I connected the call, holding my breath. "Hello, Portia."

"Hi, Della. I have good news. Can you meet me tomorrow for lunch? I'm bringing you your bonus check... and a job offer."

I closed my eyes in abject, utter, total, complete relief. "I'll be there."

November 30, Thursday

I WAS SO EXCITED, my feet barely touched the ground as I made my way to meet Portia. The only unexciting part was we were meeting at Charlie's restaurant, but that would be the perfect time and place to tell him sleeping with him had been a big, fat mistake.

No pun intended.

Actually, for a big man, though, Charlie was nimble. And strong. He hadn't missed a beat when he'd lifted me off my feet and onto his—

Okay, I had to stop replaying that scene in my head.

Especially since I was mere minutes away from getting my old life back.

A block away from the restaurant, I passed an alley and noticed one of the boys from the group of teens that always hung together—the handsome, surly boy—talking to a man.

Hm, hadn't he told Charlie he and the other kids had made a pact not to separate? As I watched them, the man grabbed the boy's arm and began leading him toward an alley. From my vantage point, I saw a van parked a few yards inside. The boy struggled and I wondered if perhaps the man was a parent or other relative who'd come to take him home. I couldn't blame a parent for being assertive about reclaiming their runaway kid.

Ain't got no home, I remembered the boy saying. But wasn't anything better than being on the streets?

The man swung his head in my direction, and when I got a good look at him, I froze.

It was the man from the video—Zenith what's-his-name, the human trafficker and Elena's presumed killer. The boy yelled and tried to wrench away. Then the man jabbed him with something, and the boy's body went limp.

I didn't think, I just ran toward the alley, shouting, "Stop! Let him go!" My recent running gigs had helped a little—I sprinted across the space in record time, even in heels. Still, by the time I reached them, the man was shoving the boy into the back of the van.

Too late, I realized I hadn't thought of what I'd do when I got there. There was no one else in the alley. I opened my mouth to scream, but when the man turned his ugly black eyes on me, my body seized in terror and my voice died in my throat.

He grabbed my arm and yanked me toward the open van door. I fought him and kicked, then I felt a sharp sting in my back, then... nothing.

I didn't want to be a hero.

DECEMBER

December 1, Friday

WHEN I OPENED my eyes, I was utterly disoriented. My throat ached and I couldn't feel my arms. I tried to move, but I was paralyzed. In the pitch blackness, my mind reeled—I knew something was terribly wrong, but it took my memory several long minutes to catch up.

I'd been walking… on my way to meet someone… my former boss Portia… for a late lunch… then I'd seen something… no— some*one*… one of the teenage boys who hung out around Triangle Point. And he'd been with another person… a man… a bad man...

The man from the video who had climbed out of Elena Padilla's car in the parking garage, after killing her, most likely.

Z-something-or-other. Zenith... Vargo. Detective Jack Terry had said the man was a known human trafficker. When I'd seen him jab the boy with something that made him go limp, I'd run toward them screaming for him to let the boy go.

And it appeared I'd been exceedingly unsuccessful.

Ack, what had the man injected into me? My brain was positively gluey.

I moved my throbbing head and felt scratchy carpet beneath my cheek. I was lying face-down with my wrists bound behind me. I tried to roll my stiff body, and discovered my ankles were also bound. I turned my head painfully and blinked wide until my eyes adjusted to the dark and I could make out a few shapes in my surroundings.

Since my face was inches away from a wheel hump, I concluded I was in the back of a parked panel van—presumably the same one the man had thrown the boy into. From the absence of outdoor noise, I surmised the van was sitting inside and from the pervasive chill, had been for some time. I mustered my strength and managed to roll over... into another person.

I sucked in a choking breath, unable to scream past a constricted throat. A good thing, I realized a half-second later. If Vargo was in the vicinity, I didn't want to alert him I was awake.

I'd bumped into the teenage boy, I realized, and since he didn't react, he must still be unconscious.

I hoped.

"Hey," I whispered in a croaky voice. "Are you awake?"

He didn't respond.

We were lying back to back. I pulled against my hand restraints, but there was no give. I wiggled my numb fingers until the needles of returning sensation subsided and I could feel his hands behind mine. I carefully found his wrist and pressed a finger into it, relieved when I felt a faint but steady pulse. I yanked on his hands. "Hey—wake up."

But he didn't move.

I reasoned either he'd gotten a bigger dose than I had, or my bigger body had burned through the tranquilizer more quickly.

So maybe the pounds I'd been packing on lately had *one* benefit.

I wriggled onto the wheel hump for elevation and after much huffing and puffing, managed to lift myself to a seated position. The head rush almost made me pass out. I sat and breathed deeply until the sensation passed, then assessed my physical condition.

I was still clothed, thank God, in the dress and jacket I'd been wearing for my meeting. The straps on my high-heeled sandals had kept them on my feet during the scuffle. My purse was missing, along with its contents, including my wallet and phone. My kidnapper could use both to find out everything about me, if he cared to know, including the fact that I was financially strapped.

I was so thirsty, I could barely swallow. Conversely, my bladder was uncomfortably full. I wondered how long I'd been in here, then remembered I'd felt a watch on the teen's wrist. I wriggled back over to him and blindly stabbed at his cheap rubber watch until a tiny light illuminated the face.

1:27 a.m.

I winced. I'd been here over twelve hours.

Had anyone missed me? Or would I, like Elena, go missing for days—weeks—before anyone even noticed?

I'd missed the meeting with Portia, but she might've thought I'd changed my mind about the promised new position with Traxton Pharmaceuticals. At the most, she would've left a message on my phone.

My roommate and former personal assistant Anthony had known I was going to meet Portia, but if I didn't show up at the condo for a couple of nights, he might simply think I was staying with my fiancé Kyle.

Meanwhile, my fiancé Kyle wasn't accustomed to seeing me more than once or twice a week, and recently, we'd fallen into the routine of spending Sundays together. So theoretically, it could be another two or three days before he questioned my whereabouts. My fingers were stiff and cold, but I felt my finger with my thumb and was relieved to find the ring intact. The stone was turned to the underside of my finger—maybe the Zenith character had overlooked it in his haste to truss me up like a pig.

My boss at the Anita Temp Agency, Joon-woo, knew my plan all along had been to go back to work for Traxton, so she wouldn't worry if she didn't see me for a while, especially since I'd cost her a couple of accounts lately—the gym and the drycleaners.

And suddenly, I remembered where I recognized Zenith Vargo from. He was one of the men standing on the loading dock of the drycleaner's the day I'd futilely waited for Amy—another teen who'd hung around Triangle Point—to leave from her job in the oppressive backroom operations.

And the light from the boy's watch revealed our bindings were plastic bags. On closer inspection, I noticed familiar markings— I'd spent hours operating the spinner rack of garments covered with those bags.

Was the drycleaners a front for a human trafficking ring?

I'd found Elena's missing earring wedged under a door there, where she'd performed cleaning services as part of her employment through Joon-woo's agency. Had she stumbled onto something while working at the drycleaners that had put her life in jeopardy?

The sound of muffled voices reached me, sending my vital signs into overdrive. I wriggled back down to the floor, closed my eyes, and went limp just as the rear van doors opened.

"Are they dead?" a man's voice asked. His tone indicated it wouldn't be the end of the world if we were.

"No," another man said more harshly. Zenith Vargo, I presumed.

I felt a sharp smack to my bare leg. I had to fight my urge to recoil.

"Wake up," Vargo shouted, then smacked my leg again.

My heart was pounding so hard I was sure they could hear it, but I didn't move. A noise sounded as if they'd hit or punched the teenage boy. He didn't respond either.

"Give 'em another hour," Vargo said.

From the echo of the men's voices, I guessed we were in some kind of parking garage or warehouse. But where? In twelve hours, the man could've driven to Miami or Chicago or Detroit.

Or across the Mexican border. The thought sent a chill up my spine.

"Isn't she a little old for this?" the first man remarked.

Great—judgmental kidnappers.

"I had to take her," Vargo said. "She tried to interfere."

"Think we can find a buyer? She's kind of porky."

Somewhere the girl working the gym counter was smiling.

"Some men like the fatties," Vargo said. "I don't mind a juicy rump myself on occasion."

Fear washed over me. Was this how my life was going to end? Indentured sex slave to some dominating man or, *gulp*, group of men? I was positive the reality would not be the titillating experience described in popular novels.

"Well, since she's asleep..." the first man offered.

When his vile suggestion sank in, my heart seized. With my hands and feet bound, I'd be unable to fight them off. My only hope was they would find my industrial-strength shapewear too much to deal with.

"Quiet," Vargo bit out, his voice alert. "What was that?"

"I didn't hear anything."

"Shut up. Someone's outside."

I strained my ears and heard a distant, unintelligible noise.

"Go see," Vargo said.

I heard the sound of running feet as the man obeyed, then the unmistakable *chick, chick* of an automatic weapon being checked. My blood ran cold.

The first man pounded back. "Cops! Fucking everywhere! What are we gonna do?"

"We're going to be quiet," Vargo said calmly. "This is a big facility. They can't check every storage unit, not without a warrant. They'll never know we're here." He closed the van doors with a quiet *thunk*.

My heart raced. Help was nearby, so now was the time to raise an alarm. But how?

The horn. If I could get to the steering wheel, I could make some noise. But that meant getting over the seat into the cab. And if by some miracle, the key was in the ignition, I could drive it through a door if I had to. But I needed to at least free my ankles to be ready to drive—or run.

Adrenaline forced me back to a seated position, my mind sprinting as to how I could cut the plastic bag that bit into my ankles as surely as a cord. I needed something sharp... or jagged.

My engagement ring.

Hoping the stone or the prongs would be strong enough to compromise the cinched plastic, I lumbered to my knees to position my bound hands behind my back over my bound ankles. I was sweating, knowing Vargo and his crony could return any second and decide my chunky ass wasn't worth saving to sell.

There was no finesse involved—I dragged my ring across the ties on my ankles, hacking away, missing more times than I made contact. Within a minute or so, my arm muscles were screaming. I'd been kicked out of the gym a lousy two weeks ago, and atrophy was already setting in.

At last I heard a satisfying rip of plastic and a few more hacks loosened the binds enough to pull them apart. My relief was so complete, I went limp a few seconds before remembering my mission. I lumbered forward on my knees, falling on my face twice before reaching the front seat. I lasered in on the ignition, but to my supreme disappointment, there were no keys. The horn was my only hope.

I propelled myself over the seat and struggled to reach the horn. I managed to stab it with my elbow, but it took a few tries to make solid contact. When the horn first blasted, it scared even me. But I knew I had only a few seconds before Vargo would be back to silence me. Too late, I realized I should've locked the doors first.

Dammit, the next time I was kidnapped, I would be better prepared.

I leaned on the horn, gratified the metal walls of the storage facility amplified the noise.

Suddenly the driver side door opened and Vargo treated me to a string of expletives. He dragged me out of the cab and I landed hard on the concrete floor on my back. Before I had time to process the pain, Vargo pulled a handgun out of his belt and aimed it at me. On pure instinct, I rolled under the van.

Vargo was incensed, now screaming at me. He stuck the gun under the van and fired blindly. The bullet pinged off metal near me and I screamed as loudly as I could past my painful throat.

Vargo's mean face appeared under the van, and he leveled the gun at me. "Die, bitch."

My life flashed before me and sadly, I realized most of it had not been happy. If I'd known I was going to die young, I would've loved more easily... and eaten more cheesecake.

When the shot sounded, I reasoned he'd shot a part of me that was numb from lack of circulation. So... as it turned out, dying wasn't so bad. I waited for the white light, and the voice of God... or the other guy. It could go either way.

"Della?"

Wow, I hadn't expected God to sound like Detective Jack Terry.

"Della?"

I turned my head to see him lying on the ground, staring at me. "Are you okay?"

"V... argo?" I managed.

"He's not getting up anytime soon. Are you injured?"

I shook my head, and burst into tears.

"There now... it's all over. I'm going to pull you out slowly.

Let me know if anything hurts."

I let him drag me from under the van like a sack of crying potatoes. He sat me up and cut the binds around my wrists.

"We need an ambulance," he called to someone, then he looked back to me and smiled. "There are a lot of people looking for you."

"My boss reported me missing?" I croaked.

"No—your boyfriend."

"Kyle?"

Jack squinted. "I thought his name was Charlie."

December 2, Saturday

"OH, MY GAWD, this is the most exciting thing that's ever happened," Anthony said, bouncing in the visitor chair next to my hospital bed. "You're a freaking hero, Della."

I shook my head. "Just in the wrong place at the right time. But I'm still a little foggy on how the police knew I was missing."

"Portia was waiting for you at Graham's Eatery, and Charlie recognized her. She said you'd missed your meeting and she couldn't reach you. Charlie called, too, and when you didn't answer, he went to the temp agency. Joon-woo hadn't seen you, so she called me. I hadn't seen you, so I called Kyle. He hadn't seen you, so Charlie called the police, and a detective there knew your name. He set things in motion, checked camera surveillance and saw you get snatched. He must've mobilized the entire police force to find you."

Dear man. If he hadn't, who knew where I'd be right now. "I have a lot of people to thank."

"Are you sure you're okay?" Anthony asked, his face creased in concern.

I nodded. "The doctor said he would release me later today."

A knock sounded on the door and when it opened, Charlie stood there holding a small vase with a single stem—a perfect white lily. My heart stuttered a bit, then fell back into rhythm.

"How's the girl of the hour?" Charlie asked.

"Amazing, like always," Anthony chirped. Then he looked at me and pushed to his feet. "Call me if you need a ride home." He blew me a kiss, then gave Charlie a smirk as the men passed.

Charlie was silent until the door closed. "Hi."

"Hi," I said.

He walked forward and placed the vase on the window sill.

"Thank you."

He smiled. "You're welcome."

"And I understand I have you to thank for raising the alarm."

"No thanks needed. I'm just glad you're okay."

"So am I," I said with a laugh.

He studied me until I squirmed, covering the bruises at my wrists. "I must look a sight."

"In the best possible way. Anthony is right—you are amazing, Della."

My heart rate was up again. "Everyone is giving me too much credit."

"You led the police to a human trafficking kingpin and busted up an entire crime organization. That's pretty good work for a Temp Girl."

I shook my head, but my face warmed under his praise.

He wet his lips. "When I realized you'd been kidnapped, I nearly went out of my mind."

I metered my words. "I'm sorry to have caused you concern."

His mouth twitched. "I'm still waiting for your answer."

My mouth watered. I swallowed. I was beyond dismayed I couldn't stop thinking about our one encounter.

The door swung open and Kyle stepped in carrying a huge bouquet of flowers. He grinned. "How's my girl?"

I smiled back. "Fine."

He swept in and handed me the flowers, then kissed me. "You gave everyone quite a scare."

"Yes, she did," Charlie piped up.

"Hello, Charlie," Kyle said, extending his hand. "Thank you for letting everyone know Della didn't make that lunch meeting. You've been a good friend to us."

Charlie clasped his hand. "Don't mention it."

"You should come to our wedding," Kyle said, then looked to me for confirmation.

Inside I winced. "Yes, of course."

Charlie gave us a wry smile. "So you set a date."

"December thirtieth," Kyle said. "At Chateau Elan, north of the city."

Charlie nodded. "I'm familiar with their wines."

"Good," Kyle said. "Hope to see you there."

"I'll check my calendar," Charlie said, then pointed to the door. "I should be going."

"Don't leave on my account," Kyle offered.

"I was just checking in with Della," Charlie said, then turned his dark gaze on me. "But I can see you have everything you need."

He walked to the door, then exited.

December 3, Sunday

"AND LIKE A SCENE out of a Hollywood thriller," Kyle read from the *Atlanta Journal-Constitution*, "Culpepper used the diamond setting of her engagement ring to cut through her ankle bindings, allowing her to reach the van's steering wheel to sound the horn for help."

Kyle looked up and grinned at the small crowd gathered in his sunroom. They cheered enthusiastically, although I noticed Libby Lakes chose to instead lift her glass for another drink.

"Go, Della!" Kyle's sister Helen said, pumping her fist. She was still pale from her metals poisoning ordeal, but she was much recovered, and happily reconciled with Reggie.

"And go Kyle," Libby offered dryly, "for buying a diamond large enough to be used as a tool."

Laughter rang out and Kyle took a little bow. "Which reminds me—Della and I will be getting married the last Saturday of the month, on the thirtieth, at Chateau Elan."

More cheering and clapping sounded.

"Are we all invited?" Libby asked with a mocking smile.

"Of course," I said evenly.

Kyle read aloud the rest of the article, which offered history into the sex trafficking ring that had been thwarted and the charges against the ringleader Zenith Vargo, who was in critical condition in a prison infirmary from injuries sustained during the standoff with police. If he recovered, no less than three countries were fighting over the right to try Vargo on capital murder and other offenses.

The article had been written by none other than Rainie Stephens, who, after recording the facts of the kidnapping, couldn't help but try to pump me for more information about the possible side effects of the weight-loss drug I used to sell, Beltina. I'd told Rainie not only did I have no such proof, but on Tuesday I would be meeting with my former boss about going back to work for Traxton. The dogged reporter had had the good grace to wish me well.

"You're a celebrity," Kyle said to me later when the crowd had dissipated and we were alone.

"The only celebrity in the room is Libby," I demurred.

He smiled, then looked serious. "Still, when I think of how close I came to losing you..." He gave me an urgent kiss, then cupped my cheek. "We have to talk."

His tone sent a knot to my stomach. "What about?"

"When Anthony called me Thursday to ask if I knew where you were, I realized I don't even know how to reach your family in the event of an emergency. That's just not right. I want to meet your family—*before* the wedding."

"I'll have to check with them—" I began.

"No more stalling. I promise not to embarrass you. I was thinking we'd go visit Christmas Day."

I managed a smile. "That sounds... great." But my intestines cramped at the thought of making the introductions. And since Kyle was insisting on meeting my family before the wedding, I wondered if he sensed something was askew with the Culpepper clan.

December 4, Monday

"THANKS FOR COMING in today to give a formal statement, Ms. Culpepper." Detective Jack Terry waved me into a chair in a private room at the precinct.

"I'm glad to be here to give it," I said wryly.

He took a chair opposite me. "The assistant D.A. and a court reporter will be here shortly." Then he smiled. "Before we get started, may I say you look better than the last time I saw you. How are you doing?"

"Everyone keeps asking me that, but I'm fine."

"You've been through a terrible ordeal. Don't be afraid to ask for help if you need it."

"I'm stronger than I look, Detective."

"That, I believe." Then he scratched his temple. "In fact, lately I'm starting to question which gender is the weaker sex."

Why did I get the feeling that last statement had a little to do with me and a lot to do with the Carlotta woman he seemed obsessed with? "No question there, Detective. Men have always been the weaker sex."

He laughed. "And today you'll get no argument from me. The mayor wants to give you a special commendation."

I frowned. "Me? You were the one who took down Vargo."

"By the way, in case you haven't heard, Vargo died a few hours ago."

"I can't imagine there will be too many mourners at his grave."

"He won't be missed," Jack confirmed with a nod. "Vargo regained consciousness long enough to give a video statement." The detective wet his lips. "He confessed to killing Elena Padilla. She stumbled onto a young woman being held against her will at the drycleaners and freed her. Vargo followed Elena to her car and made her drive to the parking garage. He said he gave her the chance at an easy life, to become some man's kept woman, but she spit in his face, so he killed her."

I blinked back horrified tears, then swallowed to compose myself. "Why do you need my statement if Vargo won't be prosecuted?"

"The charges will be filed posthumously... and the information could be used to charge his co-conspirators, such as Lela Gladstone." He shifted in his chair. "But back to the commendation. I was just doing my job. You were the one who risked your life to help that boy." He gave me a disapproving frown. "Which was pretty foolish, by the way."

Water under the bridge. "How is the young man? I'm sorry, I don't know his name."

"Toby Hess. He's doing fine and reunited with his parents in

North Carolina."

"That's good news."

"And there's more where that came from. Penny Essex and Amy Rocha were rescued from a hotel in Peachtree City where they were being held against their will, along with almost two dozen other teens and—" He grunted. "—kids who were even younger."

I closed my eyes at the unspeakable horrors they must've been subjected to.

"You'll be happy to know Penny has been reunited with her baby."

My heavy heart lifted a bit. "She has?"

"In fact, the foster family caring for the baby has agreed to take in Penny, too, so they can be together."

I exhaled. "That's wonderful."

"Well done, Ms. Culpepper."

But I didn't feel deserving of praise—far from it. "Detective, will you do me a favor?"

"Name it."

"Make sure that commendation is made out to Elena Padilla. She's the hero here, not me."

Jack considered me for a few seconds, then he dipped his chin in concession.

December 5, Tuesday

MY NERVOUS EXCITEMENT as I walked to the rescheduled meeting with Portia was tempered by an overwhelming sense of déjà vu. The last time I'd walked this route, I'd tried to intervene in an assault and had been kidnapped for my trouble.

In broad freaking daylight.

Beneath a chilly sky, my skin prickled with awareness, and I couldn't help but react to every sudden sound—an impatient car horn, blaring holiday music, the ringing bell of the Salvation Army bucket volunteer.

The drycleaners had been boarded up, with a neon sticker on the door announcing it was a federal crime scene and trespassers would be, basically, shot. When I thought of what had been going on right under everyone's noses—including mine—I shuddered. I wondered if Cheater Boss had been in on the operation. And I marveled over the irony that Lela Gladstone's unwillingness or inability to hire full-time workers had led to hiring temp workers like me and Elena, which had ultimately led to the downfall of her black market empire.

My head swung from side to side, taking in every face I passed on the sidewalk, looking for... who? Zenith Vargo? Lela Gladstone? They were both in places where they couldn't bother anyone, so why was I jumpy?

The ring of my phone startled me to the point that I cried out. When I checked the screen and saw Rainie Stephens's name, I frowned. She knew I was meeting with my former boss today and was determined to ruin it for me. I hit the decline button, then gave myself a mental shake and picked up my pace. The sooner our meeting took place, the sooner I'd have my bonus check of thirty-two grand in my hot little hand. Between the payment the Dewdrop bank needed on my mother's house and my own accumulating bills, most of it was spoken for. But if the job offer was as lucrative as I hoped, I'd be back to earning a decent salary again soon.

I wasn't thrilled Portia and I were meeting at Charlie's restaurant again, but I reminded myself if we'd planned to meet somewhere else last time, I might not have been missed. I at least owed Charlie my patronage.

I walked into Graham's Eatery a few minutes early, and asked the hostess to seat me where I could see Portia when she arrived. The lunch crowd had dissipated, but business was still brisk. I was happy for Charlie. He deserved good things...

He deserved someone who would love him better than I could.

"Your server will be right out," the hostess said.

"I've got this one, Annie."

I looked up to see Charlie making rounds in his chef's jacket. He offered me a smile. "Hi, there."

"Hi."

"Are you recovered?"

I held up my wrists. "The bruises are fading."

"But are you recovered?"

I squirmed under his penetrating gaze. "Of course." I

squinted. "You shaved your beard."

He reached up to stroke his bare jaw. "Yeah. Just needed something new."

But it had felt so good—no, I refused to go there... ack, too late.

And the tongue maneuver...

"Della?"

I blinked. "Huh?"

He indicated the seat opposite mine. "I said, are you waiting for someone?"

"My former boss."

He nodded. "She and I met last week when you... when you didn't show."

My hand moved on its own volition to touch his arm. "Thank you again for what you did, Charlie."

He looked at my hand, then covered it with his, entwining our fingers. Our gazes locked and the emotion I saw in his gray eyes scared me more than anything I'd been through the past five months.

Flustered, I retrieved my hand. "She's bringing me a job offer." I felt a tiny bit vindicated since he'd witnessed my firing in July.

"Ah. So you'll pick up where you left off and your fiancé won't ever have to know about your temp work."

I pushed my tongue into my cheek. Just when I'd begun to think him tolerable.

"Della, there you are," Portia Smithson announced as she strode up to the table, looking like she'd stepped out of a window on Rodeo Drive.

Caught off guard, I stood shakily to extend my hand to my former boss, but she bypassed it for a hug. I'd taken the hug as a good sign the last time we'd met. Now I was wary. "Hello, Portia."

"What a relief you're okay. I read the account in the *AJC*— how utterly horrific."

"Thanks," I murmured, then indicated Charlie. "I understand you met the chef and owner here, Charlie Graham."

"Yes, last week," Portia said, shaking Charlie's hand. "But when I left, I had no idea what had happened to you, Della."

"Good to see you under better circumstances," Charlie said.

"Likewise," she said, sliding into her seat without pulling out the chair. Portia was whip-thin and she moved like water.

I self-consciously reclaimed my seat, feeling every ounce of the weight I'd gained. "I know you have a return flight to catch. Shall we go ahead and order lunch?"

"That would be nice," she agreed.

"Would you like to hear our specials?" Charlie asked.

"No, thank you," Portia said primly. "I'll have a lettuce wedge, with vinaigrette dressing on the side, please."

Charlie nodded. "Very good. And for you, Della?"

I didn't miss her gaze flitting over my newly rounded figure. "The same," I murmured.

His mouth flattened. "Coming right up."

He walked away and Portia smirked. "I think the chef has been sampling too much of his own cooking."

I gave her a tight smile. "He's stocky, but he's solid. Or so I've been told," I added.

"I guess chefs can get away with extra pounds that the rest of us can't afford to carry around." She sipped her water with lemon.

I swallowed hard. "I guess so."

"Now then, let's get down to business," she said, lifting her briefcase to the table. She removed a file folder and opened it, then gave me a wide smile. "Here is your bonus check."

I reached for it, relief flooding my body. I studied the amount with satisfaction: Thirty-two thousand and no/100 dollars. Then I realized the check wasn't attached to a statement, but a letter.

"What's this?"

Portia's smile grew. "The terms of your new position with Traxton. You'll be Sales Manager of the Southern Region for a new drug that comes on the market in January."

I was shot through with gratitude that she'd come through on her promise of a promotion. "That sounds like a terrific opportunity. What's the new drug?"

"It's the replacement for Beltina," she said brightly. "So you're a perfect fit."

My smile dimmed. "Replacement?"

"More like a reformulation." She gave a dismissive wave. "You'll learn all about it when we roll out the marketing collateral.

I think you'll find the base salary and bonus potential quite an improvement over your territory sales job."

I skimmed the payment package and pursed my mouth—wow. Excitement began to well in my chest when I realized the kind of lifestyle the new position would afford me and Kyle. He could invest his profits back into the practice and buy his father out sooner than he'd planned.

The next paragraph of the letter was a little unsettling.

Employee agrees to maintain an appropriate weight and professional appearance in keeping with the branding and image of the product represented.

Back to monthly weigh-ins.

Although, admittedly, the regular weigh-ins had been good incentive to keep my weight down, so it was hard to argue their effectiveness.

But the next paragraph stopped me.

Employee agrees not to discuss or disclose any information about a former Traxton product known as "Beltina." This agreement extends beyond the employment period to include the natural life of the employee, plus thirty years. Violation of this agreement could result in criminal and/or civil prosecution of the employee by Traxton and/or third parties.

So I couldn't talk about Beltina, even if I died and came back as a zombie.

The final paragraph further unnerved me.

Cashing the attached check will be deemed acceptance of these employment terms.

And the offer expired midnight December 31.

I lifted my gaze to Portia and she beamed. "Can you start January 1?"

I tried to mirror her enthusiasm. "I'm so grateful for this opportunity, Portia. But I'd like to have my bonus now, and think about the terms of the new position for a couple of days."

She made a rueful noise, but maintained her smile. "I'm afraid that's not possible, Della. You only get your bonus if you come back to work for Traxton."

"But this is money I've already earned."

"Which Traxton isn't obligated to pay you," she said lightly. "Especially considering you lied on your original employment application."

I straightened. "That's not true. I would never lie on an application."

She removed another sheet of paper from the file and slid it across the table. "Under question eight, you checked the box that you'd never before interviewed or applied for a job at Traxton."

Dread began to build in my bowels.

"But that's not true, is it?" she asked.

When I didn't respond, she pulled another piece of paper from the bottomless folder and placed it in front of me. It was notes from my disastrous interview as Mae Culpepper, complete with a photograph of me at more than two hundred fifty pounds, hiding in a voluminous dress that made me look even bigger. My hair was dirt brown and over-long. My eyes looked sad.

A hot flush scorched my face. The fact that I'd lied on my application paled in comparison to the fact that Portia had seen this photograph.

"Here we are," Charlie said, setting our lettuce wedges on the table. I glanced up just as his gaze landed on the photograph. I saw his shock the instant recognition registered.

I looked away. My mortification was complete.

"Everything okay here?" he asked mildly.

"We're good," Portia assured him, then picked up her utensils and began eating her lettuce wedge.

I stared at his shoes. He hesitated, then moved away from the table.

"I have to hand it to you, Della—that's some makeover." Portia gave a little laugh. "Because I do not remember that interview. When Legal sent this over, I couldn't believe it."

Now I remembered checking the box "no" on my second application. I'd rationalized the lie by telling myself I was no longer that person who had initially applied, although I was sure it wouldn't make a difference to Portia, or to the company.

"There's no reason to be upset," she said between bites. "Cash the check and come back to work for Traxton, and all will be forgotten."

Cash the check... pay off my bills... make my mother's house payment... get a promotion... go back to my old life, except better... and Kyle would never know about this six-month career detour.

All in return for my loyalty… and my silence.

Portia set down her silverware and pushed her plate of half-eaten lettuce wedge to the side. She retrieved the old interview notes with the photo and my illicit application, and returned them to the file. The file went back into her briefcase. Then she stood and tossed enough cash on the table to cover the check. "Sometimes, Della, the easy thing is the right thing. And this is one of those times. Cash the damn check."

She jammed on her sunglasses, then walked out the door.

December 6, Wednesday

"BUSINESS HAS BEEN good," Joon-woo said to the group of us temp employees gathered around the table in the back room, "but expenses keep going up—insurance, utilities… and I'm facing another rent increase in January. So, it's with great disappointment that I announce the Anita Temp Agency will close December thirty-one."

Gasps and groans of protest sounded. Casey looked especially stricken.

Joon-woo offered a regretful smile. "I'm sorry for the short notice, but I'm happy to talk with my clients about full-time opportunities they might be able to offer. And I'll give reference letters to anyone who needs them. I'll be meeting with each of you one-on-one to figure out how you can best transition into another job. Meanwhile, it's work as usual."

"But what will *you* do, Joon-woo?" Anthony asked.

She gave a little shrug. "Don't worry about me. I'll figure out something."

She smiled like everything was coming up roses, but I could see the extra moisture in her eyes.

"Meeting adjourned," she said, then jerked a thumb toward her office. "I have a ton of paperwork to do, so please keep it down."

"What are you going to do?" Casey asked me.

Anthony gave a wave. "Don't cry for Mae—she's got a great sales job waiting for her." Then he grinned. "Which means I'll have a job again, too, as her personal assistant."

I'd told my roomie about the job offer, but not the strings attached. Of course most people might not see the stipulations as strings. I was still on the fence, which was why I hadn't yet cashed the bonus check. I broke away from the group and made my way down the hall to Joon-woo's office, hoping to ask her advice on the check and letter I carried in my bag. I stopped and rapped on the door. On the other side, I heard scrambling and nose-blowing.

"Yes?" she called.

I opened the door and stuck my head inside. Joon-woo had been crying, although she was valiantly trying to keep it hidden. Still, I didn't have the heart to ask her for advice when she was dealing with her own problems, which were more immediate and more far-reaching than mine.

"Did you need something, Mae?"

"I… just wanted to tell you I'm getting married December thirtieth."

She grinned. "That's fantastic news. Congratulations."

"Thanks." I reached into my bag and withdrew an invitation to hand to her. "I hope you can come, but I understand if you don't, considering the timing."

"Looks like it'll be new beginnings for both of us," she said cheerfully.

I tried to match her mood. "Right. But I can work job assignments up until the twenty-ninth, if you have enough to go around."

"I will," she said. "I expect employees will start to jump ship, which I understand. In a week or so, I'll probably have way more jobs than people to cover them."

"Do you have anything for me today?"

She angled her head. "Are you sure you're ready to come back? You've been through a lot, Mae. Maybe you should take a few days off to regroup."

I shook my head. "I'd rather be busy."

"Okay. The toy store needs a worker, and they requested you."

A smile overtook me. "I'm there."

December 7, Thursday

I WAS LYING on my bed studying the bonus check, talking myself into cashing it one minute, then talking myself out of it the next. When my phone rang, I welcomed the distraction... until I saw Charlie's name on the screen.

I had hightailed it out of his restaurant right after Portia, loath to sit there and wait for Charlie to come around and ask me about my "before" picture, or worse—to act as if he hadn't seen it. And I still wasn't ready to talk about it.

I hit the decline button, then set the phone down.

A minute later, my phone buzzed with a text. I picked it up to see a text from Charlie.

You screening calls?

I sighed, then typed in *Yes*

Finally some honesty

I rolled my eyes. *Do u need something?*

So many things...

My pulse spiked higher.

But for now, wanted to talk to u abt TP biz coalition work pgm

Surely that wasn't disappointment pulling at me because Charlie wasn't text-flirting? I remembered he had mentioned he was trying to get the Triangle Point business coalition to establish a work program for at-risk kids. In the wake of the human trafficking case, things must have accelerated. *What abt it?*

Need volunteer to help me w/teen signups Sat morning... u available?

I worked my mouth back and forth. It was for a good cause... but it meant spending time with Charlie... but it was for a good cause... but it meant spending time with Charlie...

U still there?

Yes... I'm available

Great... meet me at the music store @ 10

Ok

xxx

I frowned. He was sending kisses? *???*

What?

I asked you first—what's with the three kisses? I'm engaged

Those are hugs—I thought maybe you could use one

X's are kisses
No, O's are kisses X's are hugs—the arms are open wide
No, LOL
Lots of love? Thought you were engaged
NO! LOL is laugh out loud—ur a menace texter
XXX LOL

I frowned—wait, was he sending kisses now, or hugs? And laugh out loud, or lots of love?

I smacked the phone down on my dresser. Ooh!

December 8, Friday

I WAS SITTING AT my desk staring at the check, trying to decide if I should cash it and get on with my life... yet wondering why I was holding off.

After all, if I didn't take the job with Traxton, I had no ready alternatives since Joon-woo was closing the temp agency.

I reached down and unbuttoned my jeans so I could breathe.

Although I could always start selling off my skinny clothes.

I signed on to check the balances of my bank accounts and credit cards, hoping they would push me in one direction or the other. But my penny-pinching was paying off. For the first time in years, I had a positive cashflow in my checking account, and I was paying down my credit balances.

Mind-boggling.

But, I told myself as I reached for my phone, I still didn't have enough leeway coming or going to make the five-thousand-dollar payment to the Dewdrop bank for the note on my mother's house this month. This phone call would probably leave me no choice but to cash the Traxton check right away. I punched in the number and waited for it to connect.

"Dewdrop bank, Vernetta speaking."

Vernetta Kolb, who lived on Rapid Ridge. Her son Kenny had been one grade ahead of me in school, and had been equally overweight. People had always tried to pair us up, but I'd resisted—not because of Kenny's weight, but because of his professed predilection for farm animals.

"Hi, Vernetta. This is MaeDella Culpepper."

"Hidy-ho, MaeDella. You calling from Atlanta?"

"That's right. Donnie told me another payment is due on the note on Mom's house. Can you check for me?"

"That's so nice of you, MaeDella, looking out for your mom like that. Alright, give me just a minute to pull it up here on my computer. Did you know my Kenny is president of the bank now?"

"No, I didn't know. That's... great."

"He always had such a crush on you, MaeDella."

I was positive he hadn't. "I'm sure Kenny's married by now."

"No, but he's got himself a nice farm up on the ridge. Prettiest herd of dairy cows you ever saw."

"I'll just bet."

"Lisa said you're all skinny and gorgeous now, and you're engaged to a *doctor*."

"Yes, I'm engaged.... to a doctor."

"When are you going to bring him to Dewdrop and show him off, girl?"

"Uh... we're planning to drive down Christmas."

"Oh, that's so nice." Vernetta made a rueful noise. "I'm looking at the account, hon. Lisa has fallen way behind on the interest payments. She must not be getting many hours at the diner, huh?"

"I suppose not."

"Okay, tell you what—I'll get Kenny to waive the last two months' interest payments, but looks like you need to make a payment of fifty-two hundred by the end of the month, or the bank will start foreclosure procedures."

"By the end of the month?" I'd almost hoped she was going to say within the next couple of days.

"Well, the last day of the month is on a Sunday, so it'll be the next day. But the next day is New Year's Day and we're closed, so how about January second? Will that work for you?"

I sighed. The universe was not going to help me make a quick decision.

December 9, Saturday

I JOGGED UP to Phil's Music Emporium at ten. When I didn't see Charlie, I walked inside. My teenaged stoner boss Blowz was coming in from the backroom, his hand stuck in a big bag of chips. He reeked of weed. When he saw me, he froze.

"Hi," I said, and I'm sure the disapproval was written all over my face.

He lifted a hand. "I didn't know you were working today, Mae."

"I'm not wearing my work clothes. But then, I guess you're too loaded to tell."

"Hey," he said slowly, like The Fonz. "I'm not loaded."

"*Yes*, you are. What the heck are you thinking? What if Phil decided to actually show up for once and found you like this?"

"Yeah... he won't."

"How do you know?"

"Because I'm Phil."

I blinked. "You're Phil? *You* own this place?"

He nodded.

"How?"

He shrugged. "I'm a trust fund kid."

I took in the disheveled, smelly zoned-out teen. This walking mess was a trust fund kid? "Well, you don't get a pass just because you have money. Where are your parents?"

"I don't know—somewhere in Europe. I think."

My heart squeezed for this teen who was in desperate need of guidance.

He teared up. "Please don't arrest me."

I frowned. "What?"

"You said you weren't an undercover cop, but I know you are. I saw in the *AJC* where you took down my dealer."

My eyes boinged open in surprise. "Wait—you read the newspaper?"

"When I change out the cage liner for my bird."

Okay, that made more sense. Then I saw an opportunity to use my superpowers of bullshit for good. I drew myself up and tried to look fierce. "You won't be arrested, Blowz—*if* you clean up your act."

He sniffed. "What do I have to do?"

"Flush your weed down the toilet."

He grimaced. "All of it? That's going to stop up the toilet."

I pinched the bridge of my nose. "A little at a time."

"That'll take a while, but okay."

I sniffed. "And burn your clothes."

He lifted his sleeve for a snort, then nodded. "Okay."

"And check yourself into a rehab program. If you need help finding one, let me know."

I expected him to push back, but he straightened and nodded. "Alright."

"Now go take a shower and get presentable."

"Okay," he said, then turned toward the restroom.

"Wait." When he turned back, I snatched the bag of chips. "I'll take these... as evidence."

He looked contrite. "Thanks, Mae, for giving a crap about me." He trudged away, but his shoulders were back and his head a little higher.

I dug into the chips, marveling over the imbalances in the world. Everyone was dealing with something. I was starving, I realized, and wolfed down a couple of handfuls of the chips. I still hadn't cashed the Traxton check. I teetered between worrying Portia would rescind her offer, and hoping she would. Then I wouldn't have to make a decision.

As I mulled my choices, the chips dwindled. When the door chime sounded, I was holding the bag upside down to pour the crumbs into my mouth. I swung my head to see Charlie standing there, an amused expression on his face. "Breakfast of champions?"

I crunched the bag closed and wiped my mouth with my sleeve. "You're late."

He held up a box. "Sorry, these flyers took longer to copy than I expected."

I nodded toward the restroom. "I can't leave until Blowz comes back."

"Do you think the owner would agree to passing out flyers about the work program? I'll bet every kid we're trying to reach eventually finds this place."

"I can almost promise you he will. Give me a stack."

Charlie opened the box and pulled out an inch of the neon yellow flyers. "Thanks for agreeing to do this."

"No problem," I said lightly. "It's for a good cause." But I could feel his gaze on me, could sense unasked questions in the air that had nothing to do with the work program.

He cleared his throat. "So... about the other day with your boss. I know it's none of my business, but—"

"I used to be fat," I blurted. "I was a fat kid and fat all through school and college. I was bullied and taunted and miserable. And lonely. Then I decided to take control of my life and I lost the weight. And now I'm not." I swallowed. "Not lonely, I mean."

He stared at me, then nodded. "Okay. Well, that wasn't what I was going to ask."

"Oh." I straightened. "What were you going to ask?"

"If you're going back to work for that company. Because their tactics seem a little... cruel. Adults can be bullies, too, you know."

I bristled at his patronizing tone. I hated how this man had insinuated himself into my life, and had appointed himself my keeper. He had no idea what I owed to Traxton—every success I'd had, they had made possible. Who was he to judge?

"But like you said, Charlie, it's none of your business."

He absorbed the hit, then gave me a curt nod. "I didn't mean to offend you, Della. I'm sorry."

But I was tired of his interference in my life's plan. "I don't think I'll be able to help with the flyers after all."

He studied me for a few seconds, then his face gave way to a big, disarming smile. "No worries. Have a good day."

I watched him leave, then stamped my foot. Ooh!

December 10, Sunday

KYLE STROKED MY CHEEK. "I'll need to administer the injectable soon so the bruising will have time to heal before the wedding."

"Don't you think I'm a little young to start these procedures?"

He looked affronted. "Darling, you know how I feel about

this. Women should begin a regime before they need it so it's not such a drastic change. If done properly, no one will suspect a thing. I know you want to look your best in our wedding photos."

A picture of Helen's red, swollen face after being subjected to the injectable came to mind. "I appreciate your thoughtfulness, Kyle, but I have a lot of obligations between now and the wedding, and I don't think I'll have any down-time."

He shifted on the large chaise where we lounged in the sunroom. "I understand, and I think I have a solution. What if we wait to have the wedding photos taken at a later date?"

I squinted. "A later date?"

He nodded. "Perhaps in the spring... when we've had time to catch our breath."

"I guess it could be fun to recreate the day."

He lowered a kiss to my cheek. "Right. And it would give you time to lose a few pounds."

I blinked. I'd planned to lose weight, but his words still cut deep. "I haven't had time to go to the gym lately."

He grinned and moved his hand across my sweater to cup my breast. "I can think of a good way to burn a few calories."

I knew he meant for it to sound sexy, but something about building a cardio workout into lovemaking just killed it for me.

I stilled his hand with mine. "Actually, I'd like to hold off until our wedding night to make it more special."

Kyle sighed, but nodded. "Okay."

Besides, if he saw my two layers of Spanx, he'd probably call off the wedding.

December 11, Monday

I STEPPED INTO a consultation room at the Triangle Point weight-loss center and closed the door behind me. The employees weren't supposed to take up a room when things were busy. And since the holidays were synonymous with overeating, the place was fairly vibrating.

But I was having my own little crisis.

I stared at the scale with something akin to hatred. The brutal machine had been dictating my mood and my self-esteem my entire life. It didn't seem fair that something mechanical could wield so much power.

I stepped out of my shoes and onto the plate, then slid the weighted needle across the numbers on the top of the scale, down, then back up... up... up... up... and up.

145.

I choked back a sob. I'd suspected as much from the clothes I could no longer wear—or wear comfortably—but seeing the proof was like a punch to my expanding gut.

A knock on the door sounded. I jumped off the scale and back into my shoes before it opened. Casey stood there with a clipboard. "Mae?"

"Yeah."

"I could use your help in the round room."

I hesitated. The round room was the place where clients talked about their food issues publicly. Lots of crying, lots of blaming. I avoided it like the plague.

"Is there anything else I can do?" I asked hopefully.

Casey made a face. "The toilet in the women's bathroom is stopped up, but it's a toxic waste dump in there."

I swallowed hard. "Where's the plunger?"

December 12, Tuesday

HAVE I MENTIONED how much I hate running outside in the cold?

Yet another reason to cash that bonus check and get back on board with Traxton—they would reinstate my gym membership, and pay for a personal trainer to keep me honest.

I thought of my last personal trainer Jan, who had been the first person who'd expressed concern I was taking Beltina, but without coming out and saying anything. I'd given her name and number to Rainie Stephens but apparently their conversations hadn't produced anything concrete.

I stopped for a red light and pulled out my phone. The text I'd written to Rainie about a possible link between Beltina and high copper levels—i.e., acquired Wilson's Disease—was still saved in Draft mode. Rainie said she protected her sources. My finger hovered over the Send button.

Then the light changed, so I stowed my phone and went back to torturing myself. I'd never been a great runner with great form, so running with the extra weight was killing my joints. I tried to compensate, then landed badly and twisted my knee.

"Dammit!" I shouted, trying to walk it off.

I looked up to get my bearings, and gave a little laugh. I was in front of a branch of my bank. The bonus check was tucked inside my wallet in my running backpack. It would be so easy to walk over to the ATM and deposit the check… and put this ugly, messy, fat chapter of my life behind me.

It seemed like a message from the universe, so with my knee still pinging, I made a split-second decision to do just that.

I limped toward the ATM, then noticed something about the customer using it seemed familiar.

Charlie Graham turned, then waved.

I closed my eyes briefly, muttered an expletive, then resumed running, painful knee and all.

December 13, Wednesday

ADMITTEDLY, WORKING at the pet store as an assistant dog groomer was one job I would not miss.

It was my job to hold the unwilling animals while the groomer washed them with expensive detergents meant to curb fleas and parasites and leave a shiny coat. I wore padded gloves up to my armpits to protect me from being bitten, but some of the little terrors managed to get in nips here and there anyway.

Have I mentioned I'm not a pet person?

If the smell of dank fur wasn't bad enough, I also got sprayed and doused with enough shampoo that I was fairly confident I would never have a tick problem. The only highlight of the job was the groomer I worked with today—Myron—was a congenial guy who seemed to think there was no higher calling than washing a dang dog.

It takes all kinds.

"Only one more client today," Myron said, consulting a whiteboard. He actually looked sad about it, whereas I was watching the clock like a hawk. He walked to a door and called for Howard.

I grimaced. Male dogs were usually more difficult to control.

But when he brought in the animal—a pug—I squinted in recognition. It looked like my neighbor Mindy Chasen's dog. I scrolled back in my memory to when my brother Donnie had asked its name.

Howard... he's my little angel.

And apparently Howard recognized me, too, because the minute he spotted me he started snarling and jumping as if he was going to eat my arm off.

"Whoa, Howard," Myron said, trying to calm him down. "What's wrong, buddy?"

"We have history," I muttered. "He belongs to a neighbor of mine."

No matter what Myron tried to do to soothe him, the pug continued to bark and snarl as if it was in distress. In fact, he grew louder and more frantic as the minutes wore on. The shrill decibels were dancing on my nerves. I was wet and clammy and smelly and hairy, and this was not the life I'd signed up for. The minute I got out of this place I was going to deposit that damn bonus check.

But meanwhile, something inside me snapped.

I opened my mouth and began to snarl and bark at the pug, being just as loud and just as obnoxious as he'd been. I yelped and snorted and growled, spewing spittle and tossing my head. And once I started, I couldn't seem to stop. All the pent up anger of the past six months—getting fired and fighting to get what Traxton owed me, having to take shit jobs like this one, living a double life, covering for Gil Malone's jackassiness, finding Elena murdered in her car, discovering an abandoned baby, watching homeless kids suffer, being kidnapped—came pouring out of me in the form of a woofing, baying, howling alter ego. And species.

When I finally stopped, Myron and the dog both were staring at me as if I'd lost my mind. Howard cowered against Myron's shoulder, who had backed up a few steps himself.

I exhaled slowly, then tossed my wet bangs out of my eyes. "I think I'll be going now."

"I think that's a good idea," Myron said, speaking carefully.

As I turned toward the door, I heard Howard scramble and jump to the floor.

"Watch out," Myron called.

But when I looked back, Howard was sniffing at me and whimpering. Then he gave a happy little yap.

I reached out my hand and he licked it, then nuzzled my fingers.

"Will you look at that?" Myron said.

The door opened and Mindy Chasen stuck her head inside the room. "I heard loud barking. Is everything okay?" Then she looked at me and her eyes widened. During the fit I'd thrown, the glasses and bandanna had been displaced. "Della?"

"Hi, Mindy." I scratched Howard's ears, to his leg-jerking delight. "Everything is fine."

But I was still a little stunned at my own emotional lapse. Was this why Detective Terry had suggested I ask for help after the kidnapping? Did he know I would be a live grenade, ready to go off any minute?

I felt markedly calmer, and the urge to cash the bonus check had passed. I still had two weeks to make up my mind.

December 14, Thursday

I WALKED ACROSS THE lobby, still breathing hard from a run, waved at Henry the concierge, then went into the mail room to check my box. When I saw Charlie, I considering going the other way, but he saw me, so I had no choice but to offer a neutral smile.

He closed his box and walked over. "How are things progressing with the wedding plans?"

"Fine," I said. In truth, I'd left pretty much everything up to Kyle and Anthony. And since Libby had taken an interest in certain details I couldn't have cared less about, I let her handle them. If she was going to be the face of Kyle's practice, she and I would have to be friendly.

"Will you be keeping your condo?" Charlie asked.

"No. I'll be moving in with Kyle."

"I guess I won't be seeing you around here, then."

"I guess not."

"So you've already put your unit on the market?"

I banged the door of my mailbox closed. "Not yet. My roommate Anthony still has to find a place to live." I walked toward the elevators, and he followed.

"Where are you and Keith going on your honeymoon?"

"*Kyle* and I are going to France."

"Nice," he said, nodding. "Very romantic."

"Yes." I didn't volunteer that Keith—dammit, *Kyle* would be attending a skin care conference while we were there. When the doors opened, I walked onto the car, and Charlie followed.

When the doors closed, he pressed the button for his floor and I pressed the button for mine.

"By the way, I appreciate the invitation," Charlie said, "but I won't be coming to your wedding."

I hadn't expected him to. "Okay."

"But I'll send a gift, perhaps something for the kitchen."

"That's not necessary," I murmured.

"With your cooking skills, I believe it is."

I pursed my mouth, remembering how he'd saved my Thanksgiving dinner... and how we'd banged like teenagers the following evening when I'd returned his knife. I squirmed.

"I'm thinking about it, too," he said.

I turned my head to admonish him, but the doors opened and he walked off.

Ooh!

I stabbed the button to close the doors and rode up to my unit. I was still fuming when I walked into my bedroom, locked the door and used my pink vibrator to get off, promising myself it would be the last time I'd think about Charlie Graham and his magic tongue.

I was lying on my bed, spent and heaving, when my phone pinged a text notification.

It was from Charlie.

I just did it, too

I flopped back, exasperated. Ooh!

December 15, Friday

I WAS STANDING IN front of the bank, counting to ten before going in to cash my bonus check.

One...

I was simply putting off the inevitable... and why?

Two...

The inevitable was good and stress-free and shiny.

Three...

And skinny.

Four...

And I deserved it.

Five...

Once I cashed this check...

Six...

I would have everything I'd ever wanted.

Seven...

And my doctor husband...

Eight...

Would never have to know...

Nine...

I'd had a job cleaning up dog piddle and poo.

Ten...

I stepped forward, and an alarm sounded. I stopped, confused. Was it a car alarm?

The door of the bank burst open and a masked man came running out, carrying a duffel bag—and a handgun. He turned and shot back toward the bank, shattering a window. When a security guard appeared brandishing his own weapon, I hit the dirt.

I heard bullets pinging around me. I alternately cursed and prayed, thinking what an ironic end—to die from indecision.

Another shot sound, followed by a howl of pain, then the sound of a body falling like a sack of rocks. I could hear sirens in the distance, then they grew louder, screaming onto the scene. I didn't dare lift my head until I heard voices yell, "All clear!"

When I looked up, two uniformed officers were leading the wounded robber to a police car, while a dozen more officers swarmed into the bank. One officer outside was already unrolling crime scene tape.

And I had the distinct feeling the bank would be closed for the rest of the day.

I looked to the sky. "Loud and clear... not today."

December 16, Saturday

I WAS ON THE SIDEWALK in front of my condo building, stretching and trying to get psyched up for a run, but not really feeling it. I was still shaken by the previous day's events and marveling over how much danger and chaos I'd experienced in the last six months, when I looked up to see Charlie—Mr. Chaos himself—emerge wearing similar workout gear.

This I did not need.

And the sentiment must've shown on my face because he pulled a white handkerchief from his back pocket and waved it. "Truce?"

I narrowed my eyes. "What does that mean?"

He walked closer. "It means I stop being an ass and a flirt. I'm sorry—I'm a bad loser when it comes to you. But I hope we can be friends." He grinned. "At least today, because I really could use some company for a run."

I shrugged. "Okay. Me, too. How far are you going?"

"I'll let you set the pace."

I set off in the direction of my usual route, and he matched my shorter stride. We jogged along in companionable silence for a while, then stopped at a red light.

"How is the work program going?" I asked.

"Good," Charlie said. "Your buddy Blowz at the music store has been a big help to get the word out."

"His name is Phil, and he owns the place."

"No kidding?"

"Yeah. And if he says something about me being a cop, play along,"

Charlie laughed. "Okay. When it comes to you, nothing surprises me anymore. Hey, how's your brother?"

"He's good. I'll be seeing him at Christmas."

"That's nice. Will you tell him I've added beef jerky to the bar menu?"

I grinned. "The Professor will be ecstatic to hear that. He'll want to come and try it."

"Tell him to stop by anytime—I'd be happy to see him."

I smiled. "I will. Thanks."

"So you're going to spend Christmas with your family?"

I nodded. "Kyle and I are driving down for the day."

"Does he get along well with your family?"

"We'll see," I said lightly. Before he could comment on my eleventh hour introduction, I asked, "What will you do for Christmas?"

"Drive to Nashville, spend the day with my mom and brothers and their families."

"Sounds nice."

"It usually is. I'm eager to give Mom her ring I had repaired."

"I'm sure she'll be happy to get it back."

"Yeah, she misses my dad."

"Were they together a long time?"

"Fifty-five years."

"Wow... that's... great."

"How about your parents?"

"No dad that I remember," I said, surprised at how calmly it came out. "Mom wasn't the most stable parent. Donnie and I fended for ourselves."

"I'm sorry," he said.

I gave a little laugh. "It's not your fault."

"I mean, I'm sorry things were rough for you. It explains a lot."

I glanced at him sideways.

"I meant it as a compliment," he said. "It explains why you're tough. And fearless. And... guarded."

I didn't respond, but I did pick up the pace.

He laughed. "That's my punishment for getting too personal? Okay, I'll stop. You talk."

"About what?"

"Tell me what it was like when you were kidnapped."

I swallowed hard to get a deep breath. "I was out cold most of the time. When I woke up, it was only an hour or so before I was rescued."

"Were you scared?"

I hesitated. "Terrified."

"Do you want to talk about it?"

I was quiet for a while. I hadn't talked to anyone about my ordeal beyond reciting facts to Detective Terry, the Assistant D.A., and Rainie Stephens. Anthony had been satisfied with the highlights. Even Kyle hadn't asked for details, seemed happier not knowing.

"You don't have to," Charlie said.

"No... I'd like to." I turned my head and gave him a grateful smile. "I need to."

December 17, Sunday

"JUST THINK," Helen said, her eyes shining, "two weeks from now you'll be married and on your honeymoon!"

"Oh, I'm so jealous," Libby said.

We both turned to look at her.

She laughed. "That you'll be in Paris, I mean. What a beautiful place to be with the man you love."

I smiled. "Yes. I can't wait."

"What does your dress look like?" Helen asked.

"I... am keeping it a secret," I said evasively. If I told the women I hadn't yet bought a wedding dress, they would stroke out. But in truth, I dreaded trying to squeeze into a dress with my ever-expanding curves.

And I was terrified if I bought one now, I would outgrow it in another two weeks.

"I got my dress," Helen said, "and it's beautiful."

I was happy to see Helen reverting to her old self.

"But," she said patting her flat stomach, "I've gained weight on the metal detox program the doctors have me on—so much fat and dairy. So I was hoping, Della, you could set me up with more Beltina samples?"

I balked. Helen wanted to go back on Beltina? I was still uneasy about its possible connection to her copper poisoning... and I wasn't ready to endorse its reformulation I would be selling January 1. "Helen, you don't need to lose any weight. Besides, I'm all out of samples at the moment."

"Oh, yes, I do," Helen insisted. "But that's okay. Julie said I could have some samples she got from her doctor."

Julie, one of the two women taking Beltina who'd gotten into a knock-down drag-out on Kyle's boat.

I opened my mouth to say I didn't think that was a good idea, then Libby leaned in. "Don't be silly—I have lots of samples left that Della gave me. You can have them, Helen."

I exhaled in relief. The "samples" I'd given Libby were empty gelatin capsules—placebos.

"Okay," Helen said happily.

Then Libby smirked. "Beltina didn't really work for me."

Okay, I felt the teeniest bit guilty for giving Libby the placebos that kept her from losing weight to get the part she'd auditioned for.

Then she grinned. "Although it kind of worked in reverse. My agent called today—I got the part! The director said my curvy figure made him rethink the character's entire persona!"

I exhaled in relief. "Congratulations, Libby." And I actually meant it.

"Wonderful news," Helen agreed, raising her glass. "And good news for Kyle's business, too," she murmured to me.

Phew. Things seemed to be falling into place.

December 18, Monday

THE WORST THING about weighing yourself on a digital scale was the way the numbers fluctuated wildly before giving a final reading

143... 152... 146... 144...

149.

I clapped my hand over my mouth, fighting back tears. I was up almost thirty pounds. None of my regular clothes fit anymore—I was relegated to wearing yoga pants and sweaters, but my increasing girth had seriously shortened the hem of the exercise bottoms to high-water pants.

It was time.

I heaved a sigh and trudged toward the narrow closet in the spare room like a woman going to the gallows. I had once used the second bedroom for a glorious, decadent closet, but now Anthony slept here. He was out with Casey, so I didn't have to worry about him finding me out.

I removed the key from its hiding place in the molding, then unlocked the closet door. When it creaked open, it was as if the ghost of MaeDella emerged. I flipped on the light, my stomach churning as I surveyed the racks of clothes. How was it possible that mere garments could stir up such unsettling emotions?

"Whatcha doin'?" Anthony said.

I nearly jumped out of my skin. Hand over my racing heart, I turned to him. "I thought you were out."

"I was. Now I'm back in." Anthony stepped behind me to glance over the clothing inside. "What's all this?"

I wet my lips, remembering a conversation with Anthony several months ago about the burden and shame of maintaining lots of different sized wardrobes. "These are... my fat clothes."

Anthony frowned, then laughed. "What? You've never been fat."

"Oh, yes, I have," I murmured. "You've only known me at this size—and smaller. But I struggled with my weight most of my life, as you can see." I removed a dress that held particularly painful memories—the voluminous dress I'd been wearing when I'd first interviewed for Traxton as Mae Culpepper.

Anthony's mouth was agape. "I can't believe this. Do you have pictures?"

I winced and nodded, then reached into a box and withdrew a photo album. Page after page of the old me—overweight and smiling through the pain, both physical and emotional.

"You look like a different person," Anthony said.

"I know. I made myself over from MaeDella Culpepper to Della Culpepper. And I locked all these things away because I didn't want to think about that person." I teared up. "But I'm falling back into my old habits and I'm terrified I'm going to wind up like that again. And if I do, Kyle won't want me."

Anthony turned me to face him and gave me a little shake. "Shush now. You are beautiful and spirited, and if Kyle falls out of love with you over a few extra pounds, then he's not in love with you to begin with. Look at Casey—she's big and beautiful inside and out, and I love her so much it hurts. I made myself sick trying to get skinny, and she's been on countless fad diets, too. Now we're trying to get healthier together—isn't that what's most important?"

I nodded.

"You need to let Kyle see the real you—what you came from and where you are now. If you're going to make a life with him, there can be no secrets, Della."

Deep down I knew that... but what if secrets were all I had to hang onto?

December 19, Tuesday

"ANOTHER PRODUCTIVE day," Constance Hanlon pronounced as we walked to the elevator. "I'm sorry we won't get to work together again, Mae."

"So am I," I said. "I hate that Joon-woo is closing the agency. But it's time for me to move on anyway."

"Back to pharmaceutical sales?"

I nodded. "Unless something better comes along." I had harbored a secret hope Constance would offer me a job as her permanent assistant. I knew the pay wouldn't compare to what I could make at Traxton, but I'd learned so much about business in the short time I'd spent with her. And more than that, I felt as if she was doing important work, building ideas and relationships that mattered.

Constance gave me a little smile. "If circumstances were different I'd hire you in a minute. But I'm moving on myself. I've decided to retire. I have four grandchildren in Oklahoma I want to watch grow up."

"Grandchildren?"

She angled her head. "You're disappointed that I'd walk away from all this—" She gestured to the lobby of the Battlecoin Building, still bustling with activity. "—to do something so domestic?"

"I'm just surprised, that's all." And disappointed for myself as a possible alternative to working for Traxton evaporated.

"All this is great," she said, glancing around. "And I've enjoyed every minute of it. But successful women need love in their life, too. By the way, Joon-woo told me you're getting married?"

I nodded. "In two weeks."

She smiled wide. "Congratulations. I hope he is the love of your life."

I smiled back. I hoped so too.

December 20, Wednesday

"WE THOUGHT YOU'D found another hair salon," Johna said. "Didn't we, Faye?"

"Sure did," Faye said.

I made a rueful noise. "I'm sorry. I ran into some financial problems and I couldn't really afford all your nice services."

"Did you try selling your dirty underwear online?" Johna asked.

"Um, no... thankfully things didn't get that dire."

"Honey, if you're coloring your own hair at home in the sink, things are dire."

"Actually, my roommate Anthony did it for me."

She held up a few strands of my honey blond hair. "He did a pretty good job. This is a nice color for your skintone."

"But my roots are growing out, and I want my hair to look nice for my wedding in two weeks."

"Two weeks?" Faye shrieked. "Girl, there is still time to change your mind."

I laughed. "He's a doctor."

"But do you love him?" Johna asked.

"I... sure."

She narrowed her eyes at me. "You don't hesitate when you truly love someone."

"That's right," Faye said. "When you're really in love, it's whole hog."

Johna leaned in. "But if he's a doctor, half a hog will do."

"Or even a hamhock," Faye said.

They laughed uproariously, then Johna got serious. "Okay, what are we doing for your special day? You going back to platinum?"

It had been my first instinct, but now I was having second thoughts. "I don't think so."

"Keep it this color?"

I bit into my lip. "I'm thinking darker."

Her eyebrows shot up. "Back-to-nature dark?"

I nodded. "Let's do it."

December 21, Thursday

"MAY I HELP YOU?"

I smiled at the sales associate in Dorman's formal wear department. "I'm looking for a dress."

She glanced over my temp work attire—I'd just left the gift-wrapping department—and her mouth quirked. "A special occasion, I assume?"

I pulled the bandanna from my hair and tried to fluff it a little. "Um, yes... a wedding dress."

"Lovely. What size?"

Ack, my day of reckoning. "Twelve?"

She studied my figure. "Possibly, with shapewear."

I didn't argue.

"And are you thinking white?"

"I was thinking off-white." A flush climbed my neck at the way it sounded. "Or white would work, too."

"No, I think off-white for your skintone," she agreed. "And it's more slimming than white."

And just like that—I was back in the range of sizes where salesclerks made subtle suggestions about how to make everything appear smaller.

She led me to a long rack of dresses in every possible shade of off-white—ivory, cream, beige, buff, and blush.

I was instantly overwhelmed. Me, Della Culpepper, official clotheshorse and shopper extraordinaire, was having a hard time picking out her wedding gown. Out of sheer desperation, I selected a few random styles and carried them to a changing room. Once there, I used the bandanna to scrub away my extra eyebrows, and ditched the big glasses. I was still getting used to my darker hair—again. It was the shade I'd been born with, and Johna had declared it perfectly perfect with my eyes and skin.

But perhaps I'd made a mistake—platinum blond hair might've taken some attention away from my curvier figure.

I undressed slowly, kicking myself for not wearing shapewear. But depending on the cut of the gown, I might have to get something special to go with it anyway.

"Here you go," the sales associate said, handing me several sets of shapewear to try.

I was having problems with bras, too, as my breasts expanded along with the rest of me, but at a slightly faster rate.

"I have another customer," the woman said, "I'll be back as soon as I can."

I felt a little bereft. It was the state of brick-and-mortar retail these days—every store operated with a skeleton staff—but I was hoping to have someone to weigh in on what looked good.

Although I suspected most stores assumed brides would bring someone with them—a mother, a sister, a friend. In hindsight, it was something I probably should've invited my mom to help with, but things were still sticky with the whole Gil Malone fiasco, so a fitting could've gone sideways.

Anthony or Casey or even Joon-woo probably would've been glad to accompany me, but I was so self-conscious about my weight gain, I was trying to keep the dress shopping as low key as possible.

I pulled on the first gown, a simple princess style, with a high waist and scoop neck.

And sighed. It was okay... maybe.

My phone pinged with a text and I brightened. Maybe it was someone who could help.

But when I saw it was Charlie, my hopes were dashed.

Whatcha doing?

I hesitated, then typed in *Trying on wedding gowns, u?*

Same thing, what r the chances?

That made me laugh, but I refrained from sending "LOL" lest he think it meant "lots of love." Instead I sent *Laughing*

R u alone?

Yes, not the best plan

Need a second opinion?

I peeked out the door, but didn't see the salesclerk. *Sure.* I took a photograph in the dressing room mirror, then sent it.

Dress too plain, but I like your hair

I smiled, and reached up to touch my dark locks. *Thx*

I removed the dress and put on the next one, and the next, and the next.

Too fussy

Just wrong

Maybe for the honeymoon, not for the wedding

The thing was, I agreed with him each time. The store was getting ready to close and I was ready to admit defeat.

And then I noticed an ivory-colored dress that had been left in the dressing room by someone else. It was a simple halter style with a flared skirt, the kind of dress that didn't look great on a hanger, but I loved the feel of the fabric. And it was the right size.

As soon as I pulled it over my head, I had a good feeling, and when I'd fastened it around my neck and at the waist, I exhaled. I loved it. I snapped a picture and sent it to Charlie, and waited.

That's the one. Wow, sorry I will miss it

I pressed my lips together. I was sorry, too.

December 22, Friday

I WALKED THROUGH THE DOOR of ATA, summoned by Joon-woo. I glanced around the front counter area, nursing pangs of sadness. The place was already feeling empty.

I made my way to the back room where a handful of employees were cleaning out their workstations in preparation for the business to close in a few days' time. The mood was subdued, and when I saw Joon-woo, I could tell she'd been crying again, even though she gave me a big everything's-fine smile.

"A package came for you," she said, handing me a small box.

"For me?" I couldn't fathom who would be sending me something. But when I saw the return address was Mexico City, I had a feeling it was from Elena's family. I unwrapped the brown paper, then opened the card inside. The message was printed in block letters.

Miss Culpepper,

Thank you for caring for our mother, Elena Padilla. She was a good mother, we love and miss her. She would want you to have these earrings. Please accept with our love and gratitude. The family of Elena Padilla

From the box I lifted the pair of dangly silver earrings, perfectly repaired and polished to a sheen.

They would be beautiful with my wedding gown, I decided.

December 23, Saturday

"PLEASE, MAE, I'M BEGGING you," Casey said. She stood in front of the reception desk of the Triangle Point weight-loss center.

"You know how I feel about working the round room," I said. "Give me something else, anything else."

"Everything else is done for the day, except the round room. This time of year, it's open every day anyway to help clients cope with holiday eating issues, but now it's in crisis mode. I need another body in there with me—I can't do this alone."

I sighed. "What's the crisis?"

"One of the members had a breakdown, was checked into a psychiatric hospital. All her friends are beyond upset... I'm afraid this is going to cause a chain reaction."

"I don't—"

"She was taking Beltina."

I swung my head around. "The girl who had the breakdown was taking Beltina?"

"Her file doesn't show it, but her friend swears she was getting it on the black market."

I was already up and moving toward the round room. I remembered one of the clients in the waiting room talking about a psychiatric hospital in south Georgia with an entire wing of Beltina patients.

"Do you know where she was taken?" I asked Casey.

"Battenburg Hospital, in south Georgia."

December 24, Sunday

CHRISTMAS EVE at Kyle's parents' mansion in Buckhead was a winter wonderland of lights and gifts and champagne and entertainment... but I couldn't enjoy any of it for thinking about the anguished stories I'd heard last night in the round room of the weight-loss center.

It was as emotional and unsettling as I thought it would be, listening to the hurt and loneliness pouring out of the women sitting in a circle of chairs that were barely big enough to support the bodies that had become traps... traps that perpetuated the cycle of hurt and shame and self-loathing every waking minute of their days.

I knew their stories... because they were my stories.

I surveyed the unbelievable spread of decadent food, from caviar to lobster rolls to trays of cheese and sweetbreads. If it was chocolate you desired, there were three fountains—milk chocolate, white chocolate, and dark chocolate, with unlimited cakes and fruits for dipping. Cheesecake? Eight varieties.

For normal people, buffets of this proportion were more for spectacle than anything else—a visual delight of bountiful treats, meant to be sampled and admired.

But to someone suffering from food addiction, a buffet like this, especially at a social event, could send them into a downward spiral that could last for days... or weeks.

"Della, my dear, you look so pensive."

I lifted a smile to Kyle's parents, the epitome of grace and old money in their preserved states. "It's a lovely party. I'm afraid I'm a little preoccupied."

"With the wedding plans, I'm sure," his mother said. "I can't wait to meet your family. Kyle says you're driving down tomorrow to spend the day with them."

"That's right."

"Please give them our best," Kyle's father said. "We're looking forward to merging our families."

I maintained my smile until after they moved away, then I upended my glass of wine and downed it.

"Are you okay?" Helen asked next to me with a laugh.

I turned and blushed sheepishly. "Fine."

"You're not getting cold feet, are you?"

I shook my head. "I just hope our families will... mesh."

Helen gave a dismissive wave. "We love you, so we'll love your family."

"I'm glad you're feeling better, Helen."

She laughed, then turned sideways. "And the Beltina samples Libby gave me are already working."

I smiled. "Good."

"Your hair looks nice in that darker shade, by the way."

I fingered the ends. "Thanks... I needed a change."

"Most brides go lighter for their wedding pictures, but there you go, bucking the trend."

I maintained my smile, but inside, I wavered. Some part of me wondered if I was trying to prepare Kyle to see the real me.

"I'm going to find Reggie," Helen said. "Enjoy!"

But how could I? This time tomorrow, Kyle would know all about me... and it was about as far apart from this life as one could get.

I walked by the buffet toward the wine, when a server walked by with a tray of cheesecakes. "Would you like one, ma'am?"

My mouth watered, and I felt an old compulsion rise in my chest. "Actually, I was looking for something to take to the children in the playroom. Would it be alright if I took the entire tray?"

"Of course, ma'am." He handed it off to me, then went on his way.

I carried the tray in the direction of the children's playroom, but sidestepped into a bathroom, then closed and locked the door behind me.

December 25, Monday

"I COULD'VE SWORN you said you grew up in Dewberryville," Kyle said.

"No," I murmured. "Dewdrop."

"Okay, I guess I misunderstood. How much farther?"

"Maybe twenty minutes."

The closer we got, the quieter I got. My stomach was pitching and churning, partly from the tray of cheesecake I'd inhaled last night, and partly for what was about to happen. When we reached the exit, I gave Kyle directions to my mother's home with a shaky voice.

"This is more rural than I expected," Kyle said with a little laugh. "You didn't tell me you were a farm girl. Now I know where you got your freckles."

I scrunched my nose. "I have freckles?"

"The darker hair makes them more noticeable, I suppose." Then he winked. "You're quite the chameleon."

He had no idea. By the time we turned down the road that led to the house I grew up in, I was about to throw up.

"Kyle," I said, giving in to the panic. "I haven't been completely honest with you about... some family things."

He pulled up to the green clapboard house that wasn't especially pretty in the summertime, but was downright bleak in the wintertime. Three beater cars sat in the dirt driveway. Tacky blowup Christmas decorations dotted the scraggly yard.

"Is this it?" Kyle asked in a high voice.

"Yes," was all I could say.

He looked at me and I expected him to recoil. Instead he gave me a little smile. "You get the food and I'll get the gifts."

I exhaled in abject relief, thinking maybe I had underestimated Kyle. Maybe he did love me no matter what, and would accept my inferior relations.

My sweet brother Donnie bounded out of the house to greet us. "Hi, Sis!"

"Hi, Professor. Meet Kyle, my fiancé."

I could tell the instant Kyle realized Donnie wasn't a professor, but he recovered quickly and made conversation when Donnie asked him about his luxury sedan. My mom came out and shyly invited Kyle to come inside. If he was surprised by her harsh appearance or heavily accented language, he didn't let on.

I was still holding out hope that things might be okay... until I walked through the door of the shabby little house to find Gil Malone sitting in the living room wearing a Santa hat and drinking a beer.

"Hiya, MaeDella," he said happily.

I thought my head might pop off my shoulders. "Where's my money, Gil?" I asked through gritted teeth.

"Easy, woman," he said, raising his hands. "Before you start ramming my truck or slashing my tires like you did in Atlanta, I want to tell you that I made the payment to the bank for this month. And I'm gonna pay you back, every red cent, with interest."

I glared. "How are you going to do that?"

He grinned. "I invested the money in a porta-john cleaning business. Me and another guy go around with a truck and hose and suck the shit out of porta-johns on construction sites all over Atlanta. We're already making money!"

Barely through the door and we were already talking about a shit-cleaning business.

"I see that look on your face," Gil said, wagging his finger at me. "I see you looking down on me. Well, Miss Uppity MaeDella Culpepper, maybe you'd like to explain why you told everyone you have a big fancy job in Atlanta selling pharmaceuticals, but your real job is being a dang parking attendant at the mall." Gil looked triumphant.

Until I dove for him.

December 26, Tuesday

WE WERE DRIVING BACK after spending the night in a hotel outside of Dewdrop. Kyle hadn't said a word in miles, and I was marinating in misery.

It was quite possibly the worst Christmas ever... a veritable smorgasbord of all my family redneckedness, and all my warts, too.

I lowered the ice bag from my bruised eye. "Say something, Kyle. Please."

After several long minutes, he grunted. "Why did you feel as if you had to lie to me about so many things? Your family... your job... God knows what else."

"It's not obvious? Do you think I'm proud of everything you witnessed back there?"

"It's one thing to not be proud, but you don't have to be

ashamed."

I felt contrite.

"And how could you not tell me you were downsized in the company re-org?"

"I didn't want you to think something was wrong with Traxton and sell your stock while it was climbing." I hadn't yet told him about the suspicions surrounding Beltina—I didn't want to pile on and put him in a more compromising situation. "But I'm going back to work for Traxton as soon as we return from our honeymoon, and everything will get back to normal."

"Including your weight?" he bit out.

He was apparently still traumatized over the pictures of me at two hundred fifty pounds hanging on the walls at my mother's house. So was I.

"Yes," I whispered. "Traxton will be paying for the gym and a personal trainer, and monitoring my weight. I won't have a choice."

"I shouldn't have said that," he said, pulling his hand down his face. "I love you, Della, no matter what size you are..."

The unspoken words hung in the air. *To an extent.*

How could I blame him when I felt the same way about myself? I took a deep breath. "I understand, Kyle, if you don't want to marry me, or if you want to postpone the wedding."

He looked over. "What? No, of course I want to marry you. And everything is all set to go for a beautiful wedding on Saturday. We'll make this work, Della. That's what marriage counselors are for."

I sniffed mightily. "And what about our families getting along?"

He sighed and reached over to clasp my hand. "We'll figure it out. All I know is I'm marrying you, not your family."

I gave him a tremulous smile. He was a good man... he did love me. And it would help that my mother had decided it would be best if she and Donnie skipped the wedding. We'd find a way to introduce the two disparate groups on a less stressful day.

"Okay?" he asked.

I blew my nose. "Okay."

I'd settled back in the seat to enjoy the ride home when a sign up ahead made me lunge forward. "Wait, slow down."

"What is it?" Kyle squinted at the sign. "Battenburg Hospital, next exit."

"Take it," I said. "And I can't tell you why… you'll just have to trust me."

He gave an exasperated sigh, then put on his signal. "Okay."

December 27, Wednesday

I STUDIED THE text to Rainie Stephens I'd saved in Draft mode.

Check into Beltina-copper link, esp Wilson's Disease

My finger hovered over the Send key

I switched to Edit mode and added *Battenburg Hospital special wing*

My finger twitched. I hadn't even told Kyle the purpose of our little side trip. Bless him, he'd simply waited in the parking lot while I'd poked around and plied orderlies for information about the wing of patients who'd freaked out while taking a popular weight-loss drug. My time as Mae had taught me some helpful tips about flying under the radar.

I tore my gaze from the drafted text to look at the bonus check from Traxton with all its lovely zeros, and wavered. My life hung in the balance.

Sometimes, Della, the easy thing is the right thing.

Those patients were receiving treatment, and the Beltina they'd taken had been pulled from the market.

I pressed my lips together, then hit the Delete key and set my phone aside.

December 28, Thursday

"THE WAY I SEE IT," Joon-woo said, studying the bonus check and the attached letter, "is if you cash it and Traxton goes down for a Beltina scandal, you could be found complicit."

I swallowed hard. "Complicit? You mean prosecuted?"

"Possibly. But I'm not a criminal attorney. This letter could also constitute extortion on the part of the company." She handed the documents back to me. "Although generally extortion implies someone is trying to get you to do something you don't want to do… and I gather you're eager to go back to work there."

I nodded.

"Okay. And from what you've told me, it sounds as if you're the key to Traxton going down on this." She shrugged. "So if you keep quiet, it's possible no one will ever know."

"Except me… and you."

"I'm your lawyer, so I can't tell anyone."

"But if I did come forward with what I know, what would happen?"

Joon-woo lifted her hands. "An investigation."

"Which will probably take a while."

"You can bet on it. When a drug turns out to have dangerous side effects, the company behind it could be fined and receive a lot of bad publicity, and there would be civil lawsuits. But Traxton could probably recover."

Except I'd never work there again.

"If on the other hand," she continued, "they *knowingly* sold a drug that was harmful, that's a whole other ball of wax."

My mind was circling in figure eights, stopping on optimism. "They did reformulate the drug," I offered. "So hopefully the danger is over."

She nodded. "That could be the case."

I sat back, still undecided, and glad I still had a couple of days to think things through. "So enough about me. Are you doing okay with closing the business?"

She looked around her empty office and sighed. "I guess I have to be. I was so close to making it, but I just ran out of resources and credit."

I frowned. "How close were you?"

Joon-woo pointed to the check I held and gave a little laugh. "That check would've saved me." Then she shrugged. "But life goes on, right?"

I nodded slowly. "Right."

December 29, Friday

I STOOD IN FRONT OF MY BANK, this time resolute.

I turned the bonus check over and wrote the appropriate words on the back.

Then I walked past the bank to the post office and addressed an envelope to Rainie Stephens at the *AJC*. Before I stuffed the check inside, I reread the words I'd written on the back.

I have reason to believe there is a link between the weight-loss drug Beltina and copper accumulation/acquired Wilson's Disease. Check the special wing at the Battenburg Hospital in south Georgia.

I dropped the envelope in the mail, but I was despondent. Now I couldn't help Joon-woo. I was out of a job at Traxton, and I had no temp work either.

And I was getting married tomorrow.

As I turned toward home, my phone rang and I was surprised to see Jack Terry's name on the screen.

"Hi, Detective. What's up?"

"Hi, Ms. Culpepper. Just checking to see when you're going to claim your reward for leading to the arrest of Zenith Vargo."

I frowned. "Reward?"

"You didn't know? FBI was offering one hundred thousand for his capture. And it's all going to you."

I couldn't speak.

"Are you still there?"

"Detective, I'll have to call you back." I ended the call and punched in Joon-woo's number.

"Hi, Della. Can this wait? I'm packing up my office to go home, and I'm tired." Her voice did sound weary.

"Joon-woo, I have a business proposition. How would you feel about a partner?"

December 30, Saturday

I WAS STANDING TALL in my beautiful wedding gown, waiting to go down the aisle.

But when the doors to the chapel opened and I looked ahead to see Kyle at the altar, my feet wouldn't move. The music kept playing, and the guests were standing, turned toward me... and my feet wouldn't move.

Finally, Kyle came down the aisle to get me.

"Della, what's wrong?" he hissed. "Everyone is waiting."

"I can't do this," I told him. "I'm so sorry. Please forgive me, Kyle." I removed my engagement ring and folded it into his hand. "I hope this will cover some of your losses."

He frowned. "What losses?"

"Goodbye, Kyle." He would find out when the news about Beltina hit in the next few days.

I walked to the door of the chapel, then twisted for one last look at Kyle, and saw Libby walking toward him, hands outstretched. I nodded, then turned and walked out to the parking lot. I scanned for an Uber sign in the windows of the string of waiting cars, found one, and climbed inside.

When I gave the driver the address, he winced.

"Lady, that's an hour drive."

"I know." I settled back in my seat. I could afford it, thanks to the FBI.

"Is the address a house?"

"No. It's a restaurant. Could you hurry, please?"

During the ride my mind reeled over what a difference six months had made. I'd learned so much about myself—my strengths, and especially my weaknesses. And what I did and didn't want out of life. I was about to go into business with Joon-woo to reopen the temp agency, and I was taking a big risk that the man I loved would still want me.

When I walked into Graham's Eatery, my heart was lodged in my throat. Charlie was sitting at the bar, having a drink—or three, based on the empties.

He looked up, did a double take, then grinned. "Nice dress."

I grinned back, giddy with relief and gratitude to the universe in general. "Thanks."

"So... you're not getting married?"

"Not to Kyle."

Charlie patted the stool next to him. "Have a seat."

But before I sat down, he leaned back, and gave my backside a satisfied smile.

December 31, Sunday

SWALLOWING MY trepidation, I walked into the crowded round room of the weight-loss clinic and took a chair. New Year's Eve was a veritable minefield of temptation for food addicts, so many members had come for a dose of courage.

Casey gestured. "Counselors sit over here, Mae."

"Today I'm a member," I whispered. My life was finally falling together, but I knew I had to do one more thing to get on a healing path. Before I could lose my nerve, I pushed to my feet and everyone quieted. "Hello. Most of you know me as Mae, but my name is really MaeDella."

"Hi, MaeDella," people in the room chorused.

I flinched, but forged ahead. "I... I have an unhealthy relationship with food. It's led to so many poor decisions in my personal and professional life, you have no idea... and I want to change."

I looked around at the encouraging faces of the people gathered and exhaled, releasing a lifetime of pent up unhappiness and false control. "I need your help."

-The End-

A NOTE FROM THE AUTHOR

Thank you so very much for taking the time to read my story TEMP GIRL. I hope you've enjoyed Della's fall and subsequent recovery—I've certainly enjoyed writing it! Della reminds me a bit of Scarlett O'Hara in terms of steamrolling through life to get what she wants, but unlike Scarlett, Della got her happily ever after. Although I suspect her relationship with Charlie will be fiery, don't you?

Reviews are so important to authors and our books. Reviews help me to attract new readers so I can keep producing more stories for you. Plus I really want to know if I'm keeping you entertained! If you enjoyed TEMP GIRL and feel inclined to leave a review at your favorite online bookstore, I would appreciate it very much.

If you'd like to sign up to receive notices of my future book releases, please visit www.stephaniebond.com and join my email list. I promise not to flood you with emails and I will never share or sell your address. And you can unsubscribe at any time.

Thanks again for your time and interest, and for telling your friends about my books.

Happy reading!
Stephanie Bond

OTHER WORKS BY STEPHANIE BOND

In the Body Movers humorous mystery series, an Atlanta woman works for Neiman Marcus by day and helps her younger brother move bodies from crime scenes by night!

PARTY CRASHERS (full-length prequel)
BODY MOVERS
2 BODIES FOR THE PRICE OF 1
3 MEN AND A BODY
4 BODIES AND A FUNERAL
5 BODIES TO DIE FOR
6 KILLER BODIES
6 ½ BODY PARTS (novella)
7 BRIDES FOR SEVEN BODIES
8 BODIES IS ENOUGH

Other humorous romantic mysteries:

COMA GIRL—*You can learn a lot when people think you aren't listening...*
COMEBACK GIRL—*Home is where the hurt is.*
TWO GUYS DETECTIVE AGENCY—*Even Victoria can't keep a secret from us...*
OUR HUSBAND—*Hell hath no fury like three women scorned!*
KILL THE COMPETITION—*There's only one sure way to the top.*
I THINK I LOVE YOU—*Sisters share everything in their closets...including the skeletons.*
GOT YOUR NUMBER—*You can run, but your past will eventually catch up with you.*
WHOLE LOTTA TROUBLE—*They didn't plan on getting caught...*
IN DEEP VOODOO—*A woman stabs a voodoo doll of her ex, and then he's found murdered!*
VOODOO OR DIE—*Another voodoo doll, another untimely demise...*

Romances:

ALMOST A FAMILY—*Fate gave them a second chance at love...*
LICENSE TO THRILL—*She's between a rock and a hard body...*
STOP THE WEDDING!—*If anyone objects to this wedding, speak now...*
THREE WISHES—*Be careful what you wish for*

ABOUT THE AUTHOR

Stephanie Bond was seven years deep into a corporate career in computer programming and pursuing an MBA at night when an instructor remarked she had a flair for writing and suggested she submit material to academic journals. But Stephanie was more interested in writing fiction—more specifically, romance and mystery novels. After writing in her spare time for two years, she sold her first manuscript; after selling ten additional projects to two publishers, she left her corporate job to write fiction full-time. To-date, Stephanie has more than seventy published novels to her name, including the BODY MOVERS humorous mystery series and the COMA GIRL daily serial. Her romantic comedy STOP THE WEDDING! is now a Hallmark Channel movie. For more information on Stephanie's books, visit www.stephaniebond.com.